INNOCENT BLOOD

INNOCENT BLOOD

The Order of the Sanguines Series

JAMES ROLLINS
and Rebecca Cantrell

WM

WILLIAM MORROW

An Imprint of HarperCollinsPublishers

INNOCENT BLOOD. Copyright © 2014 by James Czajkowski and Rebecca Cantrell. All rights reserved. Printed in the United States of America. No part of this book may be used or reproduced in any manner whatsoever without written permission except in the case of brief quotations embodied in critical articles and reviews. For information address HarperCollins Publishers, 10 East 53rd Street, New York, NY 10022.

HarperCollins books may be purchased for educational, business, or sales promotional use. For information please e-mail the Special Markets Department at SPsales@harpercollins.com.

FIRST EDITION

Designed by Lisa Stokes

Library of Congress Cataloging-in-Publication Data

Rollins, James, 1961–
   Innocent blood : the order of the sanguines series / James Rollins.
      pages cm — (The Order of the Sanguines)
   ISBN 978-0-06-199106-6 (hardback)
   1. Archaeologists—Fiction. 2. Jesus Christ—Miracles—Fiction. 3. Bible. Gospels—History of Biblical events—Fiction. 4. Good and evil—Fiction. 5. Christian sects — Fiction. I. Cantrell, Rebecca. II. Title.
   PS3568.O5398I66 2014
   813'.54—dc23
                                                                                    2013031951

   ISBN 978-0-06-232523-5 (international edition)

14 15 16 17 18 OV/RRD 10 9 8 7 6 5 4 3 2 1

James

To Carolyn McCray, for her inspiration, encouragement, and boundless friendship

Rebecca

To my husband, son, and Twinkle the Cat

Behold, God received your sacrifice from the hands of a priest—that is to say from the minister of error.

—GOSPEL OF JUDAS 5:15

PROLOGUE

Midsummer, 1099
Jerusalem

As the screams of the dying rose up toward the desert sun, Bernard's bone-white fingers clutched the cross hanging from his neck. The touch of its blessed silver seared his sword-calloused palm, branding his damned flesh. He ignored the smell of his charred skin and tightened his grip. He accepted the pain.

For this pain had a purpose—to serve God.

Around him foot soldiers and knights washed into Jerusalem on a wave of blood. For the past months, the Crusaders had fought their way across hostile lands. Nine out of every ten men were lost before ever reaching the Holy City: felled by battle, by the pitiless desert, by heathen diseases. Those who survived wept openly upon seeing Jerusalem for the first time. But all that blood spilt had not been in vain, for now the city would be restored to Christians yet again, a harsh victory marked by the deaths of thousands of infidels.

For those slain, Bernard whispered a quick prayer.

He had time for no more.

As he sheltered beside the horse-drawn wagon, he drew the rough cowl of his hood lower over his eyes, cloaking his white hair and pale face deeper into shadow. He then took hold of the stallion's bridle and stroked the beast's warm neck, hearing the thunder of its heart as much with his fingertips as his ears. Terror stoked the steed's blood and steamed from its sweating flanks.

2 | *James Rollins and Rebecca Cantrell*

Still, with a firm tug, the animal stepped forward next to him, drawing the wooden cart over the blood-soaked paving stones. The wagon's bed held a single iron cage, large enough to imprison a man. Thick leather wrapped the cage tightly, hiding what was inside. But he knew. And so did the horse. Its ears flicked back anxiously. It shook its unkempt black mane.

Ranged in a tight phalanx ahead of him, Bernard's dark brethren—his fellow knights from the Order of the Sanguines—battled to clear a path forward. All valued this mission more than their own existence. They fought with strength and determination no human could match. One of his brothers vaulted high into the air, a sword in each hand, revealing his inhuman nature as much by the flurry of his steel as by the flash of his sharp teeth. They were all once unholy beasts, like the one caged in the wagon, stripped of their souls and left forsaken—until offered a path back to salvation by Christ. Each made a dark compact to slake his thirst no more upon the blood of man, but only upon the consecrated blood of Christ, a blessing that allowed them to walk half in shadow, half in sunlight, balanced on a sword's edge between grace and damnation.

Sworn now to the Church, each served God as both warrior and priest.

Those very duties had drawn Bernard and the others to the gates of Jerusalem.

Through the cries and carnage, the wooden cart rolled at a steady pace. Bernard willed the wheels to turn faster as dread clutched him.

Must hurry . . .

Still, another need rang through him just as urgently. As he marched, blood dripped down the walls around him, ran in rivers across the stones underfoot. The iron saltiness filled his head, misting the very air, igniting a bone-deep hunger. He licked his dry lips, as if trying to taste what was forbidden him.

He wasn't the only one suffering.

From the dark cage, the beast howled, scenting the bloodshed. Its cries sang to the same monster still hidden inside Bernard—only his monster was not caged by iron, but by oath and blessing. Still, in response to that scream of raw hunger, the points of Bernard's teeth grew longer and sharper, his craving keener still.

Hearing these screams, his brothers surged forward with renewed strength, as if fleeing their former selves.

The same could not be said for the horse.

As the beast howled, the stallion froze in its harness.

As well it should.

Bernard had captured the caged fiend ten months ago at an abandoned wooden stable outside Avignon in France. Such cursed creatures went by many names over the centuries. Though once men themselves, they were now a scourge that haunted dark places, surviving on the blood of man and beasts.

Once Bernard had the fiend trapped inside the cage, he had swaddled its new prison with layers of thick leather so that not a mote of light could penetrate. The shielding protected the beast from the burning light of day, but such protection came with a price. Bernard kept it ravenous, feeding it only enough blood to survive, but never enough to sate it.

Such hunger would serve God this day.

With their goal agonizingly close, Bernard attempted to get the horse moving again. He stroked a soothing hand down its sweat-stained nose, but the animal would not be calmed. It heaved against one side of the traces, then the other, struggling to break free.

Around him, Sanguinists swirled in the familiar dance of battle. The shrieks of dying men echoed off the uncaring stone. The beast inside the cage beat the leather sides like a drum and screamed to join the slaughter, to taste the blood.

The horse whinnied and threw its head in fright.

By now, smoke rolled out from neighboring streets and alleys. The smell of burnt wool and flesh stung his nostrils. The Crusaders had begun to torch sections of the city. Bernard feared they might raze the only part of Jerusalem he needed to reach—the part where the holy weapon might be found.

Recognizing the horse was of no more use, Bernard drew his sword. With a few deft strokes, he severed its leather harness. Freed, the stallion needed no urging. With a leap out of its traces, it knocked aside a Sanguinist and bolted through the carnage.

Godspeed, he willed it.

He moved to the rear of the wagon, knowing none of his brothers could be spared from the battle. These last steps he must take alone.

As Christ had with his heavy cross.

He sheathed his sword and put his shoulder to the back of the cart.

He would push it the remaining distance. In a different life, when his heart still beat, he was a strong, vigorous man. Now he had strength beyond that of any mortal.

With the tang of blood becoming a humid stew in the air, he drew a shaky breath. Red desire ringed the edges of his vision. He wanted to drink from every man, woman, and child in the city. The lust filled him near to bursting.

Instead, he gripped his searing cross, allowing the holy pain to steady him.

He took a slow step, forcing the cart's wheels forward one revolution, then another. Each turn brought him closer to his goal.

But a gnawing fear grew with every step gained.

Am I already too late?

As the sun sank toward the horizon, Bernard finally spotted his goal. He trembled with exertion, nearly spent of even his fierce strength.

At the end of the street, past where the last of the city's defenders fought intensely, the leaden dome of a mosque rose to an indifferent blue sky. Dark blotches of blood marred its white facade. Even from this distance, he heard the frightened heartbeats of men, women, and children sheltering within the mosque's thick walls.

As he strained against the wagon, he listened to their prayers for mercy from their foreign god. They would find none from the beast in the cart.

Nor from him.

Their small lives counted little against the prize he sought—a weapon that promised to purge all evil from the world.

Distracted by this hope, he failed to stop the front wheel of the cart from falling into a deep crack in the street, lodging stubbornly between the stones. The wagon jolted to a stop.

As if sensing their advantage, the infidels broke through the protective phalanx around the cart. A thin man with wild black hair rushed toward Bernard, a curved blade flashing in the sun, intending to protect his mosque, his family, with his own life.

Bernard took that payment, cutting him down with a lightning stroke of steel.

Hot blood splashed Bernard's priestly robes. Though it was forbidden except for extreme circumstance and need, he touched the stain and brought his fingers to his lips. He licked crimson from his fingertips. Blood alone would lend him the strength to push forward. He would do penance later, for a hundred years if necessary.

From his tongue, fire ignited through him, stoking renewed strength into his limbs, narrowing his vision to a pinpoint. He leaned his shoulder to the cart and, with a massive heave, got the wagon rolling again.

A prayer crossed his lips—pleading for his strength to hold, for forgiveness for his sin.

He rushed the cart forward as his brothers cleared a path for him.

The doors to the mosque appeared directly ahead, its last defenders dying at the threshold. Bernard abandoned the wagon, crossed the last strides to the mosque, and kicked open the barred door with a strength no mere man could muster.

From within, terrified screams echoed off ornate walls. Heartbeats ran together in fear—too many, too fast to pick out a single one. They melted into one sound, like the roar of the sea. Frightened eyes glowed back at him from the darkness under the dome.

He stood in the doorway that they might see him backlit by the flames of their city. They needed to recognize his priest's robes and silver cross, to understand that Christians had conquered them.

But more important, they must know that they could not flee.

His fellow Sanguinists reached him, standing shoulder to shoulder behind him in the entrance to the mosque. No one would escape. The smell of terror filled the vast room, from the tiled floor to the vast dome overhead.

In one bound, Bernard returned to the cart. He lifted the cage free and dragged it up the stairs to the door, its iron bottom screeching, scoring long black lines in the stone steps. The wall of Sanguinists opened to receive him, then closed behind him.

He rocked the cage upright atop the polished marble tiles. His sword smote through the lock's hasp in a single blow. Standing back, he swung open the rusty cage door. The creak drowned out the heartbeats, the breathing.

The creature stepped forth, free for the first time in many months. Long arms felt the air, as if seeking long familiar bars.

Bernard could scarcely tell that this thing had once been human— its skin paled to the hue of the dead, golden hair grown long and tangled down its back, and limbs as thin as a spider's.

Terrified, the crowd retreated from the sight of the beast, pressing against the far walls, crushing others in their fear and panic. The delicate scent of blood and fear billowed from them.

Bernard raised his sword and waited for the creature to face him. The creature must not escape into the streets. Its work was here. It must bring evil and blasphemy to this sacred site. It must destroy any holiness that might remain. Only then could the space be consecrated again for Bernard's God.

As if the beast heard his thoughts, it raised its wrinkled face toward Bernard. Twin eyes shone milky white. Long it had been kept from the sun, and old it had been when it was turned.

A baby whimpered from the room ahead.

Such a beast could not resist that temptation.

With a flash of skeletal limbs, it twisted away and lunged for its prey.

Bernard lowered his sword, no longer needing it to hold the monster at bay. The promise of blood and pain would imprison it within these walls for the time being.

He forced his feet forward, following behind the murderous beast. As he crossed under the dome, he blocked his ears from the screams and prayers. He turned his sight from the torn flesh, from the bodies he stepped over. He refused to respond to the blight of blood hanging in the air.

Still, the monster inside him, freshly stoked with a few drops of crimson, could not be entirely ignored. It longed to join this other, to feed, to lose itself in simple need.

To be sated, truly sated, for the first time in years.

Bernard stepped faster across the room, fearful of losing control, of succumbing to that desire—until he reached the stairs on the far side.

There the silence stopped him.

Behind him, all heartbeats had ceased. The stillness imprisoned him and he stood, unable to move, guilt ringing through him.

Then an unnatural scream echoed off the dome, as the Sanguinists killed the beast at last, its purpose fulfilled.

God, forgive me . . .

Freed from that silence, he ran down the steps and through
winding passageways far underneath the mosque. His path drew
him deeper into the bowels of the city. The thick stink of the slaughter chased him, a wraith in the shadows.

Then finally a new scent.

Water.

Dropping to his hands and knees, he crawled into a tight tunnel
and discovered firelight flickering ahead. It drew him forward like a
moth. At the tunnel's end, a cavern opened, tall enough to stand up in.

He clambered out and to his feet. A torch made of rushes hung
on one wall, casting a flickering glow across a pool of black water.
Generations of soot tarnished the high ceiling.

He began to step forward, when a woman rose from behind a
boulder. Shiny ebony tresses spilled to the shoulders of her simple
white shift, and her dark umber skin gleamed smooth and perfect.
A shard of metal, the length of her palm, dangled from a thin gold
chain hung around her slender neck. It fell to rest between well-
formed breasts that pushed against a sheer linen bodice.

He had long been a priest, but his body reacted to her beauty.
With great effort, he forced his gaze to meet hers. Her bright eyes
appraised his.

"Who are you?" he asked. He heard no heartbeat from her, but
he also knew innately she wasn't like the caged beast, nor even like
himself. Even from this distance, he felt the heat coming from her
body. "Are you the Mistress of the Well?"

It was a name he had found written upon an ancient piece of
papyrus, along with a map to what lay below.

She ignored his questions. "You are not ready for what you
seek," she simply said. Her words were Latin, but her accent sounded
ancient, older even than his.

"I seek only knowledge," he countered.

"Knowledge?" That single word sounded as mournful as a dirge.
"Here you will find only disappointment."

Still, she must have recognized his determination. She stepped
aside and beckoned him to the pool with one dusky hand, her fingers

long and graceful. A thin band of gold encircled her upper arm.

He stepped past her, his shoulder nearly brushing hers. The fragrance of lotus blossoms danced on the warm air that surrounded her.

"Leave behind your clothing," she ordered. "You must go into the water as naked as you once came from it."

At the water's edge, he fumbled with his robe, struggling against the shameful thoughts that crowded his mind.

She refused to look away. "You have brought much death to this holy place, priest of the cross."

"It will be purified," he said, seeking to appease her. "Consecrated to the one God."

"Only *one*?" Sorrow wakened in those deep eyes. "You are so certain?"

"I am."

She shrugged. The small gesture shed her thin shift from her shoulders. It whispered to the rough stone floor. Torchlight revealed a body of such perfection that he forgot his vows and stared baldly, his eyes lingering on the curve of her full breasts, on her belly, on the long muscular line of her thighs.

She turned and dove into the dark water, barely causing a ripple.

Alone now, he hurriedly unbuckled his belt, yanked off his bloody boots, and tore off his robe. Once naked, he sprang to follow, diving deep. Icy water washed away the blood on his skin, and baptized him into innocence.

He blew the air from his lungs, for he had no need for it as a Sanguinist. He sank quickly, swimming after her. Far below him, bare limbs shone white for a flash—then she flitted to the side, quick as a fish, and vanished.

He kicked deeper, but she had disappeared. He touched his cross and prayed for guidance. Should he search for her or continue his mission?

The answer was a simple one.

He turned and swam onward, through twisting passages, following the map in his head, one learned from those ancient scraps of papyrus, toward the secret hidden deep beneath Jerusalem.

He moved as swiftly as he dared, into utter darkness, through complex passageways. A mortal man would have died many times over. One hand brushed rock, counting passages. Twice, he reached dead ends and had to backtrack. He fought panic, telling himself that he had misread the map, promising himself that the place he searched for existed.

His despair grew to a sharp point—then a figure swept past him in the icy water, felt as a flow across his skin, heading back the way he had come. Startled, he went for his sword, remembering too late that he had left it in a pile with his robes.

He reached for her, but he knew she was gone.

Turning in the direction from whence she had come, he kicked with renewed vigor. He pushed through the rising dread that he would swim forever in the darkness and never find what he sought.

He finally reached a large cavern, its walls sweeping wide to either side.

Though blind, he knew he had found the right place. The water here felt warmer, burning with a holiness that itched his skin. Swimming to the side, he lifted trembling hands and explored the wall.

Under his palms, he felt a design carved into the rock.

At last . . .

His fingertips crawled across the stone, seeking to understand the images etched there.

Images that might save them.

Images that might lead him to the sacred weapon.

Under his fingers, he felt the shape of a cross, found a figure crucified there—and rising above it, the same man, his face raised high, his arms outstretched toward heaven. Between the bodies, a line connected this rising soul to the nailed body below.

As he followed this path, his fingertips burned with fire, warning him the line was made of purest silver. From the cross, the fiery path flowed along the curved wall of the cavern to a neighboring carving. Here, he found a cluster of men with swords, come to arrest Christ. The Savior's hand touched one of the men on the side of the head.

Bernard knew what this depicted.

The healing of Malchus.

It was the *last* miracle that Christ performed before His resurrection.

Swimming along the wall, Bernard traced the silver line through the many miracles that Jesus had performed during His lifetime: the multiplication of the fishes, the raising of the dead, the curing of the lepers. He drew each in his mind, as if he had seen them. He strove to contain his hope, his elation.

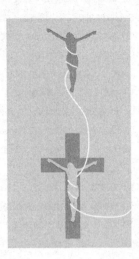

At last, he came to the depiction of the wedding at Cana, when Christ turned water into wine. It was the Savior's *first* recorded miracle.

Still, the silver path headed outward again from Cana, burning through the darkness.

But to where? Would it reveal unknown miracles?

Bernard quested along it—only to discover a wide swath of crumbling rock under his fingers. Frantic, he swept his palms along the wall in larger and larger arcs. Shards of twisted silver embedded in the stone scored his skin with fire. The pain brought him to his senses, forcing him to face his greatest fear.

This portion of the carving had been destroyed.

He spread both hands across the wall, groping for more of the design. According to those ancient pieces of papyrus, this history of Christ's miracles was supposed to reveal the hiding place of the most sacred weapon of all—one that could destroy even the most powerful damned soul with a touch.

He hung in the water, knowing the truth.

The secret had been destroyed.

And he knew by whom.

Her words echoed in his head.

Knowledge? Here you will find only disappointment.

Finding him unworthy, she must have come straight here and defaced the sacred picture before he could see it. His tears mingled with the cold water—not for what was lost, but from a harsher truth.

I have failed.

Every death this day has been in vain.

PART I

I have sinned in that I have betrayed the innocent blood.
And they said, What is that to us?

—Matthew 27:4

1

December 18, 9:58 A.M. PST
Palo Alto, California

An edge of panic kept her tense.

As Dr. Erin Granger entered the lecture hall on the Stanford campus, she glanced across its breadth to make sure she was alone. She even crouched and searched under the empty seats, making certain no one was hiding there. She kept one hand on the Glock 19 in her ankle holster.

It was a beautiful winter morning, the sun hanging in a crisp, cloud-studded blue sky. With bright light streaming through the tall windows, she had little to fear from the dark creatures that haunted her nightmares.

Still, after all that had befallen her, she knew that her fellow man was just as capable of evil.

Straightening again, she reached the lectern in front of the classroom and let out a quiet sigh of relief. She knew her fears were illogical, but that didn't stop her from checking that the hall was safe before her students trooped in. As annoying as college kids could be, she would fight to the death to keep each one of them from harm.

She wouldn't fail a student again.

Erin's fingers tightened on the scuffed leather satchel in her hand. She had to force her fingers to open and place her bag next to the lectern. With her gaze still roaming the room, she unbuckled the satchel and pulled out her notes for the lecture. Usually she memorized her presentations, but she had taken over this class for a professor on maternity leave. It was an interesting topic, and it kept her from dwelling on the events that had upended her life, starting with the loss of her two graduate students in Israel a couple of months before.

Heinrich and Amy.

The German student had died from injuries sustained following an earthquake. Amy's death had come later, murdered because Erin had unwittingly sent forbidden information to her student, knowledge that had gotten the young woman killed.

She rubbed her palms, as if trying to wipe away that blood, that responsibility. The room seemed suddenly colder. It couldn't have been more than fifty degrees outside and not much warmer in the classroom. Still, the shivers that swept through her as she prepared her papers had nothing to do with the room's poor heating system.

Returned again to Stanford, she should have felt good to be home, wrapped in the familiar, in the daily routines of a semester winding toward Christmas break.

But she didn't.

Because nothing was the same.

As she straightened and prepared this morning's lecture notes, her students arrived in ones and twos, a few climbing down the stairs to the seats in front, but most hanging back and folding down the seats in the uppermost rows.

"Professor Granger?"

Erin glanced to her left and discovered a young man with five silver hoops along one eyebrow approaching her. The student wore a determined expression on his face as he stepped in front of her. He carried a camera with a long lens over one shoulder.

"Yes?" She didn't bother to mask the irritation in her voice.

He placed a folded slip of paper atop the wooden lectern and slid it toward her.

Behind him, the other students in the room looked on, nonchalant, but they were unconvincing actors. She could tell they watched her, wondering what she would do. She didn't need to open that slip of paper to know that it contained the young man's phone number.

"I'm from the *Stanford Daily*." He played with a hoop in his eyebrow. "I was hoping for one quick interview for the school newspaper?"

She pushed the slip of paper back toward him. "No, thank you."

She had refused all interview requests since returning from Rome. She wouldn't break her silence now, especially as everything she was allowed to say was a lie.

To hide the truth of the tragic events that had left her two students dead, a story had been put out that she had been trapped three days in the Israeli desert, entombed amid the rubble following an earthquake at Masada. According to that false account, she was discovered alive, along with an army sergeant named Jordan Stone and her sole surviving graduate student, Nate Highsmith.

She understood the necessity of a cover story to explain the time she had spent working for the Vatican, a subterfuge that was further supported by an elite few in the government who also knew the truth. The public wasn't ready for stories of monsters in the night, of the dark underpinnings that supported the world at large.

Still, necessity or not, she had no intention of elaborating on those lies.

The student with the line of eyebrow rings persisted. "I'd let you review the story before I post it. If you don't like every single bit, we can work with it until you do."

"I respect your persistence and diligence, but it does not change my answer." She gestured to the half-full auditorium. "Please, take your seat."

He hesitated and seemed about to speak again.

She pulled herself up to her full height and fixed him with her sternest glare. She stood only five foot eight, and with her blond hair tied back in a casual ponytail, she didn't strike as the most intimidating figure.

Still, it was all about the attitude.

Whatever he saw in her eyes drove him back to the gathering students, where he sank quickly into his seat, keeping his face down.

With the matter settled, she tapped her sheaf of notes into a neat pile and drew the class to order. "Thank you all for coming to the final session of History 104: Stripping the Divine from Biblical History. Today we will discuss common misconceptions about a religious holiday that is almost upon us, namely *Christmas*."

The bongs of laptops powering up replaced the once familiar sound of rustling paper as students prepared to take notes.

"What do we celebrate on December twenty-fifth?" She let her gaze play across the students—some pierced, a few tattooed, and several who looked hungover. "December twenty-fifth? Anyone? This one's a gimme."

A girl wearing a sweatshirt with an embroidered angel on the front raised her hand. "The birth of Christ?"

"That's right. But when was Christ actually *born*?"

No one offered an answer.

She smiled, warming past her fears as she settled into her role as teacher. "That's smart of you all to avoid that trap." That earned a few chuckles. "The date of Christ's birth is actually a matter of some dispute. Clement of Alexandria said . . ."

She continued her lecture. A year ago, she would have said that no one alive today knew the actual date of Christ's birth. She couldn't say that anymore, because as part of her adventures in Israel, Russia, and Rome, she had met someone who *did know*, someone who was alive when Christ was born. In that moment back then, she had realized how much of accepted history was *wrong*—either masked by ignorance or obscured by purposeful deceptions to hide darker truths.

As an archaeologist, one who sought the history hidden under sand and rock, such a revelation had left her unsettled, unmoored. After returning to the comfortable world of academia, she discovered that she could no longer give the simplest lecture without careful thought. Telling her students the truth, if not the whole truth, had become nearly impossible. Every lecture felt like a lie.

How can I continue walking that line, lying to those I'm supposed to teach the truth?

Still, what choice did she have? After having that door briefly opened, revealing the hidden nature of the world, it had been shut just as soundly.

Not shut. Slammed in my face.

Cut off from those truths hidden behind that door, she was left on the outside, left to wonder what was real and what was false.

Finally, the lecture came to an end. She hurriedly wiped clean the whiteboard, as if trying to erase the falsehoods and half-truths found there. At least, it was over. She congratulated herself on making it through the final lecture of the year. All that was left now was to grade her last papers—then she would be free to face the challenge of Christmas break.

Across that stretch of open days, she pictured the blue eyes and hard planes of a rugged face, the full lips that smiled so easily, the smooth brow under a short fall of blond hair. It would be good to see Sergeant Jordan Stone again. It had been several weeks since she had last seen him in person—though they spoke often over the phone. She wasn't sure where this relationship was going long term, but she wanted to be there to find out.

Of course, that meant picking out the perfect Christmas gift to express that sentiment. She smiled at that thought.

As she began to erase the last line from the whiteboard, ready to dismiss the students behind her, a cloud smothered the sun, cloaking the classroom in shadow. The eraser froze on the board. She felt momentarily dizzy, then found herself falling away into—

Absolute darkness.

Stone walls pressed her shoulders. She struggled to sit. Her head smashed against stone, and she fell back with a splash. Frantic hands searched a black world.

Stone all around—above, behind, on all sides. Not rough stone as if she were buried under a mountain. But smooth. Polished like glass.

Along the top of the box was a design worked in silver. It scorched her fingertips.

She gulped, and wine filled her mouth. Enough to drown her.

Wine?

A door at the rear of the hall slammed shut, yanking her back into the classroom. She stared at the eraser on the whiteboard, her fingers clutched tightly to it, her knuckles white.

How long have I stood here like this? In front of everyone.

She guessed no more than a few seconds. She'd had bouts like this before over the past few weeks, but never in front of anyone else. She'd dismissed them as posttraumatic stress and had hoped they would go away by themselves, but this last was the most vivid of them all.

She took a deep breath and turned to face her class. They seemed unconcerned, so she couldn't have been out of it for too long. She must get this under control before something worse happened.

She looked toward the door that had slammed.

A welcome figure stood at the back of the hall. Noting her attention, Nate Highsmith lifted up a large envelope and waved it at her. He smiled apologetically, then headed down the classroom in cowboy boots, a hitch in his step a reminder of the torture he had endured last fall.

She tightened her lips. She should have protected him better. And Heinrich. And most especially Amy. If Erin hadn't exposed the young woman to danger, she might still be alive today. Amy's parents wouldn't be spending their first Christmas without their daughter. They had never wanted Amy to be an archaeologist. It was Erin who finally convinced them to let her come along on the dig in Israel. As the senior field researcher, Erin had assured them their daughter would be safe.

In the end, she had been terribly, horribly wrong.

She tilted her boot to feel the reassuring bulge of the gun against her ankle. She wouldn't get caught flat-footed again. No more innocents would die on her watch.

She cleared her throat and returned her attention to the class. "That wraps it up, folks. You're all dismissed. Enjoy your winter holidays."

While the room emptied, she forced herself to stare out the window at the bright sky, trying to chase away the darkness left from her vision a moment ago.

Nate finally reached her as the class cleared out. "Professor." He sounded worried. "I have a message for you."

"What message?"

"Two of them, actually. The first one is from the Israeli government. They've finally released our data from the dig site in Caesarea."

"That's terrific." She tried to fuel her words with enthusiasm, but failed. If nothing else, Amy and Heinrich would get some credit for their last work, an epitaph for their short lives. "What's the second message?"

"It's from Cardinal Bernard."

Surprised, she faced Nate more fully. For weeks, she had attempted to reach the cardinal, the head of the Order of Sanguines in Rome. She'd even considered flying to Italy and staking out his apartments in Vatican City.

"About time he returned my calls," she muttered.

"He wanted you to phone him at once," Nate said. "Sounded like an emergency."

Erin sighed in exasperation. Bernard had ignored her for two months, but now he needed something from her. She had a thousand questions for him—concerns and thoughts that had built up over the past weeks since returning from Rome. She glanced to the white-board, eyeing the half-erased line. She had questions about those visions, too.

Were these episodes secondary to posttraumatic stress? Was she reliving the times that she spent trapped under Masada?

But if so, why do I keep tasting wine?

She shook her head to clear it and pointed to his hand. "What's in the envelope?"

"It's addressed to you." He handed it to her.

It weighed too much to contain just a letter. Erin scanned the return address.

Israel.

Her fingers trembled slightly as she slit open the top with her pen.

Nate noted how her hand quivered and looked concerned. She knew he was talking to a counselor about his own PTSD. They were two wounded survivors with secrets that could not be fully spoken aloud.

Shaking the envelope, she slid out a single sheet of typewritten paper and an object about the size and shape of a quail's egg. Her heart sank as she recognized the object.

Even Nate let out a small gasp and took a step back.

She didn't have that luxury. She read the enclosed page quickly. It was from the Israeli security forces. They had determined that the enclosed artifact was no longer relevant to the closed investigation of their case, and they hoped that she would give it to its rightful owner.

She cradled the polished chunk of amber in her palm, as if it were the most precious object in the world. Under the dull fluorescent light, it looked like little more than a shiny brown rock, but it felt warmer to the touch. Light reflected off its surface, and in the very center, a tiny dark feather hung motionless, preserved across thousands of years, a moment of time frozen forever in amber.

"Amy's good luck charm," Nate mumbled, swallowing hard. He had been there when Amy was murdered. He kept his eyes averted from the tiny egg of amber.

Erin placed a hand on Nate's elbow in sympathy. In fact, the talisman was more than Amy's good luck charm. One day out at the dig, Amy had explained to Erin that she had found the amber on a beach as a little girl, and she'd been fascinated by the feather imprisoned inside, wondering where it had come from, picturing the wing from which it might have fallen. The amber captured her imagination as fully as it had the feather. It was what sparked Amy's desire to study archaeology.

Erin gazed at the amber in her palm, knowing that this tiny object had led not only to Amy's field of study—but also to her death.

Her fingers closed tightly over the smooth stone, squeezing her determination, making herself a promise.

Never again . . .

2

Sergeant Jordan Stone felt like a fraud as he marched in his dress blues. Today he would bury the last member of his former team—a young man named Corporal Sanderson. Like his other teammates, Sanderson's body had never been found.

After a couple of months of searching through the tons of rubble that had once been the mountain of Masada, the military gave up. Sanderson's empty coffin pressed hard against Jordan's hip as he marched in step with the other pallbearers.

A December snowstorm had blanketed the grounds of Arlington National Cemetery, covering brown grass and gathering atop the branches of leafless trees. Snow mounded across the arched tops of marble grave markers, more markers than he could count. Each grave was numbered, most bore names, and all these soldiers had been laid to rest with honor and dignity.

One of them was his wife, Karen, killed in action more than a year before. There hadn't been enough of her to bury, just her dog tags. Her coffin was as empty as Sanderson's. Some days Jordan couldn't believe that she was gone, that he would never bring her flowers again and get a long slow kiss of thanks. Instead, the only flowers he would ever give her would go on her grave. He had placed red roses there before he headed to Sanderson's funeral.

He pictured Sanderson's freckled face. His young teammate

had been eager to please, taken his job seriously, and done his best. In return, he got a lonely death on a mountaintop in Israel. Jordan tightened his grip on the cold casket handle, wishing that the mission had ended differently.

A few more steps past the bare trees and he and his companions carried the casket into a frigid chapel. He felt more at home within these simple white walls than he had in the lavish churches of Europe. Sanderson would have been more comfortable here, too.

Sanderson's mother and sister waited for them inside. They wore nearly identical black dresses and thin formal shoes despite the snow and cold. Both had Sanderson's fair complexion, with faces freckled brown even in winter. Their noses and eyes were red.

They missed him.

He wished they didn't have to.

Beside them, his commanding officer, Captain Stanley, stood at attention. The captain had been at Jordan's left hand for all the funerals, his lips compressed in a thin line as coffins went into the ground. Good soldiers, every one.

He was a by-the-book commander and had handled Jordan's debriefing faultlessly. In turn, Jordan did his best to stick to the lie that the Vatican had prepared: the mountain had collapsed in an earthquake, and everyone died. He and Erin had been in a corner that hadn't collapsed and were rescued three days later by a Vatican search party.

Simple enough.

It was untrue. And unfortunately, he was a bad liar, and his CO suspected that he hadn't revealed everything that had happened in Masada or after his rescue.

Jordan had already been taken off active duty and assigned psychiatric counseling. Someone was watching him all the time, waiting to see if he would crack up. What he wanted most was to simply get back out in the field and do his job. As a member of the Joint Expeditionary Forensic Facility in Afghanistan, he'd worked and investigated military crime scenes. He was good at it, and he wanted to do it again.

Anything to keep busy, to keep moving.

Instead, he stood at attention beside yet another coffin, the cold from the marble floor seeping into his toes. Sanderson's sister shivered next to him. He wished he could give her his uniform jacket.

He listened to the military chaplain's somber tones more than his words. The priest had only twenty minutes to get through the ceremony. Arlington had many funerals every day, and they set a strict schedule.

He soon found himself outside of the chapel and at the gravesite. He had done this march so many times that his feet found their way to this grave without much thought. Sanderson's casket rested on snow-dusted brown earth beside a draped hole.

A cold wind blew across the snow, curling flakes on the surface into tendrils, like cirrus clouds, the kind of high clouds so common in the desert where Sanderson had died. Jordan waited through the rest of the ceremony, listened to the three-rifle volley, the bugler playing "Taps," and watched the chaplain give the folded flag to Sanderson's mother.

Jordan had endured the same scene for each of his lost teammates.

It hadn't gotten any easier.

At the end, Jordan shook Sanderson's mother's hand. It felt cold and frail, and he worried that he might break it. "I am deeply sorry for your loss. Corporal Sanderson was a fine soldier, and a good man."

"He liked you." His mother offered him a sad smile. "He said you were smart and brave."

Jordan worked his frozen face to match that smile. "That's good to hear, ma'am. He was smart and brave himself."

She blinked back tears and turned away. He moved to take a step after her, although he didn't know what he would say, but before he could, the chaplain laid a hand on his shoulder.

"I believe we have business to discuss, Sergeant."

Turning, Jordan examined the young chaplain. The man wore dress blues just like Jordan's uniform, except that he had crosses sewn onto the lapels of his jacket. Looking closer now, Jordan saw his skin was too white, even for winter, his brown hair a trifle too long, his posture not quite military. As the chaplain stared back at him, his green eyes didn't blink.

The short hairs rose on the back of Jordan's neck.

The chill of the chaplain's hand seeped through his glove. It wasn't like a hand that had been out too long on a cold day. It was like a hand that hadn't been warm for years.

Jordan had met many of his ilk before. What stood before him was an undead predator, a vampiric creature called a *strigoi*. But for this one to be out in daylight, he must be a Sanguinist—a *strigoi* who had taken a vow to stop drinking human blood, to serve the Catholic Church and sustain himself only on Christ's blood—or more exactly, on *wine* consecrated by holy sacrament into His blood.

Such an oath made this creature less dangerous.

But not much.

"I'm not so sure that we have any business left," Jordan said.

He shifted away from the chaplain and squared off, ready to fight if need be. He had seen Sanguinists battle. No doubt this slight chaplain could take him out, but that didn't mean Jordan would go down easy.

Captain Stanley moved between them and cleared his throat. "It's been cleared all the way up to the top, Sergeant Stone."

"What has, sir?"

"He will explain everything," the captain answered, gesturing to the chaplain. "Go with him."

"And if I refuse?" Jordan held his breath, hoping for a good answer.

"It's an order, Sergeant." He gave Jordan a level glare. "It's being handled way above my pay grade."

Jordan suppressed a groan. "I'm sorry, sir."

Captain Stanley quirked one tiny corner of his mouth, equivalent to a belly laugh from a jollier man. "That I believe, Sergeant."

Jordan saluted, wondering if it was for the last time, and followed the chaplain to a black limousine parked at the curb. It seemed the Sanguinists had barreled into his life again, ready to kick apart the rubble of his career with their immortal feet.

The chaplain held open the door for him, and Jordan climbed in. The interior smelled like leather and brandy and expensive cigars. It wasn't what one expected from a priest's vehicle.

Jordan slid across the seat. The glass partition had been rolled up, and all he saw of the driver was the back of a thick neck, short blond hair, and a uniform cap.

The chaplain lifted his pant legs to preserve the crease before sliding in. With one hand, he closed the door with a dignified thump, trapping Jordan inside with him.

"Please turn up the heat for our guest," the chaplain called to the driver. Then he unbuttoned the jacket of his dress blue uniform and leaned back.

"I believe my CO said that you would explain everything." Jordan folded his arms. "Go ahead."

"That's a tall order." The young chaplain poured a brandy. He brought the glass to his nose and inhaled. With a sigh, he lowered the glass and offered it toward Jordan. "It's quite a fine vintage."

"Then you drink it."

The chaplain swirled the brandy in the glass, his eyes following the brown liquid. "I think you know that I can't, as much as I'd like to."

"About that explanation?" he pressed.

The chaplain raised a hand, and the car slid into motion. "Sorry about all this cloak-and-dagger business. Or perhaps *robe-and-cross* might be the more apt term?"

He smiled wistfully as he sniffed again at the brandy.

Jordan frowned at the guy's mannerisms. He certainly seemed less stuffy and formal than the other Sanguinists he had met.

The chaplain took off his white glove and held out his hand. "Name's Christian."

Jordan ignored the invitation.

Realizing this, the chaplain lifted his hand and ran his fingers through his thick hair. "Yes, I appreciate the irony. A Sanguinist named *Christian*. It's like my mother planned it."

The man snorted.

Jordan wasn't quite sure what to make of this Sanguinist.

"I think we almost met back in Ettal Abbey," the chaplain said. "But Rhun picked Nadia and Emmanuel to fill out the rest of his trio back in Germany."

Jordan pictured Nadia's dark features and Emmanuel's darker attitude.

Christian shook his head. "Hardly a surprise, I suppose."

"Why's that?"

The other raised an eyebrow. "I believe I'm not sackcloth and ashes enough for Father Rhun Korza."

Jordan fought down a grin. "I can see how that would bug him."

Christian set the brandy in a tray near the door and leaned forward, his green eyes serious. "Actually Father Korza is the reason I'm here."

"He sent you?"

Somehow Jordan couldn't picture that. He doubted Rhun wanted anything more to do with Jordan. They hadn't parted on the best of terms.

"Not exactly." Christian rested skinny elbows on his knees. "Cardinal Bernard is trying to keep it quiet, but Rhun has disappeared without a word."

Figures . . . the guy was hardly the forthcoming sort.

"Has he contacted you since you left Rome in October?" Christian asked.

"Why would he contact me?"

He tilted his head to one side. "Why wouldn't he?"

"I hate him." Jordan saw no point in lying. "He knows it."

"Rhun is a difficult man to like," Christian admitted, "but what did he do to make you hate him?"

"Besides almost killing Erin?"

Christian's eyebrows drew down in concern. "I thought he saved her life . . . and yours."

Jordan's jaw tightened. He remembered Erin limp on the floor, her skin white, her hair soaked with blood.

"Rhun bit her," Jordan explained harshly. "He drained her and left her to die in the tunnels under Rome. If Brother Leopold and I hadn't come upon her when we did, she'd be dead."

"Father Korza fed upon Erin?" Christian rocked back, surprise painted on his face. He scrutinized Jordan for several seconds without speaking, plainly floored by the revelation of this sin. "Are you certain? Perhaps—"

"They both admitted it. Erin and Rhun." Jordan folded his arms. "I'm not the one lying here."

Christian raised his hands in a placating gesture. "I'm sorry. I didn't mean to doubt you. It's just that this is . . . unusual."

"Not for Rhun it's not." He put his hands on his knees. "Your golden boy has slipped before."

"Only once. And Elizabeth Bathory was centuries ago." Christian picked up the glass of brandy and studied it. "So you're saying that Brother Leopold *knew* all about this?"

"He certainly did."

Apparently Leopold must have covered for Rhun. Jordan felt disappointment, but not surprise. The Sanguinists stuck together.

"He fed on her . . ." Christian stared at the glass as if he might find the answer there. "That means Rhun is full of her blood."

Jordan shuddered, disturbed by that thought.

"That changes everything. We must go to her. Now." Christian leaned over and rapped on the partition to gain the driver's attention. "Take us to the airport! At once!"

Instantly obeying, the driver accelerated the car, its bottom scraping when it crested a hill and headed out of the cemetery.

Christian glanced to Jordan. "We'll part ways at the airport. You can get home from there on your own, correct?"

"I could," he agreed. "But if Erin is involved in any of this, I'm going with you."

Christian drew in a long breath and let it out. He pulled a cell phone from his pocket and punched in numbers. "I'm sure Cardinal Bernard gave you the whole speech last time about your life and soul being in danger if you involve yourself in our affairs?"

"He did."

"Then let's save time and pretend I gave it again." Christian lifted the phone to his ear. "Right now I must charter a plane to California."

"So you don't object to me going with you?"

"You love Erin, and you want to protect her. Who am I to stand in the way of that?"

For a dead guy, Christian was turning out to be okay.

Still, as the limousine sped across the snow-swept city, Jordan's anxiety grew sharper with every passing mile.

Erin was in danger.

Again.

And likely all because of the actions of Rhun Korza.

Maybe it would be better if that bastard stayed lost.

3

Cardinal Bernard rearranged the newspapers atop his polished desk, as if organizing them into neat lines might change the words they contained. Horrifying headlines screamed from the pages:

Serial Killer Loose in Rome
Gruesome Murderer Savages Young Women
Police Stunned by Brutality

Candlelight reflected off the bejeweled globe next to his desk. He turned the ancient sphere slowly, longing to be anywhere but here. He glanced at his antique books, his scrolls, his sword on the wall from the time of the Crusades—items he had collected during his centuries of service to the Church.

I have served long, but have I served well?

The smell of newspaper ink pulled his attention back to the pages. The details disturbed him further. Each woman had her throat sliced open, and her body drained of blood. They were all beautiful and young, with black hair and blue eyes. They came from every station in life, but they had all died in the oldest quarters of Rome, in the darkest hours between sunset and sunrise.

Twenty in all, according to the newspapers.

But Bernard had managed to conceal many more deaths. It

amounted to a victim claimed nearly every day since the end of October.

He could not escape the timing.

The end of October.

The deaths had started just after the battle waged in the crypts below St. Peter's Basilica, a fight for possession of the Blood Gospel. The Sanguinists had won that battle against the Belial, a joint force of humans and *strigoi,* led by an unknown leader who continued to plague his order.

Shortly after that battle, Father Rhun Korza had vanished.

Where was he? What had he done?

Bernard shied away from that thought.

He eyed the pile of newspapers. Had a rogue *strigoi* escaped that battle and hunted the streets of Rome, preying on these young girls? There had been so many beasts in the tunnels. One could have slipped through their net.

A part of him prayed that was true.

He dared not consider the alternative. That fear kept him waiting, indecisive, as more innocent girls died.

A hand tapped on the door. "Cardinal?"

He recognized the voice and the sluggish heartbeat that belonged to it.

"Come in, Father Ambrose."

The human priest opened the wooden door with one hand, his other clasped in a loose fist. "I am sorry to disturb you."

The assistant did not sound sorry. In fact, his voice rang with ill-disguised glee. While Ambrose clearly loved him and served the cardinal's office diligently, there remained a petty streak in the man that found perverse enjoyment in the misfortunes of others.

Bernard stifled a sigh. "Yes?"

Ambrose entered the office. His plump body leaned forward like a hound on a scent. He glanced around the candlelit room, probably making certain that Bernard was alone. How Ambrose loved his secrets. But then again, maybe that was why the man so loved Bernard. After so many centuries, his own veins ran as much with secrets as with black blood.

Finally satisfied, his assistant bowed his head in deference. "Our people found *this* at the site of the most recent murder."

Ambrose stepped to his desk and held out his arm. Slowly, he turned his hand over and uncurled his fingers.

In his palm rested a knife. Its curved blade resembled a tiger's claw. The sharp hook bore a hole in one end, where a warrior could thread a finger through, allowing its wielder to whip the blade into a thousand deadly cuts. It was an ancient weapon called a *karambit,* one that traced its roots back centuries. And from the patina that burnished its surface, this particular blade was ancient—but this was no museum piece. It was plainly battle scarred and well used.

Bernard took it from Ambrose's hand. The heat against his fingertips confirmed his worst fear. The blade was plated with silver, the weapon of a Sanguinist.

He pictured the faces of the murdered girls, of their throats sliced from ear to ear.

He closed his fingers over the burning silver.

Of all the holy order, only one Sanguinist carried such a weapon, the man who had vanished as the murders began.

Rhun Korza.

4

Astride her favorite horse, Erin cantered across meadows turned golden brown by the dry California winter. Responding to the slightest shift of her weight, the black gelding lengthened his stride.

Attaboy, Blackjack.

She kept her horse boarded at a set of stables outside of Palo Alto. She rode him whenever she got a chance, knowing he needed the exercise, but mostly for the pure joy of flying over fields atop the muscular steed. Blackjack hadn't been ridden in a few days and was bouncy with energy.

She glanced back over a shoulder. Nate rode not far behind her, atop a gray named Gunsmoke. Growing up in Texas, he was a skilled rider himself and was clearly testing the mare.

She simply let Blackjack run out his high spirits, trying to concentrate on the wind across her face, the heady smell of horse, the easy connection between herself and her mount. She had loved riding ever since she was a little girl. It helped her think. Today she wondered about her visions, trying to figure out what to do about them. She knew they weren't just PTSD. They meant something more.

In front of her, the edge of the sun touched the top of rolling hills.

"We should head back soon!" Nate called to her. "Sun will be down in another half hour!"

She heard the trace of anxiety in his voice. Back in Rome, Nate had been trapped in darkness for days, tortured in those shadows. Night probably held a certain terror for him.

Recognizing this now, she knew she shouldn't have agreed to let him come along. But, earlier in the afternoon, after failing to reach Cardinal Bernard by phone, she had headed out of her office to burn off some of her anxiety. Nate had asked her where she was going, and foolishly she had allowed him to accompany her.

These last months, she had trouble saying no to him. After the tragic events in Israel and Rome, he continued to struggle, even more than she did, although he rarely spoke about it. She tried to be there for him, to help him bear the memories that had been thrust upon him. It was the least that she could do.

In the past, their relationship had been an easygoing one—as long as she pretended not to notice his attraction to her. But since she had fallen for Jordan, Nate had retreated into remote professionalism. But was it because of hurt feelings, anger, or something else?

Sadly, after tonight, it probably wouldn't matter.

She inwardly sighed. Maybe it was just as well that Nate had accompanied her on this ride. This moment offered her the perfect opportunity to speak to him in private.

She slowed Blackjack with a slight tension on the reins. Nate drew alongside her with Gunsmoke. He grinned at her, which broke off a piece of her heart. But he had to be told. Better to tell him now, before Christmas break, to give him time to get used to the idea.

She took a deep breath. "Nate, there's something I want to talk about."

Nate tilted his straw Stetson up and looked sidelong at her. Their horses walked side by side on the wide path. "What is it?"

"I talked to the dean this morning. I suggested the names of other professors whom you might be interested in working with."

His eyebrows pinched with concern. "Did I do something wrong? It's been tough since we got back, but—"

"Your work has always been excellent. It's not about you."

"Feels like it might be, seeing as how I'm involved and all."

She kept her eyes focused between her horse's soft black ears. "After what happened in Israel . . . I'm not so certain I'm the best choice for you."

He reached for Blackjack's bridle and slowed both horses to a stop. "What are you talking about?"

Erin faced him. He appeared both worried and angry. "Look, Nate. The university isn't happy that I lost two grad students."

"Hardly your fault."

She talked over him. "The dean feels that it might be best if I took a sabbatical to clear my head."

"So I'll wait." Nate folded his hands atop his saddle horn. "Not a problem."

"You don't understand." She fiddled with her reins, wanting to snap them and flee this conversation on horseback, but she let the hard truth hold her in place. "Nate, I think this is the first step toward the university letting me go."

His mouth dropped open.

She spoke quickly, getting it all out. "You don't need your dissertation tied to a professor about to be booted out. You're a brilliant scientist, Nate, and I'm sure we can find you a more suitable adviser—someone who can open doors for you that I can't anymore."

"But—"

"I appreciate your loyalty," she said. "But it's misguided."

Outrage flared from him. "Like hell it is!"

"Nate, it won't help me if you stay. Whatever is going to happen to my career will happen."

"But I picked you as my adviser because you're the best in your field." The anger drained from him, leaving him sagging in the saddle. "The *very* best. And that hasn't changed."

"Who knows? This may blow over in time."

Truthfully, Erin didn't expect it would, and down deep, she wasn't even sure she wanted it to. Earlier in her career, academia had offered her a haven of rationality after her strict religious upbringing, but it didn't feel like enough anymore. She remembered her difficulty with her classes this past semester. She couldn't keep teaching lies.

And she couldn't be any less truthful with Nate now.

"Even if it does blow over," she said, "you will have lost valuable opportunities while it does. I won't let that happen."

Nate looked ready to argue, to protest. Perhaps sensing his stress, his mare tossed her head and danced slightly on her forelegs.

"Don't make this any harder than it already is," she finished.

Nate rubbed his top lip, unable to look at her. Finally, he shook his head, turned Gunsmoke, and galloped away without a word, heading back toward the stable.

Blackjack whinnied after them, but she held the horse firm, knowing Nate needed some time alone. She gave them a good lead before letting Blackjack walk back along the trail.

The last rays of the day finally slipped behind the hill, but enough light remained to keep Blackjack from stepping into a gopher hole. Uncomfortable, she shifted on the horse. She felt Amy's lucky charm in her front pants pocket. She had forgotten she had put it there, still unsure what to do with it. She had considered returning it to Amy's parents, but would that be doing them any favors? The chunk of amber would always be a reminder that their daughter had chosen a profession that ended up killing her, her blood spilling away on foreign sands.

Erin couldn't do that to them—nor did she want to keep the talisman herself, this heavy token of her role in Amy's death.

Still not knowing what to do with it, she turned her thoughts back to Nate. Back in Rome, she had saved Nate's life, and now she would do what she could to save his career, no matter how angry that made him. Hopefully Nate would be more resigned to her request by the time she got to the stable. Either way, she would send him an e-mail later this evening with her list of names. They were solid archaeologists, and her recommendation would carry weight with them.

Nate would be all right.

And the farther he got away from her, the better off he would be.

Resigned and resolved, she patted Blackjack's neck. "Let's get you some oats and a good rubdown. How'd you like that?"

Blackjack's ear flicked back. He suddenly tensed under her.

Without thinking, she tightened her knees.

Blackjack snorted and danced sideways, rolling his eyes.

Something had him spooked.

Erin took in the open grasslands with one quick sweep. To her right stretched a shadowy stand of live oaks, their branches hung with clouds of silvery mistletoe. Anything could be hidden inside there.

From the tree line, she heard *crack!,* as the snap of a twig cut across the quiet evening.

She drew her pistol from the ankle holster and clicked off the safety, searching the live oaks for a target. But it was too dark to see anything. With her heart thundering in her ears, she cast a glance toward the distant stables.

Nate was probably there by now.

Blackjack suddenly reared, almost tossing her from the saddle. She leaned low over his neck as he tore away toward the stables. She didn't try to slow or stop him.

Fear tightened her vision, while she struggled to search in all directions. She tasted blood on her tongue as she bit her lip.

Then the smell of wine filled her nostrils.

No, no, no . . .

She fought to keep from slipping away, sensing another attack coming on. Panic tightened her grip on Blackjack's reins. If she lost control now, she'd pitch to the ground.

Then came a worse terror.

A low growl rumbled out of the night, rolling across the hills toward her. The guttural cry rose from no natural throat, but something horrid—

—and close.

5

Rhun lurched up and away. His head smashed against smooth stone. The blow opened a wound on his temple and knocked him back into the scalding bath of wine with a splash. He had awakened like this many times, trapped inside a stone sarcophagus, his body half submerged in wine—wine that had been blessed and consecrated into Christ's blood.

His cursed flesh burned in that holiness, floating in a sea of red pain. Part of him wanted to fight it, but another part of him knew that he had earned it. He had sinned centuries ago, and now he had found his true penance.

But how much time had passed?

Hours, days, years?

The pain refused to abate. He had sinned much, so he must be punished much. Then he could rest. His body *craved* rest—an end to pain, an end to sin.

Still, as he felt himself slipping away, he fought against it, sensing he must not surrender. He had a duty.

But to what?

He forced his eyes to stay open, to face a blackness even his preternatural vision could not pierce. Agony continued to rack his weakened body, but he beat it back with faith.

He reached a hand for the heavy silver cross he always wore on his breast—and found only wet cloth. He remembered. Someone had stolen his crucifix, his rosary, all the proofs of his faith. But he did not need them to reach the heavens. He breathed another prayer into the silence and pondered his fate.

Where am I? When ...

He had a weight of years behind him, more than humans could fathom.

Lifetimes of sin and service.

The memories plagued him as he hung within that burning sea. He drifted into and out of them.

... a horse cart stuck in the mud. He shoved bark under the wooden wheels while his sister laughed at him, her long braids flying from side to side.

... a gravestone with a woman's name on it. That same laughing sister. But this time he wore the garb of a priest.

... gathering lavender in a field and talking of court intrigues. Pale white hands placed the purple stalks into a handwoven basket.

... trains, automobiles, airplanes. Traveling ever faster across the surface of the earth, while seeing ever less.

... a woman with golden hair and amber eyes, eyes that saw what his could not.

He pulled free of the crush of these memories.

Only *this* moment mattered.

Only *this* place.

He must hold on to the pain, to his body.

He felt around, his hands plunging into cold liquid that burned as if it boiled. He was a Knight of Christ, ever since that moonlit evening he had visited his sister's grave. And while Christ's blood had sustained him over the long centuries since, the same consecrated wine blazed against him always, its holiness at war with the evil deep inside him.

He took a deep breath, smelling stone and his own blood. He stretched his arms and ran his palms along the polished surfaces around him. He stroked the marble—slick as glass. Across the roof of his prison, his fingertips found a tracery of inlaid silver. It burned his fingertips.

Still, he pressed his palms to that design and pushed against the sarcophagus's stone lid. He vaguely sensed he had done this many times before—and like those prior attempts, he failed again. The weight would not be shifted.

Weakened by even this small effort, he collapsed limply back into the wine.

He cupped his hands and lifted the scalding bitter liquid to his lips. The blood of Christ would lend him strength, but it would also force him to relive his worst sins. Steadying himself against the penance that must follow, he drank. As his throat burned with fire, he folded his hands in prayer.

Which of his sins would the wine torture him with this time?

As he drifted into it, he realized his penance was revealing a sin that was hundreds of years old.

The servants of Čachtice Castle huddled outside the steel door of the windowless tower room. Inside, their former mistress had been imprisoned, charged with the deaths of hundreds of young girls. As a member of Hungarian nobility, the countess could not be executed, only shut off from the world for her crimes, where her bloodlust could be bottled up behind brick and steel.

Rhun had come here for one purpose: to rid the world of this creature, to atone for his role in her transformation from a woman of sweet spirit, one skilled in the healing arts, into a beast who ravaged the surrounding countryside, stripping young girls of their lives.

He stood before the countess now, locked inside the room with her. He had bought the servants' silence with gold and promises of freedom. They wanted her gone from the castle as much as he.

They, too, knew what she was and cowered outside.

Rhun had also arrived with a gift for the countess, something she had demanded to gain her cooperation. To appease her, he had found a young girl, sick with fever, soon to die, in a neighboring orphanage, and brought her to this monster.

Standing beside the prison cot, Rhun listened as the young girl's heart stumbled and slowed. He did nothing to save her. He could not. He must wait. He hated himself, but he remained still.

At last, the weak heart stuttered its final beat.

You will be the last one she kills, *he promised.*

Near to death herself, starved for so long in this prison, the countess raised her head from the girl's throat. Pearls of blood dripped from her white chin. Her silver eyes held a dreamy and sated look, an expression he had seen there once before. He would not dwell on that. He prayed that she was distracted enough for him to end this, and that he would be strong enough to do so.

He could not fail again.

He bent to the cot, untangled her thin limbs from the dead girl. He gently lifted the countess's cold form in his arms and carried her away from the soiled bed.

She leaned her cheek against his, her lips near his ear. "It is good to be in your arms again," she whispered, and he believed her. Her silver eyes shone up at him. "Will you break your vows once more?"

She favored him with a slow, lazy smile, mesmerizingly beautiful. He responded, trapped for a moment by her charm.

He remembered his love for her, how in a moment of hubris he had believed himself capable of breaking his vow as a Sanguinist, that he could lie with her like any ordinary man. But in his lust of that moment, locked to her, inside her, he had lost control and let the demon in him burst its bonds. Teeth ripped her soft throat and drank deeply until that font was nearly empty, the woman under him at death's door. To save her, he had turned her into a monster, fed her his own blood to keep her with him, praying she would take the same vows he did and join the Sanguinist order alongside him.

She did not.

A rustle on the far side of the thick door brought his thoughts back to this room, to the dead girl on the bed, to the many others who had shared her fate.

He knocked on the door with the toe of his boot, and the servants unlocked the way. He shouldered it open as they fled down the dark stairs of the tower.

Left behind in their wake, placed outside the door, a marble sarcophagus rested atop the rush-covered floor. Earlier, he had filled the coffin with consecrated wine and left it open.

Seeing what awaited her, she raised her head, dazed by bloodlust. "Rhun?"

"It will save you," he said. "And your soul."

"I don't want my soul saved," she said, her fingers clutching to him.

Before she could fight him, he lifted her over the open sarcophagus and plunged her down into wine. She screamed when the consecrated wine first touched her skin. He set his jaw, knowing how it must pain her, wanting even now to take the agony from her and claim it for himself.

She thrashed under his hands, but in her weakened state, she was no match for his strength. Wine splashed over the sides. He forced her against the stone bottom, ignoring the fiery burn of the wine. He was glad he could not see her face, drowned under that red tide.

He held her there—until at last, she lay quiet.

She would now sleep until such a time as he could find a way to reverse what he had done, to return life to her dead heart.

With tears in his eyes, he fitted the heavy stone lid in place and secured it with silver straps. Once done, he rested his cold palms against the marble and prayed for her soul.

And his own.

Slowly Rhun returned to himself. He remembered fully how he had come to be here, imprisoned in the same sarcophagus he had used to trap the countess centuries ago. He recalled returning to his sarcophagus, to where he had entombed the coffin inside a bricked-up vault far beneath Vatican City, hiding his secret from all eyes.

He had come here upon the words of a prophecy.

It seemed the countess still had a role to play in this world.

Following the battle for the Blood Gospel, he had ventured alone to where he had buried his greatest sin. He had hammered through the bricks, broken the seals of the sarcophagus, and decanted her from this bath of ancient wine. He pictured her silver eyes opening for the first time in centuries, gazing into his. For that brief moment, he allowed his defenses to fall, slipping back to long-ago summers, to a time when he dared to believe that he could become more than what he was, that one such as he could love without destruction.

In that lapse, he had failed to see the shattered brick clutched in her hand. He moved too slowly as she swung the hard rock with a hatred that spanned centuries—or perhaps he simply knew he deserved it.

Then he awoke here, and now he finally knew the truth.

She sentenced me to this same prison.

While a part of him knew he deserved this fate, he knew he must escape.

If for no other reason than that he had loosed this monster once again upon the unsuspecting world.

Still, he pictured her as he once knew her, so full of life, always in sunlight. He had always called her *Elisabeta,* but history now christened her by another name, a darker epitaph.

Elizabeth Bathory—*the Blood Countess.*

2:22 A.M. CET
Rome, Italy

As befit her noble station, the apartment Elisabeta had chosen was luxurious. Thick red velvet drapes cloaked tall arched windows. The oak floor beneath her cold feet glowed a soft gold and breathed warmth. She settled into a leather chair, the hide finely tanned, with the comforting scent of the long dead animal under the chemical smell.

On the mahogany table in front of her, a white taper sputtered, near to expiring. She held a fresh candle to its dying flame. Once the wick caught fire, she pressed the tall taper into the soft wax of the old one. She leaned close to the small flame, preferring firelight to the harsh glare that blazed in modern Rome.

She had claimed these rooms after killing the former tenants. Afterward, she had ransacked drawers full of unfamiliar objects, trying to fathom this strange century, attempting to piece together a lost civilization by studying its artifacts.

But her clues to this age were not all to be found in drawers.

Across the table, candlelight flickered over uneven piles, each gathered from the pockets and bodies of her past kills. She turned her attention to a stack crowned by a silver cross. She reached toward it but kept her fingers from the fiery heat of the metal and the blessing it carried.

She let a single fingertip caress the silver. It burned her, but she did not care—for another suffered far more because of its loss.

She smiled, the pain drawing her into memory.

Strong arms had lifted her from the coffin of wine, pulling her from her slumber, awakening her. Like any threatened beast, she had stayed limp, knowing stealth to be her best advantage.

As her eyes opened, she recognized her benefactor as much from his white Roman collar as from his dark eyes and hard face.

Father Rhun Korza.

It was the same man who had tricked her into this coffin.

But how long ago?

As he held her, she let her arm fall to the ground. The back of her hand came to rest against a loose stone.

She smiled up at him. He smiled back, love in his shining eyes.

With unearthly speed, she smashed the stone against his temple. Her other hand slipped up his sleeve, where he always kept his silver knife. She palmed it before he dropped her. Another blow, and he fell.

She quickly rolled atop him, her teeth seeking the cold flesh of his white throat. Once she pierced his skin, his fate lay at her mercy. It took strength to stop drinking before she killed him, patience to empty half the wine from the coffin before she sealed him inside it. But she must. Fully immersed in wine, he would merely sleep until rescued, as she had done.

Instead, she had left only a little wine, knowing he would soon wake in his lonely tomb and slowly starve, as she had while imprisoned in her castle tower.

Lifting her finger from his stolen cross, she allowed herself a moment of cold satisfaction. As she moved her arm, her fingers dragged over a battered shoe atop another pile.

This tiny bit of leather marked her first kill in this new age.

She savored that moment.

As she fled the dark catacombs—blind to where she was, when she was—rough stones cut through the thin leather soles of her shoes and sliced her feet. She paid them no heed. She had this one chance of escape.

She knew not where she ran to, but she recognized the feel of holy ground underfoot. It weakened her muscles and slowed her steps. Still, she felt more powerful than she ever had. Her time in the wine had strengthened her, how much she only dared to guess.

Then the sound of a heartbeat had stopped her headlong flight through the dark tunnels.

Human.

The heart thrummed steady and calm. It had not yet sensed her presence. Faint with hunger, she rested her back against the tunnel wall. She licked her lips, tasting the Sanguinist's bitter blood. She lusted to savor something sweeter, hotter.

The flicker of a faraway candle lightened the darkness. She heard the pad of shoes drawing nearer.

Then a name was called. "Rhun?"

She flattened against the cold stone. So someone was searching for the priest.

She crept forward and spotted a shadowy figure stepping around a far corner toward her. In one raised hand, he carried a candle in a holder, revealing the brown robes of a monk.

Failing to see her, he continued forward, oblivious of the danger.

Once close enough, she sprang forward and bore his warm body to the floor. Before the man could even gasp, her teeth found his luscious throat. Blood surged through her in wave after wave, strengthening her even more. She reveled in bliss, as she had every time since the first. She wanted to laugh amid this joy.

Rhun would have her trade this power for scalding wine, for a life of servitude to his Church.

Never.

Spent, she released the human shell, her curious fingers lingering on the fabric of the robes. It did not feel like linen. She detected a slipperiness to it, like silk, but not like silk.

A trickle of unease wormed through her.

The candle had snuffed when the man fell, but the ember at the wick's tip glowed dull red. She blew on it, brightening its color to a feeble orange.

Under the dim light, she patted down the cooling body, repulsed again by the slippery feel of the fabric. She discovered a silver pectoral cross but abandoned its searing touch.

She reached down his legs and pulled a shoe from one lifeless foot, sensing strangeness here, too. She held it near the light. The top was leather, scuffed and unremarkable, but the sole was made of a thick spongy substance. She had never seen its like. She pinched the material between her thumb and forefinger. It gave, then sprang back, like a young tree.

She sat back on her haunches, thinking. Such a peculiar substance had not existed when Rhun had tricked her into the coffin of wine, but now it must be commonplace enough for a lowly monk to wear.

She suddenly felt like screaming, sensing the breadth of the gulf that separated her from her past. She knew she had not slumbered for days, weeks, nor even months.

But years, decades, perhaps centuries.

She accepted this brutal truth, knowing one other.

She must take extra care in this strange new world.

And she had. Moving from the shoe, she picked up a white ball with a red star on it from the tabletop. Its surface felt like human skin, but smoother. It repulsed her, but she forced herself to hold it, to toss it in the air and catch it again.

Upon leaving the catacombs, she had been so frightened.

But soon others became frightened of her.

She had crept through the tunnels, expecting more monks. But she had encountered none as she followed the whisper of distant heartbeats ever higher.

Eventually she reached a thick wooden door and broke through it with ease—and stepped into unfettered air. It caressed her body, dried the wine on her dress, and carried with it the familiar smells of humans, of perfumes, of stone, of river. But also odors she had never scented before—acrid stinks she imagined only existed in an alchemist's workshop. The stench drove her against the door, almost back across the threshold and into the shelter of the dark tunnels.

The foreignness terrified her.

But a countess never cowers, never shows fear.

She straightened her back and stepped forward as a lady must, her hands folded in front of her, her eyes and ears alert to danger.

As she moved away from the door, she immediately recognized the columns to either side, the massive dome rising to the left, even the obelisk in the plaza ahead. The Egyptian spire had been erected in the piazza the same year that her daughter Anna was born.

She relaxed upon seeing all this, knowing where she was.

St. Peter's Square.

Sardonic amusement warmed her.

Rhun had hidden her under the Holy City.

She kept to the edge of the piazza. Tall poles illuminated the square with a harsh, unnatural flame. The light hurt her eyes, so she shied away from it, staying near the colonnade that framed the plaza.

A couple strolled past her.

Ill at ease, she slipped behind a marble column. The woman wore breeches, like a man. Her short hair brushed the top of her shoulders, and her partner held her hand as they talked together.

She had never seen a woman so tall.

Hidden by the column, she studied other figures shifting out on the square. *All brightly dressed, bundled in thick coats that looked finely made. Out on a neighboring street, strange wagons glided along, led by unnatural beams of light, pulled by no beasts.*

Shivering, she leaned against the column. This new world threatened to overwhelm her, to freeze her in place. She hung her head and forced herself to breathe. She must shut it all out and find one simple task . . . and perform that task.

The reek of wine struck her nose. She touched her sodden garment. It would not do. She looked again out at the plaza, at the women in such strange garb. To escape from here, she must become a wolf in sheep's clothing, for if they guessed what she was, her death would follow.

No matter how many years had passed, that certainty had not changed.

Her nails dug deep into her palms. She did not want to leave the familiar. She sensed that whatever lay beyond the plaza would be even more foreign to her than what lay inside.

But she must go.

A countess never shirked from her duty.

And her duty was to survive.

Sensing she had hours before dawn, she lowered herself into the shadows of the colonnade. She sat not breathing, not moving, as motionless as a statue, listening to chaotic human heartbeats, the words from many tongues, the frequent laughter.

These people were so very different from the men and women of her time.

Taller, louder, stronger, and well fed.

The women fascinated her the most. They wore men's clothing: pants and shirts. They walked unafraid. They spoke sharply to men without reprimand and acted as if they were their equals—not in the calculated way she had been forced to use in her time, but with an easy manner, as if this was commonplace and accepted.

This era held promise.

A young mother approached carelessly with a small child in tow. The woman hunched in a burgundy-colored woolen coat and wore riding boots, although by the smell of them they had never been near a horse.

Small for a woman of this time, she was close to Elisabeta's own size.

The child dropped a white ball with a red star on it, and it rolled into the shadows, stopping a handsbreadth from Elisabeta's tattered shoes. The ball smelled like the bottom of the priest's shoes. The child refused to go after the plaything, as if sensing the beast hiding in the shadows.

Her mother coaxed her in queer-sounding Italian, waving toward the forest of columns. Still, the little girl shook her head.

Elisabeta ran her tongue across her sharp teeth, willing the mother to come in after the toy. She could take the woman's life, steal her finery, and be gone before the motherless child could cry for help.

From the shadows, she savored the child's terrified heartbeats, listening as the mother's tones grew more impatient.

She waited for the proper moment in this strange time.

Then sprang.

Elisabeta lowered the ball to the table, sighing, losing interest in her trophies.

Standing, she crossed over to the vast wardrobes in the bedroom, stuffed with silks, velvets, furs, all stolen from her victims these many weeks. Each night, she preened before the perfect silver mirrors and selected a new set of clothes to wear. Some of the garments were almost familiar, others as outlandish as a minstrel's garb.

Tonight she chose soft blue pants, a silk shirt that matched her silver eyes, and a pair of thin leather boots. She ran a comb through her thick black hair. She had cropped it to her shoulders, matching the style of a woman whom she had killed under a bridge.

How very different she looked now. What would Anna, Katalin, and Paul say if they saw her? Her own children would not recognize her.

Still, she reminded herself, *I am Countess Elisabeta de Ecsed.*

Her eyes narrowed.

No.

"Elizabeth . . ." she whispered to her reflection, reminding herself that this was a new time and, to survive it, she must abide by its ways. So she would take on this more modern name, wear it like she wore her new hair and clothing. It was who she would become. She had played many roles since she had been betrothed to Ferenc at age eleven—an impulsive girl, a lonely wife, a scholar of languages, a skilled healer, a devoted mother—more roles than she could count. This was but another one.

She turned slightly to judge her new self in the mirror. With short hair and wearing pants, she looked like a man. But she was no man, and she no longer envied men their strength and power.

She had her own.

She walked to the balcony windows and drew back the soft curtains. She gazed at the blaze of glorious man-made lights of the new Rome. The strangeness still terrified her, but she had mastered it enough to eat, to rest, to learn.

She took strength in one feature of the city, the one rhythm that survived unchanged across the centuries. She closed her eyes and listened to a thousand heartbeats, ticking like a thousand clocks, letting her know, in the end, that the march of time mattered little.

She knew what time it was, what time it *always* was for a predator such as she.

She pushed open the balcony doors upon the night.

It was time to hunt.

6

As twilight swept over the hills and meadows, Erin thundered down the last of the trail toward the stables. With no urging, Blackjack galloped at full speed into the yard.

She kept one hand on the reins and the other on her pistol. As her gelding skidded and stuttered to a stop in the dusty yard, she twisted in her saddle. She pointed her weapon toward the black hills.

While racing here, she had failed to spot the creature that had spooked her horse, but she had *heard* it. Sounds of branches cracking, of brush being trampled, had chased them out of the hills. She couldn't shake the feeling that the shadowy hunter was playing with them, waiting for full night to attack.

She wasn't about to give it that chance.

She trotted Blackjack past her old Land Rover, only to discover a new car—a black Lincoln town car—on its far side, parked a distance away. She passed closer to it on the way to the stables, spotting a familiar symbol on its door: two crossed keys and a triple crown.

The papal seal.

The fear inside her stoked higher.

What is someone from the Vatican doing here?

She searched and saw no one and urged Blackjack forward toward the stables. Once at the sliding doors of the barn, she reined in the horse. Coughing from the dust, she slid from the saddle and kept hold of both Blackjack's lead and her pistol. Seeking answers as well as shelter, she hurried to the doors and reached for the handle.

Before her fingers could touch it, the door slid open on its own. A hand burst out, grabbed her wrist in an iron grip, and hauled her across the threshold. Startled, she lost her grip on Blackjack's lead, fighting just to keep her footing.

Her attacker pulled her into the darkness of the stable, and the door slammed closed behind her, leaving her horse on the outside. Gaining her feet, she twisted to the side and kicked hard, her boot striking something soft.

"Ow. Take it easy, Erin."

She immediately recognized the voice, though it made no sense. "Jordan?"

Hands released her.

A flashlight clicked, and a white glow illuminated Jordan's face. Past the sergeant's shoulder, she spotted Nate, safe but looking pale, his eyes too wide.

Jordan rubbed his stomach and flashed her that crooked grin of his, immediately drawing a large amount of the tension from her bones. He stood there in dress pants and a white shirt, unbuttoned at the collar with the sleeves rolled up, displaying his muscular tanned arms.

She leaped to him and hugged him hard. He felt warm and good and natural, and she loved how easy it was to fall into his arms again.

She spoke into his chest. "I can't believe it's you."

"In the flesh . . . though after that kick of yours, maybe a tad more sore."

She leaned back to take him in. A day's worth of stubble shadowed his square chin, his blue eyes smiled at her, and his hair had grown out longer. She threaded her fingers through that thick wheat-blond hair and pulled him down into a kiss.

She wanted nothing more than to lengthen it, to linger in his arms, maybe show him the empty hay loft upstairs, but she stepped back, drawn away by a larger concern.

"Blackjack," she said. "My horse. We have to get him inside. Something's out there in the hills."

She turned to the door—as a horse's scream erupted, ripping through the night and quickly cutting off. Before anyone could move, a heavy object thudded against the neighboring wall. They fled deeper into the stables, to where the other horses were boarded in stalls. She looked toward the door.

No, please, no . . .

She pictured her large gelding, with his trusting eyes and soft nose, the way he pranced when happy, and his gentle neighs that greeted her whenever she entered the barn.

Jordan readied his black Heckler & Koch MP7, a mean-looking machine pistol.

She lifted her small Glock 19, recognizing a problem. "I need something bigger."

Jordan handed his flashlight to Nate and reached to his belt. He pulled out his Colt 1911 and passed it to her, the same gun he had loaned to her often in the past. She wrapped her fingers around the grip and felt safer.

She turned to give her Glock to Nate, to offer him some protection—when a stranger appeared, stepping out of the deeper shadows behind him and startling her. The man wore a formal dark blue uniform, with two gold crosses embroidered on his lapels.

A chaplain?

"I hate to interrupt your happy reunion," the stranger said. "But it's time we thought about leaving here. I searched for other exits, but the main door remains the wisest path."

"This is Christian," Jordan introduced. "Friend of Rhun's, if you get my drift."

In other words, *Sanguinist.*

Nate's voice trembled. "The professor's car is parked about fifty yards away. Could we make it that far?"

As answer, an unnatural screeching pierced the night.

From the stalls all around, the horses stamped and shouldered into their gates, whinnying their growing terror. Even they knew escape was the only hope.

"What's waiting for us out there?" Jordan asked, his weapon fixed on the door.

"From its smell and hisses, I believe it's a cougar," Christian said. "Albeit a tainted one."

Tainted?

Erin went colder. "You're talking about a *blasphemare.*"

The chaplain bowed his head in acknowledgment.

Blasphemare were beasts that had been corrupted by the blood of a *strigoi*, poisoned into monstrous incarnations of their natural forms, with hides so tough that Sanguinists made armor out of their skins.

Nate sucked in a quick breath. She touched him with one hand and felt him shiver. She didn't blame him. A *blasphemare* wolf had once savaged him badly.

She had to get Nate out of here.

A ripping, splintering sound erupted to their left. Nate swung the flashlight toward the noise. Four hooked claws shredded through the thick redwood wall. Panicked, Nate fired the Glock at it.

The claws vanished, followed by another yowl, sounding angrier.

"I think you pissed it off," Jordan said.

"Sorry," Nate said.

"No worries. If you hadn't fired, I would've."

The cat bowled into the same wall, shaking the rafters, as if trying to break inside.

"Time to go," Christian said and pointed to the door ahead. "I'll exit first, try to draw it off, and you follow in a count of ten. Make straight for Erin's Land Rover and get moving."

"What about you?" Jordan asked.

"If I'm lucky, pick me up. If not, leave me."

Before anyone could argue, Christian covered the distance to the door in a breath. He grabbed a handle and shoved open the front doors. In front of him stretched an expanse of dust and grass. In the distance stood her beat-up Land Rover and the shiny Lincoln town car. Both looked much farther away than when she had ridden up on Blackjack a moment ago.

Christian stepped into the night, illuminated by a lamp over the door. A flash of silver showed that he'd drawn a blade, then he vanished to the left.

Jordan kept his gun up, plainly starting a countdown in his head.

Erin turned away, remembering Blackjack. She hurried along the line of six stalls and began releasing the catches, swinging the doors open. She wouldn't leave the horses trapped in here to die as Blackjack had. They deserved a chance to run.

Already frightened, the horses thundered out of the stalls and swept between Jordan and Nate. Gunsmoke followed last. Nate ran his fingers along the mare's sweating flanks as the horse raced by, as if longing to accompany her. Reaching the door, the horses fled out into the night.

"That's a ten count," Jordan said and waved his free arm toward the open door.

The three of them rushed forward, following the dust-stirred trail of the horses out into the yard. Jordan kept to their left, pointing his gun in the direction Christian had vanished.

As Erin sprinted with Nate toward the Land Rover, motion drew her attention back to the stable. From around the far corner, Christian came tumbling back into the yard, landing in a crouch.

From that same corner, a monstrous beast stalked into view.

Erin gaped at the sight.

Nate tripped, crashing down to one knee.

The cougar padded into the yard, its tail lashing back and forth. It stretched nine feet, well over three hundred pounds of muscle, claws, and teeth. Tall, tufted ears swiveled, taking in every sound. Red-gold eyes shone in the darkness. But the most striking feature was its ghostly gray pelt, like a shred of fog made flesh.

"Go," Jordan urged, seeing her slow to help Nate. "I got him."

But who has you?

She stayed with them, keeping her Colt high.

Across the yard, the beast snarled at Christian, revealing long fangs—then lunged. But it was a feint. It jumped past the Sanguinist chaplain and headed straight for them.

By now, Jordan had Nate back on his feet, but the two men would never get out of the way in time. Standing her ground in front of them, she squeezed off a shot. The bullet struck the animal on the forehead, but it merely shook its head and kept coming.

She kept firing as it barreled toward her.

She couldn't run, not until Nate was safe.

She squeezed the trigger over and over again—until finally the Colt's slide locked back. Out of bullets.

The cat bunched its back legs and bounded across the last of the distance.

Vatican City

Rhun's muscles stiffened with terror.

She's in danger . . .

He pictured wisps of blond hair and amber eyes. The scent of lavender filled his nostrils. Pain kept her name from him, leaving him only need and desire.

Must reach her . . .

As panic thrummed through his body, he thrashed over onto his stomach in the burning wine, fighting through the agony, trying to think, to hold one thought in his head.

He could not let her die.

He pushed himself onto his hands and knees and braced his back against the stone lid of the sarcophagus. Gathering his faith, his strength, and his fear, he pushed against the marble slab.

Stone grated on stone as the lid shifted. A mere finger's breadth, but it moved.

He gritted his teeth and pushed again, straining, tearing his robe. The silver inlaid into the marble slab above branded his exposed back. He smelled his skin burning, felt his blood flowing.

Still, he strained with every last fiber of muscle, bone, and will.

His existence became one agonizing note of desire.

To save her.

Santa Clara County, California

Jordan bowled into Erin, sweeping her legs out from under her.

As she crashed onto her back, the *blasphemare* cat sailed over them both. A back paw slammed near Jordan's head, knocking up dust. The cougar spun around, hissing a scream of thwarted desire.

Still on the ground, Jordan rolled to a shoulder and pointed his Heckler & Koch machine pistol and fired on full automatic. He blazed a trail along its flank as it turned, stripping tufts of fur, drawing some blood, but not much.

He emptied his entire forty-round box magazine in less than three seconds.

And only succeeded in pissing off the cat.

The cougar faced them, crouched low, claws dug deep into the hard clay. It growled, hissing like a steam engine.

Jordan repositioned his empty weapon, ready to go caveman and use it as a club.

Then in a flash of blue, a small shape landed atop the creature's head. A silver knife slashed through its ear. Dark blood oozed out.

The cat yowled, rolling, twisting its head, trying to reach Christian.

But the Sanguinist was fast, sliding off the rear of the cat, dodging the tail.

"Get to the Rover!" Christian yelled, ducking as a hind paw kicked at him and slashed the air with razor claws.

Jordan hauled Erin to her feet and sprinted toward the Land Rover.

Ahead, Nate had already reached the SUV and pulled open both the driver's door and the rear door—then climbed into the backseat.

Good man.

Jordan raced alongside Erin. Once they reached the Rover, he dove into the driver's seat at the same time she lunged into the back to join Nate. Both doors slammed in unison.

Erin reached over the seat back and slapped cold keys into his open, waiting palm.

He grinned savagely. They made a good team—now to make sure that team stayed alive. He keyed the ignition, gunned the engine, and sped in reverse, fishtailing to the side.

As he swung around, his headlamps found the cougar. Its ghostgray pelt glowed in the light. The cat turned toward the car like a churning storm cloud, squinting its red-gold eyes against the glare.

Christian stood a few paces behind it.

The cougar growled and bounded toward the Land Rover, drawn by the sound and motion.

Typical cat . . .

Jordan sped away in reverse, trying to keep the light in the cat's eyes.

Momentarily free, Christian sprinted for his black sedan.

The cat gained on them, running full tilt. Jordan feared the beast could easily outrun them on these country roads. Proving this, the beast leaped and crashed its front half onto the hood. Claws tore through the metal. A heavy paw batted at the windshield. Cracks splintered across the glass.

Another blow like that, and it would be in the front seat.

Then a car horn blasted loudly, incessantly.

Howling at the sudden noise, the cougar bounded off the hood like a startled tabby. It landed, twisting to face the new challenge, its ears flattened in fury.

Past the beast's bulk, Jordan spotted Christian. The Sanguinist crouched inside the back of his town car. He leaned over the front seat, an arm stretched to the steering wheel, and laid into the car horn, pressing it over and over again.

All the sedan's windows were down.

What are you doing?

The cat bounded toward the noise.

Jordan braked hard and shoved the car out of reverse and back into drive. He sped after the cougar, chasing its tail. He knew he couldn't reach the car before the beast did, but he intended to be there to help Christian.

The cougar slammed into the flank of the town car, knocking it aside a full foot, denting it deeply. Christian was bowled across the backseat. The blare of the horn immediately died away, leaving only the growling hiss of the monstrous cat.

The cougar spotted its prey inside and forced its head and shoulders through the window, going after the priest.

Jordan floored the gas, intending to ram the beast from behind if necessary.

Get out of there, buddy!

The cat squirmed and kicked its hindquarters, pulling its full length through the back window and into the car. It was a tight squeeze, but the beast was determined.

Then on the other side, Christian squirted out of the far window.

"There!" Erin yelled, spotting him, too.

Jordan turned and skidded the Rover past the rear bumper of the sedan.

Christian stumbled away from the town car, pointing the key fob back at the car. He pressed a button—and all the windows rolled up, and the car beeped twice.

Jordan stifled a laugh at Christian's sheer audacity.

He'd locked the cougar in the car.

The cat snarled and furiously flung itself about inside, rocking the sedan.

Jordan pulled up next to Christian. "Need a lift?"

Christian opened the front passenger door and climbed inside. "Drive. And fast. I don't know how long my trap will hold it."

Jordan understood. He gunned the engine, raced the Land Rover out of the stable yard, and ricocheted along the dirt road toward the highway. He needed to put as much distance as possible between them and that angry cat.

Christian pulled a cell phone out of his pocket and barked orders in Latin.

"What's he saying?" Jordan asked Erin.

"Calling for backup," she said. "For someone to dispatch that cougar."

Christian finished his call, then glanced back at the stable. "I hope the beast doesn't have enough space inside that car to get up a good enough swing to break through the safety glass."

Erin cleared her throat. "But why was it even here? Why was it after me?"

Jordan glanced over to Christian.

"My apologies," Christian said, looking crestfallen. "But I believe someone must have caught wind that Jordan and I were seeking your help. Word might have reached the wrong ears. As you know, the order has suspicions that there are Belial traitors hidden among our fold. I fear I might not have been careful enough."

The Belial . . .

She pictured that force of *strigoi* and humans, united under a mysterious leader. Even the tight ranks of the Sanguinist order were not impervious to that group's reach and infiltration.

"It might not be you," Erin said, reaching forward and squeezing his shoulder. "Cardinal Bernard called for me earlier today, too. Maybe he let something slip. But either way, let's table this until we get Nate somewhere safe."

"Don't I get a say in this?" Nate sounded aggrieved.

"You do not," Christian answered. "My orders are clear and specific. I am to take Erin and Jordan back to Rome. That's it."

Jordan wondered if that was true, or if he was just trying to take the pressure off Erin.

"Why Rome?" Erin asked.

Christian swung to face her. "It seems, in all this tumult, we've forgotten to tell you. Father Rhun Korza has gone missing. He vanished shortly after that bloody battle in Rome."

Glancing in the rearview mirror, Jordan noted the concern in Erin's eyes, the way a hand rose to her throat. She still had scars there from where Rhun had bitten her, fed on her. But from her worried expression, she plainly cared deeply for the Sanguinist priest.

"What does that have to do with me?" she asked.

Christian smiled at her. "Because you, Dr. Granger, are the only one who can find him."

Jordan didn't care about the disappearance of Rhun Korza. As far as he was concerned, the guy could stay lost. Instead, there remained only one mystery he wanted solved.

Who sent that damned cat?

7

December 19, 4:34 A.M. CET
Rome, Italy

With a pair of antique watchmaker's tweezers in hand, the leader of the Belial hunched over the workspace on his desk. He pinched a magnifying loupe to one eye. With exquisite care, he carefully wound a tiny brass spring inside the heart of a thumbnail-size mechanism.

The spring tightened and caught.

He smiled his satisfaction and closed the two halves of the mechanism, forming what appeared to be the metal sculpture of an insect, with six jointed legs and an eyeless head. The latter was spiked with a needle-sharp silver proboscis and crowned by the gentle sweep of a pair of feathery brass antennae.

Blessed with steady hands, he shifted to another corner of his workspace and tweezed up the disarticulated forewing of a moth from a bed of white silk. He lifted the iridescent petal toward the glow of his halogen work light. The moth's scales shone silvery green, barely hiding the delicate lace of its internal structure, marking the handsome pattern of *Actias luna*, the luna moth. With a total wingspan of four inches, it was one of the world's largest moths.

With patient and clever motions, he fitted the fragile wing into tiny clips lining the brass-and-silver thorax of his mechanical creation. He repeated the same with the other forewing and two more hind wings. The mechanism inside the thorax held hundreds of gears, wheels, and springs, waiting to beat life back into these beautiful organic wings.

Once finished, his eyes lingered on each piece. He loved the precision of his creations, the way each cog caught another, meshed into a larger design. For years he had made clocks, needing to see time measured on a device as it was not measured on his own body. He had since moved his interest and skill toward the creation of these tiny automatons—half machine and half living creatures—bound for eternity to his bidding.

Normally he found peace in such intricate work, settling into easy concentration. But this night, that perfect calm escaped him. Even the soft tinkling of a neighboring fountain failed to soothe him. His centuries-old plan—as intricate and delicate as any of his mechanisms—was at risk.

As he made a tiny correction upon his latest creation, the end of the tweezers quivered, and he tore the delicate forewing, sprinkling iridescent green scales upon the white silk. He uttered a curse that had not been heard since the days of ancient Rome and threw the tweezers to his glass desktop.

He drew in a long breath, searching again for that peace.

It eluded him.

As if on cue, the telephone on his desk rang.

He rubbed his temples with his longer fingers, seeking to work calm into his head from the outside. "*Sì*, Renate?"

"Father Leopold has arrived in the downstairs lobby, sir." The bored tone of his beautiful receptionist strummed through the speaker. He had rescued her from a life of sexual slavery on the streets of Turkey, and she repaid him with loyal, yet indifferent, service. In the years he had known her, she had never once expressed surprise. A trait he respected.

"Allow him up."

Standing, he stretched and walked to the bank of windows behind his desk. His company—the Argentum Corporation—owned the tallest skyscraper in Rome, and his office took up its uppermost floor. The penthouse looked out upon the Eternal City through windowed walls of ballistic glass. Underfoot, the floor was polished purplish-red marble, imperial porphyry, so rare it was found in only one site in the world, an Egyptian mountain the Romans called *Mons Porphyrites*. It had been discovered during Christ's lifetime and became the marble of kings, emperors, and gods.

Fifty years before, he had designed and engineered this spire with a world-renowned architect. That man was dead now, of course. But he remained, unchanged.

He studied his reflection. In his natural lifetime, scars from a childhood scourge had pocked his face, but the imperfections had disappeared when the curse of endless years found him. Now he could not remember where those scars had been. He only saw smooth, unblemished skin, a set of small wrinkles that never deepened around his silver-gray eyes, a square rugged face, and a mass of thick gray hair.

Bitter thoughts swept through him. That face had been called many names over the centuries, worn many identities. But after two millennia he had returned to the one his mother had given him.

Judas Iscariot.

Though that name had become synonymous with betrayal, he had come full circle from denial to accepting that truth—especially after discovering the path to his own redemption. Centuries ago, he had finally discovered *why* Christ had cursed him with immortality.

So he could do what he must do in the coming days.

Shouldering this responsibility, he leaned his forehead against the cool glass. Once he had a manager who was so terrified of falling that he could not stand within six feet of the window.

Judas had no such fear of falling. He had fallen to what should have been his death many times.

He gazed through the glass to the city below, its glittering streets known for its decadence since before the time of Christ. Rome had always been ablaze at night, although white-hot electricity had long replaced the warm yellow fire of torches and candles.

If his plan worked, all those lights would finally go dark.

Glitter and fire were characteristics that modern people thought belonged to them, but man had brightened the world with his will long ago, too. Sometimes for advancement and sometimes triviality.

Standing there, he remembered the sparkling balls he had attended, centuries of them, all the partygoers certain that they had reached the peak of glamour. With his looks and wealth, he had never lacked for invitations, nor for female companionship, but those companions had often demanded more than he had to give.

He had watched too many lovers age and die, dimming any hope of lasting love.

In the end, it had never been worth the price.

Except once.

He had attended a ball in medieval Venice where a woman had caught his eternal heart and showed him that love was worth any price. He stared down at the colored lights of the city until they blurred together and carried him into memory.

Judas paused at the edge of the Venetian ballroom, letting the colors swirl in front of him. Crimson reds, deepest golds, indigos that matched the evening sea, blacks that ate the light, and the pearly radiance of bare shoulders. Nowhere did the women dress as brightly, and display as much skin, as in Venice.

The ballroom looked much as it had one hundred years before. The only changes were the three new oil paintings hung on its stately walls. The paintings depicted stern or jolly members of this Venetian family, each dressed in stylish finery of their day. All were now long dead. At his right hand was a painting of Giuseppe, gone thirty years, his face frozen at forty by the oils and talent of a long dead painter. Giuseppe's brown eyes, ready always for fun, belied the stern brow and stolid posturing. Judas had known him well, or as well as it was possible to know someone in ten years.

That is all Judas allowed himself to stay in any one city. After that, people might wonder why he did not age. A man who did not wrinkle and die would be called a witch or worse. So he traveled north to south, east to west, in circles that widened as the edges of civilization spread. In some cities he played the recluse, in others the artist, in still others the gadabout. He tried on roles like cloaks. And wearied of each one.

His stylish black leather boots crossed the wooden floor with practiced ease. He knew each creaky board, each almost imperceptible cove. A masked servant appeared with a tray laden with wineglasses. Judas took one, remembering the strength of his long-ago host's cellar. He sipped, let the flavors caress his tongue—thankfully Giuseppe's cellars had not gone into decline with his death. Judas emptied the glass and took another.

In his other hand, hidden behind his back, his fingers clutched tightly around a narrow black object.

He had come here for a purpose larger than this ball.

He had come to mourn.

He slipped between masked dancers on his way to the window. The long nose of his mask curved downward like the beak of a crow. The smell of the well-crafted leather from which it was made filled his nostrils. A woman swept by, her heavy scent lingering in the air long after she and her partner had moved away across the floor.

Judas knew these dances and countless more. Later, after more wine, he would join them. He would choose a young courtesan, perhaps another Moor if he could find one. He would try his best to lose himself in the familiar steps.

Fifty years ago, in his last pass through Venice, he had met the most enchanting woman he had seen in his long life. She, too, had been a Moor—dark-skinned, with luminous deep-brown eyes and black tresses that spilled over her bare shoulders to her slender waist. She wore an emerald-green dress with gold trim, pinched in at the waist as was the fashion, but between her breasts, hanging from a slender gold chain around her neck, rested a shard of bright silver, like a piece of a broken mirror, an unusual adornment. The scent of lotus blossoms, a fragrance he had not enjoyed since his last sojourn in the East, lingered around her.

He and the mysterious woman had danced for hours, neither needing a different partner. When she spoke, she had a curious accent that he could not place. Soon he forgot that and listened only to her words. She knew more than anyone he had ever met—history, philosophy, and the mysteries of the human heart. Serenity and wisdom rested in her slim form, and he wanted to borrow her peace. For her, perhaps, he might find a way to rejoin the simple cares of mortal men.

After the dancing, at this very same window, she had raised her mask that he might see the rest of her face, and he had lifted his as well. He had gazed at her in a silent moment more intimate than he had ever shared with another. Then she had handed him her mask, excused herself, and disappeared into the crowd.

Only then did he realize that he did not know her name.

She never returned. For more than a year he had searched Venice for her, paid ridiculous sums for incorrect information. She was the granddaughter of a doge. She was a slave from the Orient. She was a Jewish girl who escaped from the ghetto for a night. She was none of those.

Heartbroken, he fled the city of masks and strove to forget her in the arms of a hundred different women—some dark as Moors, others fair as snow. He had listened to a thousand stories from them, helped some and forsaken others. None had touched his heart, and he left them all before he had to confront their aging and deaths.

But now he had returned to Venice to banish her from his thoughts, fifty years after he had danced with her across these floorboards. By this time, he knew, she was likely dead, or a wizened and blind old woman who had long forgotten their magical night. All he had left of it himself was his memory and her old leather mask.

He turned the mask over in his hands now. Black and glossy, it was a thick flat ribbon of leather that slashed across her eyes, with a tiny paste jewel glittering near the corner of each eye. A daring design, its simplicity at odds with the ornate masks worn by the women of those times.

But she had needed no further adornment.

He had returned to these bright halls to cast that dark mask into the canal tonight and banish her ghost to the library of his past. Gripping the old leather, he glanced out the open window. Below, a gondolier poled his slim craft through the dark water, ripples lit silver by moonlight.

Beyond the canal's banks, figures hurried across stone tiles or over bridges. People on mysterious errands. People on everyday ones. He did not know, did not care. Like everything else, it wearied him. For one moment, he had believed that he might find connection, until she left.

Reluctant now to part with it, he stroked the mask with his index finger. It had rested in the bottom of his trunk for years, wrapped in the finest silk. At first he'd been able to smell the scent of lotus blossoms, but even that had faded. He brought the mask now to his nose and sniffed—one last time—expecting to inhale the odors of old leather and cedar from his trunk.

But the scent of lotus blossoms bloomed instead.

He turned his head, fearful of looking, the movement so slow that he would not startle even a timorous bird. His heart thumped in his ears, so loud that he expected the sound to draw all eyes to him.

She stood before him, unmasked and unchanged, her serene smile the same as a half century before. The mask slipped from his fingers to the floor. His breath held in his throat. Dancers swirled around, but he remained motionless.

It could not be.

Could this be the same woman's daughter?

He dismissed this possibility.

Not with such an exact likeness.

A darker thought intruded. He knew of the ungodly beasts that shared his march through time, as undying as himself, but of craven bloodlusts and madness.

Again he banished this prospect from his mind.

He could never forget the heat of her body through her velvet dress when he danced with her.

So what was she? Was she cursed like him? Was she immortal?

A thousand questions danced in his head, replaced finally by the only one that truly mattered, the question he had failed to ask fifty years ago.

"What is your name?" *he whispered, afraid to shatter the moment into shards like the one that she wore around her slender neck.*

"This evening, it is Anna." *Her voice sounded with the same, queer accent.*

"But that is not your real name. Will you share it with me?"

"If you will."

Her glittering brown eyes looked long into his, not flirting, instead assessing his measure. He slowly nodded his agreement, praying she would find him worthy.

"Arella," *she said in hushed tones.*

He repeated her name, matching her voice syllable for syllable. "Arella."

She smiled. She had probably not heard her name spoken aloud by another in many mortal lifetimes. Her eyes sought his, demanding he settle the promised price for learning her one true name.

For the first time in a thousand years, he said his aloud, too. "Judas."

"The cursed son of Simon Iscariot," *she finished, looking unsurprised, wearing only a faint smile.*

She held out a hand toward him. "Would you care to dance?"

With secrets revealed, their relationship began.

But those secrets hid others, deeper and darker.

Secrets without end, to match each eternal life.

Oversize doors swung open behind him, reflected in the window, drawing him back from ancient Venice to modern-day Rome. Judas tapped his fingers against the cold ballistic glass, wondering what the medieval Venetian glassblowers would have made of it.

In the reflection, he watched Renate stand framed in the doorway. She wore a mulberry-colored business suit and a brown silk top. Even though she had grown from a young woman to middle-aged in his service, he found her attractive. He realized suddenly that it was because Renate reminded him of Arella. His receptionist had the same brown skin and black eyes, the same calm.

How have I not seen this before?

The blond monk stepped into the room behind her, wearing a face much younger than his years. Nervous, the Sanguinist pinched the edge of his small spectacles. His round face fell into lines of worry that looked out of place on one so youthful, betraying a hint of the hidden decades behind that smooth skin.

Renate left and soundlessly closed the door.

Judas waved him forward. "Come, Brother Leopold."

The monk licked his lips, smoothed the drape of his simple hooded brown robe, and obeyed. He passed the fountain and came to a stop in front of the massive desk. He knew better than to sit without being told.

"As you ordered, I took the first train from Germany, *Damnatus*."

Leopold bowed his head, using an ancient title that marked Judas's past. The Latin roughly translated as the *condemned*, the *wretched*, and the *damned*. While others might take such a title as an insult, Judas wore it with pride.

Christ had given it to him.

Judas shifted a chair behind his desk, returning to his workspace, and sat. He kept the monk waiting as he focused his attention back on his earlier project. With deft and practiced skill, he unclipped the forewing he had ripped earlier and dropped it onto the floor. He opened his specimen drawer and removed another luna moth. He detached its forewing and used it to replace the one he had damaged, returning his creation to flawless perfection.

Now he must repair something else that was broken.

"I have a new mission for you, Brother Leopold."

The monk stood silent in front of him, with the stillness that only Sanguinists could attain. "Yes?"

"As I understand it, your order is certain that Father Korza is the prophesied *Knight of Christ* and that this American soldier, Jordan Stone, is the *Warrior of Man*. But there remains doubt as to the identity of the *third* figure mentioned in the Blood Gospel's prophecy. The *Woman of Learning*. Am I to understand that it is *not* Professor Erin Granger, as you originally surmised during the quest for Christ's lost Gospel?"

Leopold bowed his head in apology. "I have heard such doubts, and I believe that they may be true."

"If so, then we must find the *true* Woman of Learning."

"It will be done."

Judas pulled a silver razor from another drawer and sliced the tip of his finger. He held it over the moth he had constructed of metal and gossamer wings. A single shiny drop of blood fell onto the back of his creation, seeping through holes along the thorax and vanishing away.

The monk stepped back.

"You fear my blood."

All *strigoi* did.

Centuries ago, Judas had learned that a single drop of his blood was deadly to any of these damned creatures, even those few who had converted to serve the Church as Sanguines.

"Blood holds great power, does it not, Brother Leopold?"

"It does." The monk's eyes darted from side to side. It must trouble him to be close to something that could put an end to his immortal life.

Judas envied him his fear. Cursed by Christ with immortality, he would have sacrificed much to have the choice to die.

"Then *why* did you not tell me that the trio is now bonded by blood?"

Judas slid careful fingers under his creation. It shook itself to life in his palm, powered by his own blood. The whirring of tiny gears vibrated, barely audible under the fountain. The wings rose up and came together on its back, then extended out straight.

The monk trembled.

"Such a beautiful creature of the night, the simple moth," Judas said.

The automaton flapped its wings and lifted from the bed of his palm. It slowly circled his desk, its wings catching every mote of light and casting it back with every beat.

Leopold followed its path, plainly wanting to flee but knowing better.

Judas lifted his hand, and the moth came again to light atop Judas's outstretched fingertip. Its metal legs brushed light as spider silk against his skin.

"So very delicate, yet of immense power."

The monk's eyes fixed on the bright wings, his voice trembling. "I'm sorry. I did not think it mattered that Rhun had fed upon the archaeologist. I . . . I thought that she was not the true Woman of Learning."

"Yet, her blood flows in Rhun Korza's veins and—thanks to your ill-advised blood transfusion—the blood of Sergeant Stone now flows in hers. Do you not find such happenstance strange? Perhaps even significant?"

Obeying his will, the moth rose again from Judas's finger and flitted around the office. It danced across the currents of air just as Judas had once danced around the ballrooms of the world.

The monk swallowed his terror.

"Perhaps," Judas said. "Perhaps this archaeologist *is* the Woman of Learning after all."

"I am sorry—"

The moth descended out of the air and settled to the monk's left shoulder, its tiny legs clinging to the rough cloth of his robe.

"I tried to kill her tonight." Judas toyed with the tiny gears on his desk. "With a *blasphemare* cat. Do you imagine that such a simple woman could elude such a beast?"

"I do not know how."

"Nor do I."

With the slightest provocation, the moth would stab the monk with its sharp proboscis, releasing a single drop of blood, killing him instantly.

"Yet she survived," Judas said. "And she is now reunited with the Warrior, but not yet the Knight. Do you know why they are not reunited with Father Rhun Korza?"

"No." The monk dropped his eyes to his rosary. If he died now, in sin instead of in holy battle, his soul would be damned for all eternity. He must be thinking about that.

Judas gave him an extra moment to dwell on it, then explained. "Because Rhun Korza is missing."

"Missing?" For the first time, the monk looked surprised.

"A few days after Korza fed on her, he disappeared from the view of the Church. And all others." The moth's wings shivered in the air currents. "Now bodies litter the streets of Rome, as a monster dares to prey along the edge of the Holy City itself. It is not a *strigoi* under my control or under theirs. They fear it might be their precious Rhun Korza, returned to a feral state."

Brother Leopold met his eyes. "What would you have me do? Kill him?"

"As if you could. No, my dear brother, that task goes to another. Your task is to watch and report. And never again keep any detail to yourself." He lifted his hand, and the moth took flight from the monk's shoulder and returned to its creator's outstretched palm. "If you fail me, you fail Christ."

Brother Leopold stared upon him, his eyes looking both relieved and exultant. "I will not falter again."

8

At least the restaurant is empty.

Erin heaved a sigh of relief as she sat down with Christian and Jordan at a small battle-scarred booth in the Haight-Ashbury district. They had dumped Nate off at his campus apartment at Stanford, then whisked away into the anonymity of San Francisco, taking a circuitous path to the small diner.

She picked up the menu—not that she was hungry, just needing something to do with her hands. The weight of her Glock was again in her ankle holster. She carried Jordan's Colt in the deep pocket of her winter jacket. Their combined weight helped ground her.

She studied the ramshackle eatery, with its black-and-white paintings of skulls and flowers. The only nods to Christmas were ragged plastic poinsettias gracing each table.

Jordan took her right hand in his left. Even in the harsh, unflattering light, he looked good. A smudge of dust ran across one cheek. She reached out with her napkin and wiped it away, her fingers lingering there.

His eyes darkened, and he gave her a suggestive smile.

Across the booth, Christian cleared his throat.

Jordan straightened but kept hold of her hand. "Nice place you picked out," he said, craning to look around at the tie-dyed rainbows that decorated the back wall. "So were you a Deadhead in a past life or just stuck in the sixties?"

Hiding a smile behind her menu, Erin saw the fare was all vegan. *Jordan's going to love that.*

"This place is far nicer now than it was in the sixties," Christian said, revealing a hint of his own past, of a prior life in the city. "Back then, you could barely breathe from the fog of pot smoke and patchouli in here. But one thing that hasn't changed is the establishment's contempt for authority. I'm willing to bet my life that there aren't any surveillance cameras in this building or electronic monitoring devices. The fewer prying eyes, the better."

Erin appreciated the Sanguinist's level of paranoia, especially after the attack.

"Are you truly that worried about a mole in your order?" Jordan asked.

"Someone knew Erin would be alone at that ranch. For now, it's best we fly under the radar. At least until we reach Rome."

"That sounds fine to me," Erin said. "What did you mean when you said I'm the only one who can find Rhun?"

During the ride to the restaurant, Christian had refused to talk. Even now, he glanced once around the room, then leaned forward. "I have heard from Sergeant Stone that Rhun fed on you during the battle below St. Peter's. Is that true?"

She let go of Jordan's hand, studying the napkin in her lap so that he couldn't see her expression when she thought of the intimacy that she had shared with Rhun. She flashed to those sharp teeth sinking into her flesh, balancing between pain and bliss as his lips burned her skin, his tongue probing the wounds wider to drink more deeply.

"He did," she mumbled. "But he had to. There was no other way to catch the grimwolf and Bathory Darabont. Without our actions, the Blood Gospel would have been lost."

Jordan slipped his arm around her shoulders, and she shrugged it off. Surprise flashed across his eyes. She didn't want to hurt him, but she didn't want anyone touching her right now.

"I am not here to judge Rhun," Christian said. "The situation was extraordinary. You don't need to explain it to me. I'm more interested in what's happened to you *after* that."

"What do you mean?"

"Have you had visions? Feelings that you cannot explain?"

She closed her eyes. Relief flooded through her. So there might be an explanation for her blackouts.

I'm not going crazy after all.

Christian must have noticed her reaction. "You have had visions. Thank God."

"Someone want to explain this to me?" Jordan asked.

In retrospect, she should have told him about the blackouts. But she hadn't wanted to think about them, let alone share them.

Christian explained to both of them. "When a *strigoi* feeds on someone and the victim lives—which is a rare occurrence—the blood forms a bond between them. It lasts until the *strigoi* feeds again and erases that bond with a wash of new blood."

Jordan looked sick.

A young server came by at that moment, his hair in blond dreadlocks, with a pad in hand, a pencil behind his ear. He was waved off after a round of black coffee was ordered.

Erin waited until the kid was out of earshot, then pressed on. "But what I've been experiencing makes no sense. It's dark. Totally black. I have an intense claustrophobic feeling of being trapped. It's as if I'm encased in a sarcophagus or coffin."

"Like back in Masada?" Jordan asked.

She took his hand again, appreciating the heat of his palm, partially apologizing for snubbing him a moment ago. "That's what I thought. I thought it was a panic attack. I dismissed the episodes as flashbacks to that moment when we were stuck in that ancient crypt. But certain details of those visions had struck me as odd. The box was cold, but it felt like I was lying in acid. It soaked through my clothes and burned my skin. And even stranger, everything smelled like wine."

"Wine?" Christian asked, sitting straighter.

She nodded.

"If you were channeling Rhun during those visions, a bath of consecrated wine would burn." Christian fixed her with his sharp green eyes. "Do you have any idea where this box might be? Could you hear anything?"

She slowly shook her head, trying to think of more details, but failing. "I'm sorry."

All she remembered was that pain, sensing that what she had felt was only the tiniest fraction of what Rhun must be experiencing. How long had he been trapped there? Christian had said Rhun had gone missing shortly after the battle. That was two months ago. She couldn't abandon him to that.

Another insight chilled her. "Christian, with each of these visions I feel weaker, more leaden. In the last, I could barely lift my arms."

Christian's expression confirmed her worst fear.

It likely meant Rhun was dying.

Christian reached and touched her arm, trying to reassure her. "The best plan is to get to Rome. Cardinal Bernard has more knowledge of this kind of bond than I do. It was more common in the early days of the Church."

They were scheduled to leave by chartered plane in another two hours.

"And if we do find Rhun," Erin asked, "what do we do after that?"

She feared she would be tossed aside again, summarily dismissed, like before.

"Then we all go in search of the First Angel," Christian said.

The First Angel.

She knew all too well the prophecy concerning that mythic figure. She pictured the words inscribed on the first page of the Blood Gospel, words written by Christ, a prediction of a coming war—and a way to avert it.

A great War of the Heavens looms. For the forces of goodness to prevail, a Weapon must be forged of this Gospel written in my own blood. The trio of prophecy must bring the book to the First Angel for his blessing. Only thus may they secure salvation for the world.

"The time for waiting is past," Christian pressed. "Especially after someone moved against you, Erin. They clearly know now how valuable you are."

"Valuable?" She couldn't keep a scoffing, bitter tone from that word.

"The prophecy says the trio must carry the book to the First Angel. The Knight of Christ, the Warrior of Man, and the Woman of Learning. Jordan and you are the last two. Rhun the first."

"But I thought it was clear that I am *not* the Woman of Learning." She kept her voice steady and forced out the next sentence. "I'm pretty sure I killed her."

Jordan squeezed her hand. She had shot Bathory Darabont in the tunnels under Rome. Not only had she taken the woman's life, but the Bathory family was long thought to be the true line from which the Woman of Learning would emerge. Erin's bullet had ended that line, murdering the last living descendant.

"Darabont is indeed dead and with her that cursed line." Christian sighed, leaning back with a shrug. "So it looks like you're the best we've got, Dr. Erin Granger. What's the point in second-guessing?"

The coffee finally arrived, allowing them to collect their thoughts.

Once the server was gone, Jordan took a sip, winced at the blistering heat, and nodded to Christian. "I agree with him. Let's go find this angel dude."

As if it could be so easy.

No one had the faintest idea who the First Angel was.

9

December 19, 6:32 A.M.
The Arctic Ocean

Tommy Bolar's teeth ached from the cold. He hadn't known that was possible. Standing at the ship's rail in the darkness of the early Arctic morning, a rigid wind burned his exposed cheeks. White ice stretched to the horizon ahead. Behind the ship, a crushed wake of blue ice and black water marked the passage of the icebreaker through the frozen landscape.

He stared out, despairing. He had no idea where he was.

Or for that matter, *what* he was.

All he knew was that he was no longer the same fourteen-year-old boy who had watched his parents die in his arms atop the ruins of Masada, victims of a poison gas that killed them and healed him. He glanced at the bit of bare skin showing between his deerskin gloves and the sleeves of his high-tech down parka. Once, a brown patch of melanoma had stuck out on his pale wrist, showing his terminal condition—now it was gone, along with the rest of his cancer. Even his hair, lost to chemo, had begun to grow back.

He had been cured.

Or cursed. Depending on how you looked at it.

He wished he had died on that mountaintop with his parents. Instead, he had been kidnapped from an Israeli military hospital, stolen from the faceless doctors who had been trying to understand his miraculous survival. His latest jailers claimed he had more than *survived* the tragedy at Masada, insisted he had been more than *cured* of his cancer.

They said he could never die.

And worst of all, he had begun to believe them.

A tear rolled from his cheek, leaving a hot trail across his frozen skin.

He wiped it away with the back of his glove, growing angry, frustrated, wanting to scream at the endless expanse—not for *help*, but for *release,* to see his mother and father again.

Two months ago, someone had drugged him, and he woke up here, on this giant icebreaker in the middle of a frozen ocean. The ship was newly painted, mostly black, the cabins stacked on top like red LEGO bricks. So far he had counted roughly a hundred crewmembers aboard, memorizing faces, learning the ship's routine.

For now, escape was impossible—but knowledge was power.

It was one of the reasons he spent so much time in the ship's library, sifting through the few books in English, trying to learn as much as he could.

Any other inquiries fell on deaf ears. The crew spoke Russian, and none of them would talk to him. Only two people aboard the icebreaker ever spoke to him—and they terrified him, though he did his best to hide it.

As if summoned by his thoughts, Alyosha joined him at the rail. He carried two rapiers and passed one over. The Russian boy looked the same age as Tommy, but that face was a lie. Alyosha was lots older, decades older. Proving his inhumanity, Alyosha wore a pair of gray flannel pants and a perfectly pressed white shirt, open at the collar, exposing his pale throat to the frigid wind that raked across this empty corner of the icy deck. A real person would freeze to death in that outfit.

Tommy accepted the rapier, knowing that if he touched Alyosha's bare hand, he would find it as cold as the ice crusting the ship's rail.

Alyosha was an undying creature called a *strigoi.*

Immortal, like Tommy, but also very different from himself.

Shortly after Tommy's kidnapping, Alyosha had pressed Tommy's hand to his cold chest, revealing the creature's lack of a heartbeat. He had shown Tommy his fangs, how his canine teeth could push into and out of his gums at will. But the biggest difference between them was that Alyosha fed on human blood.

Tommy was nothing like him.

He still ate regular food, still had a heartbeat, still had his same teeth.

So what am I?

It seemed even his captor—Alyosha's master—didn't know. Or at least, never shared this knowledge.

Alyosha clouted him on the head with the hilt of his rapier to gain his attention. "You must attend to what I am saying. We must practice."

Tommy followed him out onto the makeshift fencing strip on the ship's deck and took his position.

"No!" his competitor scolded. "Widen your stance! And keep the rapier *up* to cover yourself."

Alyosha, apparently bored on the giant ship, was teaching him the manners of a Russian nobleman. Besides these fencing lessons, the boy taught him a lot of terms for horses, horse tack, and cavalry formations.

Tommy understood the other's obsession. He had been told Alyosha's real name: Alexei Nikolaevich Romanov. In the library, he had found a text on Russian history, discovered more about this "boy." A hundred years ago he had been the son of Czar Nicholas II, a royal prince of the Russian Empire. As a kid, Alyosha had suffered from hemophilia, and according to the book, only one person could relieve him of his painful bouts of internal bleeding, the same man who would eventually become his master, turning the prince into a monster.

He pictured Alyosha's master, with his thick beard and dark face, hidden elsewhere aboard the ship, like a black spider in a web. He was known in the early 1900s as the Mad Monk of Russia, but his real name was Grigori Yefimovich Rasputin. The history texts detailed how the monk had made friends with the Romanovs, becoming an invaluable counselor to the czar. But other sections hinted at Rasputin's sexual weirdness and political intrigues, which eventually led to an assassination attempt by a group of nobles.

The monk had been poisoned, shot in the head, beaten with a club, and dumped in a frozen river—only to come back up sputtering, still alive. The books said he eventually drowned in that river, but Tommy knew the truth.

It wasn't so easy to kill a monster.

Like the boy-prince, Rasputin was a *strigoi*.

Quick as a cobra strike, Alyosha lunged across the fencing strip, feinting right, then moving left, almost too fast to see. The tip of his rapier landed in the center of Tommy's chest, the point poking through his parka and piercing his skin. These were not practice swords with blunted ends. Tommy knew Alyosha could have skewered his heart if he had wanted to.

Not that it would have killed Tommy.

It would have hurt, likely left him bedridden and weak for a day or two, but he would have healed, cursed as he was atop Masada with an immortal life.

Alyosha smiled and stepped back, sweeping his rapier with a triumphant wave. He was close to Tommy's height, with wiry arms and legs. But he was far stronger and faster.

Tommy's curse offered him no such advantages of strength and speed.

Still, he did his best to parry the next few attacks. They danced back and forth along the fencing strip. Tommy quickly grew exhausted, sapped by the cold.

As they paused for a breath, a loud *crack* drew Tommy's attention past the starboard rail. The deck canted underfoot. The bow of the ship rose slightly, then crashed down onto thick plates of ice. Its giant engines ground the ship forward, continuing its slow passage through the Arctic sea.

He watched great sheets of ice shear away and scrape along the hull and wondered what would happen if he jumped.

Would I die?

Fear kept him from testing it. While he might not be able to die, he could suffer. He'd wait for a better chance.

Alyosha burst forward and slapped him across the cheek with his sword.

The sting reminded him that life was pain.

"Enough!" Alyosha demanded. "Keep alert, my friend!"

Friend . . .

Tommy wanted to scoff at such a label, but he kept silent. He knew in some ways this young prince was lonely, enjoying the companionship, even if forced, of another kid.

Still, Tommy wasn't fooled.

Alyosha was no boy.

So he returned to a defensive stance at his end of the strip. That was his only option for now. He would bide his time, learn what he could, and keep himself fit.

Until he could escape.

10

The hunter had become the hunted.

Elizabeth sensed the pack trailing her across the dark narrow streets and alleys, growing ever larger in her wake. For now, they remained back, perhaps wanting strength in numbers. These were no human curs, no brigands or thieves seeking the soft target of a lone woman on these predawn streets. They were *strigoi,* like her.

Had she intruded upon their hunting grounds? Broken some rule of etiquette in her feeding? This age held many pitfalls for her.

She glanced to the east, sensing the winter sun was close to rising. Fear trickled through her. She wanted to return to her loft, to escape the burning day, but she dared not lead this pack to her home.

So, as the day threatened, she continued down a narrow street, her shoulder close to the cold stucco wall, ancient cobblestones uneven under the soles of her boots.

The hours before the dawn had grown to be her favorite in this modern city. At this early time, the growling automobiles fell mostly silent, their breath no longer fouling the air. She took care to study the men and women of the night, recognizing how, in many ways, little had changed from her century, easily spotting harlots, gamblers, and thieves.

She understood the night—and she had thought she owned it alone.

Until this morning.

In the corners of her eyes, shadowy wraiths shifted. They numbered more than a dozen, she knew, but how many *more* she could not say. Without heartbeats or breaths, she could not be confident until they were upon her.

Which would not be long.

The beasts circled, drawing their net ever tighter.

It seemed they believed that she had not marked them. She allowed them this belief. Deception might yet save her, as it had so often in the past. She drew them onward, toward her own choice of battleground.

Her destination was far. Fearing they might attack before she reached it, she quickened her steps, but only a little, for she did not want them to know that she had sensed their presence.

She needed an open area. Trapped in these narrow alleys, it was too easy for the pack to fall upon her, to overwhelm her.

At last, her boots drew her toward the Pantheon at the Piazza della Rotonda. The square was the closest patch of free ground. The gray light of the pearling sun lightened the shadows on the Pantheon's rounded dome. The open eye of the *oculum* on top waited for the new day, blind in the dark.

Not like her. Not like them.

The Pantheon was once the home of many gods, but it was now a Catholic Church dedicated to only *one*. She avoided that sanctuary. The holy ground inside would weaken her—likewise those that hunted her—but after being reborn to this new strength, she refused to forsake it.

Instead, she kept to the open square in front.

On one side, a row of empty booths waited for daylight to transform them into a bustling Christmas marketplace. Their festive golden lights had been turned off, and large white canvas umbrellas dusted with frost protected empty tables. Elsewhere, restaurants stood lightless and shuttered, their diners long abed.

Behind her, shadows shifted at the edges of the square.

Knowing her time ran short, she hurried to the fountain in the center of the square. She rested her palms on the basin's gray stone. Near at hand, a carved stone fish spat water into the pool below. In the center rose a slim obelisk. Its red granite had been quarried under the merciless Egyptian sun only to be dragged here by conquerors.

Hieroglyphs had been cut in its four sides and reached to its conical tip: moons, birds, a sitting man. The language was old gibberish, as meaningless to her as the modern world. But the images, carved by long dead stonemasons, might yet save her this night.

Her gaze rose to the very top, to where the Church had mounted a cross to claim the power of these ancient gods.

Behind her came the squeak of leather, the scrape of cloth against cloth, the soft fall of hair from a turned head.

At last, the pack closed in.

Before any of them could reach her, she vaulted over the side of the basin and onto the obelisk, clinging like a cat. Her strong fingers found purchase in those ancient carvings: a palm, a moon, a feather, a falcon. She clambered upward, but as the pedestal grew thinner, the climbing grew harder. Fear pushed her to the very top.

Perched there, she braced herself against the searing pain and grabbed the cross with one hand. She spared a quick glance downward.

Shadows boiled up the obelisk like ants, befouling every inch of granite. Their clothes were tatters, their limbs skeletal, their hair matted and grimed. One beast tumbled back into the fountain with a splash, but others poured into the space it left.

Turning away, she glanced at the nearest house across the plaza and gathered her strength around her like a cloak.

Then leaped.

7:18 A.M.

Far below St. Peter's Basilica, Rhun crawled on all fours down a dark tunnel, his head hanging so low his nose sometimes brushed the stone floor.

Still, he whispered prayers of thanks.

Erin was safe.

The urgency that had shattered him out of his agonizing prison had faded. Sheer will alone now drove him to lift each bloody hand, to drag each raw knee. Foot by foot, he crossed along the passageway, seeking light.

Taking a moment to rest, he leaned his shoulder against the stone wall. He touched his throat, remembering the wound, now healed. Elisabeta had taken so much of his blood. She had purposefully left him helpless but alive.

To suffer.

Agony had become her new art. He pictured the faces of the many young girls who died in her experiments. This dark incarnation of his bright Elisabeta had learned to sculpt pain as others did marble. All those horrible deaths remained on his conscience.

How many more deaths must he add to that toll as she ran wild in the streets of Rome?

While entombed, he caught whispers of her delight, of the elation of her feeding. She had drained him, carried his blood inside her, binding them.

He knew she had crafted that connection on purpose.

She had wanted to drag him along on her hunts, forcing him to witness her depravations and murder. Thankfully, as she fed, washing new blood over old, that bond weakened, allowing only the strongest of her emotions to still reach him.

As if stoked by these thoughts, Rhun felt the edges of his vision narrow, fraught with panicked fear—not his own, but another's. As weak as that bond was, he could have resisted her pull, but such a fight would risk further sapping his already-drained reserves.

So he let himself be taken away.

Both to conserve his strength and for another purpose.

Where are you, Elisabeta?

He intended to use this fraying bond to find her, to stop this rampage once he found the light again. For now, he fell willingly into that shared darkness.

A tide of black beasts rose toward him. White fangs flashed out of that darkness, ravenous, ready to feed. He leaped away, sailing through the air.

The sky brightened to the east, promising a new day.

He must be locked away before that happened, shuttered against the blazing sun.

He landed on a roof. Terra-cotta tiles broke under his boots, his hands. Pieces skittered over the edge to shatter on the gray stone of the square below.

He ran across the roof, sure-footed. Behind him, one of the hunters attempted the jump, failed, and hit the ground with a sickening thud.

Others tried.

Many fell, but a few made it across.

He had reached the far side of the roof—and vaulted to the next. Cool night air washed across his cheeks. If he forgot his pursuers, he could appreciate the beauty here, running across the top of Rome.

But he could not forget them, and so he ran onward.

Ever west.

His goal climbed high into the blushing sky.

Rhun returned to his own skin, slumped in the tunnel. He rose on hands and knees, knowing this was not enough. Tapping into the last dregs of his waning strength, he shoved to his feet. With one palm on the wall, he shambled forward.

He must warn the others.

Elisabeta was leading a pack of *strigoi* straight to Vatican City.

7:32 A.M.

She held nothing back as she fled across the rooftops, heading west, fleeing the rising sun to the east and chased by a furious horde. The surprise of her climbing the obelisk had gained her precious seconds.

If they caught her, she was dead.

She vaulted from rooftop to rooftop, breaking tiles, bending rain gutters. She had never run like this in her natural or supernatural life. It seemed those centuries trapped in the sarcophagus had made her stronger and faster.

Exhilaration washed through her, holding her fear in check.

She spread her arms to the side like wings, loving the caress of the wind from her passage. If she lived, she must do this every night. She sensed she was older than those who pursued her, faster—certainly not enough to outdistance them forever, but perhaps long enough to reach her destination.

She hurdled onto the next roof, landed hard. A flock of pigeons startled and rose around her. Feathers surrounded her like a cloud, blinded her. Momentarily distracted, her boot caught in the crack between a row of tiles. She had to halt to pull it loose, tearing the leather.

A glance behind revealed her lead was gone.

The pack was upon her, at her heels now.

She fled away, pain lancing up from her ankle. The leg would not take her weight. She cursed its weakness, jumping more than running now, pushing off with the good leg, landing on the bad, punishing it for failing her.

To the east, the sky was the same light gray as the pigeons' wings.

If *strigoi* did not strike her down, the sun would.

She hurled herself forward. She would not lie down and let those who followed claim her. Such beasts were not fit to end her life.

She focused on her goal ahead.

A few streets separated her from the walls of Vatican City.

The Sanguinists would never let such a pack of *strigoi* enter their holy city. They would cut them down like weeds. She ran toward that same death with one hope in her silent heart.

She bore the secret of where Rhun lay hidden.

But would that be enough to turn their swords from her neck?

She did not know.

11

"Help us!" a voice called at his door.

Hearing the fear, the urgency, Cardinal Bernard rose from his desk chair and crossed his chamber in a heartbeat, not bothering to hide his otherness from Father Ambrose. Although his assistant knew of the cardinal's hidden nature, he still stumbled back, looking shocked.

Bernard ignored him and ripped open the door, coming close to tearing it off the hinges.

At the threshold, he found the young form of the German monk, Brother Leopold, newly arrived from Ettal Abbey. On his other side, a diminutive novice named Mario. They carried a slack form of a priest between them, the victim's head hanging down.

"I found him stumbling out of the lower tunnels," Mario said.

The vinegary scent of old wine poured from the body, filling the room, as Leopold and Mario entered with their burden. Waxen wrists stuck out from the damp robe, the skin stretched tight over bones.

This priest had starved long, suffered much.

Bernard lifted the man's chin. He beheld a face as familiar as his own—the high Slavic cheekbones, the deeply cleft chin, and the tall, smooth forehead.

"Rhun?"

Past his shock, waves of emotions battered within him at the sight of his friend's ravaged form: *fury* at whoever had inflicted this upon him; *fear* that it might be too late to save him; and a great measure of *relief*. Both for Rhun's return and the plain evidence that he could not have murdered and drained all those girls in Rome, not in this state.

All was not yet lost.

Tortured dark eyes opened and rolled back.

"Rhun?" Bernard begged. "Who did this to you?"

Rhun forced words through cracked lips. "She comes. She nears the Holy City."

"Who comes?"

"She leads them to us," he whispered. "Many *strigoi*. Coming here."

With his message delivered, Rhun collapsed.

Leopold slipped an arm under Rhun's knees and picked him up as if he were a child. His body hung there, spent. Bernard would get nothing more from him in this state. He would need more than wine to recover Rhun from this devastation.

"Take him to the couch," Bernard ordered. "Leave him with me."

The young scholar obeyed, placing Rhun on the chamber's small sofa.

Bernard turned to Mario, who gaped at him with wide blue eyes. New to the cross, he had seen nothing akin to this. "Go with Brother Leopold and Father Ambrose. Sound the alarm, and make for the entrance of the city."

As soon as the others were out of the room, he opened the small refrigerator under his desk. It was stocked with drinks for his human guests, but that was not what he needed now. He reached behind those bottles to a simple glass jar stoppered with a cork. Every day, he refilled it. Having such a temptation near him was forbidden, but Bernard believed in the old ways, when necessity tempered sin.

He carried the bottle to Rhun and uncorked it. The intoxicating scent wafted out, causing even Rhun to stir.

Good.

Bernard tilted Rhun's head back, opened his mouth, and poured the blood down his throat.

. . .

Rhun shuddered with the bliss, lost in the crimson flow through his black veins. He wanted to rebel, recognizing the sin on his tongue. But memories blurred: his lips upon a velvety throat, the give of flesh under his sharp teeth. Blood and dreams carried away his pain. He moaned with pleasure of it, riding waves of ecstasy that pulsed through every fiber of his being.

Denied this pleasure so long, his body would not let it go.

But the rapture eventually ebbed, leaving an emptiness behind, a well of dark craving. Rhun struggled for breath to speak, but before he could, darkness overwhelmed him. As it consumed him, he prayed that his sin-filled body could withstand the penance to come.

Rhun passed through the monastery's herb garden, heading to midmorning prayers. He lingered and let the summer sun warm his face. He ran his hand along the purple stalks of lavender that bordered the gravel path, the delicate scent swelling in his wake. He brought his dusted fingers to his face to savor the fragrance.

He smiled, reminded of home.

Back at his family's cottage, his sister would often scold him for dawdling in the kitchen garden and laugh when he tried to apologize. How his sister had loved to vex him, but she always made him smile. Perhaps he would see her this Sunday, her round belly rising in front of her, full with her first child.

A fat yellow bee wandered along a dusky purple bloom, another bee landing on the same stalk. The stalk bent under their weight and swayed in the breeze, but the bees paid that no mind. They worked so diligently, sure of their place in God's plan.

The first bee lifted off the blossom and swooped across the lavender.

He knew where it was headed.

Following its meandering path, Rhun reached the lichen-covered wall at the back of the garden. The bee disappeared through a round hole in one of the golden-yellow conical hives—called skeps—that lined the top of the stone wall.

Rhun had constructed this very skep himself late the previous summer. He had loved the simple task of braiding straw into ropes, twisting those ropes into spirals, and forming them into these conical hives. He found peace in such simple tasks and was good at them.

Brother Thomas had observed the same. "Your nimble fingers are meant for this kind of work."

He closed his eyes and breathed in the rich smell of honey. The sonorous buzzing of bees enveloped him. He had other work that he could be doing, but he stood a long moment, content.

When he came back to himself, Rhun smiled. He had forgotten that moment. It was a simple slice of another life, centuries old, from before he was turned into a *strigoi* and lost his soul.

He smelled again the sweet rich scent of the honey, the light undertone of lavender. He remembered the warmth of sun on his skin, when sunlight was not yet mixed with pain. But mostly he thought of his laughing sister.

He ached for that simple life—only to recognize it could never be.

And with that hard realization came another.

His eyes snapped open, tasting blood on his tongue, and confronted Bernard. "What you did . . . it is a sin."

The cardinal patted his hand. "It is *my* sin, not yours. I'll willingly accept that burden to have you at my side for the upcoming battle."

Rhun lay still, wrestling with Bernard's words, wanting to believe them, but knowing the act was wrong. He sat up, finding renewed strength in muscle and bone. Most of his wounds had also closed. He drew in a breath to steady his riotous mind.

Bernard held out his hand, revealing a familiar curve of tarnished silver.

It was Rhun's *karambit*.

"If you are recovered enough," Bernard said, "you may join us in the battle ahead. To exact vengeance upon those who treated you so brutally. You mentioned a woman."

Rhun took the weapon, shying away from the cardinal's penetrating gaze, too ashamed even now to speak her name. He fingered the blade's sharp edge.

Elisabeta had stolen it from him.

How had Bernard found it again?

The strident clang of a warning bell shattered the moment.

Questions would have to wait.

Bernard crossed the chamber in a flash of scarlet robes and lifted down his ancient sword from the wall. Rhun stood, surprised by how light his body felt after drinking blood, as if he could fly. He firmed his grip on his own weapon.

Rhun nodded to Bernard, acknowledging that he was fit enough to fight, and they took off at a run. They sailed down the gleaming wooden halls of the papal apartments, through its front bronze doors, and out onto the square.

To avoid the eyes of the handful of people milling about the open plaza, Rhun followed Bernard into the shadowy refuge of Bernini's colonnade that bordered the piazza's edges. The massive Tuscan columns, four deep, should keep their preternaturally swift passage hidden. Bernard joined a contingent of other Sanguinists who waited in the shadows for the cardinal. As a group, they rushed along the sweep of the colonnade toward the entrance to the Holy City.

Once they reached the waist-high fence that divided the Vatican city-state from Rome proper, Rhun's eyes scanned the nearest rooftops. He remembered the shared vision he had with Elisabeta, of her leaping from rooftop to rooftop.

The furious honk of a car horn drew his eyes below, to the cobblestone street that led here.

Fifty yards away, the small shape of a woman fled down the center of Via della Conciliazione, limping on one leg. Though her hair was shorter, he had no trouble recognizing Elisabeta. A white car swerved to miss her.

She paid it no mind, intent on reaching St. Peter's Square.

Trailing behind her, a dozen *strigoi* loped and sprinted.

He longed to burst from the colonnade and run to her, but Bernard put a steadying hand on his arm.

"Stay," the cardinal warned, as if reading his thoughts. "Humans are on that street and in those houses. They will see the battle, and they will know. We have millennia of secrecy to protect. Let the fight come to us."

As Rhun watched, he recognized the pain in Elisabeta's thinned lips, her fearful glances behind. He remembered the same panic when looking through her eyes.

She is not *leading* this pack—she's *fleeing* them.

Despite all she had done to him, to the innocents of the city, a reflexive surge to protect her fired inside him. Bernard's fingers tightened on his shoulder, perhaps feeling him lean forward, ready to dash to her defense.

Elisabeta finally reached the end of the street. The other *strigoi* were almost upon her. Not slowing, she hurdled the low fence that marked the boundary of Vatican City and landed in a half crouch, facing the snarling pack.

She sneered, exposing her fangs, and taunted them. "Cross to me if you dare."

The pack pulled hard to a stop beyond the fencerow. A few took a cautious step closer, then away again, sensing the debilitating holiness of the hallowed ground on this side. They wanted her, but would they dare enter Vatican City to get her?

Holy ground was not all they had to fear here.

The Sanguinist force waited to either side of Rhun and Bernard, as still as statues among the columns. If the *strigoi* came into the city, the beasts would be pulled into this shadowy forest of stone and slaughtered.

Elisabeta retreated from the fencerow—but she put too much weight on her hurt leg, and her ankle finally gave out fully, dropping her to the pavement.

The sign of weakness was too much for the *strigoi* to resist. Like lions descending upon a wounded gazelle, the pack surged forward.

Rhun ripped out of Bernard's grip and burst into the open. He flew toward Elisabeta, as much a creature of instinct as the *strigoi*. He reached her at the same time that the pack leader, a huge figure with ropy muscles and blue-black tattoos, bounded the fence and landed on the countess's far side, baring his teeth.

More *strigoi* followed his example, flowing over the fence.

Rhun grabbed her by the arm and retreated toward the colonnade, dragging her, hoping to lure the pack into the stone forest.

The leader barked an order and an overzealous beast rushed forward.

Heaving with one arm, Rhun threw Elisabeta like a rag doll into the colonnade and slashed out with his *karambit*. The silver blade cut through the air—then through flesh. The feral youngster fell back, clutching his throat as blood and breath bubbled out of his severed neck.

Other *strigoi* surged forward as Rhun retreated—only to be met at the edge of the colonnade by Bernard and the other Sanguinists.

A brief battle raged among the columns. But with the pack caught by surprise and weakened by holy ground, it was a slaughter.

A few broke away, leaping the fence and scattering like vermin into the streets, fleeing both the fight and the sun.

Rhun found himself confronting the hulking leader. Upon his bared chest, a Hieronymus Bosch painting had been tattooed, a hellish landscape of death and punishment. It came to life as his muscles rippled, lifting his heavy blade.

Rhun's blade looked contemptibly small compared to that length of steel.

As if knowing this, spite polished the other's dark eyes to a wicked gleam. He sprang at Rhun, hacking that sword downward at his head, ready to cleave him in two.

But holiness slowed the *strigoi*'s attack, allowing time for Rhun to duck inside the other's guard. He turned the hook of his *karambit* up and sliced into the other's belly. Ripping high, he tore that grotesque canvas in half and kicked the body away.

The gutted bulk toppled to the edge of the columns, one arm flinging out into the light—into *sunlight*. The limb burst into flame. Another Sanguinist helped Rhun yank the body back into the shadows and stanched the flames before the fire drew unwanted attention.

A few faces turned toward the shadows, but most remained oblivious of the swift and deadly battle within the colonnade. As Rhun stared at the sunlight brightening the plaza, fear rang through him.

Elisabeta . . .

He turned to find Bernard looming over her huddled form, her face to the ground. She surely felt the blaze of the new day, sensed its burn. For now, her only safety lay within the shadowy shelter of the colonnade. To step beyond it would be her death.

Bernard grabbed her by the shoulder, looking ready to cast her out into the square, to face the judgment of a new day. Sanguinists crowded around him, reeking of wine and incense. None would stop the cardinal if he chose to slay her. She had led *strigoi* to the holiest city in Europe.

Bernard buried a hand in her short hair, yanked her head back, rested his blade against her soft white throat.

"No!" Rhun called out, rushing forward, shoving through the others.

But it was not his shout that halted the cardinal's blade.

7:52 A.M.

Shock froze Bernard in place—along with utter disbelief.

He stared at the woman's face as if she were a ghost.

It could not be her.

It must be a trick of light and shadow, his mind indulging in fantasy, a *strigoi* with an uncanny likeness. Still, he recognized the silver eyes, the raven color of her hair, even the indignant, haughty expression as his blade rested against her soft throat, as if she dared him to take her life.

Countess Elizabeth Bathory de Ecsed.

But she had perished centuries ago. Bernard had seen her imprisoned in her castle. He had even visited her there once, pitied her, the learned noblewoman brought low by Rhun's base desires.

But Bernard bore as much guilt for that crime. Centuries ago, he had put the woman on this cruel path when he set the countess and Rhun together, when he tried to force his will upon divine prophecy. Afterward, Bernard had begged to be the one to take her life, to spare Rhun of such a deed, knowing how much he had loved her, how far he had fallen for her. But the pope had deemed it part of Rhun's penance to end her unnatural life, to slay the monster that he had created.

Bernard had worried when Rhun returned from Hungary. Rhun had claimed the deed was done, that the countess was gone from this world. Bernard had taken it to mean she was dead, not put away like a doll in a drawer. At the time, as additional penance, Rhun had starved himself for years, mortified himself for decades, shutting himself off from the mortal world.

But plainly Rhun had not killed her.

What have you done, my son? What sin have you committed yet again in the name of love?

As horror faded, another realization took root, one full of promise.

By Rhun sparing her, the Bathory line was not dead—as Bernard had despaired these past months. He pondered what that implied.

Could this be a sign from God?

Had God's will acted through Rhun to preserve the countess for this new task?

For the first time since the Blood Gospel had delivered its message and cast doubt on Dr. Erin Granger's role as the Woman of Learning, hope surged through Bernard.

Countess Bathory might yet save them all.

Bernard stared at her beautiful face in wonder, still disbelieving this miracle, this sudden turn of good fortune. He gripped her hair tighter, refusing to lose this one hope.

She could not be allowed to escape.

Rhun appeared at his side, listing a bit on his feet, plainly succumbing to his weakened state again. Even this brief battle had quickly stanched whatever fire the blood had stoked inside him.

Still . . .

"Restrain him," Bernard ordered the others, fearing what Rhun might do. At this moment, he did not know his friend's heart. Would he kill her, save her, or try to run off with her in shame?

I do not know.

All he knew for sure was that he had to protect this wicked woman with every force he could marshal.

He needed her.

The world needed her.

The countess must have read that certainty in his eyes. Her perfect lips curved into a smile, both cunning and mean.

God help us, if I'm wrong.

PART II

For they have shed the blood of saints and prophets,
and thou hast given them blood to drink; for they are worthy.

—Revelation 16:6

12

Erin shared the backseat of the red Fiat with Jordan. Christian sat up front with the driver. The Sanguinist had his head out the open window, speaking to a Swiss guard in a midnight-blue uniform and cap. The young man carried an assault rifle over one shoulder, guarding St. Anne's Gate, one of the side entrances into Vatican City.

Normally the guards here weren't overtly armed.

So why the heightened security?

The guard nodded, stepped back, and waved their car through.

Christian whispered to the driver, and they set off into the Holy City, passing under the verdigris-green iron archway. Once they were moving again, Christian had returned his phone to his ear, where it had been glued ever since their chartered plane had landed at Rome's smaller Ciampino Airport. Their driver had been waiting for them in this nondescript Fiat and whisked them in minutes to the gates of Vatican City.

Jordan held Erin's hand in the backseat, staring out as the car slipped past the Vatican bank and post office and circled behind the bulk of St. Peter's Basilica.

She studied the ancient buildings, imagining the secrets hidden behind their bright stucco facades. As an archaeologist, she uncovered truth layer by layer, but her discovery of the existence of *strigoi* and Sanguinists had taught her that history had layers even deeper than any she had thought existed.

But one question remained foremost in her mind.

Jordan expressed it. "Where is Christian taking us?"

She was just as curious. She had thought they would be heading straight to the papal apartments to meet with Cardinal Bernard in his offices, but instead their car headed farther out into the grounds behind the basilica.

Erin leaned forward, interrupting Christian on the phone. She was too tired to be polite and irritated by all the subterfuge they'd followed to come here.

"Where are we going?" she asked, touching the Sanguinist's shoulder.

"We're almost there."

"Almost where?" she pressed.

Christian pointed his phone ahead.

Erin ducked lower to study their approach toward a building of white Italian marble with a red-tiled roof. A set of train tracks behind it revealed the structure's purpose.

It was Stazione Vaticano, the one-and-only train station on the Vatican railway line. It had been built during the reign of Pope Pius XI in the early 1930s. Today it was mostly used to import freight, though the last few popes had taken occasional ceremonial trips from here aboard a special papal train.

Erin saw that same train parked on those tracks now.

Three forest-green cars were lined up behind a black old-fashioned engine that puffed out steam. At another time, she would have been thrilled at the sight, but right now she had but one overriding concern: the fate of Rhun. During the trip here, no other visions had come, and she feared what that meant for Rhun.

The Fiat drove straight to the platform and stopped. Christian popped out his door, drawing Jordan and Erin with him. With his phone back at his ear, Christian led them up the platform. The Sanguinist had changed out of his tattered dress uniform and into a priest's shirt and black jeans. The outfit suited him better.

Upon reaching the train, he lowered his phone and pointed to the middle car with a mischievous grin. "All aboard!"

Erin glanced back toward the dome of the basilica. "I don't understand. Are we leaving already? What about Rhun?"

The slender Sanguinist shrugged. "At this point, I know as much as you do. The cardinal asked that I bring you both here and board the train. It's scheduled to be under way as soon as we are on board."

Jordan put his warm palm against her lower back. She leaned back into it, glad for the touch of the familiar, the understandable. "What else did you expect from Bernard?" he said. "If you look up *need to know* in the dictionary, you'd find his smiling face there. The guy likes his secrets."

And secrets got people killed.

Erin fingered the small marble of amber in the pocket of her jeans, picturing Amy's hesitant smile under a desert sun.

"For now," Jordan said, "we might as well do what the cardinal asks. We can always come back if we don't like what he tells us."

She nodded. Jordan could always be counted on to point to the most practical way forward. She kissed his cheek, his stubble rough under her lips, adding another soft kiss to his lips.

Christian stepped to the door and pulled it open. "To avoid undue attention, the Vatican put out a cover story that the train is being shifted to a maintenance yard outside Rome. But the sooner we're moving, the happier I'll be."

With little other choice, Erin climbed the metal steps, followed by Jordan. She stepped into a sumptuous dining car. Golden velvet curtains had been tied back next to each window, and the compartment practically glowed in the morning sunshine—from the buttery yellow ceiling to the rich oak joinery. The air smelled of lemon polish and old wood.

Jordan whistled. "Looks like the pope knows how to travel. The only thing that would make this picture better would be a steaming pot of coffee on one of those tables."

"I second that," Erin said.

"Have a seat," Christian said, passing by them and waving to a table that had been set. "I'll see about making your wishes come true."

As he headed toward the car in front, Erin found a spot bathed in sunlight and sat, enjoying the warmth after the rush across the cold city. She stroked the white linen tablecloth with one finger. Two places were set with silver flatware and fine china decorated with the papal seal.

Jordan smoothed his dress blue uniform, doing his best to look presentable as he sat next to her. Still, she caught the hard glint to his eyes as he peered out the windows, constantly on the watch for any danger, though trying not to show it.

Finally, he settled down. "Hope the food here is better than at that hippie place Christian took us to in San Fran. Vegan food? Really? I'm a meat-and-potatoes sort of guy. And in my particular case, I lean more toward the *meat* side of that equation."

"This is Italy. Something tells me you might get lucky with the food."

"Indeed you shall!" a new voice called behind them, coming from the door to the first car.

Startled, Jordan came close to bursting out of his seat and swinging around, but even he recognized the slight German accent to those few words.

"Brother Leopold!" Erin exclaimed, delighted to see the monk, along with the tray he carried, holding a coffee service.

She hadn't seen the German monk since the day he had saved her life. He looked the same—with his wire-rimmed spectacles, simple brown habit, and boyish grin.

"Never fear, breakfast will be served in a moment." Leopold lifted the tray. "But first, Christian mentioned that you were both desperately in need of a jolt of caffeine after your long journey."

"If you define *jolt* as a full pot of coffee, you are correct." Jordan smiled. "It's good to see you again, Leopold."

"Likewise."

The monk bustled over and filled their china cups with a steaming dark roast blend. The train had begun to slowly move, the timbre of the engines stoking higher.

Christian appeared again and took the seat opposite Erin, staring pointedly at the steaming cup in her hands.

Familiar with his routine, she handed him the white china cup. He brought it to his nose, closed his eyes, and sniffed deeply at the curl of steam. An expression of contentment crossed his face.

"Thank you," he said and handed the cup back to her.

As a young Sanguinist, he wasn't as far removed from simple human pleasures, like coffee. She liked that.

"Any news?" Jordan asked him. "Like where we're going?"

"I was told that once we're outside of Rome, we'll learn more. Meantime, I say we savor the calm."

"As in, *before the storm*?" Erin asked.

Christian chuckled. "Most probably."

Jordan seemed content enough with that answer. During the trip here, he and Christian had become fast friends, unusually so considering Jordan's distaste and distrust for the Sanguinists after Rhun had bitten her.

As the line of cars inched away from the station, the train headed toward a set of steel doors that blocked the tracks a few hundred yards ahead, set into the massive walls that surrounded the Holy City. The gateway sported rivets and thick doornails and looked as if it were meant to guard a medieval castle.

A train whistle sounded, and the doors rumbled ponderously apart, sliding into the brick wall. This gate marked the border between Vatican City and Rome.

Passing beneath that archway under a head of steam, the train picked up speed and headed out into Rome. The train pulled through the city, like any ordinary train—only theirs had a mere three cars: the galley in front, the dining car in the middle, and a third compartment in back. The last car looked similar to the others from the outside, but its curtains had been drawn, and a solid metal door separated that car from hers.

As she looked at that door now, she tried to ignore the tightening dread in her stomach.

What was back there?

"Ah," Brother Leopold exclaimed, drawing her attention. "As promised . . . breakfast."

From the galley, a new figure emerged, as familiar as Leopold, if not as welcome.

Father Ambrose—aide to Cardinal Bernard—stepped from the galley car with a tray of omelets, brioche, butter, and jam. The priest's round face looked even redder than usual, damp with sweat or perhaps from the steam of the galley kitchen. He didn't look happy with his role as waiter.

"Good morning, Father Ambrose," Erin said. "It's wonderful to see you again."

She did her best to make that sound genuine.

Ambrose didn't even bother. "Dr. Granger, Sergeant Stone," he said perfunctorily, inclining his head fractionally toward each of them.

The priest unloaded the food and returned to the galley car.

Clearly, he wasn't interested in conversation.

She wondered if his presence indicated that Cardinal Bernard was already on board. She glanced again to that steel door leading to the neighboring compartment.

Next to her, Jordan simply tore into his omelet, as if he might not see food again for days—which, considering their past experiences with the Sanguinists, could be true.

Following his example, she spread jam onto a slice of brioche.

Christian watched all the while, looking envious.

By the time their plates were empty, the train had threaded out of Rome and appeared to be heading south of the city.

Jordan's hand again found hers under the table. She stroked her fingertips along his palm, liking the smile it provoked. As much as the thought of a relationship scared her, for him she was ready to take the risk.

But a certain awkwardness remained between them. No matter how hard she tried not to, her thoughts often returned to the moment when Rhun had bitten her. No mortal man had ever made her feel like that. But the act had meant nothing, a mere necessity. She wondered if that bone-deep bliss was a trick of the *strigoi* to disable their victims, to turn them weak and helpless.

Her fingers inadvertently found themselves touching the scars on her neck.

She wanted to ask someone about it. But who? Certainly not Jordan. She considered asking Christian, to inquire what it had been like for him when he was first bitten. Back at the diner in San Francisco, he had seemed to sense her thoughts, but she had balked at discussing such an erotic experience with any man, especially a priest.

Still, not all her hesitation was embarrassment.

She knew a part of her didn't want to know the truth.

What if the feeling of connectedness that she had experienced wasn't just a mechanism to quiet prey? What if it was something else?

10:47 A.M.

Rhun awoke to a feeling of dread and panic. His arms flailed up and to the side, expecting to feel stone walls enclosed around him.

His memories filled back in.

He was free.

As he listened to the clack of steel wheels on tracks, he remembered the battle at the edge of the Holy City. He had suffered some minor wounds, but worst of all, the battle had drained the last dregs of his strength, returning him to a weakened state. Cardinal Bernard had insisted he rest while they waited for the arrival of Erin and Jordan.

Even now he could hear the thump of human hearts, the timpani of their beats as familiar to his keen ears as any song. He ran his palms over his body. He wore a dry set of robes, the reek of old wine gone. He eased himself upright, testing each vertebra as he did so.

"Careful, my son," Bernard said out of the darkness of the train car. "You are not yet restored to your full health."

As Rhun's eyes adjusted and focused, he recognized the papal sleeping car, outfitted with the double bed upon which he had slept. There was also a small desk and a pair of silk chairs flanking a couch.

He spotted a familiar figure standing behind Bernard at his bedside. She wore tailored leather armor and a silver chain belt. Her black hair had been braided back from the stern lines of her dark face.

"Nadia?" he croaked out.

When had she arrived?

"Welcome back to the living," Nadia said with a sly smile. "Or as close to *living* as any Sanguinist can claim."

Rhun touched his brow. "How long—?"

He was interrupted by the final figure in the room. She lounged on the couch, one leg stretched up, outfitted with a splint. He remembered her limping flight down the cobblestone street toward the Holy City.

"*Helló, az én szeretett,*" Elisabeta said, speaking Hungarian, every syllable as familiar as if he had heard them only yesterday, instead of hundreds of years before.

Hello, my beloved.

There was no warmth in her words, only disdain.

Elisabeta switched to Italian, though her dialect was old, too. "I trust you did not find your brief time in my prison too burdensome. But then again, you took my life, you destroyed my soul, and then you stole four hundred years from me." Her silver eyes glared out of the darkness at him. "So I doubt you've been punished quite enough."

Every word cut him with its truth. He had done all that to her, a woman he had once loved—still loved, if perhaps only the memory of her former self. He reached for his pectoral cross, found a new one hung around his neck, and prayed for forgiveness for those sins.

"Has Christ been much comfort to you these last hundreds of years?" she asked. "You look no happier than you did in my castle centuries ago."

"It is my duty to serve Him, as always."

One side of her mouth lifted in a half smile. "You give me the politic answer, Father Korza, yet did we not once promise to speak truth to each other? Do you not owe me at least so much?"

He owed her much more.

Nadia glared at Elisabeta with undisguised rage. "Do not forget that she left you in that coffin to suffer and die. Or all the women she killed on the streets of Rome."

"It is her nature now," he said.

And I made her so.

He had perverted her from healer to killer. All her crimes rested on his conscience—both in the past and now.

"We can control our natures," Nadia countered, touching the delicate silver cross at her neck. "I control mine every day. So do you. She is fully capable of doing the same, but she chooses not to."

"I will never change," Elisabeta promised. "You should have just killed me at my castle."

"So I was ordered," he told her. "It was mercy that hid you away."

"I trust little in your mercy."

She shifted in her seat, lifting clasped hands to brush a lock of hair from her forehead before settling them again in her lap. He saw she wore handcuffs.

"Enough." Bernard gestured to Nadia.

She stepped closer to the sofa and pulled Elisabeta none too gently to her feet. Nadia kept firm hold of her. She would not underestimate Elisabeta as he had when he took her from the wine.

The countess only smiled, baring her handcuffs toward Rhun.

"Shackled like an animal," she said. "That is what your love has brought me."

10:55 A.M.

Leopold started at one end of the dining car and worked his way to the other. He did what he was ordered to do, closing each set of curtains, pulling the panels tightly together until no scrap of sunlight came through.

The car grew dark, the only illumination coming from the electric lights mounted on the ceiling. He paused outside the door to the last car.

The two humans' hearts beat louder. He smelled the anxiety rising from them like steam. A twinge of pity flickered through him.

"What are you doing?" Erin asked, but she was no fool. From the way she glanced from the steel door to the closed windows, she must already sense that something dangerous was about to be brought in here.

"You are perfectly safe," Leopold assured her.

"To hell with that," Jordan swore.

The soldier reached across Erin to the curtain next to her and yanked it back open. Sunlight poured into the room, bathing her.

Leopold stared at Erin in the middle of the pool of sunlight, trying to decide whether to return and secure the curtain. But from Jordan's expression, he decided against it. Instead, he rapped on the thick steel door, alerting those inside that all was ready.

Christian stood, as if readying for battle, and placed himself between Erin and the door, standing half in shadow, half in light.

The door opened, and Cardinal Bernard stepped first into the car, wearing his full scarlet vestments. His eyes moved from Erin to Jordan. "First, let me apologize for such clandestine measures, but after all that has occurred—both here and in California—I thought it wiser to be cautious."

Neither of the two humans seemed overly satisfied by this explanation, plainly suspicious, but they politely remained silent.

That awkward tableau was interrupted as the galley door on the other side of the car opened, and Father Ambrose appeared. He wiped his hands on a dish towel and stepped inside, uninvited. He must have heard Bernard's voice and come to offer assistance to the cardinal—and to eavesdrop on the discussion.

Bernard strode across the car. The cardinal took Erin's hand in both of his own, then Jordan's. "You both look well."

"As do you." Erin tried to smile, but Leopold could read the worry from her face. "Is there any news on Rhun's whereabouts?"

Hope rang there. She genuinely cared for Rhun.

Leopold hardened his heart against the rising guilt inside him. He liked these two humans, cherished their vitality and intelligence, but he reminded himself for the thousandth time that his betrayal served a higher purpose. This knowledge did not make his traitorous acts any easier.

"I'll explain all in good time," Bernard promised them. His eyes turned to his assistant. "That will be all, Father Ambrose."

With a peeved sigh, his assistant retreated back into the galley, but Leopold had no doubt that the spidery priest had an ear close to that door, hanging on their every word. He was not about to be left out in the dark.

Then again, neither am I.

He remembered his promise to the *Damnatus*, felt again the touch of the dire moth on his shoulder, the flutter of its wing against his neck.

I must not fail him.

13

Once Father Ambrose was gone, Cardinal Bernard signaled to the shadows beyond the open steel door.

Erin tensed, her fingers tightening on Jordan's hand. She was suddenly very happy Jordan had yanked the curtains open. Still, despite the streaming sunlight, she felt chilled.

From out of the darkness a black-clad priest stepped into the bright car. He was skeletally thin, a gaunt pale hand held the edge of his hood against the glare. He moved in halting steps, but there remained a certain grace about him, a familiarity in his movements.

Then he dropped his hand and revealed his face. Lanky black hair hung over dark, sunken eyes. His skin was pulled tight across broad cheekbones, and his lips looked thin, bloodless.

She remembered kissing those lips when they had been fuller. "Rhun . . ."

Shock pulled her to her feet. He looked as if he had aged years.

Jordan rose and kept to her side.

Rhun waved them all back to their seats. He then hobbled, assisted by Bernard, and fell heavily into the vacant chair next to Christian. Erin noted he kept out of the worst of the bright light. While Sanguinists could tolerate sunlight, it weakened them, and clearly Rhun had few reserves to spare.

From across the table, familiar eyes locked onto hers. She read exhaustion there, along with a measure of regret.

Rhun spoke softly. "I understand from Cardinal Bernard that we have come to share a blood bond. I apologize for any suffering that might have caused you."

"It's fine, Rhun," she said. "I'm fine. But you . . ."

His pale lips lifted into a ghostly attempt at a smile. "I have felt more vigorous than I do now, but with Christ's help, I will recover my full strength soon."

Jordan took her hand atop the table, making his claim on her clear. He glared at Rhun, showing no sympathy. Instead, he turned to Bernard, who stood beside the table.

"Cardinal, if you knew Rhun was missing for so many weeks, why did you wait so long before reaching out to us? You could have called before he got into this sorry state."

The cardinal folded his gloved fingers together. "Until a few hours ago, I did not know of the dark act committed against Dr. Granger in the tunnels below St. Peter's. I could not know of any bond between him and Erin. But Rhun's actions have offered hope for the world."

Rhun dropped his gaze to the table, looking mortified.

What was the cardinal talking about?

Bernard lifted his arms to encompass the train. "With all who are gathered here—the prophesied trio—we can now seek the First Angel."

Jordan glanced around the table. "In other words, the band's back together again. The Knight of Christ, the Warrior of Man, and the Woman of Learning."

At the mention of the last of that trio, he squeezed Erin's fingers.

She slipped her hand free. "Not necessarily," she reminded everyone.

She heard that pistol blast again in her head, pictured Bathory Darabont collapsing in that tunnel. *I murdered the last of the Bathory line.*

Rhun stared at her. "The three of us have accomplished much."

In this, Jordan seemed to agree. "Damned straight."

They might be right, but it was the *damned* part that worried her.

11:15 A.M.

The train slowed and changed tracks, continuing its journey south.

Jordan glanced out the window, trying to guess their destination. Bernard had still not told them. Instead, the cardinal had vanished again into the rear car, leaving them to their own thoughts, to digest all that had happened.

It was a big meal.

A clink of metal drew his attention back to that dark doorway. Bernard emerged again, with two women in tow.

The first was tall, a dark-haired and dark-eyed Sanguinist. He immediately recognized Nadia. He eyeballed her leather armor and the length of silver belted at her waist. The latter was a chain whip, a weapon the woman was extremely skilled at wielding. She also had a long blade strapped to her side.

The phrase *dressed to kill* came to mind.

Nadia's attention stayed focused on the second woman.

Not a good sign.

The stranger was shorter than Erin, with short curly ebony hair. She wore jeans and boots, the right one torn, exposing a splint on that leg, plainly a recent injury. Over her clothes, she shouldered an old-fashioned heavy cloak that seemed to weigh her down. Her tiny hands were folded demurely in front of her, and it took Jordan a second more to see that she wore handcuffs.

In one gloved hand, Nadia held a thick chain tethered to those handcuffs.

They weren't taking any chances with this one.

Why was this woman so dangerous?

As the prisoner limped closer, Jordan saw her face. His jaw clenched to keep from gasping in surprise.

Silvery eyes met his. He studied the shape of those perfectly formed lips, the high cheekbones, the curly fall of her locks. If he changed the hue of her hair to a fiery red, she would be the spitting image of Bathory Darabont, the woman Erin had killed in the tunnel below Rome.

Erin had stiffened next to him, also recognizing the obvious family resemblance.

"You found another from the line of Bathory," Erin said.

"Yes," the cardinal said.

Jordan inwardly groaned. *Like the last one hadn't been trouble enough.*

"And she is *strigoi*," Erin added.

Jordan flinched in surprise, suddenly understanding the need for the heavy guard, the drawn shades. He should have recognized this fact himself.

The woman fixed Erin with a cold, dismissive stare, then turned to the cardinal. She spoke to him in Latin, but her accent sounded Slavic, very much like Rhun's when he got angry.

Jordan looked at the prisoner with new eyes, appraising the threat level, calculating contingencies if this monster broke free from her handlers.

Once the woman had finished, Bernard said, "It's better if you speak English. Matters will go much more smoothly."

She shrugged, turned to Rhun, and spoke in English. "You already look much refreshed, my love."

My love? What did that mean?

As a priest, Rhun wasn't supposed to take lovers.

She sniffed curtly at Erin and Jordan, as if they had both crawled out of some gutter. "It seems such low company suits you well."

Rhun gave no indication that he had heard her.

Cardinal Bernard stepped forward and made a formal introduction. "This is Countess Elizabeth Bathory de Ecsed, widow of the Count Ferenc Nádasdy Bathory de Nádasd et Fogarasföld."

Erin gasped, drawing Jordan's eye, but she simply kept staring at the woman.

In turn, the cardinal introduced both of them to the countess. Fortunately their titles were much shorter. "Allow me to present Dr. Erin Granger and Sergeant Jordan Stone."

Erin found her voice again. "Are you claiming that this is *the* Elizabeth Bathory? From the late 1500s?"

The woman bowed her head, as if acknowledging this truth.

Emotions ran across Erin's face—a mix of relief and disappointment. They both knew how convinced the Church was that the Woman of Learning would arise from the Bathory line.

"I don't understand," Jordan said. "Is this woman a *Sanguinist*?"

The countess answered, "I will have no part of that dreary order. I place my faith in passion, not penitence."

Rhun stirred. Jordan remembered the priest's story from when he was new to the Sanguinist fold. In a moment of forbidden passion, Rhun had killed Elizabeth Bathory and the only way to save her was to *turn* her, to change her into a *strigoi*. But where had this woman been for the last four hundred years? The Church had been convinced the Bathory line had died with Darabont.

Jordan could guess the answer: *Rhun must have hidden her.*

It seemed the priest had kept quiet about more than just biting Erin.

Bernard spoke. "I believe that those gathered here are our best weapons in the upcoming War of the Heavens, a battle prophesied by the Blood Gospel. Here stands the world's only hope."

Countess Bathory laughed, the noise both amused and bitter. "Ah, Cardinal, with your love for the dramatic, you should have been better served by becoming an actor on a wider stage than the pulpit."

"Nevertheless, I believe it to be true." He turned and confronted the woman's disobliging manner. "Would you rather the world end, Countess Bathory?"

"Did not my world come to an end long ago?" She glanced to Rhun.

Nadia pulled out her blade from its sheath at her hip. "We could make it a *permanent* end. After the murders you committed, you should be executed on the spot."

The countess laughed again, a musical tinkling sound that raised goose bumps on the back of Jordan's neck. "If the cardinal truly wished me dead, I would be a pile of ashes in St. Peter's Square. For all your stern words, you need me."

"That's enough." Bernard raised his red-gloved hands. "The countess has a duty to perform. She will serve as the Woman of Learning—or I will thrust her out into the sunlight myself."

11:22 A.M.

Erin steeled herself against her wounded pride.

That was a clear vote of no confidence from the cardinal.

Was Bernard really so certain of Bathory and so uncertain of her?

She had one advocate in her corner. Jordan slipped an arm around her shoulders. "Screw that. Erin proved that *she* is the Woman of Learning."

"Did she now?" Countess Bathory ran her pink tongue along her upper lip, revealing sharp white fangs. "Then it seems I am not needed after all."

Erin kept her face blank. Over the centuries, Bathory women

had been singled out for generations, trained to serve as the Woman of Learning. She had no such pedigree. Although she had been part of the trio that had recovered the Blood Gospel, it had been Bathory Darabont who actually succeeded in opening that ancient tome on the altar of St. Peter's.

Not me.

Bernard pointed a hand at the countess. "What can explain her presence here except the fulfillment of prophecy? A woman believed to be dead, but resurrected by Rhun, the indisputable Knight of Christ."

"How about poor judgment?" Christian said, coming to Erin's corner. "And blind coincidence? Not every fall of a coin is prophecy."

Jordan nodded firmly.

Rhun spoke, his voice hoarse. "It was *sin* that brought Elisabeta to this moment, not prophecy."

"Or perhaps a lack of experience with sin," the countess countered with a spiteful smile. "We could spend many idle hours speculating as to *why* I am here. None of that should obscure the fact that I *am* here. What do you wish of me, and what shall you pay for my cooperation?"

"Is it not payment enough to save the earthly realm?" Nadia asked.

"What do I owe this *earthly realm* of yours?" Bathory straightened her back. "Against my will, I was torn from it, ripped away by the teeth of one of your own. Since that time I have spent far longer locked away than free. From this moment on, I will do *nothing* that does not benefit me."

"We don't need her," Jordan said. "We have Erin."

Both Nadia and Christian nodded, and gratitude at their trust filled her.

"No," Bernard said firmly, ending the discussion with his sternness. "We need this woman."

Erin clenched her jaw. Again she was being cast aside.

The countess stared at Bernard. "Then explain this role of mine, Cardinal. And let us see if you can buy my help."

As Bernard explained about the prophecy, about the looming War of the Heavens, Erin reached down and took Jordan's warm hand. He tilted his head to look at her, and she lost herself for a moment in those clear blue eyes, the eyes of the Warrior of Man. He squeezed her hand, making a silent promise. Whatever happened, she and Jordan were in this together.

The cardinal finished his explanation.

"I see," Bathory said. "And what manner of payment might I expect if I help you find this First Angel?"

Bernard bowed his head toward the countess. "There are many rewards to be had by serving the Lord, Countess Bathory."

"My rewards for serving the Church have been scant thus far." The countess shook her head. "The glory of service does not content me."

In this one instance, Erin agreed with Bathory. The countess had certainly gotten a raw deal—turned into a *strigoi*, imprisoned first in her own castle, then in a coffin of wine for hundreds of years.

Everyone the woman knew was long dead. Everything she cared about was gone.

Except Rhun.

"My desires are of utmost simplicity." The countess held up one imperious finger. "First, the Sanguinists must protect my person for the rest of my unnatural life. Both from other *strigoi* and meddling humans."

She held up another finger. "Second, I must be allowed to hunt."

She unfolded another finger. "Third, my castle shall be restored to me."

"Elisabeta," Rhun whispered. "You do your soul a disservice by—"

"I have *no* soul!" she declared loudly. "Do you not remember the day you destroyed it?"

Rhun let out a quiet sigh.

Erin hated to see him look so defeated. She hated Bathory for causing it.

"We can reach an accommodation," the cardinal said. "If you choose to live in a Sanguinist enclave, you will be sheltered from all who wish to do you harm."

"I shall not be locked away in some Sanguinist nunnery." The countess's voice rang with anger. "Not for Christ, not for any man."

"We could give you a suite of apartments in Vatican City itself," Bernard countered. "And Sanguinists to protect you when you leave the Holy City."

"And spend eternity in the company of priests?" the countess scoffed. "Surely, you cannot imagine I would succumb to such a dreadful fate?"

A corner of Christian's mouth twitched toward a smile, but Nadia looked ready to explode.

"The Church has other properties." Cardinal Bernard seemed unperturbed. "Though none so well defended."

"And what of my hunting?"

Everyone fell silent. The train rattled against the tracks, carrying everyone south.

Bernard shook his head. "You may *not* take a human life. If you do, we shall be forced to take you down like any other animal."

"How then will I survive?"

"We have access to human blood," Bernard said. "We could supply you with enough to satisfy your needs."

The countess examined her cuffed hands. "So am I to become a cosseted prisoner, as was my fate in centuries past?"

Erin wondered how long she had spent locked in her own castle before Rhun imprisoned her in a coffin and spirited her to Rome. Certainly long enough to know what it meant to lose your freedom.

The cardinal leaned back. "So long as you do not kill, you may roam the world, live your life as you see fit."

"Tied to the Church for protection." She shook the chains that bound her. "Ever dependent upon you for the very blood that sustains my meager existence."

"Do you have a better deal?" Nadia scoffed. "Cardinal Bernard is offering you a life of ease, when you have earned only death."

"Yet could not the same be said for each Sanguinist in this room?" Her silver eyes locked on Nadia. "Or have none of you tasted sin?"

"We have turned from our sins," Nadia said. "As must you."

"Must I?"

"If you do not agree," the cardinal said, his tone brooking no argument, "we will throw you from the train into the sunlight and assume that is God's will."

The countess's eyes locked onto Bernard's face for a full minute. No one in the car spoke or moved.

"Very well," the countess said. "I accept your gracious terms."

"If she gets to name terms," Jordan spoke up, "then so do I."

Everyone stared at him, their faces incredulous.

Jordan pulled Erin closer to him. "We're in this together."

Bernard looked ready to balk.

Christian faced the cardinal. "Even if Erin is not the Woman of Learning, she still has much knowledge. We might need her. I'm certainly not part of any prophecy, but that doesn't mean I can't serve."

Erin realized he was right. It didn't matter whether or not she was the prophesied Woman of Learning. What mattered was that if she could help, she would do it. This quest wasn't about pride, it was about saving the world.

She stared down Bernard. "I want in."

Jordan tightened his grip on her shoulder and looked at the cardinal. "You heard her. That's nonnegotiable. Or I walk. And I have no aversion to sunlight."

Nadia inclined her head in Erin's direction. "I support this, too. Dr. Granger has proven herself loyal in battle and deed. While this one"—she yanked on the countess's silver chain—"has proven the opposite."

A wrinkle appeared in the cardinal's forehead. "But the fulfillment of prophecy is clear about—"

Rhun raised his head, facing Bernard. "Who are you to pretend to know the will of God?"

Erin blinked, surprised by his support, from the priest who had resurrected Elizabeth Bathory to replace her.

The cardinal lifted his hands, palms out in a conciliatory gesture. "Very well. I concede. It would be foolish of me to dismiss Dr. Granger's knowledge and keen mind. I'm sure she could assist Countess Bathory in her role as the Woman of Learning."

Erin couldn't decide whether to be relieved or terrified.

So, leaning against Jordan, she settled for both.

14

The train rocked as it continued south to points unknown.

As trees and hills rolled past the window, Jordan rested his chin on top of Erin's head. She smelled like lavender and coffee. Her shoulder and side pressed against his. He wished the chairs weren't bolted to the floor so he could pull her even closer.

Time alone with her would be great, without priests and prophecies. But that wasn't going to happen any time soon.

Ideally, he would prefer that Erin stayed as far as possible from this mess, from Sanguinist priests and *strigoi* countesses. But that wasn't going to happen either. He had spoken up for her because he knew how much she wanted to go. Additionally, if the Vatican sent her home, he wouldn't be able to protect her.

But can I protect her here?

After Karen had been killed in action, time had stopped for him, and it hadn't started again until he met Erin. He would always know that Karen had died alone hundreds of miles away from him. He would never let that happen again to someone he loved.

Someone he *loved* . . .

He had never spoken that word aloud, but it was there inside him.

He kissed the top of Erin's head, intending to stay close to her no matter what.

Erin hugged him tighter, but he saw her eyes studying Rhun.

The priest sat with his head bowed in prayer, his thin hands clasped in front of him. Jordan didn't like how Erin had been acting around Rhun ever since he bit her. Her eyes seldom left him when he was near. Her fingers often touched the two puncture scars on her neck—not with dread but with something akin to wistfulness. Something had happened in that tunnel, something she also hadn't spoken aloud about yet. Jordan didn't know what it was, but he sensed she was keeping more secrets from him than just those damned bloody visions.

But there was nothing he could do to draw her out. Whatever she was working through was clearly private, and he would give her that latitude. For now the best plan was simply to get this mission done—then get Erin as far from Rhun as possible.

To that end . . .

Jordan stirred, keeping one arm tightly around Erin. "Anybody have any idea *where* we can find the First Angel? Or even begin looking?"

Erin sat straighter. "It depends on *who* the First Angel is."

Seated at a neighboring table, the countess lifted her hands, rattling her handcuffs. "Does not the Bible teach us that the First Angel is the Morning Star, the first light of day, the son of the dawn?"

"You're talking about Lucifer," Erin said. "He went by those names, and he was indeed the first angel to *fall*. But the Bible mentions many other angels *before* him. The first angel mentioned in Genesis came to the slave Hagar and told her to go back to her mistress and bear her master's child."

"True." The countess had the coldest smile that Jordan had ever seen. "Yet how could we hope to find an angel without a name?"

"That's a good point," Erin said.

Bathory inclined her head, accepting the compliment.

Jordan noted both Rhun and Bernard studying this exchange between the two women. Christian also caught Jordan's eye, as if to say, *See, I told you they would work well together.*

In the shadows, Bathory closed her silver eyes, as if in thought. Long black lashes rested against her ashen cheeks.

Erin stared out the window toward the sunlight, as the train rattled past winter fields dotted with giant round bales of hay.

The countess opened her eyes again. "Perhaps we had best focus our search on angels that have names. The first angel mentioned by *name* in the Bible is Gabriel, the primary messenger of God. Could that be the First Angel that we seek?"

The priests at the table looked uncertain. Erin remained curiously quiet, gazing out the window.

"Gabriel the messenger?" Nadia raised an eyebrow, still standing behind Bathory holding the countess's leash. "In a war, I would think the archangel Michael would be a better ally."

Jordan surveyed the train car, suddenly recognizing the strangeness of this discussion. Even if they settled on a biblical angel, how were they going to find one and bring it the book?

"Don't angels live in another dimension or something?" Jordan asked. "One that humans can't get to? How are we supposed to reach an angel there?"

"Angels dwell in Heaven." Rhun had returned his attention to his folded hands. "Yet they may travel freely to Earth."

"Then I don't suppose you guys have some sort of angelic phone?" Jordan asked, only half joking. After all he had experienced since learning of *strigoi* and Sanguinists, who knew what other secrets the Church was keeping?

"It is called prayer," Cardinal Bernard said, frowning at his flippancy. "And I have spent many hours on my knees praying for the First Angel to reveal himself. But I do not think that this angel will do so. Not to me. He will reveal himself only to the trio of prophecy."

"If you are right, my dear cardinal," Bathory said, "then we should begin praying to Lucifer immediately. For surely only a *fallen* angel would reveal himself to the likes of your flawed trio."

Erin finally spoke, still staring out the window with that faraway look that meant she was in deep thought. "I don't think we're looking for Gabriel or Michael or Lucifer. I think we are searching for the First Angel from Revelation."

The countess laughed, almost clapping her hands. "The angel who sounds the trumpet and ends the world. Ah, what an enticing theory!"

Erin quoted from memory. "*The first angel sounded, and there followed hail and fire mingled with blood, and they were cast upon the earth: and the third part of trees was burnt up, and all green grass was burnt up.*"

Armageddon.

Those were the stakes.

Jordan tried to picture hail and fire mixed with blood and sighed. "So where do we find him?"

Erin turned back to face the car. "I think the answer is found in an earlier passage from Revelation, from before the trumpet sounds. There is a line that reads, *And another angel came and stood at the altar.* Then after another few lines, it continues, *The smoke of the incense, which came with the prayers of the saints, ascended up before God out of the angel's hand. And the angel took the censer, and filled it with fire of the altar, and cast it into the earth: and there were voices, and thunderings, and lightnings, and an earthquake.*"

Jordan grinned. "Well, at least that part is easy enough to interpret."

And he meant it.

He enjoyed the look of surprise on the Sanguinist priests' faces.

"It doesn't take a biblical scholar to figure that one out," Jordan continued. "Smoke from the angel's hand? Incense? Thunder? Earthquake?"

The others eyed him with confused expressions. The countess merely looked amused. He was supposed to be the muscle, not the brains.

Erin touched the back of his wrist, allowing him to reveal what she had already figured out.

He took her fingers and squeezed them. "That sounds exactly like what happened at Masada. Remember the boy who survived? He had said he thought he smelled incense and cinnamon in the smoke. We even found traces of cinnamon in the gas samples. And the boy also mentioned that the smoke touched his hand before everyone died from the gas and the earthquake."

"*The smoke of the incense, which came with the prayers of the saints, ascended up before God out of the angel's hand,*" Rhun repeated, his voice reverential.

"Everyone on that mountaintop died." Jordan's words came faster now. "Only something *inhuman*, like an angel, could have survived that poisonous assault."

Erin gave him a smile that warmed him to his toes. "The events match the biblical passage. More important, it points to someone whom we could actually hope to find."

"The boy," Rhun said, sounding unconvinced. "I spoke to him

atop that mountain that day. He seemed like just an ordinary child. In shock, grief-stricken after the death of his mother and father. And he was born of the flesh. How could he be an angel?"

"Remember, Christ was also born of the flesh," Cardinal Bernard countered. "This boy seems like a fine starting point to begin our search."

Jordan nodded. "So where is he? Does anybody know? The last I recall, he was being evacuated off that mountaintop by helicopter, by the Israeli army. They were taking him to one of their hospitals. It shouldn't be hard to track him from there."

"It will be harder than you think," Bernard said, suddenly looking worried.

That was never a good thing.

12:05 P.M.

"Why would it be harder?" Erin asked, sensing she wasn't going to like the answer.

Bernard sighed regretfully. "Because he is no longer in the custody of the Israelis."

"Then where is he?" she asked.

Instead of answering, the cardinal turned to Brother Leopold. The German monk had remained silent near the back of the car. "Leopold, you are the most skilled with computers. My laptop is with my luggage. Father Ambrose has my passwords. I need to access my files at the Vatican. Can you help me?"

Leopold nodded. "I can certainly try."

The monk rushed out of the dining car and headed into the galley.

Bernard turned back to the others. "We were keeping tabs on the boy, staying in contact with the Israelis who were studying him at a military hospital. His name is Thomas Bolar. The medical staff was trying to discover how he had survived the poison gas. And then—"

Leopold burst back into the car, returning with a simple black laptop in hand. He crossed to them, set it on the table, and booted it up. Adjusting his wire-rimmed glasses, Leopold typed with the speed only a Sanguinist could manage. His fingers were a blur across the keyboard, accessing the Internet, punching in passwords, connecting to a Vatican server.

Bernard looked over his shoulder, directing him every now and again.

Erin found it odd to watch these ancient men in priestly garb engaging with modern technology. It seemed like Sanguinists should be haunting churches and graveyards, not surfing the Internet. But Leopold seemed to know what he was doing. In a few minutes, he had a window open on the screen containing a grainy gray video.

Erin crowded closer to see, as did everyone else.

Only the countess hung back. From her uneasy expression, such technology must unnerve her. She had not lived through the long years like the others so that she could assimilate the changes over time. Erin wondered what it must be like to be thrust from the sixteenth century into the twenty-first. She had to hand it to the woman. As far as Erin could tell, the countess seemed to be taking it in stride, showing a surprising resilience and toughness. Erin needed to be mindful of that in her dealings with her in the future.

For now, she kept her attention fixed to the laptop.

"This is surveillance video taken from the Israeli medical facility," Bernard said. "You should watch this, then I'll explain more."

On the screen, a boy sat in a hospital bed. He was dressed in a thin hospital gown, tied in the back. As they watched, the boy wiped tears from his eyes, then got up and dragged his IV pole to the window. He leaned his head against the glass and looked out into the night.

Erin felt for the boy—both his parents had died in his arms, and now he was trapped alone in a military hospital. She was glad that Rhun had taken time to spend a few minutes talking to the child, comforting him, before everything went to hell.

Suddenly, another small figure stood next to the boy at the window. The newcomer's face was turned away from the camera. He had appeared out of nowhere, as if someone had cut out a piece of the video.

The stranger wore a dark suit coat and slacks. Thomas shrank back from him, clearly afraid. In a move too fast to follow, a knife flashed under the lights. The boy clutched his throat, blood gushing out, drenching his hospital robe.

Erin's shoulders inched up, but she didn't look away from the screen. Jordan pulled her closer to his side, supporting her. He must have seen his share of bloodshed and the murder of children in Afghanistan and knew how hard it was to watch such cruelty.

On the screen, Thomas stumbled away from the stranger. He yanked off a trail of wires attached to his chest. Lights flashed on the bedside machines. An alarm. The kid was trying to call for help.

Smart.

Two Israeli soldiers ran into the room, their weapons up and ready.

The stranger hurled a chair through the window, grabbed Thomas, and threw the boy out the window before the soldiers could open fire.

From the attacker's speed, he had to be *strigoi*.

The stranger turned to face the soldiers, finally showing his face. He looked to be a boy himself, no more than fourteen. He sketched a quick bow to the soldiers before jumping out the window himself.

"How far was the drop?" Jordan asked, watching the soldiers rush to the window and begin silently firing below.

"Four stories," the cardinal answered.

"So Thomas must be dead," Jordan said. "He can't be the First Angel."

Erin wasn't so sure. She glanced to Bernard as he whispered to Leopold. If Thomas was dead, why waste everyone's time showing this video?

"The boy survived the fall," the cardinal explained and pointed to the screen.

Another video file appeared, this one from a parking lot camera on the ground.

Caught from this angle, Thomas fell through the air, his blood-soaked hospital gown fluttering around his body like wings before he crashed headlong to the black asphalt. Shards of broken glass sparkled and danced around him.

As they watched, the boy stirred, plainly alive.

A split second later, the stranger in the suit landed, *on his feet,* next to him.

He grabbed Thomas by an arm and sprinted with him into the desert, vanishing quickly from view.

"We believe that the kidnapper was *strigoi,* perhaps in service to the Belial," the cardinal said. "But we know for certain the child who survived Masada was no *strigoi*. He was reported in sunlight. The Israeli medical machines showed he had a heartbeat."

"And I heard it, too," Rhun added. "I held his hand. It was warm. He was *alive*."

"But no human could survive a fall like that," Leopold said, awed, still typing rapidly, as if trying to search for answers.

Erin caught a glimpse of a text box being opened, a message sent, then closed again. All done so quickly, in less than two seconds, that she failed to make out a single word.

"But Thomas survived," Jordan said. "Like he did in Masada."

"As if he's under some divine protection." Erin touched Leopold's shoulder. "Show that first video again. I want to see that attacker's face."

The monk complied.

As the stranger turned toward the camera, Leopold froze the image and zoomed in. The kidnapper had an attractive face, oval, with dark eyebrows, one raised higher than the other. He had light-colored eyes, with short dark hair parted on the side.

He didn't look familiar to her, but both Rhun and Bernard tensed with recognition.

"That's Alexei Romanov," Bernard said.

Erin let the shock ring through her.

The son of Czar Nicholas II . . .

Rhun closed his eyes, clearly aggrieved by sudden insight. "That must be why Rasputin let go of the Blood Gospel so easily back in St. Petersburg. He had already put plans in motion to kidnap this boy. He was playing an entirely different game from us, keeping cards up his long sleeves. I should have suspected as much back then."

"You speak of the Romanovs," the countess interrupted. "In my time, that Russian royal family lost power and were exiled to the far north. Did they then return to the throne?"

"They ruled from 1612 until 1917," Rhun said.

"And my family." The countess leaned forward. "What became of them? Did we also return to power?"

Rhun shook his head, looking reluctant to say more.

Contrarily, Nadia was more than happy to extend the branches of the countess's family tree, to fill in her lost history. "Your children were charged with treason for your crimes, stripped of their wealth, and exiled from Hungary. For a hundred years, it was forbidden to speak your name in your homeland."

The countess raised her chin a couple of millimeters, but she gave no other sign that she cared. Yet something in her eyes cracked as she turned away, revealing a well of grief behind that cold demeanor, a peek at her former humanity.

Erin changed the subject. "So Rasputin kidnapped this boy. But why? To what end?"

No one answered, and she didn't blame anyone, remembering her own dealings with Rasputin. The monk was shrewd, conniving, and out merely for himself. To guess the twisted intentions of the Mad Monk of Russia, it would take someone equally as *mad*.

Or at least, a kindred soul.

The countess stirred and gazed around the room. "I would surmise he did it because he hates you all."

15

As the rattling set of coaches tunneled through the bright middle of the day, Elizabeth pulled on the chain that connected her manacles to the wall of the last car.

The loathsome Sanguinist woman, Nadia, had marched her back into the darkness and secured her in this coach. The chain was locked into a hasp at waist height, the links of silver so short that she was forced to stand while the room rocked around her.

Steps away, Nadia watched her, as patient as a fox watching a rabbit den.

Elizabeth twisted her arms, trying to find a more comfortable position. The silver manacles burned in a ring of fire around her wrists, but she was more at ease here than in the dining car, where the single open curtain had allowed in a stream of sunlight. She had not showed how much it had seared her eyes whenever she looked at the woman and soldier, refusing to reveal weakness before these two humans.

As the train trundled on, she set her feet farther apart to keep from being knocked about by the rocking. She would adapt. The modern world had many powerful objects, and she would master them. She would not let fear of them rule her.

With her hands pressed against the wall, she savored the warmth of the sun-heated steel against her palms. She imagined the sun blazing strong and bright outside, crossing a blue sky with sharp white clouds. She had not seen such sights for centuries, barely remembered what they looked like. *Strigoi* could not stand the sun, as Sanguinists could. She missed the day, with its heat and life and growing things. She remembered her gardens, the bright flowers, the healing herbs she once grew.

But was she willing to give up her freedom as a *strigoi* in order to see the sky again, to convert to the pious life of a Sanguinist?

Never.

She rubbed her warmed hands together and pressed them against her cold cheeks. Even if she tried to convert, she suspected God would know that her heart was black, and the blessed wine would strike her dead.

She had agreed to help the Sanguinists, but her promise had been given under threat of death. She had no intention of keeping her word if presented with a better chance at survival. An oath sworn on pain of death was not binding.

She owed them nothing.

As if hearing her thoughts, Nadia glared at her. Once Elizabeth was free, she would make the tall woman pay for her insolence. But for now she sensed that Nadia would be a difficult captor to escape. The woman plainly loathed her, and she seemed dedicated to Rhun— although more like a fellow knight, not like a woman devoted to a man.

The same could not be said of the human woman.

Dr. Erin Granger.

Elizabeth had easily spotted the telling pink scars on the other's neck. A *strigoi* had fed upon her recently and suffered her to live. A rare enough event, and certainly no ordinary *strigoi* would have left such careful marks. Those punctures spoke of control and care. From the awkward manner in which the woman and Rhun sat and did not speak, she suspected that Rhun had fallen again, fed again.

But in this instance, he had not killed the woman, nor turned *her* into a monster.

Elizabeth remembered how Erin's heart had sped when Rhun first entered the car. She recognized the anguish that poured from the woman's voice when she saw his wounds and spoke his name. This human seemed intertwined with Rhun in a deeper manner than the blood bond of feeding should foster.

Jealousy flared hot and venomous.

Rhun belongs to me and me alone.

Elizabeth had paid dearly for that love and refused to share it.

She thought back to that night, of Rhun in her arms, of their unspoken love for each other finally being expressed in the heat of lips, of the press of flesh, the soft words of love. She knew what was happening was forbidden a priest, but little did she know how much such laws chained the beast that truly lurked inside Rhun. Once broken, that face finally showed its fangs, its darker lusts, and tore her from her old life and into one of eternal night.

And now it seemed Rhun had loosed that same beast upon another woman, another whom he plainly cared for.

In that attraction, Elizabeth also saw possibility. Given a chance, she would use their feelings for each other against them, to destroy them both.

But for now, she must content herself with waiting. She must go along with Bernard's group, but she held little trust in the cardinal. Not now, and certainly not during her mortal life. Back then, she had striven to warn Rhun against Bernard, sensing the depths of secrets hidden inside his heartless, sanctimonious chest.

In the neighboring car, her keen ears picked out her name being spoken.

"We cannot risk losing her," Cardinal Bernard said. "We must know where she is at all times."

The young monk named Christian answered. "Don't worry. I've already taken measures to assure that. I will keep her on a short leash."

Another spoke with the thick tongue of the Germans, marking him as Brother Leopold. "I will see about getting more coffee."

Light footsteps left the table, heading to the coach at the front, where food was being prepared and where she could faintly make out another human heartbeat, another servant to this horde.

Those at the table sat silent, apparently having little to say, each probably pondering the journey ahead.

She decided to do the same and turned to Nadia. "Tell me of this Russian connected to the royal Romanovs . . . this Rasputin? Why does the Church have no love for him?"

Perhaps she could make an ally out of him.

Nadia sat silent as stone, but her face betrayed how she loved withholding secrets.

"Your cardinal wishes me to be part of this endeavor," Elizabeth reminded her, pressing her. "As such, I must know everything."

"Then let the cardinal tell you." Nadia folded her arms.

Realizing that no quarter would be given, Elizabeth turned her attention to eavesdropping, but she lost interest as the rattling of the train grew louder as it climbed some long hill, blotting out most sounds.

Minutes later, the steel door to her prison opened, bringing in the sharper smells of food, the blaze of sunlight, and the louder heartbeats of the humans.

Cardinal Bernard entered with the younger Sanguinist, Christian. They were followed by another priest, this one human, likely the cardinal's retainer. She recognized his sluggish heartbeat from the first car, where the food was being prepared. She was growing hungry herself—and this one had a round belly, fat cheeks, all plump with blood, a pig waiting to be slaughtered.

"We will arrive soon," Bernard informed Nadia. "Once we leave the train, I am placing you and Christian in charge of Countess Bathory."

"Do you not mean in charge of the *prisoner*?" Elizabeth corrected. "Even though I have joined your quest, do you trust me so little?"

"Trust is earned," Christian said. "And you currently have a massive trust deficit."

She held out her bound hands. "Can you not at least release me to move freely about this prison? With daylight outside, I cannot escape here. I do not see what harm—"

An explosion blasted away her words. As if struck by the hand of God, the entire coach lifted under them, riding atop a thunderous roar, accompanied by the fires of Hell.

16

Rhun moved upon the first shift of air, the first note of the explosion. He rode the blast wave as time slowed to the thickness of liquid glass.

He lunged across the table, wrapped both his arms around Erin, and hit the closed window with his shoulder. The thick curtain wrapped around his body as he crashed through. Glass raked his arms and back. Flames and roaring chased him out into the world.

At his heels as he leaped from it, the train car expanded, growing impossibly bigger until its skin split—and smoke and soot and wood burst outward in a great explosion.

Tossed high, Rhun turned his body to the side and hit the ground rolling, one arm around Erin's back, the other pulling her head close to his chest. He and Erin rolled across the stubble of a harvested field that bordered the tracks.

The brief smell of dry grass was quickly scorched away by the bitter, chalky smell of explosives, the scratch of charcoal, and the unmistakable odor of burnt human flesh.

The train had exploded.

Someone, maybe everyone, had died.

In his arms, Erin gasped and coughed.

She yet lived—and that made him far happier than it should.

He ran his hands across her body, feeling for broken bones, for blood. He found scrapes, a few cuts, and bruises. Nothing more. His fingers entwined with hers, seeking to reassure her, feeling the shock draining the heat of her body.

He pulled her tighter to him, sheltering her.

Only then did he turn back to face the disaster spread out across the fields.

Chunks of soot-streaked metal pierced the yellow grass, littered the railroad tracks, and scattered across the smoldering fields. Pieces of the black steam engine had been blown from the track. The boiler lay a hundred yards ahead, a hole torn in its metal belly gaping at the sky.

Patches of fire ate the fields, as broken glass rained from the sky, like so much crystalline hail, all mixed with blood. He remembered the biblical quote from Revelation: *There followed hail and fire mingled with blood, and they were cast upon the earth.*

Was he witnessing that now?

Dust and smoke roiled up from the tracks. A chunk of steel had landed mere feet away, steam hissing where its hot surface touched wet grass.

A high-pitched bell rang without pause in his ears. With one hand, he brushed glass from his robes and pulled pieces from his other arm. Still cradling Erin, he searched around him, but nothing moved.

What had become of the others?

He touched his rosary and prayed for their safety.

He finally untangled himself from Erin. She sat in the grass, her arms wrapped around her knees. Her limbs were streaked with mud and blood. She pushed hair back from her forehead. Her face was clean, protected as it was while he held her against his body.

"Are you hurt?" he asked, knowing he spoke loudly past the ringing of his ears.

She trembled, and he longed to take her in his arms again and quiet her, but the fragrance of blood wafted from her body, and he did not dare.

Instead, her amber eyes met his. He looked deeply into them for the first time since he had left her on the tunnel floor to die months before.

Her lips formed a single word.

Jordan.

She struggled to her feet and stumbled toward the tracks. He followed in her wake, scanning the wreckage, wanting to be near her when she found him.

He did not see how the soldier could have survived . . . how anyone could have survived.

12:37 P.M.

Elizabeth burned in the field, rolling in agony.

Sunlight seared her vision, boiling her eyes. Smoke rose from her hands, her face. She curled into a ball, ducked her chin against her chest, her arms over her head, hoping they might protect her. Her hair crackled like an aura around her.

A moment ago, the train car had exploded, bursting open with a thunderclap. She flew like a dark angel through the burning brightness. Both her hands gripped the silver chain that bound her to a useless scrap of metal. She caught a glimpse of another's hands also clasped to the chain—then the sunlight blinded her, withering her eyesight.

The mighty boom also stole her hearing, leaving behind a rushing sound inside her ears, as if the sea had torn into her skull and washed back and forth inside her head.

She tried to worm deeper into the cool mud, to escape the sunlight.

Then hands rolled her and threw darkness atop her, protecting her from the sun.

She smelled the heavy wool of a cloak and cowered beneath this thin protection. The burn quickly ebbed into an ache, giving her the hope that she might yet live.

A voice shouted near her head, piercing the sea roiling in her skull. "Are you alive?"

Not trusting her voice, she nodded.

Who had saved her?

It could only be Rhun.

She ached for him, wanting to be held and comforted. She needed him to lead her through this pain to a future that did not burn.

"I must go," yelled the voice.

As her head cleared, she now recognized that stern tone.

Not Rhun.

Nadia.

She pictured those other hands clasped to her chain, guiding her fall, covering her. Nadia had risked her life to hold on to that chain and save her. But Elizabeth knew such efforts were born not out of concern or love.

The Church still needed her.

Safe for now, new fears rose.

Where is Rhun? Did he yet live?

"Stay here," Nadia commanded.

She obeyed—not that she had any choice otherwise. Escape remained impossible. Beyond the edges of her cloak lay only a burning death.

She considered for a moment casting the cloak aside, ending this interminable existence. But instead, she curled tighter, intending to survive, wrapping herself as snugly in thoughts of revenge as in heavy wool.

12:38 P.M.

Erin stumbled across a field scarred by metal shrapnel from the train. Coughing on the oily smoke, her mind tried to sort it out, rolling the explosion backward in her head.

The blast must have centered on the steam engine because the locomotive was nearly obliterated. Black pieces of steel stuck out of the field like ruined trees. But it wasn't just scorched metal that littered the fields.

A legless body lay by the tracks. She spotted an engineer's cap.

She hurried and crouched beside him, her knees pressing into stubbly grass.

Sightless brown eyes stared at the smoky sky. A black-clad arm moved past her head and closed the dead man's eyelids. The engineer hadn't been involved in any prophecy. He'd just shown up to do an honest day's work.

Another innocent life.

When will it ever end?

She lifted her face to Rhun. The priest touched his cross to his lips, the blessed silver searing that tender flesh as he whispered prayers over the dead man.

When he finished, she stood and walked on, drawing Rhun with her.

Within a few yards she came upon the second crewman, also

dead. He had light brown curly hair and freckles, a smudge of soot across his cheek. He looked too young to be working on a train. She thought about his life. Did he have a girlfriend, parents who were still alive? Who knew how far the ripples of grief would reach?

She abandoned Rhun to his prayers, propelled by the urgency to find Jordan.

Moving down the tracks, she came upon the remains of what she suspected was the galley car. A stove had shot through the air and landed in a crater. Leopold had been in that compartment. She looked for him, too, but found no trace.

Continuing, she reached the ruins of the dining car. Although the front had peeled away, the back was intact. It had derailed and dug a deep furrow through the rich brown soil. A gold curtain flapped through a shattered window at the back.

She pictured the moment before the blast. Rhun must have sensed the explosion. He had yanked her from Jordan's arms and through that window.

Rhun's shadow fell across the earth beside her, but she didn't turn to look at him. Instead, she searched inside the dining car, fearing to find a body, but needing to know.

It was empty.

Stepping away from the dining car, she looked over to the sleeper. The last car lay on its side, one side caved and split. To its right, she spotted movement through the smoke and ran toward it.

She quickly recognized Cardinal Bernard, covered in soot. He knelt over a figure sprawled on the ground, bent in a sigil of grief. Standing vigil behind the cardinal, Christian gripped Bernard's shoulder.

She struggled across the wreckage to them, fearing the worst.

Christian must have sensed her approach, turning his head, revealing a face covered in black blood. Shocked by the sight of him, she tripped and almost fell headlong.

Rhun caught her and kept her going.

Ahead, Bernard wept, his shoulders heaving up and down.

It could not be Jordan.

It could not be.

She finally reached Christian, who sadly shook his head. She hurriedly stepped around the cardinal.

The man on the ground was unrecognizable—soot smeared his face, his clothing had been burned away. Her eyes traveled from his smudged face, to his bare shoulders, to the silver cross he wore around his chest.

Father Ambrose.

Not Jordan.

Bernard held both of the priest's burnt hands in his own and gazed upon his lifeless face. She knew Ambrose had served the cardinal for many years. Despite the priest's sour attitude to everyone else, he and the cardinal had been close. Months ago she had watched the man kneeling in the pope's blood, trying to save the old man after his attack without a thought to his own safety. Ambrose might have been a bitter man, but he was also a staunch protector of the Church—and now he had given his life to that service.

The cardinal raised his face. "I've called for a helicopter. You must find the others before the police and rescue workers arrive."

"We must also be wary of whoever blew up this train," Christian added.

"It could have been a simple, tragic accident," Bernard corrected, already turning back to Ambrose.

She left Bernard to his grief, tripping over smoking debris, walking around fires, her eyes scanning the scarred field. Christian and Rhun flanked her, moving with her, their heads swiveling from side to side. She hoped their keener senses could help her to discover any clue to Jordan's fate.

"Over here!" Christian called and dropped to his knees.

On the ground in front of him, a familiar blond head.

Jordan.

Please, no . . .

Fear immobilized her. Her breath caught, and her eyes watered. She tried to steady herself. When Rhun took her arm, she broke free of his grip and crossed the last few feet to Jordan on her own.

He lay flat on his back. His dress blue uniform jacket lay in tatters, his white shirt under it torn to pieces.

She fell to her knees next to him and grabbed his hand. With trembling fingers, she searched for his pulse. It beat steady under her fingertips. With her touch, he opened his clear blue eyes.

She wept with relief and took his warm hand in hers.

She held him, watching his chest rise and fall, so grateful to find him alive.

Jordan's gaze steadied and looked at her, his eyes mirroring her relief. She stroked his cheek, his forehead, reassuring herself that he was whole.

"Hey, babe," he mouthed. "You look great."

She put her arms around him and buried her face in his chest.

12:47 P.M.

Rhun watched Erin cling to the soldier. Her first thought had been of Jordan, as it should have been. Likewise, Rhun had responsibilities as well.

"Where is the countess?" he asked Christian.

He shook his head. "When the car blew, I saw her and Nadia thrown outside."

Into the sunlight.

Christian pointed beyond the main wreckage. "Their trajectory would have tossed them to the far side of the tracks."

Rhun glanced down to Erin and Jordan.

"Go," Erin said. She helped Jordan sit up and start gaining his feet unsteadily. "We'll meet you back by Cardinal Bernard."

Freed of this responsibility, Rhun set off with Christian. The younger Sanguinist jogged across the field, jumping holes as lightly as a colt. He seemed unaffected by the explosion, while Rhun ached everywhere.

Once beyond the tracks, Christian suddenly sped to the left, perhaps spotting something. Rhun struggled to catch up.

Out of the pall of smoke, a tall figure dressed in black limped toward them.

Nadia.

Christian reached her first and hugged her tightly. He and Nadia had often served together on prior missions for the Church.

Rhun finally joined them. "Elisabeta?"

"The demon countess still lives." Nadia pointed to a mound a few hundred yards away. "But she's badly burned."

He hurried toward her cloaked body.

Christian followed with Nadia, filling her in on the status of the team.

"And what of Leopold?" Nadia asked.

Christian's face grew graver. "He was in the galley car, closer to the explosion."

"I will continue the search for him," Nadia said. "You two can care for her majesty. Get her ready to go."

As Nadia trotted off into the smoke, Rhun crossed the last of the distance to Elisabeta. Nadia had covered Elisabeta with the countess's traveling cloak. He knelt next to the mound, smelling charred flesh.

Rhun touched the surface of the cloak. "Elisabeta?"

A whimper answered him. Pity filled him. Elisabeta was legendary for her ability to withstand pain. For her to be reduced to this, her agony must be terrible.

"She will need blood to heal," Rhun told Christian.

"I'm not offering up mine," Christian said. "And you have none to spare."

Rhun leaned down to the cloak. He didn't dare lift it to examine the extent of her injuries. Still, he slipped his hand under the cloak and found her hand. Despite the pain it must cause, she gripped his fingers, holding to him.

I will get you to safety, he promised.

He stared up at the midday skies, the crisp blue smudged by smoke. Where could they go?

12:52 P.M.

The helicopter came in fast and low and landed in an undamaged part of the field. The pilot cracked a window and waved to the group gathered at the edge of the wreckage.

"That must be our ride," Jordan said, recognizing the expensive helicopter, a twin to the one that had rescued them out of the desert of Masada all those months ago.

Jordan took Erin's hand, and together they navigated through the last of the rubble to the helicopter. He was shaky on his feet, but Erin seemed mostly fine. He recalled the blur as Rhun had torn Erin from his grasp and crashed through the window when the train exploded.

Rhun's quick reaction had likely saved her life.

Perhaps he should forgive the Sanguinist priest for his prior actions, for feeding and leaving Erin to die in the tunnels under

Rome, but he still couldn't muster up enough goodwill to do so.

Ahead, the rotors kicked up dust and pieces of grass. The pilot wore the familiar midnight-blue uniform of the Swiss Guard and gestured to the back, indicating they should climb in.

Erin clambered aboard first and reached a hand down to Jordan.

Forgoing pride, he took it and allowed her to help him inside.

Once buckled in, he glanced out the open door toward the other Sanguinists. Swirling dust obscured all but the approaching forms of Christian and Rhun. Slung between them, they hauled a ragged black bundle, fully covered in a cloak.

The countess.

Bernard followed next out of the dust behind them. He carried Father Ambrose's body. Behind him, Nadia trailed.

Christian and Rhun climbed inside. Once seated, Rhun took possession of Bathory's form, cradling her on his lap, her draped head resting on his shoulder.

"No sign of Leopold?" Jordan asked Christian.

The young Sanguinist shook his head.

Bernard arrived and held out his bundle. Christian took it, and together the two strapped Ambrose's body to a stretcher, their movements quick and efficient, as if they had done this a thousand times before.

And they probably had.

The cardinal stepped back from the helicopter, allowing Nadia to board. She tapped the pilot on the shoulder and pointed her thumb up to indicate that he should take off.

As planned, Bernard would remain behind to explain everything to the police, to put a public face on this tragedy. It would be a tough job, especially as he was clearly still grieving.

The rotors sped up with a roar of the engine, and the helicopter lifted.

Once high enough, it swept over the carnage.

Faces pressed to the windows, everyone searched below and came to the sad and inevitable conclusion.

Brother Leopold was gone.

17

Erin gripped Jordan's arm as the helicopter sped toward a quaint stone village nestled among pines and olive groves next to a large lake. Its cobalt waters reminded her of Lake Tahoe, stirring a longing to be back in California—protected from all this death and chaos.

Not that trouble couldn't find me there, too.

She remembered Blackjack, heard the screams of the *blasphemare* cat.

She knew any lasting peace would escape her until this was over.

But would it ever be truly over?

The pilot aimed for the edge of the lush volcanic crater that overlooked the lake and the village square. Surmounting its stony crest like a crown sat a massive castle with red tile roofs, two leaden domes, and massive balconies. The grounds themselves were just as impressive, divided into private manicured gardens, contemplative fishponds, and tinkling fountains. Avenues were lined by pine trees or dotted with giant holm oaks. She even spotted the ruins of a Roman emperor's villa.

She had no trouble recognizing the pope's summer residence.

Castel Gandolfo.

As their aircraft descended toward a neighboring helipad, she wondered about this destination. Had the residence always been their goal or was this simply a quick and convenient hideout after the explosion?

Ultimately she didn't care. They needed rest and a place to recuperate.

Any port in a storm . . .

She glanced at her fellow passengers, recognizing this truth. Jordan looked haggard under a mask of soot and grime. Nadia's stern countenance was set, but shadowed with sadness. Christian still had traces of blood streaked in the creases of his face, making him look much older, or maybe it was just exhaustion.

Across from her, Rhun hadn't taken his eyes off the bundle in his arms, looking stricken and worried. He cradled Bathory's cloaked head against his shoulder with one hand. The countess lay still as death in his arms.

As soon as the skids touched ground, the Sanguinists rushed Erin and Jordan off the helipad. Ambrose's body remained on board, although each Sanguinist touched him as they disembarked, even Rhun. According to Christian, the pilot and copilot would attend to the priest's body.

Erin and Jordan followed the others down a gravel path through a rose garden, the plants long off their bloom. A few minutes later, they reached a spade-shaped door set into the stucco garden wall. Christian opened it and led them down a corridor with a gleaming terrazzo floor. Salons and rooms opened to either side, decorated with medieval tapestries and gilt-edged furniture.

At an intersection, Nadia beckoned Rhun to the left with his burden. Christian pointed Erin and Jordan to the right.

"I'm taking you to rooms where you can wash up," he said.

"I'm not letting Erin out of my sight," Jordan said.

She tightened her grip on his hand. She wasn't letting him out of her sight either.

"Already figured as much," Christian said. "And I'm not letting either of you out of my sight until you are safe in that room. The plan is to wait for the cardinal's return. We'll recover and regroup, then figure out what to do next."

With the matter settled, Jordan followed Christian. Tall windows on one side of this corridor looked out over the lake. White sails glided across the blue water, and seagulls soared above. It was a serene view, almost surreal after all the devastation and death.

Jordan was clearly less captivated, his mind elsewhere. "What do you think happened to Leopold?"

Christian touched his cross. "He was closer to the source of the explosion. His body may never be found. But the cardinal will keep searching until rescue personnel and police arrive. If Leopold's body is found, the cardinal will claim him and bring him here."

Reaching an oaken door, Christian unlocked it and ushered them both through, then followed them inside. He quickly crossed and closed the shutters over the windows that looked out upon the lake. He switched on a few wrought-iron lamps. The room held a double bed with a white duvet, a marble fireplace, and a seating area in front of the windows.

Christian disappeared through a small side door. Erin followed after him, trailed by Jordan. She found a simple bathroom with white walls, toilet, and sink. A shower stood in the corner, tiled in the same marble as the floor. Two thick towels rested on a low wooden table, topped by a fresh change of clothes.

It looked like she would be wearing tan pants and a white cotton shirt. Jordan would have on jeans and a brown shirt.

Hanging against the back of the bathroom door were a pair of familiar leather jackets. On their prior mission, she and Jordan had worn this very set of outerwear, constructed from the hides of grimwolves—slash-proof and tough enough to withstand *strigoi* bites. She stroked her hand down the battered brown leather, remembering the battles of the past.

Christian opened the medicine cabinet and took out a first-aid kit. "This should have what you need."

He turned and marched back to the hall door. He lifted up a stout brace that leaned against the wall next to the exit and handed it to Jordan. "This is reinforced with a core of steel."

Jordan hefted the bar. "Feels like it."

"Once I'm on the other side, use it to brace the door." Christian pointed to a chest at the foot of the bed. "You'll also find weapons there. I don't expect you'll need them, but it's better not to be caught off guard."

Jordan nodded, eyeing the chest.

"Let no one in besides me," Christian said.

"Not even the cardinal or Rhun?" she asked.

"No one," Christian repeated. "Someone knew we were on that train. My best advice for both of you is to trust no one except each other."

He stepped through the door and closed it behind him. Jordan lifted the heavy bar and secured it in place.

"So much for Christian's pep talk," she said. "That wasn't exactly reassuring."

Jordan moved to the chest and opened it up. He took out a machine gun and examined it. "Beretta AR 70. At least this is reassuring. Fires up to six hundred fifty rounds per minute." Then he checked the ammunition supply in the chest and smiled as he came up with another weapon, a Colt 1911. "It's not my own pistol, but it looks like someone did their research."

He handed it to her.

She checked the magazine. The bullets were made of silver—fine against humans, essential against *strigoi*. The silver reacted with their blood, helping to even the odds. *Strigoi* were hard to kill—tougher than humans, able to control their blood loss, and possessing supernatural healing abilities. But they weren't invulnerable.

Jordan next eyed the bathroom. "I'll let you take first crack at the shower, while I see about getting a fire started."

It was a fine plan, the best she had heard all day.

But first, she stepped close to him, inhaling his musky scent, smelling soot underneath. She tilted up and kissed him, glad to be alive, to be with him.

As she leaned away, Jordan's eyes were pinched with concern. "You okay?"

How could I be? she thought.

She was no soldier. She couldn't walk through fields of bodies and keep going. Jordan had trained himself, the Sanguinists, too, but she wasn't so sure she ever wanted to be that tough, even if she could. She remembered the thousand-yard stare that Jordan sometimes got. It cost him, and she bet it cost the Sanguinists, too.

He whispered, still holding her, "I don't mean about today. I feel like you've been holding something back since we met in California."

She slipped out of his embrace. "Everyone has secrets."

"So tell me yours."

Panic fluttered in her chest.

Not here. Not now.

To hide her reaction, she turned and headed for the bathroom. "I've had my fill of secrets today," she said lamely. "Right now, all I want is a hot shower and a warm fire."

"I can't argue with that." But despite his words, he sounded disappointed.

She entered the bathroom and closed the door. She gladly shed her clothes, happy to rid herself of the smell of soot and smoke and replace it with lavender soap and a citrus shampoo. She stood for a long time under the hot spray, letting it burn away the day, leaving her skin raw and sensitive.

She toweled and slipped into a soft robe. Barefooted, she returned to the main room. The lamps had been switched off, and the only illumination came from the crackling fire.

Jordan straightened after jabbing and rolling a log into better position in the flames. He had shed his suit coat and shredded shirt. His skin shone in the firelight, bruised and crisscrossed with scratches and cuts. Across the left side of his chest, his tattoo almost seemed to glow. The artwork wrapped around his shoulder and sent tendrils partway down his arm and across part of his back. It looked like the branching roots of a tree, centered on a single dark mark on his chest.

She knew the history of that mark. Jordan had been struck by lightning when he was in high school. He had died for a short period of time before being resuscitated. The surge of energy had left its fractal mark across his skin, bursting capillaries, creating what was called a Lichtenberg figure, or a lightning flower. Before it faded, he had the pattern tattooed as a reminder of his brush with death, turning the near tragedy into something beautiful.

She drew closer, as if drawn by that residual energy.

He faced her, smiling. "Hope you didn't use all the hot—"

She put a finger to his lips, silencing him. Words weren't what she wanted right now. She tugged her belt loose and shrugged out of the robe. It slithered to the floor, brushing against her breasts and pooling at her ankles.

With one hand, he stroked her hair back from her neck. She arched her throat in invitation. He took it, trailing slow kisses down to her collarbone. She moaned, and he drew back, his eyes dark with passion and an unspoken question.

In answer, she pulled him by the waistband of his pants toward the bed.

Once there, he shed the last of his clothes, ripping them off and kicking them away.

Naked, aroused, he lifted her up in his arms. Her legs wrapped around his muscular thighs as he lowered her to the bed. He loomed over her, as wide as the world, shoving away everything, leaving only them, this moment.

She pulled him down for an urgent kiss, tasting him, her teeth finding his lower lip, his tongue with her own. His warm hands ran over her skin, across her breasts, leaving a trail of electricity in their wake—then slid around to her lower back to lift her higher.

She arched under him, needing him, knowing she would always need him.

His lips moved to her throat, brushing across the scars on her neck.

She moaned, pulling his head hard against her, as if begging him to bite her, to open her again. A name rose to her lips, but she trapped it inside before it escaped into the world.

She remembered Jordan begging for her secret.

But the deepest secrets are the ones we don't know we're keeping.

His lips moved to below her ear, his breath heating the nape of her neck. His next words groaned out of him, full of his truth, felt in the bones of her skull.

"I love you."

She felt tears rise to her eyes. She drew his mouth to hers and whispered as their lips brushed. "And I love you."

It was her truth, too—but perhaps not her whole truth.

18

Rhun carried Elisabeta down a dark passageway that smelled of wood and aged wine. This corner of the castle's subterranean levels had once served as the pope's personal wine cellar. Some long-forgotten rooms still held huge oak casks or racks of green bottles thick with dust.

He followed Nadia down yet another set of stairs, heading toward the floor reserved for their order. He felt his arms trembling as he held Elisabeta. He had taken a quick sip of consecrated wine aboard the helicopter. It had fortified him enough to make this journey below, but weakness still plagued him.

At last, passing down a stone passageway dug out of the volcanic bedrock, Nadia stopped at a bricked-up archway, a seeming dead end.

"I can pay the penance," Rhun offered.

Nadia ignored him and touched four bricks, one near her head, one near her stomach, and one near each shoulder—forming the shape of a cross.

She then pressed the centermost stone and whispered words that had been spoken by members of their order since the time of Christ, "Take and drink you all of this."

The center brick slid back to reveal a tiny basin carved in the brick below it.

Nadia unsheathed her dagger and poked its tip into the center of her palm, in the spot where nails had once been driven into the hands of Christ. She cupped her palm until it held several drops of her blood, then tipped the crimson pool sideways into the basin.

In his arms, Elisabeta tensed, likely smelling Nadia's blood.

He stepped back a few paces, allowing Nadia to finish.

"For this is the Chalice of My blood," she said, "of the new and everlasting Testament."

With the last word of the prayer, cracks appeared between bricks in the archway, forming the shape of a narrow door.

"*Mysterium fidei,*" Nadia finished and pushed.

Stone grated against brick as the door swung inward.

Nadia slipped through first, and he followed, taking care not to brush Elisabeta's body against the walls to either side. Once across the threshold, Elisabeta softened in his arms. She must have sensed that she was deep underground now, where sun could never reach her.

Nadia's thin form glided ahead, revealing how much effortless speed and strength of limb she possessed compared to him. She hurried past the entrance to the castle's Sanguinist Chapel and led Rhun toward a region seldom trespassed—toward the prison cells.

He followed. No matter how grievous her wounds, Elisabeta remained a prisoner.

Though the cells were rarely used in this age, the stone floor had been worn smooth and shiny by the centuries of boots passing this way. How many *strigoi* had been imprisoned down here and put to the question? Such prisoners entered as *strigoi* and either accepted the offer to join the Sanguines or they died down here as damned souls.

Nadia reached the nearest cell and hauled open a thick iron door. Its heavy hinges and stout lock were strong enough to hold even the most powerful *strigoi*.

Rhun carried Elisabeta inside and placed her atop the single pallet. He smelled fresh straw and bedding. Someone had made the room ready for her. Next to the bed, a beeswax candle sat atop a rough wooden table, casting a flickering light across the cell.

"I will fetch healing ointments for her burns," Nadia said. "Are you safe to be alone with her?"

At first, anger rose in him, but he brought it under control. Nadia was correct to worry. "Yes."

Satisfied, she swept away, the door thudding closed behind her. He heard the key turn in the lock. Nadia was taking no chances.

Alone now, he sat next to Elisabeta on the pallet and gently shifted the cloak to expose her small hands. He winced from the fluid leaking from broken blisters, the skin beneath them burned pink. He felt the heat radiating from her body, as if it were trying to expel the sunlight.

He drew the rest of the cloak off, but she turned away, her head hidden in the hood of her velvet cape.

"I don't wish you to see my face," she said, her voice a harsh rasp.

"But I can help you."

"Let Nadia do it."

"Why?"

"Because"—she shifted farther away—"my appearance will disgust you."

"Do you think I care about such things?"

"*I* care," she whispered, her words barely louder than a breath.

Honoring her wishes, he left her hood alone and took one of her burnt hands in his, noticing her palm was untouched. He pictured her clenching her hands in agony as the sunlight engulfed her in fire. He leaned against the stone blocks and rested, keeping hold of her hand.

Her fingers slowly closed over his own.

A deep weariness filled the marrow of his bones. Pain told him where he had been wounded—lacerations across his shoulders, scrapes on his forearms, a few burns on his back. His eyes began to drift closed when a quick knock thumped the door. A key turned in the lock, and the hinges complained.

Nadia stepped into the room. She frowned upon seeing Rhun's hand clasped to Elisabeta's, but she said nothing. She carried an earthenware bowl covered with a brown linen cloth. The smell rolled across the cell, filling the space.

His body quickened, and Elisabeta growled next to him.

Blood filled that bowl.

Warm, fresh, *human* blood.

Nadia must have collected it from a volunteer among the castle staff.

She crossed to the pallet and handed him the bowl.

He refused to take it. "Elisabeta would prefer it if you tend to her wounds."

Nadia arched one eyebrow. "And I would prefer *not* to. I already saved her royal life. I will do no more." She slipped free a leather flask and held it out to him. "Consecrated wine for you. Do you wish to drink it now or after you have tended to Countess Bathory?"

He set the flask down on the table. "I will not let her suffer a moment longer."

"Then I will fetch you soon." She retreated to the door and out again, relocking the cell.

A moan from Elisabeta returned him to his task.

He soaked the linen cloth in the bowl, sopping it heavily with blood. The iron scent drifted into his nostrils, even as he held his breath against it. To steady himself against a craving that rose from his bones, he touched his pectoral cross and muttered a prayer for strength.

He then picked up the hand he had been holding and slid the cloth along it, the fabric grazing her skin.

She gasped, her voice muffled by the hood.

"Have I hurt you?"

"Yes," she whispered. "Don't stop."

He bathed one hand, then the other. Where he touched, blisters fell away and raw skin healed. Once done, he finally reached for the edge of her hood.

She grabbed his wrist with her bloodstained fingers. "Look away."

Knowing he could not, he drew the hood back, revealing first her white chin, streaked with grime and pink from the burn. Her soft lips had cracked and bled. The blood had dried in black rivulets from the corners of her mouth.

He steeled himself and pulled the hood fully away. Candle-light fell on her high cheekbones. Where once clear white skin had invited his touch, now he saw blackened and blistered ruin, all over-laid with soot. The soft curls of her hair were mostly gone, burned away by the sun.

Her silver eyes met his, the corneas cloudy, nearly blind.

Still, he read the fear there.

"Am I hideous to you now?" she asked.

"Never."

He soaked the cloth and brought it to her ravaged face. Keeping his touch light, he ran it across her forehead, down her cheeks and throat. Blood smeared her skin, soaked into blisters, and stained the white pillow under her head.

The smell intoxicated him. Its warmth tingled his cold fingers, heated his palms, inviting him to taste it. His whole body ached for it.

Just one drop.

He stroked the cloth down her face again. The first pass had mostly just washed the soot away. He now attended to her damaged skin. He bathed her face over and over again, watching in wonder each time as he wiped away the damage—and unblemished skin slowly appeared. A field of black curls took root, shadowing her scalp with the promise of new growth. But it was her face that enchanted him, as flawless as the day he had fallen in love with her, in a long dead rose garden beside a now ruined castle.

He traced her lips with the soft fabric, leaving behind a thin sheen of blood. Her silver eyes opened to him, clear once again, but now smoky with desire. He bent his head toward her lips and crushed them with his own.

The taste of the crimson fire spread through his body, as swiftly as a match set to dry grass. She threaded blood-wet fingers through his hair, enfolding him in a cloud of hunger and desire.

Her mouth parted under his kiss, and he lost himself in her scent, her blood, her softness. He had no time for gentleness, and she asked for none. He had waited so long to join with her again, and she with him.

He promised himself in that moment that he would exact swift vengeance on whoever had sent her blazing into the sunlight.

But until then . . .

He fell atop her, letting fire and desire burn away all thought.

19

Burrowed deep in the giant hay bale, Leopold strove for a comfortable position. Straw pierced his robe and gouged his tender burns. Still, he dared not leave this shelter.

As the train had exploded, he had jumped clear, riding the blast wave across an expanse of stubbly fields. Only by the hand of God had he been standing in the lee of the boiler when it blew. The metal tank bore the brunt of the explosion, saving him from being incinerated on the spot.

Instead, he had been blown free of the car. He had tumbled through the air, burnt and bleeding, and skidded into the cold mud of the winter fields. Dazed and deafened, he had crawled into a hay bale to hide, to think, to plan.

He did not know then if he was the only survivor.

While he waited, he had stanched the blood flowing from his many wounds. Finally, as the ringing in his ears faded, he heard the rhythmic sound—*thump, thump, thump*—of a helicopter landing, muffled by the straw surrounding him.

He did not know if the aircraft had been summoned by the cardinal or if it marked the arrival of rescue workers. Either way, he kept hidden. Though he had not set the bomb himself, he knew he bore the blame for the attack. As soon as he had texted the *Damnatus*, informing him that everyone was on board, along with sharing their theory concerning the identity of the First Angel, the train had exploded—catching Leopold entirely by surprise.

Perhaps he should have expected as much.

Whenever the *Damnatus* spotted what he wanted, he moved in for the kill.

Never any hesitation.

After the helicopter lifted off and headed away, he heard Cardinal Bernard calling his name, the grief plain in his voice. Leopold longed to go to him, to assuage his sorrow, to beg for forgiveness, and to truly rejoin the Sanguinists.

But, of course, he did not.

Though brutal, the *Damnatus*'s goal was right and pure.

Over the next hour, more helicopters arrived, followed by rescue vehicles with sirens and shouting men and tromping feet. He curled smaller in the straw. The commotion should mask any sounds he made when he did his penance.

Finally, he could drink the holy wine and heal.

With some difficulty, he freed his leather wine flask and brought it to his lips. Using his teeth, he unscrewed the top and spit it out, and drank deeply, allowing the fire to take him away.

Far beneath the city of Dresden, Leopold knelt in a dank crypt lit by a single candle. Since the air-raid siren had sounded, no one dared show a light, fearful of drawing the wrath of the British bombers down upon them.

As he listened, a bomb detonated far overhead, the boom shaking loose pebbles from the ceiling. The church above had been struck weeks ago. Only this crypt was spared, the entrance dug out from the inside by the Sanguinists who lived there.

Leopold knelt between two other men. Like him, they were both strigoi, *preparing to take their final vows as Sanguinists on this dark and violent night. Before him stood a Sanguinist priest, dressed in fine robes and cupping a golden chalice in his clean white palms.*

The strigoi *next to him trembled. Was he afraid that his faith was not strong enough, that the first sip of Christ's blood would be his last?*

When it came to his turn, Leopold bowed his head and listed his sins. He had many. In his mortal life, he had been a German doctor. Early in the war, he had ignored the Nazis, resisted them. But eventually the government drafted him and sent him into battlefields to care for young men ripped apart by guns and bombs or brought low by disease, starvation, and cold.

One winter night, a rogue pack of strigoi set upon his small unit in the Bavarian Alps. The half-frozen soldiers fought with rifles and bayonets, but the battle lasted no more than a handful of minutes. In the first sweep by the beasts, Leopold had been wounded, his back broken, unable to fight or move. He could only watch the slaughter, knowing his turn would come.

Then a strigoi the size of a child dragged him into the empty cold forest by his boots. He died there, his blood steaming holes into dirty white snow. All the while, the child sang in a high clear voice, a German folk song. That should have been the end of Leopold's miserable life, but the boy had chosen to turn him into a monster.

He fought against the blood being poured into his mouth—until revulsion became hunger and bliss. As Leopold drank, the child continued to sing.

In the end, wartime was a strigoi's paradise.

To Leopold's great shame, he feasted.

Then one day he met a man he could not bite. His senses told him that a drop of that man's blood would kill him. The stranger intrigued him. As a doctor, he wanted to understand this one's secrets. So he sought him out night after night, watching him for weeks before daring to speak. When he finally did confront the stranger, the man listened to Leopold's words, understood his disgust over what he had become.

In turn, the stranger offered him his true name, one so cursed by Christ that Leopold still dared only to think of him as the Damnatus. At that moment, Leopold was offered a path to salvation, a way to serve Christ in secret.

That was what brought him to this crypt beneath Dresden.

On his knees, listing his sins, alongside these others.

Leopold had been instructed to seek out the Sanguinists, to enfold himself among them, but to remain the Damnatus's eyes and ears within the order.

He swore his allegiance back then—as he must do again this night.

Another bomb fell above, shaking dirt from the crypt's roof. The penitent on his left yelped. Leopold remained silent. He did not fear death. He had been called for a greater purpose. He would fulfill a destiny that had spanned millennia.

The penitent pulled himself back under control, crossed himself, and finished his litany of sins. Eventually, his words stopped. He had given his sins up to God. He could be purified now.

"Do you repent of your sins out of the truest love to God and not out of fear of damnation?" the Sanguinist priest intoned to Leopold's neighbor.

"I do," the man answered.

"Then rise and be judged." The priest's face was invisible under his cowl.

The penitent rose, trembling, and opened his mouth. The priest lifted the golden chalice and poured claret-red wine onto his tongue.

Immediately the man began screaming, smoke roiling from his mouth. Either the creature had not fully repented or he had lied outright. No matter the reason, his soul was judged stained, and his body could not accept the holiness of Christ's blood.

It was a risk they all took to join the order.

The creature fell to the stone floor and writhed, his shrieks echoing off the bare walls. Leopold bent to touch him, to still him, but before his hand reached him, the body crumbled to ash.

Leopold said a prayer for the strigoi *who had sought to change his ways, even if his heart was impure. He knelt then, and once more folded his hands.*

He finished his own long confession and waited for the wine. If his path was righteous, he would not burn to ash before this holy Sanguinist. If he and the one he served were wrong, a single drop of wine would reveal it.

He opened his mouth, allowing Christ to be poured into his body. And lived.

Leopold came back into his trembling body, pressed on all sides by the sharp hay. He had never considered his conversion from *strigoi* to Sanguinist as a sin, something that needed penance.

Why had God sent this vision to him?

Why now?

For a sickening moment, he worried that it was because God knew that his conversion was done under false pretenses, knew Leopold was destined to betray the order, like the *Damnatus* had with Christ.

He lay there for a long time, thinking upon this, then swallowed back his fears.

No.

He had seen the vision precisely *because* his mission was true.

God had spared his life back then to serve the *Damnatus,* and He spared it again today. Once the sun sank and the rescue workers left for the night, he would leave the hay bale under the cover of dark and continue his purpose, no matter the cost.

Because God told him so.

20

Atop the Tiber River, Judas drew back on the sculls, and his slim wooden boat shot a gratifying distance across the water. Sunlight reflected off the silvery river and dazzled his eyes. This late in the year he savored both its light and its fading warmth.

A flock of crows circled overhead, disappearing into the bare branches of a riverside park before rising up against the bright winter sky.

Below, he kept his body working in rhythm, moving down the Tiber, stroking harder as he battled the wake of a passing boat. Larger crafts plowed through the river around him. His fragile wooden hull could easily be smashed to matchsticks in an instant. This time of year, he was the only rower who braved the frigid winter temperatures and the risk of being run down by speedboats, ferries, and cargo ships.

His phone buzzed with another text message from his receptionist.

Sighing, he knew what it said without reading it. He had watched it on the news before he climbed into his boat. The papal train had been destroyed. The cardinal alone had survived. Everyone else aboard had died.

He stroked the sculls through the water again.

With the prophesied trio gone, nothing stood in his way.

Brother Leopold's last text message had mentioned the First

Angel, the one who was destined to use the book as a weapon in the coming War of the Heavens. With the prophecy broken, this angel likely posed no further threat, but Judas did not like loose ends.

A ferry captain tooted his horn, and Judas raised a hand in greeting. The man straightened his black cap and waved back. They had greeted each other almost every day for twenty years. Judas had watched him grow from a thin young buck, uncertain on the controls, to a portly old man. Still, he had never learned his name.

He had grown to understand solitude as he watched his family and friends die. He had learned to keep his distance from others after generations of friendships had ended in death.

But what of this immortal boy Leopold had spoken of?

Thomas Bolar.

Judas wanted him. He would bargain with Rasputin, pay whatever the monk desired, and fetch this immortal child to his home. His heart quickened at the thought of meeting another like himself, but also from knowing the role that the boy was destined to play.

To help bring about the end of the world.

It was a shame he hadn't met this boy earlier in his long life, to have someone to share his endless span of years, another who was as ageless and as unfettered by time.

Still, Judas had been offered such a chance centuries before, and he had wasted it.

Perhaps this is my penance.

As he pulled on the oars, he pictured Arella's dark skin and gold eyes. He remembered the first ride that he had taken with her, the night they were reunited at the Venetian masquerade. Then, too, he had manned a wooden boat, driven the craft where he wanted it to go, never sensing how little control he had.

Their gondola glided over the calm water of a dark canal, the stars shining above, a full moon beckoning. As he poled the craft through a light mist, passing alongside a grand Venetian house, the reek of excrement and waste washed over their craft, intruding on their pleasant night like some sulfurous shade.

He scowled at the sewage pipe leaking tepidly into the canal.

Noticing his attention and expression, Arella laughed. "Is this city not refined enough for your tastes?"

He gestured at the rooms above full of laughter and decadence, then to the sludge fouling the water below. "There are better ways of ridding such waste."

"And when it is time, they will find them."

"They have found them and lost them." Judas's voice held the bitterness he had acquired from watching the fate of men.

She trailed long dark fingers along the hull's black lacquer. "You speak of the former wonders of Rome, when the city was at its splendorous best."

He poled the boat away from the lighted houses and back toward his inn. "Much was lost when that city fell."

She shrugged. "It shall be regained. In time."

"In times past, the healers of Rome knew how to cure diseases from which the men of this era still suffer and die."

He sighed at how much had been lost to the darkness of this age. He wished that he had studied medicine, that he could have preserved such knowledge after the libraries burned and the men of learning were put to the sword.

"This age will pass," Arella assured him. "And the knowledge will be found again."

Silvery moonlight shone on her hair and her bare shoulders, leaving him wondering about this beautiful mystery before him. After discovering each other again, they had danced most of the night away, sweeping across wooden floors, until finding themselves here as dawn neared.

He finally broached the subject that he had been reluctant to raise all evening, fearful of the answer.

"Arella . . ." He slowed the pace of the boat and let it drift through the mists on its own, as undirected as a leaf. "By my name alone, you know my sin, my crime, and the curse laid upon me by Christ, to march these endless years. But how are you able . . . what are you . . . ?"

He could not even form the question fully on his lips.

Still, she understood and smiled. "What does my name tell you?"

"Arella," he repeated, letting it roll off his tongue. "A beautiful name. Ancient. In old Hebrew, it means a messenger from God."

"And it is a fitting name," she said. "I have often carried messages from God. In that way also, we two are alike. Both servants to the heavens, bound to our duty."

Judas snorted softly. "Unlike you, I have received no special messages from above."

And how he wished he would have. After the bitterness of his curse waned, he had often wondered why this punishment had been exacted upon his flesh, leaving it undying. Was it merely penance for his sin or was it for some purpose, a goal he had not yet come to understand?

"You are fortunate," she said. "I would gladly accept such silence."

"Why?" he pressed.

She sighed and touched the silver shard hanging from around her neck. "It can be a curse to see dimly into the future, knowing of a tragedy to come but not knowing how to avert it."

"So then you are a prophetess?"

"I was once," she said, her dark eyes flicking up to the moon and back. "Or should I say, many times. In the past, I once bore the title of the Oracle of Greece, another time the Sibyl of Erythraea, but throughout the ages, I was called countless other names."

Shocked, he sank to the seat before him. He kept a grip on the pole in the water, while he took her hand in his. Despite the cool night, he felt the heat coming off her skin, far warmer than the touch of most men and women, beyond that of any human.

Her lips curved into the already familiar half smile. "Do you doubt me? You who have lived to see the world change and change again?"

The most remarkable thing was that he did not.

As the gondola drifted silently in the moonlight, a half smile played across her lips, as if she knew his thoughts, guessing what he had begun to suspect.

She waited.

"I do not pretend to know such things," he started, picturing her in his arms, dancing with her. "But . . ."

She shifted in her seat. "What do you not pretend to know?"

He squeezed the fierce heat of her palm and fingers.

"The nature of one such as you. One given messages from God. One who endures across the ages. One of such perfection."

He blushed as he said these last words.

She laughed. "Am I then so different from you?"

He knew deep in his bones that she was—both by nature and

by character. She was an embodiment of good, whereas he had done terrible things. He gazed at the wonder before him, knowing another name for a messenger of God, *another name for the word* Arella.

He forced himself to state it out loud. "You are an angel."

She folded her hands in front of her, as if in prayer. Slowly, a soft golden light emanated from her body. It bathed the gondola, the water, his face. The warmth of its touch suffused him with joy and holiness.

Here was another eternal being—but she was not like him.

Where he was evil, she was good.

Where he was dark, she was light.

He closed his eyes and drank in her radiance.

"Why have you come to me? Why are you here?" He opened his eyes and looked at the water, the houses, the sewage in the canal, then back to her—back to a beauty beyond measure. "Why are you on Earth and not in Heaven?"

Her light dimmed, and she resembled an ordinary woman again. "Angels may descend and visit Earth." She looked up at him. "Or they *may* fall."

She stressed that last word.

"You fell?"

"Long ago," she added, reading the shock and surprise in his face. "Alongside the Morning Star."

That was another name for Lucifer.

Judas refused to believe she had been cast out of Heaven. "But I sense only goodness in you."

She gazed at him, her eyes patient.

"Why did you fall?" he pressed, as if this were a simple question on a simple night. "You could not have done evil."

She looked down at her hands. "I kept my knowledge of Lucifer's pride hidden in my heart. I foresaw his coming rebellion, yet stayed silent."

Judas tried to fathom such an event. She had kept a prophecy concerning the War of the Heavens from God, and for that she was cast down.

Arella raised her head and spoke again. "It was a just punishment. But unlike the Morning Star, I did not wish ill of mankind. I chose *to use my exile to watch over God's flock here, to continue to serve Heaven as I could."*

"How do you serve Heaven?"

"However I can." She brushed a speck from her skirt. "My greatest act was during your age, when I protected the Christ child from harm, watching over him while he was but a babe, defenseless in this hard world."

Judas bowed his head in shame, reminded how he had failed to do the same when Jesus was older. Judas had betrayed not only the Son of God—but also his dearest friend. He felt again the weight of the leather bag of silver coins that the priests had given him, the warmth of Christ's cheek under his lips when he kissed him to mark him to his executioner.

Unable to keep the envy from his voice, he asked, "But how did you protect Christ? I do not understand."

"I came before Mary and Joseph in Bethlehem, shortly after Christ was born. I told them what I foresaw, of the coming slaughter of innocents by King Herod."

Judas gulped, knowing this story, recognizing anew who shared his boat.

"You were the angel who told them to flee to Egypt."

"I also led them there, taking them to where their son could grow up sheltered from harm."

Judas now understood how very different she was from him.

She had saved Jesus.

Judas had killed him.

His breathing grew heavier. He had to stand again, to move. He returned to slowly poling the gondola down the canal, trying to picture her life here on Earth, a stretch of time far longer than his brief span.

He finally asked another question, one just as important to him. "How do you stand the time?"

"I pass through it, just as you do." Again, she touched the shard on her neck. "For time beyond measure, I have served mankind as a seer, a prophetess, an oracle."

He imagined her in this role, wearing the simple robes of a Delphic priestess, sharing words of prophecy. "Yet you do this no more?"

She stared out across the dark waters. "I still see occasional glimpses of what is to come, of time rolling ahead of me as surely as it trails behind me. I cannot stand against these visions." A line of sorrow appeared between her brows. "But I no longer share them. To know my prophecies has brought more suffering to mankind than pleasure, and so I keep such futures a secret."

The inn appeared through the mists. He steered his gondola toward the stone dock. Once he drew abreast of it, two men in livery hurried to secure the boat. One held out a gloved hand to the beautiful lady. Judas steadied her with a palm held against the small of her back.

Then shadows fell out of the darkness above and landed on the dock, forming the shapes of men—but they were not men. He saw the sharp teeth, the pale, feral faces.

Many times he had fought such creatures, and many times he had lost. Still, with his immortality, he always healed, and his tainted blood always destroyed them.

He pulled Arella behind him in the boat, letting the beasts take the men from the hotel. He could not save them, but perhaps he might save her.

He swung his pole like a club, while her beautiful hands fumbled with the ropes that secured them to the dock. Once free, he pushed the gondola away. It heeled to one side, then righted itself.

But they were not fast enough.

The creatures sprang across the water. It was an impossible leap for a man, but a simple one for such beasts.

He yanked a dagger from the sheath in his boot and thrust it deep into the chest of the larger of the two. Cold blood washed across his hand, down his arm, and soaked into his fine white shirt.

No man would have survived the blow, but this creature barely slowed, knocking his arm aside and pulling out the dagger from its own belly.

Behind him, the second beast had Arella on her back and crawled across her soft body.

"No," she whispered. "Leave us be."

She pulled the silver shard from her throat and slashed its sharp edge across the creature's neck.

A scream ripped from its severed throat, followed by flames that quickly swept its cursed form. Entirely on fire, it leaped for the cool darkness of the canal, but only ash fell to the water, the body already completely consumed.

Seeing this, the larger beast vaulted high, hit the neighboring bank, and bounded into the darkness of the city.

Arella dipped the shard into the canal and dried it on her skirt.

He scrutinized the sliver in her hands. "How?"

"This is a piece of a sacred blade," she explained and hung it around her neck again. "It kills any creature it pierces."

Judas's heart quickened.

Could it kill the unkillable—like him?

Or her?

Sorrow crossed her face as if she knew his thoughts, confirming what he had just imagined. She wore the instrument of her own destruction around her slender neck, a way to escape this prison of endless years. And from her expression, she must have been sorely tempted occasionally to use it.

He understood that desire. For years uncounted, he had sought to end his life, enduring unspeakable pain in the attempts. And still he lived. The simple right of death was granted to all other creatures. Even the beasts they had fought here could simply walk into the sunlight and end their unholy existence.

His gaze fell again on the silver shining between her breasts, knowing that the death he had sought for so long was close. He only had to take it.

He reached out—and took her hand instead, drawing her up to him, to his lips.

He kissed her, so very glad to be alive.

Upon the Tiber, in the brightness of the midday sun, Judas thought back to that moment, to that kiss in the dark. Regret swelled inside him, knowing what would follow, that their relationship would end so badly.

Perhaps I should have grabbed that shard and not her hand.

He had never learned where she had obtained it, nor anything else about that sacred blade. But in the end, they each had their secrets to keep.

He touched his breast pocket and removed an ice-cold stone roughly the size and shape of a deck of cards. It was made of a clear green crystal, like an emerald, but deep in its heart was a flaw, a vein of ebony black. He lifted the stone toward the sun, turning it this way and that. The black flaw shivered in the brightness, waning to a pinpoint, but still there. Once he returned the crystal to the shadows of his pocket, the flaw would grow again.

Like a living thing.

Only this mystery thrived in darkness, not light.

He had found the stone during the years that followed after Arella, after he had discovered *why* he walked this long path on Earth. During that dark time of his life, he had lost himself to the study of alchemy, taught by the likes of Isaac Newton and Roger Bacon. He had learned much, including how to animate his clockwork creatures, how to manipulate the power found inside his blood.

He had come upon the crystal while searching for the mythical philosopher's stone, a substance said to grant eternal life. He had hoped it would offer a clue to his own immortality. He had unearthed the crystal from under the cornerstone of a ruined church.

In the end, it wasn't the philosopher's stone—but something far more powerful, tied to *death* not immortal *life*. He rubbed his thumb across the mark carved on the underside of the stone. After years studying both this symbol and the stone, he knew many of its secrets—but not all.

Still, he knew in the right hands this simple green stone could upset the balance of life on Earth. For centuries, he had waited for the right time to release its evil into the world, to accomplish what he had been put on Earth to do.

He pocketed the stone and stared up at the sun.

At last, it was now time.

But first he needed to secure two angels.

One from the past, one from the present.

21

Far above the deck of the icebreaker, Tommy gripped the metal cross braces of a red crane, holding tightly with his thick gloves. He had no fear of death, knowing a plunge to the hard steel below wouldn't kill him—but he could do without the pain of a shattered back, pelvis, and skull.

Instead, he carefully pulled himself higher.

His captors let him climb whenever he wanted.

They also had no fear of Tommy's death—or escape.

He worked his way around to the back of the crane. Even with the biting wind, he loved being up here. He felt free, leaving his fears and concerns below.

As the Arctic sun sat leadenly on the horizon, refusing to fully rise this time of year, Tommy stared at the endless spread of sea ice, at the dark trail of open water forged by the bow of the ship. The only living things for miles around were the crew of the icebreaker. He wasn't sure if Alyosha or the kid's master counted as living things.

A creak of a door drew his gaze from the horizon back to the deck. A dark shape stepped through a hatch, having to bend his tall form to exit. He held the edges of his robe against the fierce wind—not because he was cold, but simply to restrain the wool from whipping about his body. It was easy to spot the thick beard, the dour expression.

It was Alyosha's master.

Grigori Rasputin.

The Russian monk held a satellite phone in one hand.

Curious, Tommy climbed toward him, intending to eavesdrop from above.

Aboard the ship, everyone went dead silent whenever Tommy entered a cabin. They looked at him as if he were an alien creature—and maybe he was now. But from up here, unseen, he could hear and watch ordinary life pass below. It was another reason he liked climbing up here. It comforted him to watch somebody smoke or whistle or joke, even if he couldn't understand the Russian.

Quietly, he worked his way down until he reached a perch close enough to listen, while keeping out of direct view of Rasputin.

The monk paced below him, muttering in Russian and glaring out at the ice. He kept checking his phone, as if expecting a call. Something clearly had the guy agitated.

Finally, the phone rang.

Rasputin snapped the phone to his ear. "*Da?*"

Tommy kept very still on his braced perch. He prayed the person on the other line spoke English. Maybe he could learn something.

Please . . .

Rasputin cleared his throat after listening for a full minute and spoke with a heavy accent. "Before we negotiate for the boy," he said, "I want a photograph of the Gospel."

Tommy was relieved to hear English, but what did Rasputin mean by *negotiate for the boy*? Was someone trying to buy him? Was this call about his freedom or another prison?

If only I could hear the other end of the conversation.

Unfortunately that wish wasn't granted.

"I know what the Gospel revealed, Cardinal," Rasputin growled. "And I won't negotiate unless I can verify that it remains in your possession."

Questions popped like firecrackers in Tommy's head: *What gospel? What cardinal? Was he talking to someone in the Catholic Church? Why?*

Tommy pictured the eyes of the priest who had comforted him after the death of his parents atop Masada. He remembered the man's concern. The priest had even offered a prayer for his mother and father, though he knew they were both Jewish.

Angry sounds erupted from the other end of the phone, loud enough to reach Tommy's perch.

Rasputin said something again, switching from English to what sounded like Latin.

He recalled the priest's prayer had also been in Latin.

Was there some connection?

"Those are my terms," Rasputin spat out and ended the call.

His pacing resumed again, until his phone beeped with an incoming text.

Rasputin looked at the screen and sank to his knees on the icy deck. His face looked rapturous as he scanned the ice, clutching the phone between his palms as if it were a prayer book.

Tommy quietly leaned out from the crane to stare down at the screen. He couldn't make anything out, but he guessed it was the photo of the gospel that Rasputin had demanded to see.

The phone pealed again.

Rasputin answered it, on his knees, plainly unable to keep the delight from his voice. "*Da?*"

A long pause followed while the monk listened.

"Very satisfactory," he said, touching his cross with a thick finger. "But, Cardinal Bernard, we could always meet in St. Petersburg for the exchange? I would love to give you a demonstration of Russian hospitality. Father Korza enjoyed it very much when he visited me last time."

Tommy jolted, almost falling off his perch.

He had forgotten the priest's name, but he recognized it upon hearing it now.

Korza.

Before he could ponder this new mystery, Rasputin bared his teeth, exposing his sharp fangs. "So then, neutral ground," he said with a chuckle. "How about Stockholm?"

Rasputin listened for a stretch, then said his good-byes and hung up the phone. The monk climbed back to his feet and stared out at the ice for a long time.

Tommy was afraid to move, so he watched and waited.

The monk tilted his head and looked up at Tommy, his smile colder than the ice surrounding the ship. Rasputin must have known Tommy had been there the entire time. He suspected the monk might have purposefully switched to English, to make sure Tommy understood the gist of the conversation.

But why?

Rasputin wagged a finger at him. "Be careful up there. You may be an angel, but you haven't got your wings yet. I'll have to see about getting you a pair before we leave."

Harsh laughter echoed across the deck.

What did he mean by that?

Tommy suddenly sensed he was in much more danger than a moment ago. He prayed for someone to rescue him, picturing the face of Father Korza.

But was that priest good or bad?

22

Lost in blood and fire, Rhun pulled his lips from Elisabeta's mouth and brought them to her throat. His tongue slid along veins that had once throbbed with her heartbeats.

She groaned under him. "Yes, yes, my love . . ."

His fangs grew, ready to pierce her tender flesh and drink what she offered.

Her alabaster throat beckoned.

At last, he would be joined with her. Her blood would flow in his veins, as his had flowed through hers. He dropped his eager lips to her welcoming throat.

He opened his mouth, baring hard teeth to soft flesh.

Before he could bite down, hands suddenly grabbed him. He was yanked off Elisabeta and slammed against the stone wall. He snarled and fought, but his captor hung on like a wolf to an elk.

He heard two *clicks*.

Then another pair of hands joined the first.

As crimson fire slowly dimmed from his vision, he saw Elisabeta handcuffed to the bed, fighting to get free. The burn of silver blistered her delicate wrists, marring what he had just healed, just kissed.

Nadia and Christian held him pinioned to the wall. At full strength, he might have been able to break free, but he was still weak. Their words penetrated his fog, revealing themselves to be prayers, reminding him who he was.

Spent, he sagged in their grasps.

"Rhun." Nadia's grip did not loosen. "Pray with us."

Obeying the command in her voice, he moved his lips, forced out words. His bloodlust slowly waned, but comfort did not return in its place, only emptiness, leaving him weary, consumed.

The two Sanguinists bore him from the cell, and Nadia locked the door.

Carried a few cells down, Christian laid him atop a bed there.

Am I a prisoner now, too?

"Heal thyself." Nadia pressed a flask of wine into his palm.

She and Christian closed and locked the cell door.

He lay on his back on the musty pallet. The mildewed scent of old straw and stone dust filled the room. He longed to return to Elisabeta's cell, to lose himself in the scent of blood. With both hands, he gripped his pectoral cross and let the silver sear his palms, but it failed to center his mind.

He knew what he must do.

He reached to the flask, opened it, and drained its entire contents in one long swallow. The fire of Christ's blood would leave no room for doubt. The holiness blazed down his throat and exploded inside him, hollowing him out, burning away even the emptiness from a moment ago.

Clutching his cross again, he closed his eyes and waited for his penance to wash over him. The price of Christ's blessing was to relive one's worst sins.

But what would the consecrated blood show him now?

What could be strong enough to match the sin in his soul?

With the moon high, Rhun crossed himself and stepped across the tavern's threshold. It was the only gathering place in a small hamlet known for the quality of its honey. As he entered, the stench of mead mingled with the iron smell of spilled blood.

A strigoi had been here. A strigoi had killed here.

A barmaid, thin and riddled with sores, lay sprawled next to the corpulent innkeeper on the filthy floor. No heartbeats echoed from their chests. They were dead and would remain so.

Broken crockery crunched under his boots.

Firelight gleamed on his silver blade.

Bernard had trained Rhun with this weapon, along with many others, readying him for his first mission as a Sanguinist. It had been a year ago to this very day that Rhun had lost his own soul to a strigoi *attack, taken down beside his sister's grave.*

Today he must begin to redeem himself.

Bernard had ordered him to find the beast that had been terrorizing the local village. The rogue strigoi *had arrived only days before but had already killed four souls. Rhun must turn its foul appetites to holy ones, as Bernard had done with him, or slay the beast.*

A creak drew his attention to the corner where a rough-hewn wooden table had been pushed up against the wall. His sharp vision picked out a shape in the darkness beneath it.

The strigoi *he sought crouched there.*

Another sound reached his ears.

Weeping.

In a single bound, Rhun crossed the distance to the table, yanked it away with one hand, and hurled it across the room. With his other hand, he dropped his blade against a dirty white throat.

A child.

A boy of ten or eleven gazed up at him, his eyes wide, his short brown hair trimmed by loving hands. Dirty fingers wrapped around his bare bony knees. Tears stained his cheeks—but blood stained his chin.

Rhun dared show no mercy. Too many Sanguinists had died because they had underestimated their prey. An innocent young face often masked a centuries-old killer. He reminded himself of that, but the child seemed harmless, piteous even.

He spared a quick glance to the dead bodies on the floor, reminding himself not to be fooled. The boy was far from harmless.

He twisted the boy around and clutched him against his chest, gripping him from behind, pinning his arms down. Rhun dragged him to the fireplace. A mirror hung above a crude wooden mantel.

The reflection showed the child to be quiet in his embrace, unresisting.

Unhappy brown eyes met his in the mirror.

"Why am I a monster?" those young lips asked.

Rhun faltered at the unexpected question, but he took strength from what he had been taught by Bernard. "You have sinned."

"But I did not, not of my own will. I was a good boy. A creature

broke through my window in the night. It bit me. It made me feed on its blood, then fled. I did not ask for that to happen. I fought against it. Fought with all my strength."

Rhun remembered his own initial struggles against the stri-goi *who had stolen his soul and how he had succumbed in the end, embracing the bliss that was offered to him.* "There is a way to stop the evil, to serve God again."

"Why would I want to serve a god who let this happen to me?"

The child didn't seem to be angry, merely curious.

"You can turn this curse into a gift," he said. "You can serve Christ. You can live by drinking His holy blood, not the blood of humans."

The child's eyes strayed to the bodies on the floor. "I didn't want to kill them. Truly, I didn't."

Rhun loosened his hold. "I know. And you can stop killing now."

"But"—the child met his gaze in the mirror again—"I liked it."

Something in the boy's eyes sang to the darkness inside him. Rhun knew this first mission was as much a test of him as it was of the boy.

"It is a sin," Rhun stressed.

"Then I will end up in Hell."

"Not if you turn from this path. Not if you dedicate yourself to a life of service to the Church, to Christ."

The child considered this, then spoke. "Can you promise me that I won't go to Hell if I do as you say?"

Rhun hesitated. He wished he could offer a sounder truth to the boy.

"It is your best hope."

Like so much in his life, it was a matter of faith.

A burning log slipped off the fire and rolled against the fireplace stones. Bright sparks flew onto the floor and extinguished there. Rhun sensed that the morning approached swiftly. The child looked toward the window, likely feeling it, too.

"You must decide soon," Rhun said.

"Does the sun burn you?" the child asked, wincing from remembered pain.

"Yes," he said. "But through Christ's blessing I can walk under the noon sun. His blood gives me the strength and holiness for such."

The boy's round eyes looked doubtful. "What if I drink His blood but don't truly believe?"

"Christ will know the falsehood. His blood will burn you to ash."

The child's small body shivered in his arms. "Will you let me go if I say no?"

"I cannot allow you to keep killing the innocent."

The boy tilted his head toward the couple on the floor. "They were less innocent than I ever was. They stole from travelers, they trafficked in whores, and they once slit the throat of a man to steal his purse."

"God will judge them."

"But you will judge me?" the child asked.

Rhun winced.

That was his role, was it not?

Judge and executioner.

His voice faltered. "We have little time. Sunrise is only—"

"I always had little time, and now I have none at all." Tears appeared and ran down his cheeks. "I will not go with you. I will not become a priest. I did nothing wrong to become this monster. So do it now. And do it quickly."

Rhun gazed into those wet but resolute eyes.

It is God's will, he reminded himself.

Still, he hesitated as the burning sun threatened.

What had this child done to deserve to be turned into a beast? He had been innocent, he had fought evil when attacked, and he had lost to it.

Rhun had been no different—except that he had chosen to serve Him.

The smell of cold blood drifted from the bodies on the floor. Such wreckage was what the boy would leave behind him to the end of his days.

"Forgive me," Rhun whispered.

The boy said one word that would haunt him for centuries to come.

In spite of that, he drew the blade across the child's throat, spattering dark blood across the mirror.

Rhun came to himself on the floor of the cell. At some point, he had crawled under the bed and curled into a ball, weeping. He lay there alone, staring at the slats of the bed, only a handsbreadth from his face.

Why was I shown this moment?

He had done as he was instructed, obeying the word of God.

How was that a sin that needed penance?

Was it because I hesitated at the end?

He climbed from under the bed and sat on its edge. He planted his elbows on his knees, dropped his head into his hands, and prayed for solace.

But none came.

Instead, he remembered the boy's clear brown eyes, his high voice, how he had nestled back against Rhun and raised his chin so that the blade would find a true home.

Rhun remembered asking him for forgiveness.

The boy had answered.

No.

Still, in the name of God, he had slaughtered the child.

Since that time many innocent faces had died under his blade. He no longer paused, no longer hesitated. He killed without a pang of regret. His years of service had led him to this place—to where he could slaughter children without remorse.

Covering his face, he wept now.

For himself, and for the boy with brown eyes.

23

Jordan stretched beneath the bedsheets, every part of his naked body in contact with Erin's. She murmured in her sleep, and he pulled her closer against him.

God, how he'd missed her.

A tap on the door woke Erin, clearly startling her. She sat up quickly. Blond hair brushed her shoulders, and the blanket fell down from her bare breasts. In the dim light coming through the shuttered windows, she looked beautiful.

He reached for her, unable to stop himself.

Christian called through the door, sounding very amused with himself. "You two have fifteen minutes! So finish what you started . . . or start what you want to finish. Either way, you've been given fair warning."

"Thanks!" Jordan called back and grinned at Erin. "You know it's a mortal sin to disobey a priest's direct order."

"Somehow I don't think that's true," she said with a relaxed smile—then pointed to the shower, to the promise of hot soapy water and naked skin. "But maybe for the sake of our souls, it's better to be safe than sorry."

He matched her grin, hauled her into his arms, and carried her toward the bathroom.

By the time Christian knocked again, they were both showered, dressed, and strapped with their new weapons. Despite the scrapes and bruises, Jordan hadn't felt so good in a long time.

Once out in the hall, Christian put a finger to his lips and handed each of them a small flashlight.

What is this about? Jordan wondered.

Still, he trusted Christian enough not to question the man's actions. Jordan and Erin followed him to the end of the corridor, down a series of stairs, and through a long tunnel that had no lights.

Jordan clicked on his flashlight, and Erin did the same.

Christian set a grueling pace down the passageway. It looked hewn out of the natural bedrock and stretched at least a mile. Finally Christian reached a steel door at the end and stopped. He entered digits in an electronic keypad and stepped back. The door swung soundlessly inward. It was a good foot thick and could probably withstand a mortar blast.

Bright sunlight flowed into the dark passageway.

Jordan smelled pine and loam.

Must be an emergency exit, one possibly designed to whisk the pope to safety in case of a threat at the castle.

Christian stepped through, then motioned for them to keep close.

Growing worried at all the subterfuge, Jordan shifted his assault rifle into a ready position and kept Erin between him and Christian. He wanted her protected front and back.

They stepped into a dense evergreen forest. It was cold beneath the shadowy bower. As he walked, his breath hung in the quiet air. A carpet of fallen pine needles muffled the sound of his feet.

Erin zipped up her wolf-leather jacket.

Even that small sound was too loud for this quiet forest.

Ahead of them, three figures melted out of the shadows. While Christian relaxed, Jordan kept firm hold of his rifle. Then he saw it was Nadia, leading Rhun and Bathory. Or at least he assumed it was the countess, as the woman was veiled from head to toe against the sun. But the silver handcuff secured to one of her thin wrists left little doubt that it was Bathory. The other cuff was fastened to Rhun.

The Sanguinists were taking no chances with the countess.

Personally, Jordan would rather be handcuffed to a cobra.

Nadia motioned Jordan behind the thick bole of a pine for a private meeting. It was unnerving that no one spoke. He gave Erin's elbow a quick squeeze, leaving her with Christian, then followed Nadia.

Once out of sight. Nadia pulled out a single thick sheet of paper, folded and sealed with red wax, bearing the insignia of a crown with two crossed keys.

The papal seal.

With one long fingernail she broke the seal and unfolded the paper to reveal a hand-drawn map of Italy. A blue line traced north from Castel Gandolfo, ending near Rome. Highway numbers were marked, along with a timetable.

Nadia lifted a lighter and rasped a flame to life, ready to burn the paper, her eyes on him.

Clearly he was supposed to commit this map to memory.

Sighing silently, he memorized the highways and timetables. Once done, he met her eyes.

She mimed a driving motion and pointed to him.

Looks like I'm driving.

She lifted the lighter to the page. Yellow flames licked up the thick paper, consuming everything to ash. The purpose of all this pantomime was plain. Jordan, and Nadia, and whoever wrote the note—probably the cardinal—were the only ones who were supposed to know their destination and route.

They weren't giving the bomber another chance to take them all out.

With the matter settled, Nadia led him back to where the others waited.

Once they were all together, they set off across the forest to a parking lot. Only two vehicles were parked there: a black Mercedes SUV with dark tinted windows and a Ducati motorcycle, also black and with lines that screamed speed.

He looked longingly at the bike, but he knew he would end up with the SUV.

Proving this, Nadia hiked a leg over the motorcycle and raised an eyebrow toward him. He grinned, remembering their wild ride through Bavaria a few months back. He'd never been so scared or exhilarated. Her preternatural reflexes had let her handle the bike at speeds he had not imagined possible.

But that wasn't going to be today.

She tossed him the keys to the SUV before starting up her bike and roaring off.

Jordan's group headed for the SUV. Rhun helped the countess into the back, flanked on her other side by Christian. Jordan held open the front passenger door for Erin. He was not about to let her sit in the back with Rhun and the countess.

Even the front seat was too close to that pair.

3:14 P.M.

As the vehicle fled up a road paved to a smooth black finish, Elizabeth clenched her free hand into a fist. Automobiles terrified her. In Rome, she had avoided their foul smells, their grumbling engines. She had no desire to get near one, and now she sat inside one.

It was very like a carriage from her day, except such carriages were never so fast. Never had a horse traveled across the ground at such a pace. How did the soldier maintain control over it? She knew the vehicle was a mechanical device, like a clock, but she couldn't help thinking of it spilling them from its warm leather cocoon and dashing their brains against the hard road.

She monitored the hearts of the humans in the front, using them to measure the potential danger. Right now, both hearts beat at a slow, relaxed pace. They did not fear this belching, growling beast.

She did her best to mirror their emotions.

If they do not show fear, she could not allow herself to either.

As the minutes passed, her initial terror dulled into simple boredom. The black ribbon of road unspooled before her with an eerie sameness. Trees, villages, and other automobiles passed to either side, unremarkable and unremarked.

Once her fear settled, her thoughts returned to Rhun. She remembered him holding her hand, his lips on her throat. He was not so passionless and dedicated to the Church as he seemed—not now or before. He had come so close again to betraying his vows in the cell.

She knew it was not mere bloodlust.

He wanted *her*.

He still loves me.

Of all the strangeness of this modern world, that struck her as the oddest. She considered this now, knowing she would wait for the right opportunity to exploit it.

To break free.

Perhaps to break them *both* free.

The automobile passed a row of rustic Italian houses. In a few windows, she glimpsed people moving about inside. She envied them the simplicity of their existence—but she also recognized how stifled they were, trapped by the span of one lifetime, living lives of frailty, forever worn down by passing years.

Such fragile and fleeting creatures, these humans were.

After more driving, the automobile entered a vast field of the same hard material as the road and pulled beside a giant metal structure with massive open doors. The soldier turned the key, and the automobile's growling ended.

"What is this place?" she asked.

Rhun answered, "A hangar. A place that houses airplanes."

She nodded. She knew airplanes, having seen their lights in the night sky often over Rome. In her small apartment, she had pored over pictures of them, fascinated by such wonders of this age.

In the shadows of the hangar, she spotted a small white airplane with a blue stripe on its hull.

From a doorway in its side, Nadia appeared at the top of a short set of stairs. Elizabeth's fangs drew a fraction longer, her body remembering the countless small humiliations the tall woman had subjected her to.

Rhun guided Elizabeth out of the automobile, their movements clumsy because of the burning shackles that bound them together. They followed the others into the deep shadows of the building.

Nadia joined them. "I've checked the aircraft thoroughly. It is clean."

Rhun turned to Elizabeth. "It is dark enough inside here. If you like, you can remove your veil for now."

Happy to do so, she reached up with her free hand and pulled the cloth away. Cool air flowed across her face and lips, bringing with it the smell of tar and pitch and other scents that were acrid, bitter, and burnt. This was an era that seemed to run on fire and burning oil.

She kept her face away from the open doors. Even the diffuse sunlight hurt her, but she did her best to conceal her pain.

Instead, she watched the soldier as he stretched his back and stamped blood back into his legs after the drive. He reminded her of a restless stallion, loosed after being stabled for too long. His title— *the Warrior of Man*—fit him well.

He kept close to the woman, Erin Granger. He was clearly besotted with her, and even Rhun seemed more aware of the woman's presence than Elizabeth liked.

Still, Elizabeth had to admit the historian had an athletic grace about her and a fine mind. In another time, another life, they might have been friends.

Nadia headed back toward the airplane. "If we're to make our rendezvous, we must leave now."

The group followed her up the stairs and into the aircraft.

Ducking inside, Elizabeth glanced to the left, to a small room with two tiny chairs, angled windows, and red and black switches and buttons.

"That's called the cockpit," Rhun explained. "The pilot flies the plane from in there."

She saw the youngest of the Sanguinists, the one called Christian, taking a seat inside. It seemed the skills of the Sanguinists had adapted to this new age.

She turned her back and headed into the main space. Rich leather seats lined each side of the small airplane with a narrow aisle down the middle. She paid heed to the small windows, imagining how it would be to view the world from the air, the clouds from above, the stars from the sky.

This was indeed a time of wonders.

Her eyes strayed past the seats and settled on a long black box in back, with handles on the ends. The box was plainly of modern construction, but its shape had not changed since long before her time.

It was a coffin.

She stopped so suddenly that Rhun collided with her.

"Forgive me," he said quietly.

Her eyes had not left the coffin. She sniffed. The box did not contain a corpse, or she would have smelled it.

Why is it here?

Then Nadia smiled—and Elizabeth immediately understood.

She lunged back, bumping hard into Rhun. With her left hand, she pulled Rhun's hooked blade from its wrist sheath. In one quick motion, she swept it at Nadia. But her target danced back, the blade catching her on the chin, drawing blood.

But not nearly enough.

Elizabeth cursed the clumsiness of her left hand.

Behind her, a door slammed. She turned and saw that Christian had stuffed the two humans in the cockpit for safekeeping. She was flattered that he thought her such a threat.

She tightened her grip on the knife and faced Nadia.

The woman had slipped free a length of silver chain, readying it like a whip, and carried a short sword in the other.

"Stop!" Rhun yelled, his voice booming in the small space.

Elizabeth held her ground. She pictured the sarcophagus from which she was birthed into this new world. She remembered the bricked-up cell in her castle tower where she had slowly starved. She could not stand to be confined again, to be trapped.

"The last time you put me in a coffin," she spat at Rhun, "I lost four hundred years."

"It's just for this trip," Rhun promised her. "The plane will be traveling above the clouds. There will be no escaping the sun where we fly."

Still, she panicked at the thought of being shut away again, unable to control herself. She thrashed against the silver that bound her to him. "I'd rather die."

Nadia stepped closer. "If you prefer."

With a quick flick of her short sword, the woman slashed Elizabeth's throat. Silver burned her skin, and blood poured from the wound, trying to purge the holiness from her body. Elizabeth stopped fighting, the blade falling from her fingertips. Rhun was there, clamping his hand over her throat, holding in the blood.

"What have you done?" he hissed at Nadia.

"She'll live," Nadia said. "I cut shallow. It will make it easier to get her into the box without more needless fighting."

Nadia lifted the hinged lid.

Elizabeth moaned, but crippled by silver, she had the strength to do nothing more.

Rhun lifted her and carried her to the coffin.

"I promise that I will fetch you from here," he said. "Within hours."

He lowered her into the coffin gently. A *click* and the manacle left her wrist.

She willed herself to sit up, to fight, but she could not summon the strength.

The lid came down on the box, smothering her again into darkness.

24

With the sun down for the past hour, Leopold haunted the edges of the papal summer residence. The grounds themselves were larger even than the entirety of Vatican City, offering plenty of places to skulk, hide, and watch. At the moment, he was up in one of the giant holm oaks that dotted the property, using its branches and thick trunk to keep hidden in the dark. The tree stood only a stone's throw from the main castle.

Earlier, as the sun went down, he had crawled out of his hay bale. Using the darkness, it was easy to slip through the police barricade around the ruins of the train. His ears easily picked out the heartbeats of the salvage investigators, allowing him to avoid them and leave unseen. From the hay bale, he had heard the cardinal mention that he would be coming to Castel Gandolfo, where he would mourn and pray for the souls who had lost their lives this day.

So Leopold followed after sunset, rushing with the speed only a Sanguinist could muster, to cross the handful of miles to reach the small village with its looming papal castle.

For the past half hour, he had watched the residence from a distance, slowly circling it completely. He dared get no closer lest the Sanguinists inside sense his presence.

But with his keen ears, he heard much from inside, bits and pieces of conversation, the flow of gossip among the staff. He slowly learned what they knew of the tragic events. It seemed only Cardinal Bernard had escaped alive. The police had found the bodies of the train engineers. Leopold remembered hearing a helicopter come and go before the rescuers arrived on scene. The cardinal must have collected his dead. Bernard would not let the bodies of Sanguinists fall into the hands of the Italian police. Leopold even heard a maid mention a body, seen briefly by her, before Bernard whisked it out of sight into the bowels of the castle.

Leopold shifted on his branch and prayed for their murdered souls. He knew the deaths were necessary, to serve a greater purpose, but he mourned Erin and Jordan, and his fellow Sanguinists—Rhun, Nadia, and Christian. Even the irascible Father Ambrose had not deserved such a fate.

Now, he listened to the sounds of a funeral Mass, the cardinal's rich Italian tones unmistakable even from such a distance. Leopold's lips moved in prayer to match, attending that Mass himself from his perch in the tree. All the while, he listened for the voices of Erin and Jordan, in case the staff were wrong. He tried to pick their heartbeats out of the tapestry of the pope's human retainers.

Nothing.

He heard only the cardinal's prayers.

As the funeral Mass finished, he climbed down the tree and retreated out of the grounds and across to the neighboring town. He searched and found a discreet telephone booth beside a gas station. He dialed a number he had memorized.

The connection was answered immediately. "You survived?" the *Damnatus* said, sounding more angry than relieved. "Did anyone else?"

Of course, that would be the *Damnatus*'s main concern. He plainly worried that if Leopold had survived, then others might have, too, like the prophesied trio. Leopold did not expect an apology from him for being caught in that same trap—as much as he might believe he deserved one. Both knew their path was a righteous one. No matter Leopold's feelings, he must work together with the *Damnatus*, even if the man had almost killed him to achieve that goal.

Knowing this, Leopold explained all he had learned. "From what I have been able to determine, only the cardinal survived. A maid spotted a body brought here from the wreckage. There may be more."

"Return to the castle and check that body," the *Damnatus* ordered. "Confirm the others are dead. Bring me proof."

Leopold should have thought of that himself, but to enter the residence would put him at great risk of discovery. Still, he made the *Damnatus* a promise. "It will be done."

Minutes later, Leopold found himself at the secret gate that led into the Sanguinists' subterranean wing of the castle. He prayed that none guarded this door. Once there, he sliced the tender flesh of his palm and dripped a few precious drops of blood into the old stone cup. He whispered the necessary prayers, then slipped through the entrance as it opened.

He paused at the threshold and stretched out his senses: listening for heartbeats, smelling for the presence of others, straining to see into each dark corner.

Once satisfied that he was alone, Leopold worked his way toward the Sanguinist Chapel. Any of the bodies recovered from the explosion would have been brought down there. He remembered listening to the funeral.

Fearing others of his order might still be about, he slipped out his short blade and tightened his hand on it. He had killed many men and *strigoi* in his long life, but he had never killed another Sanguinist. He girded himself against that possibility.

He continued silently down the final tunnel, breathing in the familiar underground smells of damp earth, rat droppings, and a hint of incense from the recent Mass. As he neared the entrance to the chapel, his steps slowed.

Quiet prayers drifted to him, stopping him.

He recognized the lone mourner's voice.

Cardinal Bernard.

Leopold crept to the closed door and peered through its tiny window. Beyond a row of pews, a white altar cloth covered a stone table, lit with beeswax candles at both ends. A golden chalice stood in the middle, brimming with wine.

The flickering firelight reflected off the stained-glass windows built into the stone walls to either side—and off an ebony coffin that rested before the altar.

He noted the simple silver cross affixed to the top.

It was a Sanguinist's coffin.

He knew the body inside must soon be shipped to Rome and entombed in the Sanctuary below St. Peter's, the one place on Earth secure enough to keep their secrets.

But one person was not yet ready to say good-bye.

Bernard knelt in front of the coffin, his white head bowed, murmuring prayers. He seemed somehow smaller, fallen from his high station as cardinal into profound and personal sorrow.

Confronted here by the physical proof of his deeds, grief cut through Leopold. A warrior of the Church lay dead, and it might as well have been by his hand. While such a death in service to the Church brought a Sanguinist his final peace, Leopold found no comfort from that thought.

Bernard's scarlet vestments wrinkled as he leaned forward and placed a hand on the side of the coffin. "Farewell, my son."

Leopold pictured his fellow Sanguinists aboard the train. From the cardinal's final words of good-bye, it must be either Rhun or Christian in that coffin.

Bernard stood and left the chapel, his shoulders bowed with grief.

Leopold retreated to a side room, stacked full of wine casks. He waited until the sound of the cardinal's footfalls had long since faded before returning to the empty chapel and entering.

He moved toward the coffin, his legs leaden with grief and guilt. He knew that the *Damnatus* would want it to be Rhun in that coffin, the prophesied Knight of Christ. The fate of the others could not be certain, but Leopold suspected there must not have been enough of their blasted remains to be carried here.

Reaching the coffin, he ran a palm across the cold smooth surface and whispered a prayer of atonement. Once done, he held his breath, lifted the lid, and looked inside, bracing himself.

It was empty.

Shocked, Leopold searched the chapel, looking for a trap, but found none.

Returning his attention to the coffin, he saw it was not entirely empty.

A single rosary lay curled with great care on the bottom, the beads well worn, the small silver cross dull from the decades of a thumb rubbing it in prayer. He pictured Bernard recovering this rosary from the cold mud of the winter fields, all that was left of the Sanguinist who had once carried it.

Leopold did not have to touch it to know to whom it belonged.

It was as familiar as his own palm.

It was his rosary, lost when he fell from the train.

He closed his eyes.

Look how far I have fallen, my Lord . . .

He remembered Bernard so bowed by sorrow, so stricken by grief.

Over me . . . a traitor.

He closed the lid and stumbled out of the chapel, out of the castle.

Only then did he weep.

PART III

He casts forth his ice like morsels;
Who can stand before his cold?

—Psalms 147:17

25

The world had become encrusted in ice.

Huddled against the implacable cold of the Swedish winter night, Erin shivered in her jacket as she strode down a street in central Stockholm. Her coat's armored leather might protect her from bites and slashes, but it did little against the frigid wind that cut through every opening afforded it. Every breath felt like she was inhaling frost. Even underfoot, the chill of the ice-glazed cobblestones seemed to seep through the soles of her boots.

She had only learned of their destination once the chartered jet was airborne, sweeping north from Rome. The flight to Sweden took about three hours, landing them in this land of snow and ice. They were now headed to a rendezvous in the city with Grigori Rasputin, to negotiate for the release of Tommy Bolar, possibly the First Angel of prophecy.

She was surprised Rasputin had agreed to meet in Stockholm, not St. Petersburg. Bernard must have pushed hard, drawing the Russian monk as far as possible from his home territory, into something that passed as neutral ground.

Still, to Erin, it didn't feel far enough.

Christian led the way. In this continuing pageant of subterfuge, the youngest Sanguinist was the only one who had been informed of the meeting place in the city, drawing the group quickly across central Stockholm. Austere buildings lined the way. The simple

Scandinavian facades were a relief after the ornamented Italianate structures of Rome. Warm light spilled into the night from most windows, reflecting off new snow that had drifted up on both sides of the street.

Erin's breath formed white clouds in the air, as did Jordan's.

If the Sanguinists breathed, there was no sign.

She noted Jordan suddenly sniffing at the air, like a dog on a scent. Then she smelled it, too: gingerbread and honey, roasted chestnuts, and the burnt smell of sugar-glazed almonds.

At the end of the street, a large square beckoned, aglow with lights. It was a Christmas market.

Christian led the way toward that haven of warmth and cheer. She and Jordan kept to his heels, trailed by Rhun and Bathory, the two again discreetly handcuffed together.

Nadia trailed behind, her attention focused on the straight back of the countess.

With every step and glance, Rhun radiated cold fury. For the entire flight, he had sat seething over Nadia's attack on Bathory. Erin could understand the logic and necessity of the woman's confinement. No one trusted the countess, fearful that she might say something to a border agent, or attack someone, or even go on a rampage aboard the jet, which from the sounds of the battle prior to taking off from Rome proved not an unjust concern.

Like Rhun, Erin still balked at the act of slicing the woman's throat.

Bathory had been nearly killed for their convenience. Erin had donated her own blood to restore the countess to health after the plane had landed, but she knew that did not undo the damage. She saw it in the countess's eyes. Nadia had cut through more than just the woman's throat, but also any trust the woman had for them.

To Erin, it was also a harsh reminder of the lengths to which the Sanguinists were willing to go to achieve their goals. She knew securing the First Angel was important to stop a holy war, but she wasn't so sure that the ends justified the means. Especially in this case. There could have been a less brutal way to secure Bathory, another means to earning her grudging cooperation, but the Sanguinists didn't seem to look for it.

Still, this deed could not be undone.

They had to move forward.

Stepping into the warmth and merriment of the Christmas market, her icy mood thawed, along with some of the cold as she passed by open braziers that glowed with roasting chestnuts and almonds.

Farther to the left, a giant pine lit with golden balls stretched snow-dusted green branches toward the night sky. Out of the darkness overhead, feathery snowflakes danced to the ground. To the right, a round jolly Santa waved from inside a booth selling Christmas candies, one hand stroking his long white beard.

Jordan seemed to note little of it. His eyes plainly appraised the square, checking the tall buildings and the crowds bustling along in their warm winter clothes. He eyeballed each shop front as if a sniper could be hiding behind it.

She knew he was right to be on guard. Reminded that Rasputin lurked somewhere nearby, the simple magic of the Christmas market quickly evaporated. Per the Russian monk's demands, their party had left their weapons inside the jet. But could they trust Rasputin to do the same? Oddly, he was known to be a man of his word—though he could twist those words in the most unexpected ways, so great care had to be taken with each syllable he uttered.

Passing alongside a stand selling wooden toys, Erin bumped against a girl wearing a blue knit cap with a white pom-pom. In her small hands, the child had been examining a marionette of an elf riding a deer. The puppet fell into the snow, tangling its strings. The proprietor of the shop did not look happy.

To avoid a scene, Erin handed him a ten-euro note, offering to pay. The transaction was made swiftly in the cold. The child offered a shy smile, grabbed her prize, and ran off.

While this was done, Jordan stood by a booth selling steaming sausages. Other links were looped over dowels near the ceiling. If there was any doubt as to what the sausages were made of, it was dispelled by the stuffed reindeer head hanging behind the apple-cheeked proprietor.

Erin joined the others, ready to apologize for the delay.

But Christian had stopped and searched around. "This is as far as I know where to go," he said. "I was told to get us from the airport to this Christmas market."

They all turned to study the spread of the festival.

The countess touched the healed wound on her neck. "A life-or-death mission, and yet you all know so little?"

Erin agreed with her, sick of so many secrets. She felt the weight of the amber stone in her pocket. She had transferred Amy's keepsake from her old clothes to the new, carrying this burden with her, reminded that secrets could kill.

She eyed everything in the square warily. A woman pushed a baby carriage, the front covered by a plaid blanket. Next to her, a four-year-old with sticky cheeks held a lollipop in his fuzzy mitten. Beyond them, a gaggle of young girls giggled next to a stand that sold gingerbread hearts, while two boys puzzled over the inscriptions written on the hearts with white frosting.

A chorus of voices rose in song, echoing across the market, coming from a children's choir singing "Silent Night" in Swedish. The melancholy notes of that Christmas favorite echoed her mood.

She craned her neck, searching for any sign of Rasputin. He could be anywhere or nowhere. She would not put it past that mad monk to not show up, to leave them hanging here in the cold.

Jordan rubbed his arms, plainly not liking them all standing out here in the open, or maybe he was merely cold. "We should make a circuit of the market," he suggested. "If Rasputin wants to find us, he will. This is clearly his game, and we'll have to wait for him to make the first move."

Christian nodded and headed out again.

Jordan slipped his gloved hand into hers. While he seemed to walk casually after the young Sanguinist, she felt the tension in his grip, knew from the set of his shoulders that he was anything but relaxed.

Together, they passed other stands selling pottery, knitted goods, and candy beyond counting. Bright colors and glowing yellow lights shone all around, but it became clear that the market was beginning to close down. More people headed out into the surrounding streets than were coming in.

There continued to be no sign of Rasputin or any of his *strigoi* followers.

Stopping by a stand that sold sweaters knitted from local wool, Erin considered buying one if they had to wait much longer. Behind her, the children's choir started again, their strong innocent voices filling the air.

She glanced to the stage at the end of the market alley.

She listened as a rendition of "Little Drummer Boy" began. Again it was in Swedish, but the melody was unmistakable, telling the story of a poor child offering up the only gift he could to the Christ child: a drum solo.

She smiled, remembering how enraptured she was as a girl, allowed to watch an animated version of this story, a rare treat in the hard religious compound where she had been raised.

Her eyes were drawn to the singers, noting they were all boys, like the subject of the Christmas carol. Then she suddenly stiffened, staring at all those innocent faces.

"That's where Rasputin will be," she said.

She knew the monk's penchant for children. His interest was not sexual, though it was still predatory in its own way. She pictured all those children of Leningrad whom the monk had found starving or near death during the siege of World War II. He had turned them into *strigoi* to keep them from dying.

Rasputin had once been a Sanguinist, but he had been excommunicated and banished for such crimes. In turn, he had set up a perverted version of their order in St. Petersburg, becoming its de facto pope, mixing human blood and consecrated wine to sustain his flock, mostly children.

"He'll be with those boys," she pressed. "Near that choir."

Bathory arched a skeptical eyebrow, but Rhun nodded. He knew Rasputin better than any of them. Rhun's gaze met hers, acknowledging her insight into the monk's psyche.

Jordan gripped her hand again. "Let's go watch the show."

8:38 P.M.

Jordan kept tightly to Erin's side as the group threaded through the thinning crowds toward the stage. His stomach ached at the smell of roasting chestnuts and mulled wine. It had been too long since he and Erin had any food. The Sanguinists often forgot that their human companions had to occasionally eat.

Once this was over, he planned on finding the largest and hottest bowl of soup in Stockholm. Or maybe *two*. One to eat and one to stick his numb feet into.

He glanced around at the civilians strolling the marketplace, carrying steaming cups, tied-up packages, or oily bags of chestnuts. What would happen to them if Rasputin attacked with his *strigoi* flock? He tried to imagine the collateral damage. It would not be good.

In fact, this entire setup stank. They had no weapons. And unreliable allies. He stared over at the countess, who strode with her hood tossed back, oblivious to the cold, her back pulled straight by her haughty, superior attitude.

If push came to shove, he didn't know which side she would pick. Then he corrected himself. He did know.

She would pick her own side.

During the flight here, he'd had a quick conversation with Christian, holing up with the guy in the jet's cockpit. Jordan had exacted a promise from Christian: that if things went to hell here, Christian would whisk Erin away as quickly as possible. Jordan wasn't risking her life any more than he had to. He would not lose her.

He glanced over at Erin's intent face. She would be mad if she knew of these plans. But he would rather have her angry at him—than gone.

Nearing the stage, Jordan passed a sign shaped like an outstretched arm. Its wooden finger pointed to a section of the market behind the choir.

Words on the sign were written in both Swedish and English, indicating the presence of an ice maze. It seemed the Swedes were definitely capitalizing on the cold.

Jordan passed the sign and approached the choir stage. Two rows of young boys wore white robes, their hands tucked into their sleeves, their noses red with cold. As they sang, he examined their earnest young faces, pale with winter. His eyes stopped on the last boy in the front row, a songbook grasped in his young hands, half obscuring his face.

This kid stuck out from the others. He looked to be thirteen or fourteen, a year or two older than the others. But that wasn't what struck Jordan as odd.

Jordan touched Christian's arm.

"The one on the end," he whispered. "That kid isn't wearing gloves."

The boy sang with the others, harmonizing well, clearly experienced with singing in a choir—just maybe not *this* one. His nearest neighbor leaned away from him, as if he didn't know him.

Jordan pictured Rasputin's stronghold in St. Petersburg—the Church of the Savior on Spilled Blood—where he conducted his own dark masses, had his own choir.

Jordan studied the singer's half-hidden features. Dark brown hair framed a face as white as his immaculate robe. There was no rosiness to those cheeks at all.

The young boy noticed his attention and finally lowered his choir book. That was when Jordan recognized him. He was the boy from the video: Alexei Romanov.

Jordan suppressed an urge to grab Erin and haul ass out of there. He examined the other kids in the choir with a keener eye. They seemed cold, tired, and human. Nobody in the neighboring crowd stood out either.

He would see how this played out before reacting.

A small girl approached their group, wearing a blue hat with a white pom-pom. She fiddled with a stringed puppet. It was the child whom Erin had bought a gift for earlier. Jordan noted the girl also wasn't wearing any gloves or mittens.

Christian followed his gaze to her bare fingers. He seemed to listen for a moment with his head slightly cocked, then nodded.

No heartbeat.

So she was another of Rasputin's *strigoi* kids, her innocent face hiding a creature twice as old as Jordan and twice as deadly.

Nadia and Rhun grew stiffer to either side, ready for a fight. The countess simply held one graceful hand to a scarf that covered her damaged throat; her other remained handcuffed to Rhun. She sized up the square in a leisurely way, as if looking for advantages instead of enemies.

As the singing ended, the choirmaster gave a speech in Swedish, wrapping things up, signaling the end of the festival for this night. More of the crowd dispersed toward the streets. A young mother picked up a white-robed boy from the stage, bundled him up in a

winter coat, and gave him a thermos full of a steaming beverage.
Lucky kid.

Other parents claimed other children until only Rasputin's boy remained. With a slight bow toward them, he jumped off the platform and strode toward them with all the pride of Russian nobility.

Christian confronted the boy as he reached them. "Where is your master?"

The kid smiled, drawing a chill down Jordan's spine. "I have two messages, but first you must answer a question. His Holiness has been watching you since you arrived. He says that you have come with *two* Women of Learning. The one he met in Russia and another from the true line of Bathory."

It unnerved Jordan to learn how much Rasputin already knew about them.

But maybe that was the monk's goal.

"And why does this concern him?" Rhun asked.

Alexei put his hands on his hips. "He said that there must be a *test*."

Jordan didn't like the sound of that.

"By his sworn word to your cardinal, His Holiness will only give the First Angel to the true Woman of Learning. Such is the bargain struck."

Rhun looked ready to argue, but Erin stopped him.

"What kind of test?" she asked.

"Nothing too dangerous," Alexei answered. "I will take two of you with *one* Woman of Learning, and Olga"—he motioned to the young girl with the blue hat—"will take two with the *other*."

"What happens then?" Jordan asked.

"The first woman to find the First Angel wins."

The countess shifted closer, sensing the game afoot, perhaps seeking a way to betray them. "What happens to the one who loses?"

Alexei shrugged. "I do not know."

"I'm not putting Erin at risk," Jordan said. "Find another way."

The girl, Olga, spoke. Her voice was childishly sibilant, but her words were much too sophisticated and formal for someone of her apparent young age. "His Holiness has informed us to remind you that he possesses the First Angel. If you do not accede to his demands, you will never see him."

Jordan frowned. Rasputin had them by the shorthairs and knew it.

"Where do we go?" Jordan asked, taking firm hold of Erin, refusing to be separated, irrevocably choosing which team he was going to play on. "Where do we begin this hunt?"

Alexei simply pointed to the sign Jordan had passed earlier.

The one shaped like an outstretched arm.

They were going into the ice maze.

26

Erin followed Olga's bobbing white pom-pom around the side of the choir stage and toward a narrow alleyway. The festival's ice maze had been constructed in a neighboring square, hidden for now by the apartment buildings to either side.

Of course, Rasputin would pick such a maze for his *test*—a place both cold and confusing. And at this late hour with the market now closed, the Russian monk would merely need to post guards at the various entrances to the maze to ensure privacy inside. But what waited for them at the heart of this labyrinth? She pictured the giant *blasphemare* bear that Rasputin had kept caged below his church in St. Petersburg. What monsters waited for them inside here?

As she headed toward the entrance to the alley, Erin was flanked by Christian and Jordan. A glance to the left showed Alexei leading Rhun, Bathory, and Nadia. They appeared on the far side of the choir stage and headed for a different street. Likely it led to another entrance to the hidden ice maze, another starting point.

Rhun glanced toward her as he reached the mouth of his alley.

She lifted an arm, wishing his group well.

Then the two teams vanished into the narrow streets, ready to face the challenge ahead, to outrace each other for the prize at the center of the maze: the First Angel.

As Erin's group entered the narrow lane, Jordan's gaze traced the straight rooflines to either side. He kept watch on the heavy doors, ready for any sudden attack. From frosted windows, light spilled onto the snowy cobblestones. Blurred shadows moved about in the warm rooms, the occupants oblivious of the danger beyond their stone walls and wooden doors, blind to the monsters that still haunted the night.

For a moment, Erin wished for such simple ignorance.

But lack of knowledge was not the same as safety.

With her hands in her pockets, she felt Amy's keepsake, the chunk of warm amber preserving a fragile feather. Her student had been equally unaware of this secret world—and it had killed her just the same.

After a few more steps, the street ended at another square. Erin stopped abruptly, halted by the sheer beauty of what lay ahead. It seemed this labyrinth was not a simple mimic of a hedge maze. Ahead rose a veritable palace of ice, filling the entire square, rising a hundred feet into the air, composed of spires and turrets all made of ice. Hundreds of sculptures topped its walls, etched with hoarfrost and dusted with snow.

Unaffected by the beauty, Olga led them toward a gothic archway in the nearest wall, one of the many entrances into the maze hidden inside. Drawing closer, Erin admired the skill of the artisans who had carved it, the clever way they had cut ice blocks and mortared them together with frozen water, like stonemasons of old.

Lit by yellow streetlights behind her, the gateway glowed citrine.

Olga halted at the entrance. "I leave you to your journeys. The angel awaits you in the center of the castle."

The girl folded her arms, stepped her legs apart, and stood as still as the statues atop the walls. Even her eyes went blank. A chill ran up Erin's spine, reminded that this little girl was a *strigoi*. The child had probably been killing for half a century or more.

"I'll go first," Christian said, stepping under the archway, his black robe dark against the gold light.

"No." Erin stopped him with a touch on his sleeve. "It's my test. I should go first. When it comes to Rasputin, we'd best follow his rules. As the Woman of Learning, I must be the one to find the safe passage to the heart of the maze."

Jordan and Christian exchanged uneasy glances. She knew that they wanted to protect her. But they couldn't protect her from this.

Erin turned on her flashlight, stepped past Christian, and entered the passageway.

Massive blue-white walls rose on both sides, about twelve feet high, looking two feet thick, open to the dark sky above. The walkway between the blocks was so narrow that she could touch both sides with her outstretched fingertips. Her boots crunched on snow turned dirty gray by countless visitors.

She shone her light around. Every few feet, the builders had inserted clear ice windows to provide distorted glimpses into neighboring passageways. She reached an archway on the left and peered through it, expecting it to be another leg of the maze, but instead she discovered a miniature courtyard garden, where all the flowers and trellises and bushes were made of ice.

Despite the danger, a smile rose on her face.

The Swedes knew how to put on a winter pageant.

Continuing on, she glanced up at the cloudy sky. There were no stars to guide her steps. A light snow now fell, quiet and clean. Reaching an intersection, she set off toward her left, running her gloved fingertips along the left wall, remembering a child's trick. The surest way to traverse all the parts of a maze was to keep a hand on one side and follow it through. She might reach dead ends, but the path would eventually end in the center.

Not the fastest route, but the surest.

With Jordan and Christian trailing, she picked up the pace, her glove gliding over ice windows, snagging on the parts of the walls made of snow. Her flashlight revealed other chambers. She came upon a space holding a sculpted four-poster bed of ice with two pillows, overhung by an ice chandelier that had been wired with real bulbs. It was dark now, but she tried to imagine it lit, its brilliance shining off all the polished ice.

In another room, she found herself staring at a massive ice elephant, its tusks toward the door, serving as a perch for a line of finely carved birds, some settled in sleep, others with wings outstretched ready to take flight.

Despite the wonders found here, trepidation inside Erin grew with every step, her eyes searching for any traps. What game was Rasputin playing here? The test could not be as simple as solving a path through this maze.

She even searched some of the graffiti carved into the ice by tourists, likely teenagers from all the inscribed hearts holding initials. She found nothing menacing, no clue to some deeper intent by the Russian monk.

She rounded another corner, sure that she was close to the center of the maze by now—then she saw it.

One of the ice windows, its surface polished to the clarity of glass, held an object frozen inside it. She lifted her flashlight in disbelief. Hanging in that window, perfectly preserved by the ice, was a dirty ivory-colored quilt, missing a square in the bottom left corner.

Horrified, Erin stopped and stared.

"What is it?" Jordan asked, adding his light.

How could Rasputin know about this? How had he found it?

"Erin?" Jordan pressed. "You look like you just saw a ghost. Are you okay?"

She peeled off her glove and pressed her bare palm against the ice, the heat of her hand melting the surface, remembering the last time she saw this quilt.

Erin's small fingertip traced across the ivory-colored muslin. Interlocking squares of willow-green fabric formed a pattern across its surface. Her mother had called the pattern an Irish chain.

She remembered helping her mother make it.

After the day's work was done, she and her mother would cut and piece squares by candlelight. Her mother's stitching wasn't as fine as it once had been, and toward the end, her mother was often too tired to work on it. So Erin took responsibility for the task, carefully sewing each square into place, her young fingers growing faster with each one.

She had finished it in time for her sister Emma's birth.

Now, only two days old, Emma lay atop that same quilt. Emma had lived her entire life wrapped in it. She was born weak and feverish, but their father forbade that a doctor be called. He decreed that Emma would live or die by God's will alone.

Emma died.

As Erin could only watch, the pink flush faded from Emma's tiny face and hands. Her skin grew paler than the ivory of the quilt underneath her. It was not supposed to happen that way. The wrongness of it struck Erin, told her that she could no longer accept her father's words, her mother's silences.

She would have to speak her heart, and she would have to leave.

Glancing over her shoulder to make sure that no one saw her, Erin pulled scissors from her dress pocket. The metal snicked together as she cut out one square from the corner of the precious quilt. She folded the square and hid it in her pocket, then wrapped her sister in her quilt for the last time, the missing corner tucked deep inside so that no one would ever know what she had done.

Her sister's body was wrapped in the quilt when her father buried her tiny body.

Through the ice, Erin traced the green Irish-chain pattern, darkened with mold and age. Her fingertips slid across ice. She had never expected to see this quilt again.

Aghast, she realized what its presence here meant.

To obtain it, Rasputin must have despoiled her sister's grave.

9:11 P.M.

Elizabeth ran through the maze, dragging Rhun along by the silver manacles. Nadia trailed, ever her dark shadow. Their human opponents could never match her group's preternatural speed. Elizabeth should have no difficulty reaching the center of the maze well ahead of the blond doctor.

Though she cared little about the ambitions of the Sanguinists, she knew she must win this contest. If Cardinal Bernard ever decided that she was *not* the Woman of Learning, her life would be forfeit. Her fingers strayed again to the soft scarf that covered the wound on her throat. It was a shallow cut, a reminder of the depths of the order's trust in her. If Bernard's faith in her faltered, the next cut would be far deeper.

So she set a swift pace, memorizing every turn in the dark. She needed no light as she sped along. But with every step, her newly healed throat ached from the cold. Erin's blood had partially revived her, but it was not enough, not nearly enough. It surprised her that the woman had offered such a boon—and even more so that Erin recognized the grievous nature of the Sanguinists' assault on her.

The woman grew ever more intriguing to her. Elizabeth had even begun to comprehend Rhun's fascination with her. Still, that would not stop Elizabeth from defeating the human in this task.

Elizabeth's boots trod across the snow, her legs hurrying her forward. She ignored the distractions along the way, those rooms that had been sculpted to draw the eye and stir the imagination. Only one chamber had slowed her progress. It was a room that held a life-size carousel of horses made of ice. She remembered seeing such a display in Paris back in the summer of 1605, when such attractions had begun to replace the old jousting tourneys. She remembered the delight on her son Paul's face upon seeing the bright costumes and prancing stallions.

An ache for her lost family, for her children long dead and grandchildren never seen, welled inside her.

Both sorrow and anger drove her onward.

Sweeping along, she peered through the many ice windows, each cunningly fashioned, but none provided clues as to which direction she should go. At a crossroads, she breathed in the smell of cold and snow, trying to judge the wind for a clue to the correct path.

Then from ahead came a faint rustling, hinting at unseen lurkers. No heartbeats accompanied the noises.

Strigoi.

She must be close to the heart of the maze.

Focusing on the sounds, she increased her pace again—then something caught the corner of her eye. Something frozen inside one of the ice windows, like a fly in amber. She stopped to study it, drawing Rhun to a halt, too.

Suspended in the middle of the ice was a rectangular object the size of her two hands put together. A shiny black cloth wrapped it snugly, tied with a dirty scarlet cord. She knew what it held.

It was her journal.

What is it doing here?

It was hard enough to imagine that the book had survived the ravages of centuries. It was even harder to fathom that someone had plucked it from its long-ago hiding place and brought it here.

Why?

The shiny cloth was oilskin. Her fingertips remembered its sticky surface, and her mind's eye saw the first page as clearly as if she had drawn it yesterday.

It was a picture of an alder leaf, along with a diagram of its roots and stems.

Those early pages had contained drawings of herbs, listing their properties, the secrets to their uses, the places where they might be gathered on her estate. She had drawn the plants and flowers herself, written the instructions in her fairest hand by candlelight during the long winter hours. But she had not stopped there, remembering when her studies had turned darker, as dark as the heart Rhun had blackened.

Elizabeth wrote the last entry while the peasant girl died in front of her, blood seeping from a hundred cuts. Elizabeth had thought her stronger than that. She had mistimed the girl's death, the outcome a failure. She felt a stab of impatience, but reminded herself that even such failures brought her knowledge.

Behind her, another girl whimpered from her cage. She would be the next subject, but her fate could wait until tomorrow. As if she sensed this, the caged girl grew quiet, wrapping her arms around her knees and rocking.

Elizabeth scribbled observations by the light of the fire, recording each detail—how quickly the first girl died, how long she could wait before turning such subject into a strigoi, *how long it took for each to die in that state.*

Over and over, with different girls, Elizabeth experimented.

Slowly and carefully, she learned the secrets of who she was, what she was.

Such knowledge would only make her stronger.

Elizabeth lifted her hand to touch the ice. She had not thought to see her journal again. She had hidden it within her castle once her trial had started. It contained more than six hundred names, many more girls than she had been charged with killing. She had secured it deep under her castle, beneath a stone so large that no mortal man could lift it.

But someone had.

Likely the same someone who brought it to this maze, left it for her to find.

Who? And why?

"What are you doing?" Rhun asked, noting her interest.

"That book is mine," she said. "I want it back."

Nadia shoved her forward. "We have no time for such diversions."

Elizabeth stepped back to the ice window, standing her ground. She wanted it back. Her work might yet have value.

"Oh, but we do," she said, scraping the edge of her manacle down the ice, removing the top layer. "I am the Woman of Learning, and I choose how we spend our time. I am the one being tested."

"She is right," Rhun added. "Rasputin would not want us to interfere. She must succeed or fail on her own."

"Then be quick about it," Nadia said.

Rhun added his strength to Elizabeth's. Together, they quickly bored through the clear ice until the book was free. With both hands, Elizabeth plucked the precious book from its cold prison.

As she held it, she noticed shadowy shapes on the far side. Though distorted by the ice, the forms clearly were men or women. Again she heard no heartbeats.

They must be the *strigoi* she had sensed before.

She suddenly realized there was no need to follow this damnable maze any longer. There was a more direct path to victory. Hauling her free arm back, she slammed her elbow into the ice window, shattering through it to the far side.

Shards of ice danced across the dirty snow of the maze's heart.

Rhun and Nadia bowed next to her, peering through the hole.

Elizabeth laughed between them. "We have won."

27

Erin tore her eyes from the frozen quilt. She could not let her personal feelings distract from her goal. She had to leave this piece of her past behind and press on. She guessed its purpose here: Rasputin wanted to throw her off balance, to slow her down.

She would not give him the satisfaction.

"Erin?" Jordan's soft voice breathed in her ear.

"I'm fine." The words sounded strange, plainly a lie. "Let's keep going."

"Are you sure?" His warm hands cupped her shoulders. Jordan knew her well enough to see through her brave words.

"I'm sure."

She sounded more confident that time. She could not let Rasputin see how he had affected her. If he sensed any weakness in her, he would use it to tear a deeper wound. So she buried that pain and kept marching.

We must be near the center by now.

She hurried forward, again running her fingertips along the left wall, moving ever closer to the heart of the maze. In another two turns of the passageway, she entered a spacious round room, the walls made of packed snow, again open to the sky above, the edges of the walls overhead crenellated.

They had reached the central turreted tower of the ice palace.

In the middle of the space rose a life-size ice sculpture of an angel.

It stood atop a plinth, also carved from ice. The craftsmanship was extraordinary. It looked as if the angel had just landed there, using its massive wings to alight on this frozen perch. Moonlight shimmered through its diamond wings, each feather perfectly defined. The body itself was glazed by frost to a pure white, its snow-dusted face turned up toward the heavens.

As beautiful as the sight was, Erin only felt disappointment.

Gathered below the sculpture was Rhun's group, with the countess wearing a smug smile.

I lost.

The judge of this contest stood beside the victor.

Rasputin lifted his arm in greeting toward her. "Welcome, Dr. Granger! About time you joined us!"

The monk looked the same as always, in a simple black robe that draped below his knees. From his neck hung a prominent Orthodox cross, in gold instead of the Sanguinist's silver. His shoulder-length hair looked oily in the dim light, but his light blue eyes stood out, dancing with amusement.

She met his gaze defiantly as she crossed toward them.

He clapped bare white hands, the sound too loud for the quiet space. "Alas, it seems you have come in second, my dear Erin. It was close, I must say."

Bathory gave her a cold triumphant smile, here again proving she was the true Woman of Learning.

Rasputin continued, turning to Jordan. "But what is that clever expression, Sergeant Stone? Close only counts with hand grenades?"

"Or horseshoes," Jordan added. "Which is this?"

Rasputin laughed, deep from his belly.

Rhun scowled. "We did not come here to play games, Grigori. You promised us the First Angel. As Bernard agreed, your home in St. Petersburg—the Church of the Savior on Spilled Blood—will be reconsecrated by the pope himself. His Holiness will also give you a full pardon and rescind your excommunication. If you wish, you may take the vows of a Sanguinist again and—"

"Why would I want that?" Rasputin said, cutting him off. "An eternity of pious suffering."

Bathory tilted her head. "Indeed."

Erin kept back, ignoring Rhun and Rasputin as their argument grew more heated. The masterful sculpture captured her attention. Closer now, she saw the expression of anguish on that white face, as if this winged creature had been cast from the heavens to land atop this plinth, banished to this earthly realm.

It was horrible and beautiful at the same time.

Rhun continued. "You may return to St. Petersburg knowing that your soul has been forgiven by the Church. But you must first deliver us the boy, Grigori."

"But I brought you what I promised," Rasputin said, waving toward the statue. "A beautiful angel."

"We did not ask for this mockery of holiness," Rhun said, taking a threatening step toward Rasputin, stirring the handful of *strigoi* who gathered at the room's edges.

"So are you then saying you don't want my gift?" Rasputin asked. "Are you declining my generous offer and breaking our bargain?"

Something in the monk's eyes went dark, hinting at a danger, a trap.

Oblivious to this, too angered to note it, Rhun began to tell Rasputin where he could shove this frozen angel.

Erin cut him off. "We want it!" she called out before Rhun could say otherwise.

Rasputin turned to her, his face going hard, angry.

Erin moved to the statue, beginning to fathom the level of the monk's cruelty. She took off her gloves and touched the angel's foot. Frost melted under the warm fingertips. She wiped her palm up the statue's leg, wiping away more of the surface to reveal the clear ice underneath.

She brought up her flashlight, shining the beam of her light into the heart of the clear sculpture. She swore and stared daggers at Rasputin.

"What is it?" Jordan asked.

She shifted aside to show him, to show them all.

Through the space she had cleared, a bare human leg shone within the ice.

A boy's leg.

A boy who could not die.

Even if frozen.

With her stomach heaving, she whirled to face Rasputin. "You froze him inside a block of ice and carved a statue out of him."

Rasputin shrugged, as if this were the most natural thing to do. "He is an angel, so of course I gave him *wings*."

9:24 P.M.

Jordan pointed to the statue and grabbed Christian by the arm. "Help me! We need to get that kid free!"

The boy must be in agony.

Frozen to death, but unable to die.

Together, they rammed their shoulders at the statue's midsection. It toppled backward off the plinth and crashed to the snow. A crack shattered down the torso. Erin joined them, dropping to her knees. They worked to clear the ice from the frozen form, each taking a side, pulling and breaking away chunks of ice.

Jordan removed a piece from the boy's chest, taking some of his skin with it.

He prayed the boy slept in this icy slumber, trying not to picture the kid being dropped into cold water, sealed there, drowning as the ice formed around him. He could only imagine the suffering.

Erin worked very gently on his face, exposing his cheeks, his eyelids, cracking ice from his hair. His lips and the tip of his nose had split, leaking blood and freezing again.

Rasputin looked on, his arms crossed. "Of course, this presents a problem," he said. "The countess reached the center of the maze first, but Erin found the angel. So then who is the winner?"

Jordan scowled at him, as if that mattered now. He watched as Erin concentrated on freeing the boy's face, pressing her hands against his cheeks and chin and across his closed eyes. It seemed a futile process. It could take hours to thaw the boy out, even with a fire nearby.

But Erin glanced over to him, her expression amazed. "His skin is frozen, but once warmed, the flesh below seems soft, pliable."

Intrigued, Rasputin stepped closer. "It seems the grace that grants Thomas his immortality resists even the touch of ice."

Still, from the grimace frozen on the boy's face, such grace had clearly not kept him from suffering.

Jordan pulled a small med kit from his pocket. He had taken it from the bathroom at Castel Gandolfo. He snapped it open and took out a syringe. "This is morphine. It'll help with the pain. Do you want me to inject it? If his core is not frozen and his heart beats—even slowly—it might offer him some relief, especially as he wakes up."

Erin nodded. "Do it."

Jordan placed a hand over the boy's bare chest, over his heart. He waited for his palm to warm the skin below. As he waited, he felt a feeble beat.

He glanced up.

"I heard it, too!" Rhun said. "He is stirring."

"Sorry, buddy," Jordan mumbled.

He lifted the syringe high and pounded the needle through the thawed palm print on his chest, aiming for the heart. Once set, he pulled back on the plunger, got a reassuring flush of cold blood into the syringe, indicating a good stick. Satisfied, he pushed the plunger home.

Erin brushed his frosty hair and whispered a litany into his cold ear, warming him with her breath. "I'm so sorry . . . I'm so sorry . . ."

They waited a full minute, but nothing seemed to happen.

After rubbing his thighs, calves, knees, Jordan worked the boy's legs, bending them with great care. Christian did the same with his arms.

Erin suddenly jerked back as his thin chest gave a heave, then another.

Jordan stared over as the boy's eyelids pulled open. Despite the dimness, the boy's pupils remained fixed and tiny, constricted by the morphine. His lips gasped open, and a gargled cry escaped, half weeping, half pain.

Erin cradled him in her lap. Jordan shed his leather jacket and wrapped Thomas's body and limbs as a violent trembling shook through his wan form.

Rhun loomed over Rasputin. "We will take the boy from here. You have won your pardon, but our business here is concluded."

"No," Rasputin said. "I'm afraid, it is not."

More *strigoi* entered from the various archways around the room, joining the handful already there, quickly outnumbering their group. Many carried automatic weapons.

The Sanguinists moved together to face the threat.

"Do you break your word?" Rhun asked.

"I almost got *you* to break it for me by nearly refusing my gift," Rasputin said with a smile. "But it seems Erin saw through my little ruse here. Which only makes your decision harder, Rhun."

"What decision?"

"I told Bernard I would hand the boy over to the Woman of Learning." He waved an arm to encompass both Erin and Bathory. "So which woman is it? You must choose."

"Why?"

"The prophecy allows for only *one* Woman of Learning," said Rasputin. "The false one must die."

Jordan stood up, moving to stand over Erin.

Rasputin smiled at this motion. "Clearly the Warrior of Man will choose his lady love, guided by his heart not his head. But my dear Rhun, you are the Knight of Christ. So you must choose. Who is the *true* Woman of Learning? Which woman shall live? Which shall die?"

"I will not become part of your evil, Grigori," Rhun said. "I will not choose."

"That is also a *choice*," Rasputin said. "Rather the more interesting one."

The monk clapped his hands once.

His *strigoi* brought up their guns.

Rasputin faced Rhun. "Pick or I will kill them both."

9:44 P.M.

Rhun glanced between Elisabeta and Erin, recognizing the cruel trap set by Rasputin. The monk was a spider who wove words to snare and torture. He knew now that Rasputin had come here as much to torment Rhun as for Bernard's promised absolution. The Russian would hand over the boy, but not before making Rhun suffer.

How can I choose?

But with the fate of the world in balance, how could he *not*?

He saw how battle lines were drawn in the snow: *strigoi* on one side, Sanguinists on the other. They were outnumbered, caught without weapons. Even if victory could be achieved, both women would likely be killed or the boy whisked away by Rasputin's forces during the fighting.

Into the silence that stretched, a strange intruder arrived in their midst, wafting through the drift of snowflakes, crossing between

214 | *James Rollins and Rebecca Cantrell*

their two small armies. The brilliance of its emerald-green wings caught every mote of light and reflected it back. It was a large moth, so strange to see in this icy landscape. Rhun's sharp ears picked out the faintest whirring coming from it, accompanied by the soft beat of its iridescent wings.

No one moved, captured by its beauty.

It fluttered closer to the Sanguinists, as if picking a side in the battle to come. It landed on Nadia's black coat, on her shoulder, displaying swallowtails at the ends of its wings, the emerald scales dusted with a hint of silver.

Before anyone could react, to speak out at the strangeness, more of its brethren blew into the space, some from the various passageways all around, some drifting down with the snowflakes from above.

Soon, the entire room stirred with these tiny shreds of brilliance, dancing about the air, alighting here and there, wings beating.

The whirring Rhun had noted before grew more evident.

Rhun studied the moth perched on Nadia, noted the metallic hue to its body.

Despite the real wings, these trespassers were not living creatures, but artificial constructs, built by some unknown hand.

But whose?

As if answering this question, a tall man entered the ice tower from the same entrance used by Erin. Rhun heard his heartbeat now, having failed to note it earlier amid all the strangeness. He was human.

The man wore a light green scarf and a gray cashmere coat that reached to his knees. The colors set off his gray hair and his silver-blue eyes.

Rhun noted Bathory stir at the sight of him, stiffening slightly, as if she knew this man. But how could she? He was plainly human, of this time. Had she met this stranger during the months that she roamed free in the streets of Rome? Had she called him here to free her? If so, this stranger could hardly hope to win against Rasputin's *strigoi* and the Sanguinists.

Yet he did not seem the least nervous.

Rasputin also reacted to the man's arrival with an expression more worrisome than Bathory's. The monk fled away, toward the farthest wall, his normal darkly amused expression turned to horror.

Rhun went cold.

Nothing of this world ever unnerved Rasputin.

Knowing this, Rhun turned a wary eye on the stranger. He shifted to stand over Erin and the boy, ready to protect them against this new threat.

The man spoke, in English with a slight British accent, formal and studied. "I have come for the angel," he said with a deadly calm.

The other Sanguinists closed ranks to either side of Rhun.

Jordan pulled Erin to her feet, clearly readying them to run or fight. The boy sat on the snow at their knees, dazed by debilitation and drugs, wrapped in Jordan's leather coat. Rhun knew Erin would not leave the boy.

In turn, the *strigoi* flocked their small forms in front of Rasputin, forming a shield between him and the mysterious man, their guns pointed toward the stranger.

The man remained unperturbed, his eyes on Rasputin. "Grigori, you are sometimes too clever for your own good." The man gestured to the boy. "You found another immortal such as I, *months* ago, and you did not tell me until *hours* ago?"

Rhun struggled to understand.

Another immortal such as I . . .

He stared at the man. How could that be?

The man scowled sadly. "I thought we had an arrangement when it came to such matters, *tovarishch.*"

Rasputin's mouth opened, but no words came out.

Another rarity for the clever-tongued monk.

Christian and Nadia exchanged a quick glance with Rhun, confirming their mutual confusion. None of them knew anything about this man, this supposed immortal.

Bathory simply watched, a small calculating crinkle between her brows. She knew something but remained silent, clearly wanting to see how this would play out before reacting.

The man's eyes found hers, and a welcoming smile softened his cold countenance. "Ah, Countess Elizabeth Bathory de Ecsed," he said formally. "You remain as beautiful as first I set eyes upon you."

"You, too, are unchanged, sir," she said. "Yet I hear your heartbeat and cannot fathom how such a thing could be so, since we met so long ago."

He clasped his hands behind his back, looking relaxed. He

answered her, but his words were for them all. "Like you, I am immortal. Unlike you, I am not *strigoi*. My immortality is a gift given to me by Christ to mark my service to Him."

Behind him, Erin sucked in a quick breath.

Rhun also could not keep the shock from his face.

Why would Jesus grant this man immortality?

Nadia spoke up, asking another question. "What service did you perform?" she pressed. "What did you do that our Lord blessed you with eternity?"

"Blessing?" he scoffed. "You know better than anyone that immortality is no blessing. It is a curse."

Rhun could not argue against that. "Then why were you *cursed*?"

A smile formed on his lips. "That is two questions buried in one. First, you are asking, what did I do to become cursed? Second, why was I given this particular punishment?"

Rhun wanted the answers to both.

As if reading his mind, that smile broadened. "The answer to the first is easy. The second was a question that plagued me for millennia. I had to walk this earth many centuries before the truth of my purpose became evident."

"Then answer the first," Rhun said. "What did you do to become cursed?"

He met Rhun's eye unabashedly. "I betrayed Christ with a kiss in the Garden of Gethsemane. Surely you know your biblical history, priest."

Nadia gasped, while Rhun stumbled back in horror.

It could not be.

Into that stunned silence, Erin stepped forward, as if to face the truth of this man's impossible existence. "And why were you given this punishment, these endless years?"

The Betrayer of Christ stared back at Erin. "By my word, I sent Christ from this world. By my actions, I will bring him back. That is the purpose of my curse. To open the gates of Hell and prepare the world for His return, for the Second Coming of Christ."

To his horror, Rhun understood.

He intends to bring about Armageddon.

28

Erin struggled against the weight of the history that stood before her, to keep it from crushing her into immobility. If this man spoke the truth and was not some deluded soul, here stood Judas Iscariot, the most infamous man in history, the betrayer who sent Christ to the cross.

She listened to his confession, to his goal to end the world.

"And you believe that is your purpose?" she challenged him. "You believe Christ set you on this long path so that you could orchestrate His return?"

In the distance came the wail of police sirens, reminding her of this modern world, of this age, where few believed in saints and demons. Yet before her was a man who claimed to encompass both. If he spoke the truth, his eyes had witnessed Christ's miracle, his ears had heard His parables and lessons, those very lips had kissed Jesus in the Garden of Gethsemane and condemned Christ to death.

The sirens grew louder, closing in on them.

Had their trespass been noted by neighbors? Had an alarm been raised?

Iscariot's eyes turned in that direction—then back to them. "The time for talk is over. I will have this angel and be gone."

Sensing a threat behind his words, both *strigoi* and Sanguinist tensed for battle.

Jordan pulled Erin behind him.

Iscariot simply lifted his index finger, as if summoning a waiter to the table—but instead he summoned the strange flock that heralded his arrival. The flutter of moths in the air settled over their gathered forces.

One landed on Erin's hand as she held up her arm, warding against whatever threat these bits of brilliance posed. Tiny brass legs danced over the wool of her glove until it reached a bare patch of skin exposed at the end of her sleeve. A tiny silver proboscis jabbed her flesh, needling deep.

She dropped her arm and shook her hand against the sting.

The moth dislodged and, with a slow beat of its wings, fluttered off. *What the hell?*

She scrutinized the drop of blood welling from the puncture wound.

Jordan swore, slapping at the back of his neck, crumpling a moth that fell to the snow. She watched as the others were similarly assaulted. She still failed to understand the threat—until she saw Olga stumble away from the cluster of *strigoi* children.

Emerald wings battered at her small cheek. Then she screamed, falling to her knees. The moth flittered up from its perch on her nose and wafted away. A black corruption started at her cheek and quickly ate away her face, exposing bone, blood boiling from cracks. Her small form convulsed. More of Rasputin's flock fell, writhing, dropping to the snow.

Erin glanced to the spot of blood on her wrist, recognizing what was happening.

Poison.

The butterflies carried some form of venom.

She rubbed at her arm, but she remained unaffected.

So did Jordan.

Rasputin fell among his flock, but he was brought low not by poison, but by grief. "Stop!" he wailed.

Erin remembered another creature that had died by a similar corruption. She pictured the grimwolf in the tunnel under the Vatican. She had shot the beast with bullets tainted by the blood of Bathory Darabont. The woman had carried some form of venom in her blood that was poisonous to *strigoi*—even to Sanguinists.

Panicked, she turned to Rhun, to the other Sanguinists.

Nadia was on her knees, cradled by Christian, while Rhun battered against the emerald storm around him, using his leather armor as a shield.

Erin rushed over, drawing Jordan with her. "Help them!" she called out. As humans, they seemed to be immune to this poison. "Keep those moths away!"

Still, she remembered the first moth, its emerald wings coming to perch on Nadia.

"It burns," the woman moaned. Her fingers clutched her blackened throat, squeezing as if to hold back the poison.

But it was useless. The darkness moved up her cheeks, consuming her—though it spread through more slowly than it did with the *strigoi,* it appeared as inevitable.

Christian looked helplessly at Erin. "What can we do?"

The answer came from the far side of the storm. "Nothing," Iscariot called, hearing his plea. "Except watch her die."

Nadia's body arched back, racking into a convulsion.

Something hit Erin from the side. A small boy clutched at her, one of the *strigoi,* half his face gone. Tears wept from his one eye. She dropped and held him, his tiny hand clutching hers, perhaps knowing that she could not save him, but not wanting to be alone. He looked up at her with an anguished sky-blue eye. She held his cold hands tightly until he went quiet, the corruption consuming him entirely.

She stared across the snow.

None of the children moved now; their ravaged bodies draped the snow.

Nadia gave one final gasp—then lay motionless in death.

Christian bent over her, his eyes shining with tears.

Erin released the *strigoi*'s tiny hands—or what was left of them.

Obeying some silent signal, the moths lifted around them, ascending high, but remaining a threat above. She counted the few survivors: Rasputin and the other Sanguinists. She suspected they only lived because their master willed it.

She stood and faced Iscariot. "Why?"

Judas held out his hand and a moth landed gracefully in his palm, silvery-green wings opening and closing. "A lesson for you all." He nodded to Nadia's body. "To prove to the Sanguinists that their blessing will not protect them from my curse, from my blood."

So it was *his* tainted blood inside the moths.

Erin watched as Nadia's form dissolved to ash and bone. The brave woman had saved her life countless times. She did not deserve such an ignominious and pointless death.

And not just her.

Rasputin moaned, on his knees among his fallen children. "Then why this? What lesson are you trying to teach me?"

"No lesson, Grigori. Only punishment. For keeping secrets from me."

Moths swirled lower again, threateningly. One wafted about Rhun's shoulder.

Erin's mind raced, sensing Iscariot was not done with them. Her best hope was knowledge. She remembered the black palm print that had decorated the throat of Bathory Darabont, marking her blood as tainted. Erin sensed that palm belonged to Iscariot. Had he used some alchemy of his own blood to corrupt the woman's, to protect her among the *strigoi* she had commanded? Darabont had served the Belial, a group of *strigoi* and humans working together, manipulated by an unknown puppet master.

Erin again pictured that black palm print and looked at Iscariot. "You are the leader of the Belial."

Her words drew his attention. "It seems your former title as the Woman of Learning was not unjustified, Dr. Granger." He faced the survivors here. "But I am not done here."

Before anyone could move, the moths fell from the skies and covered the Sanguinists, landing atop Rasputin, even Bathory, too many to stop. As they began to struggle anew, Iscariot bellowed an order.

"Stop!" Iscariot threatened. "Fight and you will all die!"

Recognizing the futility, they obeyed, going still. Moths fluttered to perch across shoulders and limbs.

"I have no wish to kill you all, but I will if forced."

Iscariot kept his gaze fixed to Rhun, who remained standing like a suit of armor, a true Knight of Christ.

He pointed a finger at Rhun. "It is now time for the Knight of Christ to join his sister of the cloth. To leave his world in peace and ascend to his place in the heavens."

Rhun's eyes flicked to hers, as if to say good-bye.

"Wait," Erin said. "Please."

Iscariot turned to her.

Erin had only one card to play, remembering Rasputin's dealings with the Belial before. Back in St. Petersburg, the monk had turned over the Blood Gospel and Erin to Bathory Darabont, but only after exacting a promise from her. Erin remembered Rasputin's words, of the debt sworn.

I promised you the book as a gesture of goodwill . . . if, in return, your master grants me the life of my choosing later.

It had been agreed.

Erin turned toward Rasputin. Would the monk be willing to call in that debt now to save Rhun? Would Iscariot honor it? She had no other choice but to make her case.

She faced Iscariot. "Two months ago, Rasputin made a deal with your Belial forces. In exchange for his cooperation, he would be granted a life of his choosing. The pact was made. It was witnessed by all."

Iscariot looked to Rasputin, who knelt among his children's bodies. Tears ran down his cheeks and disappeared in his beard. In spite of his evil, he had loved his children like a true father, and he had watched them die in agony, victims of his own plotting.

"Is that your wish then, Grigori?" Judas asked. "Will you cast this veil of protection over Rhun Korza? Is this who you will claim?"

Rasputin raised his head to meet the man's gaze.

Please, she thought. *Say yes. Save one life tonight.*

The Russian monk stared long at Iscariot, longer at Rhun. At one time, he and Rhun had been friends, working together as fellow Sanguinists.

Eventually Rasputin spoke, his voice faint with grief. "Too many have died this night."

Iscariot sighed, his lips drawing tight with irritation. "I broke my word once . . . and was cursed for it. I swore never to break it again. And will not now. Despite what you think, I am not a craven man." He inclined his head toward Rasputin. "I honor my debt and grant your wish."

Erin let out her held breath, closing her eyes.

Rhun would live.

Iscariot lifted his arm, and two burly men entered the room, one with dark hair and one with light. Both were tall and built like tanks, with thick necks and arms. They crossed toward the boy, ready to collect Iscariot's prize.

Erin moved to stop them, but Jordan gripped her arm.

This was not a battle they could win, and any aggression could end up with their friends falling dead to the moths.

The large pair examined the boy's limp body with rough attention, raising a whimper from his dazed and drugged form. They got him roughly on his feet.

"What do you want with him?" Erin asked.

"That is none of your concern."

"I think we can move him," said one of the men. "He's lost a lot of blood, but he seems strong enough."

"Very good." Iscariot lifted a hand in invitation toward Bathory. "Would you care to come with me?"

Bathory straightened. "I would be honored to make your reacquaintance." She lifted up her arm, displaying her handcuffs. "But it seems I'm bound to another at the moment."

"Release her."

Christian hesitated, but Rhun nodded to him. "Do as he says."

No one wanted to provoke this man any further. Christian dropped, fumbled in Nadia's pocket, and produced a tiny key. The countess held out her hand as if she wore an expensive bracelet. Christian unlocked the handcuffs.

Once free, Bathory stepped to join Iscariot. "Thank you, sir, for the kindness that you show me now, as you have always shown my family."

Iscariot barely noted her, which drew a small pique of irritation upon the countess's lips. Instead, the man drew out a large pistol from his pocket, pointed it forward, and fired.

Erin flinched from the noise of the gunshot—but the weapon had not been aimed at her.

Jordan's grip on her arm slipped away.

He slid to the snow beside her.

Crying out, she fell to her knees beside him. A wet stain spread from the left side of his chest. She ripped his shirt open, revealing a bullet wound. Blood pumped out of his wound, running across the blue lines of his lightning tattoo, sweeping over his chest, pooling under him.

She pressed her hands tight against the hole. Slippery warm blood coated her fingers. He would be fine. He had to be. But her heart knew better.

"Why?" she cried at Iscariot.

"I'm sorry," he said matter-of-factly. "According to the words of the prophecy, you are the only three in the world who hold any hope of thwarting me, of stopping the Armageddon to come. To break that prophecy, *one* of the trio must die. Once accomplished, the other two become irrelevant. So I give you your lives. As I said, I am not a craven man, merely practical."

He shrugged.

Erin covered her face with her hands, but she could not hide the truth so easily. She had killed Jordan with her cleverness. By saving Rhun, she had doomed the man she loved.

Iscariot would not be thwarted.

If the Knight of Christ lived, the Warrior of Man had to die.

Under her palms, Jordan's chest no longer rose and fell. Blood continued to spread, steaming across the cold snow. A snowflake fell onto his open blue eye and melted there.

He did not blink.

"You cannot help him," Christian whispered.

She refused to believe that.

I can help him. I must help him.

As tears streamed down her cheeks, she couldn't breathe. Jordan could not be gone. He was always strong, always came through. He could not die from a simple gunshot. It was wrong, and she would not let it happen.

She stared up at Christian, clutching his pant leg with a bloody hand. "You can bring him back. Make him one of you."

He looked at her in horror.

She didn't care. "Turn him. You owe him that. You owe *me* that."

Christian shook his head. "Even if it were not forbidden, I could do nothing. His heart has already stopped. It is too late."

She gaped at him, trying to make sense of his words.

"I'm sorry, Erin," Rhun said. "But Jordan is truly gone."

A crunching in the snow told her that someone moved toward her, but she did not care who. A hand, skin cracked and bleeding, touched Jordan's chest.

She raised her head to find the boy crouched next to her, barely on his feet. He slipped the coat off his shoulders—Jordan's coat—and returned it to its former owner, gently draping it over the wound.

The boy licked his cracked lips. "Thank you."

Erin knew he was thanking Jordan for far more than the coat.

"Enough," Iscariot said as the sirens crashed louder around them. "Take him."

One of his burly assistants picked the boy up as if he were a sack of potatoes, carrying him in his arms. The boy cried out at the rough handling, fresh blood dripping from his many wounds, melting holes into the snow.

Erin half stood, wanting to go to him. "Please don't hurt him."

She was ignored. Iscariot turned and held out his hand, and Bathory took it, her white hand coming to rest in his, making her choice of whom to follow.

"Stay, Elisabeta," Rhun pleaded. "You do not know this man."

The countess touched the scarf that covered the barely healed incision on her neck. "But, my love, I know *you*."

Covered in moths, Rhun could only watch as they departed.

Erin returned to Jordan's body. She caressed his lifeless cheek, his stubble rough under her fingertips. She touched his upper lip, then leaned forward, kissing him one last time, his lips already cold, more like Rhun's.

She pushed that thought roughly away.

At her shoulder, the two Sanguinists chanted a prayer. She recognized the words, but she stayed mute. Prayers did not comfort her.

Jordan was dead.

None of their words could change that.

29

Leopold stood on the shore of a blue lake in southern Italy, starlight reflecting in the quiet waters. He took in a deep breath, readying himself for what must come. He noted traces of sulfur in the air, the odor too faint for mortal senses to detect, but it was still there, revealing the volcanic nature of Avernus Lake. Thick woods rose along the ancient crater's steep banks. Across the water, a scatter of lights marked distant homesteads and farms, and much farther out the city of Naples glowed at the horizon.

In the past, the lake had once steamed heavily with volcanic gases, so strongly that birds passing overhead would drop from the sky. Even the name *Avernus* meant *without birds*. Ancient Romans came to believe that the entrance to the underworld could be found near this lake.

How true they were . . .

He studied the unruffled blue waters, picturing this peaceful place birthed out of fire, born from lava blasting into the sky, burning the land, killing every creature that crept, crawled, or flew. Now it had become a calm valley, offering a haven for birds, fishes, deer, and rabbits. The surrounding pines and shrubs teemed with new life.

He took that lesson to heart.

Sometimes fire was necessary to cleanse, to offer a lasting peace.

That was Leopold's hope, to bring salvation to the world through the fires of Armageddon.

He stared out at the lake, pausing from his task to thank God for sparing the lives of those on the train. He had called the *Damnatus* after viewing his own coffin at Castel Gandolfo, only to learn that the others had survived, that the *Damnatus* had made a pact with that Russian monk to ambush the others in Stockholm.

Resolved to do what he must, he turned his back on the lake. His leather sandals scuffed red volcanic soil as he followed a path that led toward the Grotta di Cocceio. It was an old Roman tunnel, a kilometer long, built before the birth of Christ, burrowing from the lake to the ruins of ancient Cumae on the far side of the crater wall. Damaged during World War II, the tunnel was closed to the public, serving now as the perfect place to hide secrets.

Leopold reached the entrance, an archway of dark stone sealed with an iron gate.

It took little of his strength to break the lock and slip inside. Once through, he had to crawl and traverse a broken landscape of rock, to reach the main tunnel. With the way now open, he ran through the darkness, not bothering to hide his unearthly speed. No one would see him here.

His footsteps slowed when he reached the far end, where it opened into a complex of ruins outside the crater. He stepped out into the cool breezes off the neighboring sea. Above his head, perched at the rim of the valley, was a temple to Apollo, an ancient complex of broken pillars, stone amphitheaters, and crumbling foundations of structures long gone. That was not his destination. From the tunnel entrance, he turned right, ducking into another tunnel. The passage-way here was cut through yellow stone, carved trapezoidal in shape, narrow at the bottom with walls that slanted outward.

It was the entrance to the grotto of the Cumaean sibyl, the time-less prophetess mentioned by Virgil and whose image was painted on the Sistine Chapel, marking her as one of the five seers who had predicted the birth of Christ.

Leopold had been instructed on precisely what he must do from here. By now, the *Damnatus* should have secured the First Angel. Leopold must do the same with another. A chill swept his cold skin, threatening to drive him back.

How dare I assault such a one?

But he pictured Avernus Lake, where peace and grace were

born out of fire and brimstone. He must not balk when their goal was so close.

The passageway stretched a hundred yards into the depths below the crater. According to Virgil, the path to the sibyl was a hundredfold, hinting at the maze buried beneath these ruins. What was visible to the tourists was but the tiniest fraction of the true lair of the prophetess.

Still, he reached the tunnel's end and lingered at what was considered the sibyl's inner sanctum. Standing at the threshold, he examined the carved archways and empty stone benches. Once it had been grander, filled with frescoes and flowers. Beautiful offerings would have lined the walls. Blossoms would have released their scents to the underground air. Fruit would have ripened and rotted here.

Across the way stood her carved throne, a simple bench of stone.

He pictured the Sibyl of Cumae singing her prophecies from there, imagining the stir of leaves that were said to accompany her predictions, leaves upon which she recorded her visions of the future.

Despite the ancient accounts, Leopold knew the true power did not lie in this room—but far below it. The sibyl had chosen this site because of what lay hidden at the heart of her lair, something she protected from the world at large.

Before he lost his courage, he rushed across the chamber to her throne, to the archway behind it. Drawing up to the far wall, he studied the pattern of stones found there. Following the directions given to him by the *Damnatus,* he pushed in a series of the stones, forming the rough symbol of a bowl, the ancient icon representing this sibyl.

As he pushed in the last stone, he heard a crack, and black lines formed, spilling dust, marking a door. He knew there were other secret ways to the maze below, but the *Damnatus* had been clear that he must approach her from this path. The *Damnatus* knew her from another life, learned of this sanctuary of hers. Over the centuries, he had tracked her steps across the earth, knew she resided here now, likely awaiting them.

Leopold shoved open the door with a grate of stone but remained at the threshold. He dared not enter her domain without permission. He retreated to the front of the throne and knelt before it.

He drew a knife and cut his wrist.

Dark blood welled out, letting the blessing of Christ inside him shine forth.

"Hear my prayer, O Sibyl!" he chanted. "The time has come for your final prophecy to come to fruition."

He waited on his knees for what seemed like hours, but was likely minutes.

Finally to his keen ears came the soft pad of bare feet on stone.

He looked beyond the stone seat to the dark doorway.

A shred of shadow melted out, stepping into view, revealing the lithe perfection of a dark-skinned woman. She wore a simple linen shift. Her only bits of adornment were a gold cuff upon her upper arm and a shard of silver hanging from a gold chain. Not that she needed any such decoration. Her dark beauty captured his every imagination, stirring even sinful ones. How could any man resist her? She was mother, lover, daughter, the very embodiment of womanhood.

But she was not a woman.

He heard no heartbeat as she stepped around and sat atop her throne.

She was something far greater.

He lowered his face from her beauty. "Forgive me, O Great One."

He knew her name—*Arella*—but dared not use it, finding himself unworthy.

"My forgiveness will not ease your burdens," she said softly. "You must put them down of your own accord."

"You know I cannot."

"And he sent *you* in his stead, unable to come himself."

He glanced up, noting the depth of sorrow in her eyes. "I'm sorry, my blessed lady."

She laughed quietly, a simple sound that promised joy and peace. "I am beyond your blessing, priest. But are you beyond mine? You can yet set aside the task he set for you. It is not too late."

"I cannot. From fire will come a lasting peace."

She sighed, as if scolding a child. "From fire comes only ruin. It is only love that brings peace. Did you not learn that from He who blesses the very blood you spill at my doorway?"

"We only seek to bring His love back to this world."

"By destroying it?"

He remained silent, resolute.

The *Damnatus* had tasked him with this mission—and one other.

He felt the weight of the emerald rock in the inner pocket of his robe. It would have to wait. Now, he must complete his first duty, no matter how much it pained him.

He bared his face to the sibyl.

She must have read his unwavering determination. With a look of profound sadness, she simply held out her wrists. "Then let it begin. I will not interfere. Children must make their own mistakes. Even you."

Hating himself, Leopold stood and bound her wrists in soft cords of leather. Unlike him, she had no unnatural strength to resist, to fight him. The scent of lotus blossoms floated off her skin as she pushed gracefully to her feet. He took hold of the cord that ran to her bound hands and walked her, his legs trembling at his impertinence, back to the dark doorway.

As he crossed the threshold first, a pall of sulfur and brimstone from below washed away the gentle wisp of lotus. Swallowing against it, he headed down into darkness, toward a destiny of fire and chaos.

30

He can't be gone . . .

Rhun touched Erin's arm, but she barely felt it. When he spoke, his voice sounded far away. "We must leave this place."

Sirens rang loudly all around.

The emerald butterflies had lifted a moment before, rising away upon some silent signal of their vanished master, leaving only ruin behind. There remained little of the dead, clothing and bits of blackened bone amid piles of corrupted ashes.

Nothing bound them here any longer.

Still, she clung to Jordan, unable to let go. She saw no need to leave. Everything had gone to ashes. The First Angel was gone, the Woman of Learning had abandoned them for the enemy, and the Warrior of Man lay dead at her knees.

Jordan . . .

He was far more than that prophesied title.

A sound of rushing feet drew her eyes to the side. The small shape of Alexei appeared from one of the maze archways. Though he was a monster, she was glad he still lived. He must have been left to guard the outer walls of the ice palace, escaping the slaughter here— but not the pain. He sprinted to Rasputin and fell into his arms, like any scared boy seeking the comfort of his father. Tears streamed down his face as he stared across the tattered remains of the others, his dark family.

Christian stood, holding the body of Nadia wrapped in a cloak, what little there was left of her. "There's a cathedral close by. We can seek refuge there, decide our next course of action."

"Next?" Erin still watched Alexei, reminding herself that there was *another* child at great risk. She would not abandon the boy without a fight. Anger dried her tears. Determination steeled through her grief. "We must rescue the First Angel."

Tommy, she reminded herself, not allowing herself to relegate him to a cold title. He had been given that name by a mother and father who had loved him. That was far more important than any prophesied name.

Rhun spoke, staring down at Jordan. "But with the trio destroyed, there is no—"

She cut him off. "We cannot leave Tommy in that monster's hands."

Rhun and Christian looked down at her, worry on their faces.

Let them worry.

Erin rested her hand on Jordan's shoulder. She would see to it that he was buried in Arlington, like the hero that he was. He had saved many lives, including hers. To honor that, she would save that boy.

Complete the mission.

It was what Jordan would have wanted.

She could do no less.

A snowflake fell on his cold eyelid and melted, the droplet shedding from his eye like a tear. She reached a thumb to wipe it away. As she did so, she noted that the dusting of snow on his cheeks had begun to run and slide from his skin.

"Rhun," she whispered.

She yanked her glove off and put her bare palm on his neck.

His skin was warm.

Her heart slammed against her ribs. She yanked back the grimwolf coat that Tommy had draped so gently across his body.

Blood swamped Jordan's chest, pooled in the well of his sternum. She wiped at it with her bare palm, exposing his tattoo, the stretch of skin over firm muscle. She used both hands now, smearing his chest clean.

She stared up at Rhun, at Christian.

Even Rasputin was drawn by her frantic action.

"There's no wound," she said.

Rhun dropped beside her, his hand over Jordan's ribs, but he refrained from touching the traces of blood found there. Then suddenly Jordan's chest rose under his palm, as if trying to reach the priest's hand. Rhun fell back in shock.

As Erin watched, Jordan's chest rose again.

"Jordan?" Her voice shook.

Christian spoke. "I hear a heartbeat."

How could that be?

Erin placed her palm atop his chest, wanting to feel it beat. Then Jordan's arm rose on the far side and reached for her hand, resting his warm palm over hers.

She looked up to find his eyes open, staring at her, his gaze addled, as if waking from a deep sleep. His lips parted. "Erin . . . ?"

She cupped his face in her palms, wanting to both cry and laugh.

Rhun helped pull Jordan into a sitting position. He felt for the exit wound in Jordan's back. Then simply shook his head when he found nothing.

"A miracle," Rhun breathed.

Jordan looked dazedly to her for an explanation for all the commotion.

Words failed her.

Rasputin spoke. "It must have been the touch of the First Angel. It was the boy's blood."

Erin pictured Tommy placing his bloody hand on Jordan's chest.

Could it be?

Sirens reached the square, blue and white lights flashing beyond the wall. Shouts could be heard in the distance.

Rhun helped Jordan to his feet. "Can you stand?"

Jordan rose with little effort, shivering and pulling on his jacket, staring down at his bloody shirt with a confused expression. "Why shouldn't I be able to stand?"

He clearly had no memory of getting shot.

Rhun pointed for the exit that lay farthest from the sirens and lights. "We must go."

Rasputin nodded, moving forward in that direction. "I know the path out. I have a car not far."

Christian hiked Nadia's body up, ready to run with her.

Seeing her prostrate form in the young Sanguinist's arms, Erin's joy ebbed. Rather than succumbing to grief, she took firm hold of the anger inside her. She glared down at the broken moths in the snow. Determined to better understand her enemy, to turn grief into purpose, she bent and scooped up several of the broken moths, dumping them into the pocket of her grimwolf jacket.

As she bent for a last moth, Erin looked with sorrow at the destruction left in Iscariot's wake. The bodies of the *strigoi* were beyond recognition, a mystery that would haunt Stockholm for some time. Peering that way, she noted something discarded in the snow a yard away, something dark. She crossed to it and discovered a package wrapped in oilcloth. She scooped it up and tucked it into her inner jacket.

As she straightened, fingers gripped her arm, as hard as iron.

Rhun tugged her toward the exit, as shouts of the police grew louder behind her. He herded Jordan along with her. Reaching the archway of ice, he pushed them both into the maze.

"Run!"

10:23 P.M.

Snow crunched under Rhun's feet. He listened to Erin's and Jordan's heartbeats as they ran. Steady and strong, faster because of the exertion.

Jordan's heart sounded like any other. But Rhun knew he had heard it *stop*. He had listened to the silence of his death. He had known that stilled heart would never beat again—but it had.

It was a true miracle.

He pictured the boy's face, the First Angel, imagining such grace, to bring the dead back to life. Did the boy know he held such power? Rhun knew such a miracle must ultimately come from the will of God. Was this resurrection a sign that the trio truly served His will?

But who were the *trio*?

He studied Erin's back, while recalling Elisabeta's departure. She had not even looked back when she walked away. Still, he knew he had earned that desertion.

Finally, the exit loomed. They fled the massive ice palace for the dark tangle of streets beyond. Grigori led them to a blue minivan parked in a deserted alleyway. They piled through the doors from all sides.

Grigori took the wheel and sped out into the dark city.

Christian leaned forward from the backseat. "Take us to the Church of St. Nicholas. We should be safe there for a short time."

"I will drop you off there," Grigori said, dull with the shock of his loss. "I have my own rooms."

In the rearview mirror, Grigori's shadowy blue eyes met Rhun's, apology shining there along with profound grief. Rhun wanted to lash out at the monk, for laying this trap, but his old friend had also saved him a moment ago, using the favor owed him to spare Rhun's life. In the end, there was no worse punishment than what the monk had already suffered inside that maze.

A few turns later, the minivan pulled to a stop in front of Stockholm's cathedral: the Church of St. Nicholas. The structure was simpler than the churches of Rome, built in a brick gothic style. Four streetlamps cast golden light against the yellow sides. Arched windows were set deep in the stone, flanking a large rosette of stained glass in the middle.

Rhun waited while everyone else exited. Once he was alone, he leaned forward and touched Grigori on the shoulder. "I am sorry for all you lost today. I will pray for their souls."

Grigori nodded his thanks, glancing to Alexei. The monk gripped the boy's small hand as if afraid of losing him, too.

"I did not think he would show himself," Grigori whispered. "In person."

Rhun pictured Iscariot's cold countenance.

"I only wished to challenge God," the monk said. "To see His hand in action by casting all into chaos by my own hand. To see if He would make it right."

Rhun squeezed his old friend's shoulder, knowing there would always be a gulf between them. Grigori was too angry at God, too wounded in the past by His servants on Earth. They could never fully make amends between them, but for this night, they would part as best they could.

Grigori watched Jordan walk away. "In the end, maybe I did see the hand of God."

The monk's face turned slightly toward Rhun, his cheeks stained with tears.

With a final squeeze of farewell, Rhun departed and slammed

the door. The van took off down the street, abandoning them to the night.

A step away, Christian held Nadia's covered head against his shoulder as if she slept, one palm cradling the back of her neck.

Rhun, too, had fought many battles at her side. In many ways, she had been the strongest among them, not plagued by doubt. Her dedication to her purpose was fierce and unyielding. Her loss—as both a Sanguinist and a friend—was incalculable.

"We should get off the street," Jordan warned.

Rhun nodded, and Christian headed for the side of the church, passing under the skeletal limbs of winter-bare trees. Rhun tilted his head to look up at the windows of the cathedral. The church inside was ever a beautiful space, with whitewashed ceilings and redbrick archways. Their prayers for Nadia would find a proper home here.

At the rear of the cathedral, facing a featureless wall, Rhun went through the ritual, cutting his palm and opening the secret Sanguinist door. He remembered Nadia doing the same half a day ago, neither of them knowing it would be her last time.

Christian hurried inside and down the dark steps.

Jordan clicked on a flashlight and followed. Erin held the soldier's hand with an easy intimacy. Rhun remembered listening to her heart, gauging the bottomless depth of her grief. Yet, against all expectations, Jordan had been returned to her.

Envy flashed through Rhun. Centuries ago, he had once lost his love, but when she was restored to him, she had been forever changed.

For him, there was no going back.

Rhun entered the secret chapel below. Like the church above, it had a vaulted ceiling, painted a serene blue centuries ago, to remind the Sanguinists of the sky, of God's grace restored to them. To either side, red bricks lined the walls from floor to ceiling. Ahead, the simple altar contained a picture of Lazarus rising from the dead with a resplendent Christ in front of him.

Passing ahead, Rhun smoothed the altar cloth, then Christian placed Nadia's remains gently atop it, keeping her wrapped. They prayed over her. With her death, all unholiness had finally fled her.

In death, she was free.

Erin and Jordan also bowed their heads during these last prayers, their hands clasped. Grief sounded in each breath, each heartbeat, as they mourned her, too.

Once finished, Christian stepped back from the altar. "We must go."

"We're not staying here?" Jordan asked, sounding exhausted.

"We cannot risk it," Christian said. "If we hope to rescue the boy, we should keep moving."

Rhun agreed, reminding them, "Someone within the Church remains a traitor. We dare not stay in any one place too long. Especially here."

"What about Nadia's body?" Erin asked.

"The local priests will understand," Rhun assured her. "They will see to it that she is returned to Rome."

Rhun bowed his head a final time to honor her, then left her cold body alone on the altar and followed the others out.

He must look to the living now.

31

Erin walked down a well-lit street, heading away from the shelter and warmth of the cathedral. Snow fell more thickly now, shrinking the world around her. Flakes soon dusted her hair, her shoulders. A few inches had accumulated underfoot.

A handful of cars flowed along the street at this late hour, tires rumbling over cobblestones, headlights poking holes through falling snow.

She kept a firm grip on Jordan—both to keep from slipping on the icy pavement and to make sure she was not dreaming. As they walked, she watched the warm breath huffing from his lips, turning white in the cold air.

Less than an hour ago, he had been dead—no breath and no heartbeat.

She studied Jordan sidelong.

Her logical mind struggled to understand this miracle, to put it into scientific context, to understand the rules. But for now, she simply held tight to him, grateful that he was warm and alive.

Rhun walked on the other side of her. He looked beaten down, weaker than even the recent loss of blood could explain. She could guess why. Bathory had done a great deal of damage to him—and not only to his body. He still clearly loved her, and the countess seemed intent on using those feelings to hurt him.

Finally, Christian stopped in front of a well-lit storefront.

"Where are we?" Jordan asked.

"An Internet café." Christian opened the door, tinkling a bell attached to the door frame. "It was the closest one I could find this late."

Happy to escape the snow, Erin hurried into the warm building. Inside, it looked more like a convenience store than an Internet café—shelves of food stretched off to her left and a refrigerator case covered one wall. But in the back, two metal folding chairs waited in front of computer monitors and keyboards set on a long card table.

Christian spoke to the bored woman behind the counter. She wore black, with a silver stud in her tongue that glinted as she talked. Christian purchased a cell phone, asking terse questions in Swedish. Once done, he handed her a hundred-euro note and headed for the back of the store.

At the counter, Jordan ordered four sausages from the roller grill, where it looked like they had been turning since the beginning of the millennium. Erin added two Cokes, a couple bags of potato chips, and a handful of chocolate bars to the pile.

She might not get a chance to eat again for a long time.

Jordan carried their dinner on a piled tray to the computer stations. Christian already sat in front of one monitor, his fingers flying, blurring over the keyboards.

Rhun hovered at his shoulder.

"What are you doing?" Jordan asked, wolfing down a sausage.

"Checking the contingency plan I worked out with Cardinal Bernard."

"What contingency plan?" Erin pressed, forgetting the unwrapped chocolate bar for the moment.

"The cardinal wanted our dear countess kept on a short leash," Christian explained. "In case she broke her bonds and tried to escape. I devised a way to keep track of her."

Jordan gripped the young Sanguinist's shoulder with a greasy hand, smiling. "You planted a tracking device on her, didn't you?"

Christian smiled. "Inside her cloak."

Erin matched his grin. If they could track Bathory, there was a good chance they could track the boy.

Rhun glared down at the smaller man. "Why was I never informed of this?"

"You'll have to take it up with Bernard." Christian ducked his head lower, looking chagrined at his subterfuge.

Rhun sighed heavily, shedding his anger. Erin read the understanding that came to his eyes. The cardinal had not trusted that Rhun might not escape with the countess. After Rhun had hidden Bathory for centuries, Bernard could not be blamed for this bit of caution.

"It may take a few minutes to pick up her signal and gain a fix on it," Christian warned. "So make yourselves comfortable."

Erin did exactly that, slipping her arm around Jordan's waist and resting her head against the warmth of his chest, listening to his heartbeat, appreciating each solid *lub-dub*.

After ten minutes of keyboard tapping and mumbled complaints about connection speeds, Christian pounded a fist on the table—not in anger, but satisfaction.

"Got it!" he declared. "I'm picking up her signal at the airport."

Rhun turned with a sweep of his black robe, drawing up Christian, who quickly logged out. The two Sanguinists rushed away, not bothering to hide their preternatural speed from the counter clerk.

Oblivious, the girl had her nose buried in a dog-eared paperback, her iPod earbuds firmly in place.

Jordan hurried after them, grousing. "Sometimes I really wish those guys needed to eat and sleep."

She grabbed his hand again and jogged with him toward the door, waving good-bye to the girl behind the counter. Erin was equally ignored by the disdain of youth.

She suppressed a smile, suddenly missing her students.

11:18 P.M.

Elizabeth settled into a seat by the airplane's window. The space was much like the one she had traveled in earlier to come here: rich leather seats, small bolted tables. Only this time, she was not trapped in a coffin. As she touched the scarf around her neck, anger flared inside her.

She stared out the round window. The lights of the airport glowed, each wreathed in a glittering halo of snow. She clipped the unfamiliar belt into place across her lap. She had never worn such a restraint, but Iscariot and the boy had both fastened theirs, so she assumed that she should as well.

She glanced at the child seated next to her, trying to understand what made him so special. He was the First Angel, another immortal, but he seemed outwardly to be just a normal boy. She even heard his heart beating in fear and pain. After bandaging the worst of his outer wounds, his new captors had given him a set of gray clothes to wear, soft and loose so as not to abrade his raw skin.

Sweats, they had called them.

She turned her attention to the mystery seated across from her.

Judas Iscariot.

He had removed his overcoat and wore a modern cashmere suit, well tailored. On the small table between them rested a glass box, holding his collection of moths, save three that flitted about the cabin. She knew they remained loose as a reminder of the price of any disobedience, as if she had not been paying that price for centuries.

The plane accelerated across the snowy black field. She clasped her hands in her lap, letting her cloak fall over them so that Iscariot could not see her nervousness. She tried not to imagine this metal contraption flinging itself into the air and hurling itself hundreds of miles across land and sea.

Nature never intended such a thing.

Next to her, the boy reclined his seat, clearly indifferent to the airplane and how it functioned. Several spots of crimson stained his gray sweats, weeping from the hundreds of cracks in his thawed skin. The scent of his blood filled the cabin, but oddly it held no temptation for her.

Was the blood of angels different from all others?

He brushed brown hair out of his eyes. He was older than she had first thought, perhaps fourteen. The anguish in his face reminded her of her son, Paul, whenever he was hurt. Sadness welled up in her at the memory, knowing her son was now dead, along with all her children. She wondered what had happened to her son.

Did he have a long life? Was he happy? Did he marry and father children?

She wished that she might know these simple facts. Bitterness rose in her throat. Rhun stole that from her with a single careless act.

She had lost her daughters, her son, everyone whom she had loved.

The boy shifted in his seat with a small groan. Like her, he had also lost everything. Rhun had told her how his parents had died in front of him, poisoned by a horrible gas.

She gently touched his shoulder. "Are you in much pain?"

Incredulous eyes met hers.

Of course he was in pain.

A cut above one brow had clotted and dried. Already he was healing. She touched her throat, still throbbing from the wound Nadia had given her. She was also healing, but it would take more blood.

As if reading her thoughts, Iscariot flicked her a quick glance. "Refreshments will be served in a moment, my dear."

Beyond their cabin, the engines rose in pitch, and the plane took a smooth jump into the sky. She held her breath, as if that would help hold the plane aloft. The craft rose higher. Her stomach fell and settled. The feeling reminded her of jumping her beloved mare across fences.

Finally, their course settled into a smooth glide, like a hawk through the air.

She slowly released her breath.

Iscariot lifted an arm, and the blond bear of a man who had accompanied them from the maze lumbered into the back of the plane.

"Please, Henrik, bring drinks for our guests. Perhaps something warm after all the ice and cold."

The man bowed his head and departed.

Her attention returned to the window, captivated by the lights growing smaller and smaller below. They flew higher than any bird. Exhilaration flared through her.

Henrik returned a few minutes later.

"Hot chocolate," he said, bending to place a steaming mug into the boy's hands.

He then lifted a small bowl toward her. The heady fragrance of warm blood wafted to her. She noted the white tape at the crook of the brute's thick arm, stained with a drop of blood. It seemed there was little that his servants would not do for their master. Her opinion of Iscariot grew.

She accepted the bowl and drained its warm contents in a single draught. Heat and bliss spread outward from her belly, into her arms, her legs, the ends of her fingertips. The lingering ache in her neck faded. She now throbbed with strength and delight.

How could the Sanguinists refuse such pleasure?

Rejuvenated, she turned her attention to her young companion. She remembered the conversation aboard the train. "I understand your name is Thomas Bolar."

"Tommy," he answered softly, offering something more intimate.

She offered the same. "Then you may call me Elizabeth."

His gaze focused a bit more strongly on her. In turn, she studied him. He might be a valuable ally. The Church wanted him, and if he was truly the First Angel, he might have powers that she yet failed to comprehend.

"You should drink," she said, nodding to the mug in his hands. "It will warm you."

Still looking at her, he lifted the cup and sipped gently, wincing a bit from the heat.

"Good," she said and turned to Henrik. "Fetch clean towels, hot water."

The blond man seemed taken aback at her tone. He glanced at his master.

"Bring her what she wants," Iscariot ordered.

She savored this small victory, and moments later, Henrik returned with a basin and a pile of white towels. She soaked the first towel and held it toward Tommy.

"Clean your face and hands. Gently now."

Tommy seemed ready to refuse, but she kept her arm out until, with a tired sigh, he took the towel. After placing his mug down, he wrung the towel's heat in his hands and pressed it to his face. Soon he was rubbing a second towel up his arms, tucking it under his shirt and across his chest. His face softened with the simple pleasure of the damp heat.

His gaze, also softened now, found hers again. "Thank you."

She nodded her head very slightly and turned her attention to the gray-haired man across from her. When she had last seen him, four hundred years ago, he had worn the gray silk tunic of a nobleman. It felt like only months ago, after slumbering away the centuries in Rhun's trap. Back then a ruby ring had adorned one of his fingers, a ring that he had given to Elizabeth's youngest daughter, Anna, marking his oath to protect the Bathory family.

But why?

She asked that now. "Why did you come to me when I was imprisoned in Čachtice Castle?"

He studied her for a long breath before responding. "Your fate interested me."

"Because of the prophecy?"

"Many spoke of your skills at healing, your sharp mind and keen eye. I heard whispers of the Church's interest in you, in your family. So I came to see for myself if the rumors of your wisdom were true."

So he came sniffing at the edges of prophecy, like a dog on a coattail.

"And what did you find?" she asked.

"I found the Church's interest of possible worth. I decided to watch over the women of your lineage."

"My daughters. Anna and Katalin."

He bowed his head. "And many after that."

A yearning ached in her, to fill in the gaps of her past, to know the fate of her family. "What became of them? Of Anna and Katalin?"

"Anna had no children. But your eldest, Katalin, had two daughters and a son."

She turned away, wishing she might have seen them, the seed and blood of the noble house of Bathory. Had they possessed Katalin's simple beauty and easy grace? She would never know, because they were also long dead.

All because of Rhun.

"And what of my son, Paul?"

"He married. His wife bore him three sons and a daughter."

Relief washed through her, knowing now they had all lived, had lives after her. She was afraid to ask how *long* they had lived, how their lives had unfolded. For now, she was content to know that her line had not been broken.

Tommy dropped the towel into the bowl next to his seat and leaned back in his chair, crossing his arms, looking more settled.

"You should finish your drink," she scolded him, motioning to the mug. "It will help to restore your strength."

"What do I care about my strength?" he mumbled. "I'm just a prisoner."

She lifted the mug and held it out to him. "As am I. And prisoners must keep up their strength at all costs."

He took the mug from her hands, his brown eyes curious. Perhaps he had not realized that she was as much a prisoner as he.

Iscariot shifted in his seat. "You are *not* my prisoners. You are my guests."

So said all her captors.

Tommy didn't look any more relieved than she. He swirled the mug, transfixed by the contents. Clearly he had been a much-loved boy once, anyone could see that. Then he had been taken away, been hurt, and grown wary.

Tommy finally looked up, ready to face this other. "Where are you taking us?"

"To your destiny," Iscariot answered, steepling his fingers and staring over their tips toward the boy. "You are fortunate that you came into being at such a pivotal time."

"I don't feel fortunate."

"Sometimes you cannot understand destiny until it is upon you."

Tommy simply sighed loudly and stared out the window. After a long time, Elizabeth noted him eyeing her, studying her hands, her face, trying not to show it.

"What is it?" she finally asked.

He scrunched his face. "How old are you?"

She smiled at his discourteous question, understanding his curiosity, appreciating his boldness. "I was born in 1560."

He sucked in a breath, and his eyebrow rose in surprise.

"But I have slept many of those centuries away. I do not understand this modern world as I should."

"Like the story of Sleeping Beauty," he said.

"I am not familiar with that tale," she said, earning another raised eyebrow. "Tell me it. Then perhaps you can tell me more about this age, how I might learn to live in it."

He nodded, looking happy for the distraction—and maybe she needed the diversion, too. He took a deep breath and began. As she listened attentively to his tale of magic and fairies, his warm hand stole across the armrest and nestled into hers.

She felt his warm fingers clasped to hers. Beyond his powers and unknown destiny, she saw he was also a lonely young boy, bereft of his father, his mother.

As Paul had been after her trial.

Her fingers tightened over his, an unfamiliar feeling rising in her. Protectiveness.

11:32 P.M.

In the backseat of the stolen silver Audi, Jordan clutched the car's grab bar as Rhun raced across Stockholm for the airport. He tried to ignore the red lights that they blew through. Desperate times called for desperate measures, but that didn't mean he wanted to be wrapped around a light pole.

He hoped the owner of the car had good insurance.

Now on the highway, Rhun wove in and out of lanes, as if the freeway lines were mere suggestions. Christian sat up front, oblivious to the danger, studying his new phone, using its cellular connection to keep track of the countess. A moment ago, he had reported that she was already airborne, whisking south from Stockholm over the Baltic Sea.

Rhun refused to allow her any more of a lead. He sped alongside a semitruck, the side of their car racing less than an inch from the truck's running board.

Erin clutched Jordan's arm.

"It's easier if you close your eyes," he said.

"When my death comes, I want to see it."

"I already died once today. I don't recommend it, eyes wide or not."

"Do you remember anything from when you were . . . ?" Her words trailed off.

"When I was dead?" He shrugged. "I remember feeling the kick to the chest and falling. Then everything went dark. The last thing I saw was your eyes. You looked worried, by the way."

"I was. Still am." She took his hand with both of hers. "What do you remember after that?"

"Nothing. No white light, no celestial choir. I vaguely remember having a dream about the day I got struck by lightning. The lines of my tattoo burned." He scratched at his shoulder. "Still sort of itches."

"Marking when you last died," she said, studying his face, as if looking for meaning in this detail.

"Guess Heaven didn't want me then or now. Anyway, next thing I knew I was staring into your eyes again."

"How do you feel now?"

"Like I just woke up on Christmas morning, full of energy and ready to go."

"Seeing you sitting here is like Christmas morning for me."

He squeezed her hand—as Rhun suddenly slammed the brakes, pitching Jordan against his seat belt.

"We're here," Rhun announced.

Jordan saw they were back at the airport, parked next to their jet.

They all quickly exited, hurrying to continue their chase.

Rhun and Christian led Erin toward the plane.

As Jordan followed, he felt guilty lying to Erin a moment ago—or at least not telling her the entire truth.

He rubbed his shoulder. His entire left side burned with a fire that refused to subside, tracing along the fractal lines of his lightning flower. He didn't know the significance of that blaze—only its source.

Something is inside of me.

32

As soon as the jet reached cruising altitude, Rhun unbuckled his seat. He needed to move, to pace out his frustration. Earlier, he could barely contain his anxiety while Christian performed his interminable preflight check, and Jordan examined the plane with a sensor for any hidden explosives. Both were wise precautions, but Rhun chafed against any further delays, sensing Elisabeta flying farther and farther away with every passing minute.

He pictured the smug countenance of the man who had killed Nadia. Elisabeta was now under his thumb, a man who could murder her with a single gesture

Why had he taken her?

Why had she gone with him?

Rhun at least understood the answer to that last question. He glanced back to the empty coffin in the rear of the plane, where Elisabeta had been imprisoned on the flight over.

I failed to protect her.

But who was this man truly?

While driving to the airport, Grigori had sent a text to Rhun's phone. It was a single picture of an old-fashioned anchor.

Beneath it were the words: *This is his symbol. Be wary of it.*

Needing to move, Rhun walked to the cockpit and peered inside the room lit with instruments.

"You can come in," Christian said, waving to the empty copilot's seat.

Rhun stayed in the doorway. He did not like to be close to the controls, afraid that he would inadvertently bump into something and cause havoc.

"I'm still tracking the countess's plane," Christian said. "It continues south, sticking to the prescribed air corridor. Now it's just a matter of following, seeing if we can close their lead. But should we even be attempting this?"

"What do you mean?"

"Do you truly believe the man we are chasing is the Betrayer of Christ?" Christian asked. "Not some deluded madman?"

"Elisabeta recognized him from her time, marking him as immortal. But he also has a heartbeat. So he cannot be a *strigoi*, but something else."

"Like the boy."

Rhun considered that, sensing there must be a connection between the two.

But what?

"Whether he is indeed Judas Iscariot from the Gospels or not," Rhun said, "he was granted immortality while still maintaining his humanity. Such a miracle would seemingly take the hand of God, or possibly an act of Christ as the man claimed."

"If you're right, then he must've been granted this miracle for a purpose."

"To bring about the Apocalypse?"

"Maybe." Christian looked to Rhun, touching his cross. "If you're right, are we interfering in the will of God by trying to stop him, by following him, by trying to rescue this boy?"

A stirring rose behind him. Erin unbuckled and crossed toward them, drawing Jordan with her. They had both changed into clean, dry clothes prior to taking off. The scent of lavender drifted forward with her, pushing Rhun farther into the cockpit, to better keep his distance from her.

She leaned against the door frame. "Do either of you believe it would be God's will to torture an innocent child?"

"Remember," Jordan said to her, "we're talking about *Judas*. Isn't his role always the bad guy?"

"Depends on how you interpret the Gospels," Erin said, turning to him, but her words were for them all. "In the canonical texts of the Bible, Christ knew Judas was going to betray Him but did nothing to stop it. Christ *needed* someone to turn him over to the Romans so that He could die on the cross for man's sins. In fact, in a Gnostic text—the *Gospel of Judas*—it states that Christ *asked* him to betray Him, that He said to Judas, '*As for you, you will surpass them all. For you will sacrifice the human being who bears me.*' So, at best, the character of Judas is murky."

Jordan scowled, clearly not accepting this judgment. "Murky? I saw him mow down Nadia and Rasputin's kids. He shot me in the chest. I'm not buying him as a force for good."

"Maybe," Christian said. "But perhaps God sometimes needs a force of *evil* to act. The betrayal by Judas served a higher purpose. Like Erin said, Christ needed to die to forgive our sins. Maybe this is what is happening now. An evil act that serves a greater goal."

Erin crossed her arms. "So we sit back and let evil happen on the off chance there is a positive outcome. As in, the ends justify the means."

"But what are the *ends*?" Jordan asked, homing in with his usual practicality to the heart of the problem. "We still have no idea what this bastard wants with the boy."

"He remains the prophesied First Angel," Rhun reminded them. "The boy must serve a destiny. Perhaps Judas intends to pervert it in the same way he attempted to break the trio by killing Jordan."

Jordan rubbed his chest, looking discomfited by that thought.

Erin frowned. "But what *is* Tommy? He plainly cannot die. So is he actually an *angel*?"

Rhun gave her a doubtful look. "I heard his heartbeat. It sounded natural and human, not something unearthly. At best, I suspect he carries angelic blood, some blessing cast upon him when he was atop that mountaintop at Masada."

"But why him?" Erin asked. "Why Tommy Bolar?"

Rhun shook his head, unsure. "Back at the mountain, I sought to console him, to ask him what he knew concerning the tragic events that killed so many, yet spared him. He mentioned finding a dove with a broken wing, of attempting to save it, just before the ground split open and the earthquakes began."

"A single merciful act?" Erin mumbled. "Would that be enough to earn such a blessing?"

Christian glanced back as they hit a jolt of turbulence. "The dove is often the symbol for the Holy Spirit. Perhaps that messenger sought someone deserving of such a blessing. A small test placed before him."

Rhun nodded. "He was an ordinary boy when he came to that mountain, but perhaps when he performed this merciful act in the right place at the right time, he was infused with angelic blood."

"I don't care what's in his *blood*," Jordan said. "If you're right, then he's still essentially just a boy."

"He is more than a boy," Rhun said.

"But he's *also* a boy," Erin pressed. "And we should not forget that."

Rhun could not deny her words, but none of it settled the fundamental concern raised by Christian. Rhun faced them all. "So do we risk thwarting the will of God by rescuing Tommy from the hands of Iscariot?"

"Damn straight." Jordan raised his chin, ready to fight for the boy. "My former commander drilled a quote into all of us soldiers. *All that is necessary for the triumph of evil is that good men do nothing.*"

Erin looked as resolute. "Jordan is right. It's about free will. Tommy Bolar *chose* to save that dove and was blessed for that kind act. We must allow the boy to choose his own future, not to have it stripped from him by Iscariot."

Rhun had expected nothing less from the pair and took strength from them. "Christ walked willingly onto the cross," he agreed. "We will give this boy Tommy the same freedom to decide his fate."

11:58 P.M.

As the plane hit a rough patch of turbulence, Christian sent them back to their seats. The bouncing and rocking echoed Erin's own unease, keeping her further unsettled. While buckling into the seat, she knew she should get some sleep, but she also knew any effort toward that goal would be wasted.

Jordan seemed less troubled, yawning with a pop of his jaws, his training as a soldier serving him. It seemed he could sleep under the roughest of circumstances.

As he reclined his seat, squirming his large frame into a better position, Erin stared out the window at the stretch of darkness over the midnight sea. Her mind spun on the mystery that was Tommy Bolar, on the stretch of history surrounding Judas Iscariot. Finally, needing a distraction, she reached into her coat pocket and pulled out the oilcloth-covered object she had recovered from the snow of the ice maze.

Rhun stirred across from her, his gaze sharpening at what was in her hands. "That belongs to the countess. She found it frozen in the wall of the maze. She must have dropped it during the commotion."

Erin pinched her brows, remembering finding her sister's baby quilt similarly encased in ice, planted by the Russian monk to distract and cause pain. The sight of that stained cloth had struck her deeply and personally.

Yet, still I abandoned it.

She rubbed a thumb across the oilcloth. Bathory had clearly dug her prize out. Was that the right choice in the maze? Erin had chosen to follow the dictates of necessity, rather than emotion. Yet Bathory won by crashing through the ice to reveal a shortcut. Had Grigori been testing their hearts?

Is that why I failed?

Even now a pang of regret rang through her. She should have retrieved the quilt, so it could be taken back to California and buried in her sister's grave where it belonged.

She considered the object in her hands, wondering what it held, if it had the same emotional punch for Bathory as the quilt did for her. Needing to know, she struggled to work the knot loose, her fingers slipping each time the plane bounced.

Finally, the cord loosened a fraction. She slowly worked the rest of the knot free and teased back a corner of the cloth. It looked like linen that had been treated with beeswax to make it waterproof.

"Whatever is in here," she mumbled, "must have been important to Bathory."

Rhun held out his hand. "Then perhaps it is private. And we should honor that."

Erin stayed her hand, remembering how disturbed she had been by the thought of Rasputin violating her sister's grave to obtain the quilt.

Am I performing a similar violation now?

Jordan stirred next to her, plainly awake. "Something in there may offer us a clue to that bastard's interest in the countess. It might save her life. It might save ours."

Erin raised her eyebrows at Rhun.

The priest lowered his hand to his lap, conceding the point.

While the plane pitched up and down, Erin unfolded the thick cloth with deliberate movements. She uncovered a book, bound in leather, marred by age spots. She ran a finger gently across a shield embossed on the cover.

It was a heraldic symbol of a dragon wrapped around with three horizontal teeth.

"It is the Bathory family crest," Rhun said. "The teeth allude to a dragon allegedly slain by the warrior Vitus, the founder of the Bathory line."

Even more curious now, she gently parted the cover to reveal paper darkened to a brownish cream. A clear feminine script flowed across the page, written in iron gall ink. There was also a beautifully inscribed drawing of a plant: leaves, stems, even a detailed notation of its root system.

Erin's heart quickened.

It must be her personal journal.

"What's it say?" Jordan asked, sitting straighter and leaning over.

"It's Latin." She puzzled over the first sentence, getting used to the handwriting. "It describes an alder plant, listing various properties of its parts. Including remedies and the manner in which to prepare them."

"In her time, Elisabeta was a devoted mother and a healer." Rhun spoke so softly that she barely made out his words.

"In our time, she's a killer," Jordan added.

Rhun stiffened.

Erin turned to the next page. It contained a skillful drawing of a yarrow plant. The countess had reproduced its composite blooms, its feathery leaves, its taproot rendered with tiny tendrils curling from the sides.

"It looks like she was also a gifted artist," Erin said.

"She was," Rhun agreed, looking more aggrieved, likely reminded of the goodness he had destroyed by turning her.

Erin scanned the text, reading the common medicinal uses for yarrow: as an aid in healing of wounds and to halt bleeding. A notation at the end caught her eye. *It is also known as the Devil's Nettle, due to its help in divination and to ward off evil.*

The last served as a reminder that Bathory had lived in superstitious times. Still, the countess had sought to understand plants, to bring them order, mixing science with the beliefs of her day. A grudging respect for the woman formed in her. The countess had defied superstitions of her time in order to search for ways to heal.

Erin contrasted that with her father's strict admonitions against modern medicine. He had adhered instead to superstition, grasping his beliefs with his hard-calloused hands and inflexible attitude, allowing no compromise.

Such willing blindness had killed her baby sister.

Erin settled into her seat and read, no longer noticing the turbulence as she learned about the ancient uses of plants. But halfway through, the illustrations suddenly changed.

Instead of flower petals and roots, she found herself staring at a detailed rendition of a human heart. It was anatomically perfect, like one of da Vinci's medieval sketches. She drew the book closer. Neat letters underneath the heart listed a woman's name and her age.

Seventeen.

A chill spread through her as she continued to read. The countess had turned this seventeen-year-old girl into a *strigoi*—then killed her and dissected her corpse, trying to uncover why her own heart no longer beat. The countess noted that the *strigoi* heart looked anatomically identical to a human one, but that it no longer needed to contract. Bathory noted her speculations from her experiments in the same sweet script. She hypothesized that the *strigoi* had another method of circulation.

She called it *the will of the blood itself.*

Aghast, Erin read the page again. Bathory's brilliance was undeniable. These pages predated European theories of circulation by at least twenty years. In her isolated castle, far from universities and courts, she had used macabre experiments to understand her new body in ways that few in Europe could have fathomed.

Erin searched the next pages, as Bathory's methods grew more horrific.

The countess had tortured and murdered innocents to satisfy her insatiable curiosity, turning her talents as a healer and scientist to grisly ends. It reminded Erin of what the Nazi medical researchers had done to prisoners in their camps, acts just as callous and dismissive of the suffering.

Erin touched the aged page. As an archaeologist, she was not supposed to judge. She often had to stare evil full in the face and record its deeds. Her job was to pull facts from history, to place them in a larger context, and to bring truths to light, no matter how horrible.

So despite her queasiness, she read on.

Slowly the countess's quest turned from the physical to the spiritual. Erin came upon a passage dated November 7, 1605. It concerned a conversation Elizabeth had had with Rhun, about how the *strigoi* did not have souls.

Bathory wanted to know if it was true. Erin read what she wrote.

I trust him to tell me the truth that he believes, but I do not think that he has ever turned beyond faith to seek to understand the simple mechanics of this state that has been forced upon us.

Seeking evidence of this claim, Bathory experimented and observed. First, she weighed girls before and after their deaths, to see if the soul had weight. It had cost four girls their lives to determine it did not.

On another page was an architecturally precise depiction of a sealed glass casket. Bathory had it crafted to be waterproof. She even filled it with smoke to make sure no gases could escape. Once satisfied, Bathory locked a young girl inside and let her suffocate, trying to capture the dead girl's soul inside her box.

Erin pictured the girl pounding on the glass sides, begging for her life, but the countess had no mercy. She let her die and took her notes.

Afterward, the countess kept the box sealed for twenty-four hours, examining it by candlelight, by sunlight. She found no shred of a soul in the glass box.

The countess did the same with a *strigoi* girl, mortally wounding her before sealing her to her death. Erin wanted to skip past these gruesome experiments, but her eye caught upon a passage at the bottom of the next page. Despite the horror, it intrigued her.

Upon the death of the beast, a small black shadow rose from her body, barely visible in the candlelight. Long into the night, I watched the shadow flit throughout the box, seeking an escape. But at dawn, a ray of sunlight fell upon it, and it shriveled to nothingness and vanished from my sight, never to return.

Shocked, Erin read that passage several times. Was Bathory deluded, seeing something that wasn't there? If not, what did that mean? Did some dark force animate the *strigoi*? Did Rhun know?

Erin read Bathory's conclusion.

I surmise that the human soul is invisible, perhaps too light for my eyes to see, but the souls of beasts such as I are as black as tarnished silver. In its attempt to escape, where did it seek to go? That I must discover.

Erin studied the last page, where Bathory neatly rendered a picture of her experiment. It showed a girl with fangs sprawled dead in a box. Light from a window fell across the foot of the glass coffin, while a black shadow hovered at the other end, as if trying to stay away from the light.

Rhun stared at that page, too, visibly shaken. But which upset him more: the shadow or the murdered girl? He held out his hand for the book.

"Please, may I see it?"

"Did you know about this? What she was doing? What she discovered?"

Rhun would not meet her eye. "She sought to discover what kind of creature she was . . . what manner of beast I had turned her into."

Erin flipped through the remaining pages, finding them all blank. Clearly Bathory must have been caught and imprisoned shortly after this last experiment. She was about to hand the book over to Rhun when she spotted one final drawing, on the last page, looking as if it had been drawn in great haste.

It looked like some form of cup, but what was its meaning?

"May I see it?" Rhun asked again.

She closed the book and handed it to him.

He slowly looked through the pages now himself. She watched his jaw grow tighter and tighter.

Does he blame himself for the countess's actions?

How could he not?

Rhun finally closed the book, his face lost and defeated. "Once she was not evil. She was full of sunlight and goodness."

Erin questioned how much of that was true, wondering if love blinded Rhun to the true nature of the countess. For Bathory to have performed these gruesome experiments, there must have been some shadow behind that sunlight, buried deep, but there.

Jordan scowled. "I don't care what that countess was like in the past. She's evil now. And none of us had better forget that."

He gave Rhun a scathing look, then turned his back toward them, ready to sleep.

Erin knew he was right. Given the chance, Bathory would kill them all—probably slowly, while taking notes.

PART IV

Her house is the way to hell,
going down to the chambers of death.

—Proverbs 7:27

33

With the full face of the moon shining above the midnight sea, Elizabeth stepped to the bow of the strange steel ship and searched across the timeless antiquity of the Mediterranean. She took comfort in its unchanging quality. The lights of the city of Naples vanished swiftly behind her, taking the dark coast with it.

Their plane had alighted back to the ground in the middle of the night, less than an hour ago, landing in a wintry metropolis that bore no resemblance to the city of her past.

She had to stop looking to that past.

It was a new world.

As she stood at the bow, cold wind combed through her hair. She licked salt spray from her lips, amazed at the speed of their craft. The ship hit a tall wave. It shuddered from the impact. Then it kept going, like a horse wading through deep snow.

She smiled at the heaving black waves.

This century had many marvels to offer her. She felt a fool for having confined herself to the streets of old Rome for so long. She should have thrown herself into this new world, not tried to cower in the old.

Inspired, she pulled the Sanguinist's cloak from her shoulders. It had protected her from the sunlight, but the old design and heavy wool did not belong in this world. She lifted her cloak to the wind. Black cloth flapped in the air like a monstrous bird.

She let it go, freeing herself of her past.

The cloak circled in a current of wind, then swept out and landed in the water. It rested there for a breath, a soot-black circle atop moonlit waves, before the sea dragged it down.

Now she carried *nothing* from the Sanguinists, *nothing* from the old world.

She faced forward again, running a palm along the steel rail of the vessel. She stared along the sides of the hull, at the fins upon which the craft flew over the water.

"It's called a hydrofoil," Tommy said, coming up behind her.

So caught up in the wind and wonder, she had failed to hear his heartbeat approach. "It's like a heron, skimming over the water."

She glanced back at him, laughing with the delight of it all.

"For a prisoner, you look much too happy," Tommy noted.

She reached and tousled his hair. "Compared to my old prison, this one is wonderful."

He looked little swayed.

"We must savor every moment given us," she stressed. "We know not where this journey ends, so we must wring each scrap of joy out of it while it lasts."

He stepped closer to her, and she found her arm slipping around him. Together, they shared the dark waves rising and falling in front of their ship, the cold wind tearing back their hair.

After a short time, she felt him shiver in her arms, heard his teeth chatter, remembering he did not have her impervious nature.

"We must warm you," she said. "You will catch your death of cold."

"No, I won't," he said, lifting an amused eye toward her. "Believe me."

He finally grinned.

She matched it. "Still, we should get you inside, out of this wind, where you'll be more comfortable."

She led him across the deck, through a hatch, and down into the main cabin. It smelled of men and coffee and engine oil. Iscariot sat on a bench next to a table, sipping from a thick white cup. His hulking servant hovered near a small kitchen.

"Fetch the boy hot tea," she called over to Henrik.

"I don't like tea," Tommy said.

"Then just hold the cup," she said. "That will warm you as well."

Henrik obeyed her order, arriving with a steaming mug. Tommy took it in both hands and stepped over to one of the windows, eyeing Iscariot with plain suspicion.

The man seemed oblivious, motioning with an arm, inviting Elizabeth to join his table. She accepted his offer and slid to the seat.

"What is our destination?" she asked.

"One of my many homes," he said. "Far from prying eyes."

She gazed out the window at the moonlit sea. Ahead lay nothing but darkness. This home must be far from anything. "Why do we travel there?"

"The boy must recover from his ordeal in the ice." Judas looked to where Tommy stood. "He lost much blood."

"Is his blood then of value to you?" A pang of worry for the boy shot through her.

"It is certainly of value to *him*."

She noted that he had not answered her question, but she let it go for a more pressing concern. "Will the Sanguinists find us there?"

Iscariot ran his hand through his silver hair. "I doubt that they can."

"Then what, pray tell, do you wish of me? I understand you coveting the First Angel, but of what use am I to you?"

"Nothing, my lady," he said. "But I have had a Bathory woman at my side for four hundred years, eighteen women total, and I know what powerful allies they can be. Should you choose to stay, I will protect you from the Sanguinists, and perhaps you will protect me from myself."

More riddles.

Before she could inquire further, Tommy pointed out the forward window. "Look!"

She stood to see better. Out of the darkness, lit by hundreds of lamps, a monstrous steel structure appeared out of the waves. Four gray pillars jutted up from the sea like the legs of a massive beast. These monstrous pillars supported a flat tabletop larger than St. Peter's Basilica. Atop this platform rested a nest of painted beams and blocks.

"It's an oil rig," Tommy said.

"It was *once* an oil rig," Iscariot corrected him. "I've turned it into a private residence. It is on no maps. Positioned far from the cares of the world."

Elizabeth examined the lights shining from the middle of the

262 | *James Rollins and Rebecca Cantrell*

nest atop the platform, defining the ramparts of a blocky steel castle. She glanced out at the spread of dark water all around, then back to the oil rig.

Is this to be my new cage?

2:38 A.M.

"We have a problem!" Christian called back to the jet's cabin from the cockpit.

Of course we do, Jordan thought. They were due to land in another forty minutes. Over the past couple of hours, they had been slowly closing the lead on the others. Christian had reported that Iscariot's group had gone to ground about fifteen minutes ago in Naples.

"What's wrong?" Erin yelled back.

For once, Jordan was hoping for engine trouble.

"I lost Bathory's signal!" Christian reported. "I've tried recalibrating, but still nothing."

Jordan unbuckled and hurried forward to the cockpit. He braced his arms atop the tiny doorway and leaned through. "Where'd you see her last?"

"Her group must have transferred to another vehicle. Slower than the jet, but still fast. Speedboat, helicopter, small-engine plane. Can't say. They headed away from the coast, out over the Mediterranean, moving due west. Then suddenly the signal cut out."

Erin joined him with Rhun. "Maybe they went down," she said. "Crashed."

"Maybe," Christian said. "But there are easier explanations. She might have found the tracker, or ditched the cloak where I hid it, or maybe even the battery died in the unit. I can't say."

Jordan sighed his frustration, rubbing at the burn in his shoulder. The fire blazing along his tattoo had settled into a steady heat, keeping him from truly sleeping on the flight here.

"No matter the reason, she's gone," Christian concluded, glancing back over his shoulder. "So what now?"

"We'll land in Naples as planned," Rhun said. "Contact the cardinal in Rome and decide how to proceed from there."

Resigned that the hunt had gotten much harder, Jordan headed back to his seat with the others, but first he diverted to the rear of the cabin and grabbed the first-aid kit from the bathroom.

When he returned to his seat, Erin asked, "What are you doing?"

He opened the kit on the small walnut table in front of their seats. "I want to take a look at those mechanical moths. If we're going to tangle with that bastard again, we need to find a way of neutralizing that flying threat. Or we're screwed."

He pulled on a pair of latex gloves from the medical kit and lifted up the box where Erin had stored the handful of moths she had collected from the ice maze. He tweezed one out that looked mostly intact and placed it gently on the table.

Rhun recoiled slightly in his seat.

Good instinct.

The residual venom inside could probably still kill him.

Erin shifted closer to Jordan, which he didn't mind one bit.

He examined the green wings. They definitely looked organic, likely plucked from a living specimen. He turned his attention next to the body, an amazing bit of handiwork in brass, silver, and steel. He inspected the tiny, articulated legs, the thin threads of antennae. Keeping his fingers away from the needle-sharp proboscis, he flipped the body over and probed the bottom side, discovering tiny hinges.

Interesting . . .

He sat straighter. "We know the moths have the capability to inject poison into *strigoi* or Sanguinists," he said. "But it doesn't affect us humans, so maybe there is a clue there. Time to do a little experimenting."

He glanced over to Rhun. "I'm going to need a few drops of your blood."

Rhun nodded and pulled the *karambit* from his sleeve. He cut his finger and dribbled a few crimson drops onto the tabletop where Jordan indicated. In turn, Jordan used a razor from the kit to nick his thumb and do the same.

"Now what?" Erin asked.

"Now I need some of the toxin from inside the moth." Jordan tugged back on his latex glove after placing a bandage on his thumb.

"Careful," Rhun warned.

"Trust me, during my years of forensics work with the military, I handled both poisons and explosives. I'm not taking any chances."

Bent over the brass body of the moth, he used tweezers from the medical kit to undo the hinges on the underside of the moth. Once free, he pried open the moth's body with great care, revealing tiny gears, springs, and wires.

"Looks like the inside of a watch," Erin said, her eyes shining with amazement.

The craftsmanship was exquisite.

Rhun leaned forward, too, curiosity outweighing his earlier caution.

Jordan noted a tiny glass vial occupied the anterior end of the mechanism. It had cracked, but small streaks of blood remained inside it.

"The blood of Iscariot," Erin said.

Rhun leaned back again. "Smells like death. The taint is plain."

Jordan stuck his tweezers into the broken vial and pried it farther open. Then he used two cotton swabs to scoop out droplets of the remaining stain. The first swab he pressed into his own blood.

As expected, nothing happened.

So far, so good.

He picked up the second swab and dipped it into Rhun's blood. With an audible *snap*, Rhun's blood vaporized, leaving only a smudge of soot on the walnut surface.

Into the stunned silence that followed, Jordan met the priest's wide eyes. "So Iscariot's blood is definitely inimical to the blood of a Sanguinist."

"And the blood of *strigoi*," Erin added.

One and the same in my book, Jordan thought, but he kept that to himself.

Instead, he turned to his bag of discarded winter clothes and rummaged through it until he found one of his woolen gloves. It was stained with Tommy's blood from when he had helped extract the boy out of the ice sculpture.

"What are you doing?" Erin asked.

"We know Iscariot and this kid are similarly unique immortals. I want to check if the boy's blood is toxic, too."

Rhun squeezed out a few more drops for him to test. Jordan wet a swab with the priest's blood and applied it to the gloves.

There was no reaction.

Erin's brow furrowed in thought.

Jordan sighed. "So it seems the boy's blood doesn't hurt anybody. In fact, it might have saved my life."

"Might have?" Erin said. "Something sure did."

Jordan ignored the burn blazing across his shoulder and down his back and chest. "Either way, the kid and Judas are very different, despite their shared immortality."

"So where does that leave us?" Rhun asked.

"From here, Erin and I should take point whenever those moths are around. And not just moths. We should be suspicious of anything that creeps, crawls, or flies. I also suggest you all wear thicker armor, showing less skin. Maybe even something like a beekeeper's mask to protect your faces."

Rhun nodded. "I will share this information with the cardinal, to warn any Sanguinists in the field, to ready such gear for any fight to come."

Jordan returned his attention to the moth's remains. "Which brings us next to its functional mechanism. This clockwork inside is very intricate. I suspect any foreign contamination could wreak havoc, possibly gumming up the gears. Fine dust, sand, oil."

"I will have the cardinal look into that, too."

Jordan looked at Rhun. "And for all our sakes, it would be good to have as much advance notice of this manner of assault as possible. Back in the ice maze, were you able to hear the moths when they flew through the air?"

He imagined the gears made some sort of noise.

"I remember a soft whirring, far quieter than a heartbeat. But I'd recognize it if I heard it again."

"Then that's a start," Jordan said.

But would it be enough?

34

Tommy gaped as the massive doors of the elevator cage opened into a huge room.

After the hydrofoil had docked at the foot of one of the oil rig's massive legs, the group had crossed to an industrial freight elevator. It looked old and well worn, an artifact left from the days when the rig actually sucked oil from beneath the Mediterranean Sea. The nondescript steel cage had whisked them to the towering platform above and into the superstructure built on top.

Iscariot stepped out first, flanked by his two huge men.

Tommy followed with Elizabeth.

He had expected to find the same old, industrial look here. Even from below, the superstructure on top had looked like the steel forecastle to an old sailing ship. But as Tommy entered the room now, it was like stepping onto the bridge of Captain Nemo's *Nautilus*. The room was a graceful mix of steel and wood, glass and brass, masculine yet elegant.

Directly across from the elevator rose towering windows, arched to a point like those found in gothic churches. The outermost flanking windows were even stained glass, depicting scenes of fishing, of men hauling nets, of small boats with white sails. The remaining windows opened a commanding view of the sea. Moonlight shone on white-capped black waves and thin silvery clouds.

It took some effort to tear his gaze from that view. Underfoot, a rich red carpet cushioned a floor that showed polished hardwood at its edges. Overhead, steel beams had been painted black, the rivets a rich copper. A skylight shone up there, also stained glass, displaying seabirds in flight: gulls, pelicans, herons. In the center, though, hung a white dove with emerald eyes.

Tommy tripped a step, remembering the injured dove he had sought to rescue in Masada. Iscariot caught his hand before he fell, glancing up to the same skylight, his silver-blue eyes returning to Tommy with a curious glint.

"Your hands are cold," Iscariot said. "I've had a fire stoked for our arrival."

Tommy nodded, but he had a hard time getting his legs to move. The remainder of the space was decorated with leather chairs and deeply cushioned couches, tacked with copper studs. There were also display cabinets and tables, holding brass sextants, old telescopes, a large steel bell. Standing before the center window was even a ship's massive wheel, of wood and brass, clearly an authentic antique. Hanging on the wall above that same window was an old anchor, gone green with verdigris.

Guy must like to fish, Tommy thought.

He cast a sidelong glance at Iscariot.

Judas, he reminded himself, despite the impossibility of that. But after all he had experienced of late, *why the hell not?*

Elizabeth touched his arm. "You are shivering. Let's get you before the fire."

He allowed himself to be led to a set of chairs before a massive hearth. Bookcases rose to either side, climbing from floor to ceiling, so tall that you had to scale a rolling ladder to get to them. His mother would have loved this room, a space warm and cozy, full of books to read.

"Sit," Elizabeth demanded once they reached an overstuffed chair. She tugged it closer to the fire, showing the depths of her strength.

He sank into it, staring into the flames, at the black andirons, shaped like dolphins dancing on their tails. The entire place smelled like woodsmoke, suddenly reminding him of the ski trips he had taken with his parents before he got sick.

Above a mantel rose a triptych of three maps. He leaned closer, rubbing his hands together over the crackling flames. The middle map displayed the modern world but drawn in an old-fashioned style with spidery lettering. To the left was a map that looked ancient, with vast parts of the world missing. The chart to the right was dated 1502. It showed the edge of North America, colored green, and a tiny bit of South America.

Elizabeth peered closely at that map, her voice drawn softer. "That is how the world looked when I was the same age you are now."

Her remark caught Tommy off guard as he was suddenly reminded that she was more than four hundred years old.

Tommy pointed to the center map. "That's how the world looks now. We've even mapped it from space."

"Space?" she asked, glancing back, as if to see if he was joking.

"We have giant satellites. Machines. Orbiting way up, like between here and the moon."

Her gray eyes clouded up. "Man has gone so far?"

"To the moon and back," Iscariot said, joining them. "Mankind has sent devices crawling across the surface of Mars and traveling out beyond our solar system."

Elizabeth sank back, placing a hand on the wingback of Tommy's chair to steady herself. "I have a great deal to learn," she said, looking overwhelmed.

Tommy reached up and touched her cold hand. "I'll help you."

Her fingers turned and gripped his—at first too strongly, threatening to break bones, but then she softened her hold, reining in that strength. "I would welcome that."

Iscariot sighed, looking like he wanted to roll his eyes. "Before any of that can happen, Thomas should rest, eat, recover his own strength."

Elizabeth's hand tightened slightly again on him. "And then?"

"Then at dawn, Thomas will meet his destiny. As we all must do eventually."

A chill trickled down Tommy's spine that the fire could not warm. *What destiny?*

One of Iscariot's men arrived with a tray. Tommy stirred at the sight and smells of a hamburger, french fries, and a chocolate shake.

"I thought you might enjoy such fare," Iscariot said as the tray was placed next to Tommy on a side table. "You should eat heartily. We have a long day tomorrow."

Tommy touched the tray, remembering Elizabeth's earlier warning. *Eat to stay strong.*

He knew he would need all his strength to escape.

3:32 A.M.

Elizabeth settled into a chair opposite the hearth from the boy as he ate. She held her palms toward the welcoming heat. True flames warmed her like no modern device could. She closed her eyes and allowed her body to drink in that fire, picturing sunlight on a hot summer's day.

Warm now and freshly fed, she should be content—but she was not. *I am unsafe here—as is the boy.*

She was surprised at how much that last bothered her. Iscariot had plans for the both of them, and she began to suspect that he would treat her no more kindly than the Sanguinists had.

She rotated her injured ankle. It had healed enough that it would not slow her if she needed to flee. But what about the boy? She stared over at Tommy. He displayed appalling manners, devouring everything on his plate. The smell of grilled meat and frying oil repulsed her, but she gave no outward sign. She knew much of the boy's appetite was driven by the same goal as her, to keep his strength up, to ready himself for escape.

But will the opportunity ever present itself?

Iscariot watched them like a hungry hawk, even as he ate his own meal, a blood-red steak and buttery vegetables. He used a silver fork and knife, the utensils emblazoned with an anchor.

Tommy finally sighed with great satisfaction and leaned back in his chair.

She studied his young face. Color had stolen into his cheeks again. It was uncanny, even for her, how quickly he healed. The food had clearly lent him strength.

"I can't eat any more," he declared, stifling a belch with a fist.

It turned instead into a long yawn.

"You should get some rest," Iscariot said. "We must be up again before dawn."

Tommy's tired eyes found hers. He clearly didn't know how to respond.

She gave him the smallest nod.

Now was not the time to confound their new captor.

"Okay," he said, standing and stretching his back.

Iscariot gestured to Henrik. "Show the boy to the guest room and deliver him clean clothing."

Tommy picked at his sweatpants and shirt, stained in spots by dried blood. He plainly could use fresh clothing.

Resigned, Tommy followed after Henrik, but not before casting a worried glance toward Elizabeth. It ached her silent heart.

Once he was gone, Iscariot shifted on the sofa closer to her chair. "Some sleep will do him good." He caught her gaze with his silver-blue eyes. "But you have many questions for me. Questions better asked and answered with the boy out of the room."

She folded her hands in her lap and decided to start with the past before addressing the present or future. "I would know more about the fate of my family."

He nodded, and over the course of several long painful minutes, he told stories of her children, and their children again, of marriages, births, deaths. It was a tale mostly tragic, of a family brought low, a vast tapestry woven from the threads of her sins.

This is my legacy.

She kept her face stoic and buried his words deep inside her. Bathorys did not reveal their pain. Many times she had told her children this, even when she wanted to hold them in her arms and brush away their tears. But she had not learned of comfort from her mother, and she had not taught it to her children. This strength had cost her, but it had also saved her.

Once finished describing her descendants, he asked, "But are you not curious about the modern world?"

"I am," she said, "but I am more curious about my *role* in this new world."

"And I suspect you want to know the boy's role, too."

She shrugged, admitting nothing. She let a trace of sarcasm enter her voice. "What kind of monster would I be if I did not care about such a stout lad?"

"What kind of monster indeed." A hint of a smile crossed his lips.

She read his satisfied expression, letting him believe she was the sort of monster who cared little about such a boy. For she was just such a monster—she had killed many scarcely older than Thomas. But to him she felt a strange kinship, and her kin were sacred.

Iscariot fixed her with a harder stare. "Your *role,* my dear Countess Bathory, is first and foremost to keep him calm and obedient."

So I am to play nursemaid.

Keeping ill temper from her voice, she asked, "What do you plan to do to him that you need such soothing services?"

"Near dawn, we will travel to the coast, to the ruins of Cumae. It is there he will find his destiny, a fate he may wish to fight. And while escape is impossible, if he resists, it will go hard for him."

Elizabeth turned to the flames.

The ruins of Cumae.

A chord of memory rang through her, from her time reading the ancient writings of Virgil and the histories of Europe, as all good noblewomen should. A famous seer had once lived in Cumae, a sibyl who prophesied the birth of Christ. By Elizabeth's time, the place had fallen to ruin, the city walls long destroyed.

But something else nagged at her, another story of Cumae. Fear etched into her bones, but she kept it from her face.

"What is the boy's fate in Cumae?" she asked.

And what is mine?

"He is the First Angel," Judas reminded her. "And you are the Woman of Learning. Together, we will forge the destiny that Christ has set upon me, to return Him to His world, to bring His Judgment upon us all."

She remembered Iscariot's earlier admission of such a lofty goal. "You intend to start Armageddon. But how?"

He only smiled, refusing to answer.

Still, she recalled that last detail concerning Cumae. According to Roman legend, the sibyl's throne hid the entrance to the underworld.

The very gateway to Hell.

35

Cardinal Bernard strode through the nearly deserted airport outside of Naples. Recessed lights cast a bluish tint across the few early morning travelers, lending them a look of ill health. No one gave him a second glance as he passed swiftly toward the arrivals hall. He had shed the crimson of his formal robes for the dark navy of a modern business suit.

But he had not come to Naples as a cardinal or a businessman, but as a warrior.

Beneath the silk of his suit, he wore armor.

Wary of a mole in their order, he had traveled here in secret, slipping out of Vatican City through a long unused tunnel, across the midnight streets of Rome, where he had blended in. He had flown by a commercial airline versus private jet, using false papers. He dragged a suitcase that held two sets of Sanguinist armor, specially prepared for this trip.

Near the airport exit, he immediately recognized Erin and Jordan, hearing their telltale heartbeats before they stepped through the glass doors.

Rhun and Christian flanked the pair.

Jordan reached him first, moving on his strong legs. "Good to see you again, Cardinal."

"For now, just Bernard." He glanced around, then swung the suitcase to Rhun and pointed to a bathroom. "Change. Keep the armor under your civilian clothing."

After they left, he shook Jordan's hand, noticing the fierce warmth of his palm, almost feverish, as if he were burning up. "Are you well?" he asked.

"Considering I just came back from the dead, I'm doing fantastic."

Bernard noted a slight hesitation in the man's manner. He was clearly holding something back, but Bernard let it go. "I am grateful you're safe . . . and equally grateful for your work in helping us understand this unique threat posed by Iscariot's moths."

Bernard still had trouble coming to terms with Judas Iscariot walking the earth, that Christ had cursed His betrayer with endless years. But the threat the man posed could not be denied or ignored.

"With time and better facilities," Jordan said, "I could learn more about his creations."

"It will have to do. Time runs short. We must find the First Angel and unite him with the book."

The words of the Gospel's prophecy shone in his mind's eye in lines of flaming gold: *The trio of prophecy must bring the book to the First Angel for his blessing. Only thus may they secure salvation for the world.*

Nothing else mattered.

Erin looked grim. "For that to happen, we must discover *where* Iscariot has hidden him and discern *what* he wants with the boy."

"And why the bastard came here with the kid," Jordan added.

Erin nodded. "It must be important."

Rhun and Christian returned, their robes tighter than before, hiding their new armor, a stab-resistant material suggested by Jordan as a defense against the sting of those moths.

Bernard motioned to the door. "I have hired us a helicopter to take us to the coordinates where Christian last detected the countess. We will head west over the water along that same path and search for any clues."

Leading the way, Bernard piled them into a taxi van and drove them to a neighboring airfield, where the helicopter waited. It was a blue-and-orange craft, with a curiously long nose and swept-back windows, defining a large cabin.

Christian exited the van and whistled his appreciation. "Nice. An AW-193."

"You can fly a chopper?" Jordan asked.

"Been flying them since you were still in short pants." He waved to the aircraft. "Hop in."

Erin was aboard first. She stopped short when she spotted a long black box strapped between their seats.

"I readied a coffin for Countess Bathory," Bernard explained. "In case we come upon her during this sojourn."

"We're bringing her back?" Jordan asked.

"She may still be the Woman of Learning," Bernard answered.

He was not about to take any chances.

Rhun touched the box with one hand, an aggrieved look on his face. Bernard had heard reports from Christian about Nadia slashing the woman's throat, a woman for whom Rhun still clearly had deep affection.

Bernard needed to remain wary of that bond.

4:44 A.M.

Rhun strapped in next to Erin as Christian took the pilot's seat. The engine roared to life and the blades began turning faster and faster. Moments later they were airborne and sweeping for the dark waters of the Mediterranean.

As they reached the coastline, Christian called back. "Here is where they took to the sea! I lost her signal a few miles due west from here!"

Rhun stared down at the black waves. Moonlight glinted silver off the whitecaps.

They traveled in silence for several minutes, but the waters remained empty, showing no trace of the others. He pictured Iscariot dumping Elisabeta into the dark sea, ridding himself of her.

Christian yelled. "This is the spot where the signal cut out."

He brought the craft into a slow circle over the water. All eyes searched below for any wreckage, any evidence as to where Iscariot's group had gone.

Jordan called forward. "We should consult maps of the local currents. If a boat sank or a helicopter or small plane crashed out here, we might have to follow the coastal currents—but for now I suggest that we continue along their original trajectory."

"Roger that." Christian tipped the craft to its side and flew west.

Rhun continued his vigil, his keen eyes searching every wave.

He prayed for hope.

He prayed for her.

36

Judas stood in his bedchamber, dressed again after a short hour's nap.

He felt refreshed, full of hope.

As he secured his tie, he kept his back to the room's massive four-poster bed. To assist him while dressing, he used the reflection in the giant clock that covered one wall. The crystal face stretched eight feet across. With his own hands, he had built and rebuilt it in twenty different homes. The dial of the clock was also glass, revealing its inner gears and cogs, all of brass, copper, and steel. He liked to watch the mechanisms tick away the endless passage of his life.

Now with one careful hand, he stopped the clock. He no longer needed it. His life would end soon. After years of praying for this moment, soon he would rest.

A knock on the door disturbed his thoughts.

"Enter!" he called out.

He turned to find Henrik pushing the First Angel into the room. With sunrise only a couple of hours off, he had summoned the boy to be brought before him.

Tommy rubbed his eyes, clearly still sleep addled. "What do you want with me?"

"Only to chat."

The boy looked like he would have preferred more sleep.

Judas drew him to his small desk. He had a larger office to conduct business elsewhere on the rig, but he preferred sometimes the quiet intimacy of his own chamber. "The two of us, Tommy, are unique unto this world."

"What do you mean?"

Judas picked up a sharp letter opener and pierced the center of his own palm. Blood welled thickly, but he used a handkerchief to wipe it away. The small wound sealed quickly, healing almost immediately.

"I am immortal, but not like your countess. I am like you." As proof, he took the boy's hand in his firm grip and placed his palm against his own chest. "Do you feel my heartbeat?"

Tommy nodded, plainly intimidated but intrigued.

"Like you, I was born an ordinary boy. It was a curse that granted me my immortality, but I would like to know what you *did* to be so similarly afflicted."

Judas had heard a rough accounting of the boy's story, but he wanted to hear the details from the source.

Tommy chewed on his lower lip, clearly hesitant, but the boy likely ached to understand what he had become. "It happened in Israel," he began and slowly told the story of visiting Masada with his parents, of the earthquake and the gas.

None of this accounting explained his sudden immortality.

"Tell me more about what happened *before* the earthquake," Judas pressed.

A guilty look swept his countenance. "I . . . I went into a room that I wasn't supposed to. I knew better. But there was a white dove on the floor, and I thought it was hurt. I wanted to take it out and get some help for it."

Judas's heart thumped against his ribs. "A dove with a broken wing?"

"How did you know that?" Tommy's eyes narrowed.

Judas sank back against his desk, his words full of memory. "Two thousand years ago, I saw a dove like that. When I was a boy."

He had not thought the encounter important, barely considered it, except the event occurred on the morning that he had first met Christ, when Judas was only a boy of fourteen years, when they became fast friends.

I was the same age as Tommy, he suddenly realized.

He remembered that early morning now in immediate detail: how the streets were still shadowy as the sun had not quite risen, how the sewage in the drains had stunk, how the stars still shone.

"And the dove you saw," the boy said, "it also had a broken wing?"

"Yes." Judas pictured the ghostly white of its feathers in the night, the only thing moving on that dark street. "It dragged its wing across the muddy stones. I picked it up."

He felt the plumage now, brushing his palms. The bird had lain quiet, its head against Judas's thumb, staring up at him out of a single green eye.

"Did you try to help it?" Tommy asked.

"I wrung its neck."

The boy took a half step back, his eyes wide. "Just like that?"

"There were rats, dogs. It would have been torn apart. I saved it from that misery. It was an act of mercy."

Still, he remembered how stricken he felt afterward. He had fled to the temple for comfort, to his father, who was a Pharisee. It was there he saw Christ for the first time, a lad of the same age, impressing his father and many others with His words. Afterward, the two of them became friends, seldom parted.

Until the end.

Now I must correct that.

The boy, the dove, they were all signs that his path was the correct one.

Judas drew Tommy back to the door, back into the care of Henrik. "Ready him for our departure."

Once Tommy was gone, Judas returned to his desk. He picked up a crystal block that fit neatly in his palm. It was his most prized possession. He had taken it from his office safe and would return it before he left. But he needed its reassurance this early morning, needed its physicality and weight in his hands.

The block held a fragile brown leaf suspended inside, protected across the centuries by the glass. He lifted it to his eyes and read the words that had been cut into its once green surface with a sharp stone knife.

He cupped the block in both palms, thinking of the woman who had written these words, picturing her luminous dark skin, her eyes that glowed with a peaceful radiance. Like him, she understood truths that no one else could. Like him, she had lived many lifetimes, watched many friends die. Alone on Earth, she was his equal.

Arella.

But this simple leaf had ended the best century of his long life—the one that he shared with her. It had been in Crete, where their house looked over the ocean. She hated to be far from the sea. He had moved with her from Venice to Alexandria to Constantinople to other cities that looked out over other waves. He would have lived anywhere to see her happy. That particular decade she had wanted simplicity and quiet.

So he chose Crete.

He looked out his bedroom window now, staring at the dark waves. Since those days he, too, had never been far from the sea. But back then he had watched her more often than the endlessly changing water. That night she had stood by a window with the shutters thrown open to the night.

Judas cranked his own window now and breathed in the salt air, remembering the sounds and smells of that long-ago night.

From his bed, he watched her silhouette move against the starry sky.

The scent of the ocean filled their bedroom, along with the soft hush of the waves against the sand. Close at hand, an owl called to its mate and was answered in turn. A week before, he had seen the pair in an olive tree, each bird not much larger than two fists pressed together.

"Do you hear our owls?" she asked, turning toward him.

Moonlight glinted off her ebony hair, one wayward lock falling across her face. She reached her hand to push it away, a gesture he had seen thousands of times. But her hand stopped, her body going rigid in an all-too-familiar manner.

Judas smothered a curse and quickly stood.

As he came to her, he saw her beautiful eyes were empty.

This, too, was familiar.

The prophecies would now spill through her. Each time, he hated it, for in this state she was beyond his reach, and beyond her own, swept by the waves of time, those tidal pulls that could never be resisted.

As usual, he followed her instructions. He drew fresh leaves from a rush basket in the corner and pressed them into her warm left hand. Every day she gathered leaves for this purpose, although the prophecies came but once or twice a year.

He folded the fingers of her right hand around the ancient stone knife.

Then he left her alone.

He kept a silent vigil in front of her door. Sometimes the visions lasted for mere minutes, others for hours. No matter how long, she was not to be interrupted.

Thankfully this night she was spared.

After a single minute, she came to herself and bade him to return.

As he entered the room, she lay in their bed curled into a ball. He took her in his arms and stroked her long thick hair. She turned her face into his chest and wept. He rocked her from side to side and waited for the storm to pass. He knew better than to ask the source of her sorrow. This curse she must bear alone.

Usually the leaves on which she wrote her prophecies lay scattered across the floor, and he would gather them together while she slept and burn each in a fire.

It was as she wished, as she begged of him. No good had ever come from her gift, she had told him. The prophecies were mere shadows, holding no certainty, but the knowledge of them had driven many a man to force them into being, often in their most evil guise.

Still, in secret, he read each leaf before burning it, recording many of her words, even pictures she had drawn, in a thick leather journal that he used for the household accounts. She never read from that book, never concerned herself with financial details.

She trusted him.

This night, after her breaths slowed to sleep, he disentangled himself from her embrace and rose to pick up the single leaf that lay at the edge of the fire.

Only one prophecy tonight.

The leaf felt supple under his fingertips. The smell of green trees drifted up to his nose. The scribbled phrases beckoned him. Holding the leaf near the fire's flames, he read the words that marched across its surface in uneven lines.

After His words, written in blood, are lifted from their prison of stone, the one who took Him from this world will serve in bringing

Him back, sparking an era of fire and bloodshed, casting a pall over the earth and all its creatures.

Disbelieving, he traced each word with a trembling fingertip. He read them again and again, wishing that their meaning was not so plain. He already knew that Christ had written a Gospel in His own blood and imprisoned it in stone. Judas had recorded other prophecies concerning that book that she had written over the past century, but he had not thought them important. He had never thought that her prophecies might concern him until the line that read: the one who took Him from this world.

That could be none other than the one who had betrayed Christ.

Everyone else involved in the death of Jesus was long since turned to dust, but Judas endured. He had been spared for a purpose.

For this *purpose.*

So few words, but each one confirmed his worst fears about his curse. Once the lost Gospel was unearthed, Judas must seek to bring Christ back. To do that, it was Judas's duty to start the end of days—a time of fire and blood.

A rustling of sheets drew his attention around. She sat up, as beautiful in the firelight as she was in every light.

Her eyes saw what his fingers held. "You read this?"

He looked away, but he felt her gaze burning into him.

"Have you read them all?" she asked.

He could not lie to her, turning to her. "I wanted to preserve them in case you should change your mind, so that your gift was not lost to the world."

"Gift? It is no gift. And it was my choice to decide what to do with it. I trusted you, alone of every man in the world, to understand that."

"I thought that I was serving you."

"How? When? For one hundred years, you have betrayed me."

A line of tears glistened in the firelight. She wiped the back of her hand across one smooth cheek. He had gone against her deepest wishes, again and again. He read in her eyes that there could be no forgiveness for his actions.

"I did it for you," he whispered.

"For me?" Her voice hardened. "Not for your own curiosity?"

He had no answer to that question, so instead asked another. He lifted the leaf. "How long? How long until this prophecy is fulfilled?"

"It is but a prophecy." Her face was a blank slate on which he could read nothing. "One possible shadow of the future. It is not certainty, nor necessity."

"This shall come to pass," he insisted.

He had known its truth the instant that he read her words.

He had betrayed Jesus.

Now he must betray the world of man.

"You cannot know this." She crossed the room to stand before him. "You must not do this dark thing based on my words. Nothing in this world is set. As all men, you were imbued by God with free will."

"My will does not matter. I must find Christ's Gospel. I must set these events in motion."

"A prophecy cannot be forced." Her voice rose in rare anger. "Even with all your arrogance, you must know this."

He lifted the leaf again, matching her anger. "I see this. I know this. We must do what we were created to do. I am a betrayer. *You are a* prophetess. *Did you not defy God by failing to share your prophecy of Lucifer's betrayal? Were you not cast down because of it? And now you seek to defy Him again!"*

Stricken, she stared at him. He knew that he had spoken her greatest fear aloud, and he wished that he could call his words back.

Tears shone in her bright eyes, but she blinked them away. She turned from him, lifted the hood of the cloak so that it hid her face, and ran out the door into the starry night.

He waited for her to come back to him, for her anger to be spent, that he might beg her forgiveness. But by the time the morning sun rose, she had not returned, and he knew that she never would.

Judas breathed deeply of the night air, remembering all.

After Arella left him, he traveled to Europe where he spent many years researching whispered rumors of Christ's lost Gospel. He learned of another prophecy concerning the book, one that spoke of a sacred trio.

So he sought them, too.

One fall evening, following a rumor among the Sanguinists, he sought out Countess Elizabeth Bathory—the learned *woman* married to a powerful *warrior* and bound to a *knight* of Christ.

Like the Church, he thought that these three might be the prophesied trio—until Father Korza had turned the countess into a *strigoi,* and she was supposedly slain.

Yet he remained convinced of the power of the Bathory family. Each generation, he selected a single woman from that lineage to train and protect, poisoning her blood against the *strigoi,* to ensure she would never be turned as her ancestor had been.

Most of the women had served him well, until the line had ended with Bathory Darabont. But by then the lost Gospel of Christ had been brought back into the world, heralding what Judas must do next.

He lifted the glass block and read those words.

The one who took Him from this world will serve in bringing Him back, sparking an era of fire and bloodshed, casting a pall over the earth and all its creatures.

At long last, that time had come.

37

Tommy shivered in the breezes blowing across the open platform of the oil rig, the wind driving away the last dregs of his sleepiness.

He stared across the pad to a silver helicopter parked there. It had blacked-out windows and a large radar array sprouting from its nose. From the sleek lines and unusual features, it looked custom-made and expensive. A pilot stood next to the helicopter, dressed in a black flight suit, including a helmet and gloves.

Not a scrap of skin showed, suggesting he was like Elizabeth and Alexei.

Strigoi.

Elizabeth stood next to him. Even though sunrise was two hours away, she was also encased from head to toe. She wore high boots, black pants, a long-sleeved tunic and gloves, along with a veil that covered her face. It left a slit open for her eyes, but she held a pair of sunglasses, ready for the approach of dawn.

Iscariot waved toward the parked aircraft. "Everybody get aboard."

With no choice, Tommy ducked under the rotors as they began to spin and climbed into the helicopter. Dread etched through him. Where were they taking him? He remembered Iscariot's talk of destiny, and somehow he knew he was not going to like it.

As he strapped himself in, he noted Elizabeth fussing with the shoulder and lap belts.

"Do you need help?" Tommy asked.

"It is more complex than harnessing a team of horses," she said, but she figured it out and snapped herself in place next to him.

Iscariot spoke to the pilot, then climbed into the cabin, bringing with him his two hulking bodyguards. When he closed the door, the entire cabin went pitch-black. No light came in through the windows, and Tommy could not see out. He was glad when artificial lights came on.

Elizabeth slowly took off her veil and sunglasses.

Iscariot handed them each a set of heavy wireless earphones.

Tommy put his on and Elizabeth followed his example, clearly watching his every move.

The engine volume got louder, and they lifted off from the helipad with a jerk. With the windows blacked out, Tommy used his stomach to judge how far they climbed, when they leveled out, and when they started their flight back to land.

Tommy leaned over and peered ahead. The windshield was also tinted to a solid black. How did the pilot know where they were going?

Iscariot noted where he was looking. His voice came through the earphones. "There is a digital camera mounted on the nose of the helicopter. Let me show you."

Reaching across Tommy's lap, he flicked a switch near the armrest. A monitor lowered in front of Tommy. It flickered to life, displaying a sweep of moonlit waves and a clear horizon in front.

"There's a small joystick near your right hand," Iscariot said. "You can move the camera with it."

Testing this, Tommy spun the joystick in a circle and images on the monitor swung a full 360. He watched waves chasing waves. The horizon was water and sky. Behind the helicopter, the twinkling lights of the oil rig grew smaller and smaller. As he swung the view back forward, he spotted a set of tiny lights running low over the water, heading toward them.

Another helicopter.

Iscariot sat straighter, then leaned forward toward the pilot. "Who is that?"

"Don't know," the pilot answered. "I've swept it with the night-vision scopes. No distinct markings on the hull, but it looks like a chartered aircraft. Could be tourists."

Iscariot scoffed. "Out before sunrise? Move us closer."

Their chopper dipped and dove toward the other craft, on an intercept course.

Iscariot pushed Tommy's hand off the joystick and commandeered it. He toggled a switch and the view turned brighter, in shades of silvery gray.

Night vision.

The view suddenly zoomed forward, centering on the windshield of the other aircraft.

Tommy could make out the pilot's face, remembering him from the ice maze.

The shock of recognition quickly changed to *hope*. It was one of the priests, one of those who helped free him from the ice.

They found me!

He didn't know how, but he didn't care.

Maybe they can rescue me . . . rescue us.

He glanced at Elizabeth, who was also staring at the screen. She smiled with half her mouth, as if she couldn't help herself. "The Sanguinists have tracked us."

Anger flared in Iscariot's voice and reddened his cheeks. "Take them down."

In the corner of the screen, a yellow icon of four missiles appeared. Beneath it was a single word:

Hellfire

That couldn't be good.

Tommy felt a rumbling under his seat. He imagined a hatch opening, a missile bay lowering into view.

On the screen, one of the yellow missiles turned red.

Uh-oh.

5:35 A.M.

With her face pressed to the window, Erin watched the helicopter dive toward them. Earlier, they had noted the aircraft rise like a tiny mote from the galactic cluster of an oil rig farther out to sea. It seemed headed to the coast, going wide from their position—then it had suddenly swung toward them, plainly coming in for a closer look.

Jordan had posited that it might be security for the rig, coming to investigate the approach of an unknown aircraft. These were suspicious times.

Then suddenly it dove straight at them.

Smoke flared from its underside, along with a flash of fire.

"Missile!" Christian screamed from up front.

Erin was thrown back as Christian forced the helicopter into a steep climb. Beyond the roar of the engines, a piercing scream ripped through the night. Their aircraft rolled to the right, as a whistling curl of smoke swept past the landing skid on the left.

A second later, an explosion blasted into the sea behind them, the shock wave shuddering their craft. A flume of water and smoke shot into the sky.

Christian immediately turned their helicopter into a stomach-dropping dive, trying to outmaneuver the other, but their rental aircraft was a lumbering fat bee compared to the sleek killer wasp on their tail.

Black ocean zoomed toward them.

She sucked in her breath. Jordan clutched hard against her.

Inches from the crests of the tallest waves, their craft finally pulled up, sweeping fast and low over the water. She craned her neck and saw the other helicopter behind them. It tipped up on its edge, dropping sideways toward the sea, then straightened and sped toward them, coming in higher.

They would never escape it.

"Gonna try to reach the rig!" Christian yelled. "Use its bulk as a shield."

Jordan called up. "I saw three more missiles in its bay when it swept past overhead."

Three more chances to kill them.

Christian struggled with the stick as if it had a life of its own. The helicopter zigzagged over the water, aiming for the oil rig. Another smoke trail screamed past on the right and exploded into the sea, casting a wave of smoke and water over their craft.

Two more chances . . .

The oil platform loomed ahead, a lamplit skyscraper rising out of the sea.

Erin allowed herself a moment of hope.

Then Nature slapped them down.

An extra tall wave hit the skimming skids. The machine jolted and wobbled like a tightrope walker about to lose his balance. For a sickening second, she thought that it would tip into the sea. Then the helicopter righted itself, climbing out of the waves.

She heaved out a sigh.

"Brace yourselves!" Christian bellowed.

Her throat clutched tightly, knowing they had lost too much speed. They could never outrun this next missile. Erin met Jordan's eyes—as Christian dove them lower again, this time seeming to drag the skids in the water on purpose.

Erin was thrown against her restraints as their forward momentum braked suddenly. The craft tilted up on its nose.

The missile slipped under their uplifted tail and exploded beneath them.

Fire blossomed up along both sides of the helicopter, flames covering the windows. The world spun in a dizzying wash of smoke, fire, and water. Then the chopper settled on its side in the water. Black smoke roiled into the darkened cabin.

The helicopter hung for one last breath.

Then sank into the sea.

5:37 A.M.

Judas studied the shattered wreckage, the spreading black stain on the dark water. The pilot hovered the helicopter, turning it in a slow sweep of the area, watching for survivors.

"Sir?" the pilot asked.

Judas weighed the odds of anyone surviving that last missile blast. It looked as if the strike had hit the tail of the helicopter square on. Nothing could have survived such a direct hit; even the stubborn bodies of the Sanguinists could not heal after being shredded to ribbons by ripped metal.

Besides—he checked the platinum Rolex Yacht-Master on his wrist—*none of this mattered.*

Whether there were any survivors, they could never stop him now. Dawn was less than two hours off. Even if the Sanguinists somehow survived, they could not close their lead on him.

Still . . .

"Contact the remaining crew at the rig," he ordered. "Have them comb and watch these waters."

"Aye, sir."

"Then continue to the coast."

Judas glanced at the boy, who looked ashen after the attack.

No one can save you now.

38

A racking cough tore through Erin.

She tasted blood, smelled smoke.

Jordan gripped her hand hard.

Alive—but for how long?

Water swamped the windows all round, as the craft continued its plunge into the cold depths. Red emergency lights glowed, casting the cabin into shades of crimson. Water seeped inside, slowly filling the lower half.

Rhun scrambled and splashed forward with Bernard, reaching Christian, who draped limply in his restraints. They fought to free him.

Following their example, Erin fumbled with her seat harness's quick release, which thankfully popped open. Jordan did the same, then clicked on a flashlight. He placed a hand against the window.

How far down were they?

The waters beyond the windows were as black as oil.

Jordan moved aside as Rhun came splashing to join them, hauling Christian's arms. Bernard had his legs. Blood covered the young Sanguinist's entire face.

Was he even alive?

Jordan pointed to the window. "We need to break out of here. Rhun, do you have the strength to kick out this window?"

"I believe so."

"No," Erin called. "We don't know how far down we are. The pressure could crush us. And even if we get free, I doubt we can make it to the surface in one breath."

Jordan frowned at her. "We have to try. We'll drown just as surely by doing nothing."

Rhun nodded. "Jordan is right. I will do my best to shield you both and get you to the surface. Bernard can carry Christian's body on his own."

Erin hugged her arms around her belly, looking at the rising water, already thigh-deep in the cabin by now, knowing they were wrong. She searched the space and called again. "Wait! There's another way!"

Jordan glanced at her.

"You're not going to like it," she said.

"What?" Jordan demanded.

She pointed to the long box strapped below the water, the one Bernard had brought along to secure the countess.

"It could act as our escape pod," she said.

Jordan's jaw clenched, plainly not keen on putting their hopes of survival on a *coffin*. Still, he nodded, recognizing she was right.

Rhun quickly ripped away the straps that secured the giant plastic box to the floor and it floated up to the surface, proving it was buoyant.

"It should protect us from the pressure," Erin said. "And there should be enough air in there for us to make it to the surface."

"That's a lot of *shoulds*," Jordan said.

But there was no better option.

As Rhun hauled the lid open, Jordan scrambled in first and sprawled onto his back. He lifted his arms, as if inviting her to bed. She climbed into the coffin, into his arms. He hugged her tightly.

Rhun closed the lid of the box, sealing them in darkness. She heard the latches snug into place. In the blackness, she concentrated on Jordan's heartbeat, feeling it thud against his rib cage, echoing into her. His body heat burned through his damp clothes, intense after the cold soaking. She shifted, noting his left arm felt hotter than his right.

Before she could ponder this, Rhun thumped the outside of the box, likely warning them to prepare themselves.

Jordan pulled her head down onto his chest. "It's gonna be a bumpy ride."

She heard a crash, and a solid *whump* of water striking the side of the coffin, shoving it to the other side of the cabin. She rolled and got banged about inside. It felt as if a giant dog had the box in his mouth and was shaking it like a stick. She gritted her teeth to keep from yelling.

Jordan's arms pulled her closer. "I got you," he said in her ear.

But who's got us?

5:42 A.M.

Rhun fought the pull of the sea and hauled the coffin through the shattered window. It became caught. An outer handle normally used by pallbearers snagged on a twisted piece of metal.

He glanced to the side and saw Bernard heading upward through the dark waters, kicking and hugging Christian's limp form in his arms. The cardinal also towed a sealed and deflated emergency raft, tied by a rope to his waist.

Alone, Rhun positioned his feet to either side of the coffin, bracing against the side of the wreckage as it plunged ever deeper.

Using all the strength in his legs and back, he yanked the box, bending the twisted piece of metal, watching the outer handle tear away. He feared the box might rip open and pictured water bursting inside and drowning Erin and Jordan.

He listened to the frightened timpani of their heartbeats.

He could not fail them.

He heaved again, fueled by his past failures, refusing to repeat them.

Finally, the coffin popped free—so suddenly, he lost hold of it.

He rolled back through the water and watched the box begin to float upward, slowly, too slowly. He kicked and swept his arms and got under the coffin. Pushing from below, he propelled the pod ever higher, chasing the feeble glow of a distant moon.

The surface seemed an impossible distance away, only visible because of his preternatural eyesight. He knew there was little air left in that coffin, and much of it contaminated by the smoke of the trapped cabin.

He must hurry.

All the while, he listened to their heartbeats, each distinct from the other, but sounding somehow in harmony. He prayed that their quiet chorus continued until he reached the surface.

5:45 A.M.

Jordan felt their escape pod breach the waves. The steady upward trajectory suddenly gave way, his stomach lolling to match the roll of sea beyond their prison. A moment later, he heard the latches give way, and the lid suddenly shoved open.

As they floated there, he took a deep breath of clean salt air, savoring the press of Erin's body against his. But a tremble shook through her. He rubbed his hands along her back, trying to chase away the fear. He had felt her body fighting against panic the whole time.

Rhun gripped an edge of the coffin and raised his head into view. "Are you both well?"

Jordan nodded. "Thanks for the lift."

Erin let out a small giggle, though it was less amusement at his lame joke than it was the madness of relief. It was still the best sound he'd heard in a long time. She pushed against him and sat.

Rhun pointed left. "Bernard has inflated an emergency raft. I will push you toward it."

Rhun's dark head bobbed behind them like a seal as he began kicking toward a round raft, a bright yellow wafer spinning in the water. He saw that Bernard had Christian's body sprawled atop it, a black stain against the yellow.

Worry for his new friend iced through him.

Too many Sanguinists had already died.

He scanned the horizon, but apparently the other helicopter was long gone.

But they weren't alone out here.

An echoing pitch of an engine reached them. Jordan looked beyond the raft to a single light racing toward them, bobbing over the waves. A Zodiac pontoon boat. It clearly had to come from the towering oil platform in the distance.

The same site from where the attack helicopter had risen.

Not good.

"Rhun!" Jordan called, knowing the priest was too low in the water to see. "We've got company coming at our twelve o'clock!"

If there was any question of them being friendly, it was dispelled as gunfire cracked out, pebbling the dark water, aiming for the larger, brighter target of the raft.

Bernard suddenly dove off the side and vanished, abandoning Christian.

Did that mean the young Sanguinist was already dead?

Rhun had slowed their approach to the raft. "Leave them to Bernard. But in the meantime, we should make less of a target."

Without warning, the priest upended their coffin and dumped them both into the cold sea. While Jordan understood the necessity, he didn't necessarily care for the manner. He sputtered on a mouthful of water as he came to the surface. He hurried to Erin, knowing she was not a strong swimmer, nor a fan of water in general.

But she came up smoothly, her eyes scared but determined.

Rhun joined them. "Make for the raft, but keep its bulk between you and whoever comes."

The priest led the way.

In a few strokes, their group reached their floating refuge but dared not mount it. Jordan peered over its edge as the Zodiac closed the distance, slowing. He spotted three men: a driver and two gunmen with rifles.

In the water, they were sitting ducks.

But unknown to the newcomers, there was also a *shark* in these waters.

Bernard suddenly rose on the starboard side, a long silver blade flashing in the moonlight. Moving in a blur, he slashed the length of the pontoon on their side. The Zodiac listed crookedly, the engine choking out, throwing the standing gunmen off balance. A hand lunged out of the water, grabbed an ankle, and plucked one man from the boat. He got tossed high, but not before Bernard hacked his leg off at the knee with one savage swipe.

The other rifleman fired, but Bernard was already gone.

As the Zodiac continued to wallow, the second gunman turned in a wary circle, watching the waters all around. Then suddenly the boat opened under the man, the tarp floor ripped out beneath him. His body was yanked straight through the new hole and vanished.

The last man—the driver—gunned the engine to full life and swung the boat away, clearly wanting to flee back to the safety of the oil platform. But Bernard bounded out of the sea, like a dolphin performing a trick. He landed behind the driver, gripped his hair, and slashed his neck, nearly taking the man's head off.

Bernard threw his body into the sea with one arm.

Jordan tried to balance the pious man of the cloth with this savage butcher.

"Make for the other boat!" Rhun said, loudly enough for Bernard to hear. "Quickly now. I'll grab Christian and join you there."

The priest leaped and rolled onto the raft.

Erin and Jordan swam for the Zodiac. Bernard helped them aboard the foundering craft. Jordan knew Zodiacs were tough little boats, capable of running on only one float. By the time Jordan followed Erin up, Rhun was already there, towing Christian by one arm.

He helped Rhun get the young Sanguinist aboard the boat.

"What now?" Jordan asked as Erin and Bernard attended to Christian.

"Can you pilot this craft?" Rhun asked.

"Not a problem," Jordan said.

The priest pointed to the oil rig. "We're too far from the shore. We'll never make landfall with this small engine. We must find another means of transportation to reach the coast."

Jordan stared toward the towering structure. Despite their team's firepower sunk to the bottom of the sea, they had to go into that nest of vipers.

Knowing this, Jordan crossed and took the wheel, while Erin leaned over Christian's body.

"Is he still alive?" she asked.

"It is difficult to say," Rhun admitted, kneeling between her and Bernard.

Christian's eyes remained closed. A deep gash ran along his forehead. Jordan knew it would be useless to check for a breath or a heartbeat. The Sanguinists didn't have either.

The cardinal placed his silver cross atop Christian's forehead, as if ready to administer last rites. After a moment, Bernard lifted the cross, revealing a seared mark matching its shape on the younger Sanguinist's skin.

"He lives," Bernard declared.

Rhun explained, the relief palpable in his voice. "If we die in service to the Church, we are cleansed. Blessed silver would not burn us."

Erin held Christian's hand.

"But he requires medical attention," Rhun warned, eyeing Jordan as he gunned the engine. "His life may still be forfeit."

Jordan aimed for the oil platform. "Then let's go pay our neighbors a visit."

39

As the boat fled toward the lights of the oil platform, Rhun studied Christian's pale face. He was young, relatively new to the cloth, making him brash and irreverent, but Rhun could not fault his faith and his bravery. He clenched a fist of frustration, refusing to lose another companion so soon after Nadia's death.

Bernard poured little sips of wine from his leather flask through Christian's slack lips, but most spilled down his hollow cheeks. He was still too weak to swallow.

"What if I gave him some of my blood?" Erin asked. "Like we did with the countess. Wouldn't that help revive him?"

"We will consider that only as a last resort," Bernard mumbled.

Erin looked little satisfied with that answer.

Rhun whispered to her. "The taste of blood for one as young as he risks freeing the beast inside him. We dare not risk it, especially here where we have so little means to control him. Let us see what we find at the oil platform."

"What we will *find* will surely be more enemies," Bernard added and pointed to the flask hidden and tied to Rhun's upper thigh. "We ourselves should drink, restore our strength to its fullest."

Rhun knew Bernard was correct, but he hated taking penance in front of others, knowing it often left him weeping and confused. He did not wish to display such weakness.

Still, he knew he must.

As Rhun freed his holy flask, Bernard upended his own and drank deeply, unabashedly. Bernard seemed at peace with his sins. He did his penance and was always calm moments afterward.

Rhun prayed for the same today as he lifted the flask to his lips and drank fully.

The cemetery loomed around Rhun as he lay on his back atop his sister's grave. The beast straddled him, their limbs entangled like lovers. The monster's blood filled his mouth.

Rhun had come to his sister's grave this night to mourn her passing, only to be waylaid by this beast, a monster wearing fine breeches and a studded leather tunic. Fangs had torn into Rhun's throat, draining his blood into this other's hungry mouth. But instead of dying, his attacker had offered Rhun a wrist, sliced open, pouring with the beast's black blood.

He had resisted—until cold, silken blood burst to fire on his tongue. Bliss welled through him, and with it, hunger.

He now drank fully from that crimson font, knowing it was a sin, knowing that the pleasure that pulsed through every limb in his body would damn him for all eternity. And still he could not stop. He longed to stay locked in this man's embrace forever, drowned in ecstasy with every fiery swallow.

Then his head cracked painfully against his sister's headstone. He watched the beast yanked off him. Rhun moaned, reaching again for him, wanting more of his blood.

Four priests pulled the monster from Rhun's aching body. Their silver pectoral crosses glinted in the cold moonlight.

"Run!" shouted the beast, attempting to warn him.

But how could he ever abandon such a font of bliss and blood?

His arms remained up, stretching to the other.

A blade flashed silver across the beast's throat. Dark blood exploded from the wound, staining his fine white shirt, soiling his leather tunic.

"No!" Rhun struggled to rise.

The four priests dropped the man's body to the ground. Rhun heard it hit the scattered leaves, knew without knowing how that the man was gone forever. Tears rose in his eyes at the loss of such ecstasy.

The priests sat Rhun up and wrenched his arms behind his back. Rhun fought with the ferocity of a cornered lynx, but they imprisoned him with an implacable strength for which he was no match.

He twisted, his sharp teeth seeking their necks.

His body ached for blood, any blood.

They carried him through the night without a word. But for all their silence, Rhun heard more than he ever had before in his life. He listened to each leaf crumble under their boots, the soft hush of owl wings overhead, the scurry of a mouse into its hole. Rhun's mind strained to fathom it. He could even hear the tiny beasts' heartbeats: the mouse's swift and frightened, the owl's slower and determined.

Yet when he turned his ear to the priests around him, he heard nothing.

Only a dreadful silence.

Was he so cut off from the grace of God that he could not hear holy heartbeats, only those of soulless beasts in the field?

Despairing his fate, he went limp in the priests' hands. His lips formed desperate prayers. Still, all the while, he wished only to tear out these priests' throats and bathe his face in their blood. The prayers did nothing to quiet this bloodlust. His teeth continued to chatter with longing.

Desire burned hotter than anything he had ever felt, fiercer than any love for his family, even his love for God.

The priests carried him back to the monastery, where moments before he had left as an innocent, a seminary student about to swear his holy vows. They stopped in front of a clean, bare wall that transformed into a door. During his years here, he had never known of its existence.

He had known so little of everything.

The priests bore him below to where a familiar figure sat at a desk holding a goose quill: Father Bernard, his mentor, his counselor in all things. It seemed Rhun's lessons were not yet finished.

"We bring him to you, Father," said the priest holding his right arm. "He was felled in the cemetery, but he has tasted no other blood."

"Leave him to me."

The same priest refused. "He is in a dangerous state."

"I know this as well as you." Bernard rose from his desk. "Leave us."

"As you wish."

The priest released Rhun's arm, dropping him to the stone floor, and headed away, drawing his brethren with him. Rhun lay there a long moment, breathing in the smells of stone, mildew, and old rushes.

Bernard remained silent.

Rhun hid his face from his mentor. He loved Bernard more than he had ever loved his own father. The priest had taught him of wisdom, kindness, and faith. Bernard was the man Rhun had always aspired to become.

But right now all Rhun knew was that he must slake his thirst or die trying. In one bound, he closed the space between them, knocking them both to the floor.

Bernard fell under him, his body strangely cold.

Rhun lunged for his neck, but his prey moved with an unearthly speed, rolling from Rhun's grasp and standing next to him. How could he be so quick?

"Be careful, my son." Bernard's rich voice was calm and steady. "Your faith is your most precious gift."

A hiss started low in Rhun's throat. Faith meant nothing now. Only blood mattered.

He sprang again.

Bernard caught him and bore him down to the floor. Rhun struggled, but the older man pinned him against the tiles, proving himself far stronger, stronger than the beast who had changed him, even stronger than the priests who had carried him.

Father Bernard was as hard as stone.

Was this strength proof of God's might against the evil inside of Rhun?

But his body raged against such thoughts. Throughout the long night, Rhun continued to battle this priest, refusing to listen, trying always to gain a mouthful of his precious blood.

The old man would not be taken.

Eventually, Rhun's body weakened—but not from exhaustion.

"You feel the approach of dawn," Bernard explained, holding him, pinning him. "Unless you accept Christ's love, you will always weaken with the morning, as will you die if the pure light of sun shines upon you."

A great weariness grew inside of Rhun, weighing down his limbs.

"You must listen, my son. You may view your new state as a curse, but it is a blessing for you. For the world."

Rhun scoffed. "I have become an unholy beast. I yearn for evil. It is no blessing."

"You can become more than what you are."

Bernard's voice held simple certainty.

"I wish nothing more than to drink your blood, to kill you," Rhun warned, as his strength ebbed even further. He could barely lift his head now.

"I know how you feel, my son."

Bernard finally loosened his grip, and Rhun slid to the floor.

On his hands and knees like a dog, Rhun mumbled to the tiles. "You cannot know of the lust inside of me. You are a priest. This evil is beyond your ken."

Bernard shook his head, drawing Rhun's eye. His white hair shone in the light of the dying candle. "I am like you."

Rhun closed his eyes, disbelieving. He was so tired.

Bernard shook Rhun until he opened his eyes again. The old priest drew Rhun's face to his own, as if to kiss him. Bernard parted those lips in invitation—but long sharp teeth greeted Rhun.

Rhun gaped at his mentor, a man whom he had known many years, a man who was never a man—but a beast.

"I have hungered as you have, my son." Bernard's deep voice filled Rhun with calm. "I have indulged evil appetites."

Rhun struggled to understand.

Father Bernard was good. He brought comfort to the sick and dying. He brought hope to the living. Without him, most of the priests in this very monastery would never have found their way to God.

"There is a path for us," Bernard said. "It is the most difficult road that any priest can walk, but we can do good, we can serve the Church in ways that no others can. God has not forsaken us. We, too, can live in His grace."

With those words, Rhun slipped toward a deep well of sleep, letting this lasting hope tame his bloodlust and offer him salvation.

Rhun came out of his penance, to find the cardinal leaning over him, those deep brown eyes shining with that same love and concern.

Bernard had saved him back then.

Still, Rhun now knew the misery that had followed that one act of mercy, picturing Elisabeta's eyes, her cunning smile, the deaths and suffering that followed in her wake.

Perhaps the world would have been better served if Bernard had let him die.

40

Elizabeth clutched Tommy to her side, feeling him tremble every now and then, likely still picturing the fire and explosions. She had never seen such a battle: two adversaries flying about like hawks, smoke screaming from impossible cannons in their bow, booms that shook even the air. The fighting exhilarated her, awed her—but it had terrified the boy.

He leaned against her shoulder, seeking comfort.

She remembered the other vessel exploding and rolling into the sea, sinking like a scuttled ship. She pictured Rhun torn to pieces—but oddly she found no satisfaction in the vision, only disappointment.

He should have died at my hands.

She also could not discount a sense of hollowness at his loss. She explored that emptiness now, knowing it was not grief, at least not entirely. It was more like the world was barren without him. Rhun had always filled her life, even back at the castle, before she was turned—with his frequent visits, their long conversations, their long pregnant silences. After that bloody night, he continued to define her, having given birth to her new existence. And ever since then he had plagued her shadow—even into this modern world.

Now he was simply gone.

"We're almost there," Iscariot said, waving a hand to the screen before them.

She drew her attention forward. The screen showed a dark coastline, littered with a blaze of lights. Farther to the east, she noted the skies had begun to pale with the approach of dawn. She felt its approach in the lassitude that weighed her down, making her feel sluggish.

Their craft suddenly veered away from the mass of lights that marked the city of Naples. It swung toward a shadowy stretch of coastline, overlooked by a tall hill, with a thin sandy beach at its base. The crown of the hill was scooped out, marking it as one of the many old volcanoes that dotted this region of southern Italy, but its slopes had long turned to thick forests, sheltering deep lakes.

"Where are we?" Tommy asked, stirring from her side.

"Cumae," Elizabeth answered, staring across the top of the boy's head to Iscariot.

"We're going to visit an old friend," Iscariot added cryptically.

Elizabeth had little interest in anyone whom Iscariot considered a *friend*.

As their craft reached the shore, it swept low over the sandy beach, stirring dust into a cloud. They lowered back to the land as sand rose around them in a cloud.

She felt Tommy stiffen in her arms. He must know his destiny was close at hand and rightly feared it. She remembered Iscariot's instructions to her, that she was supposed to keep the boy calm, to play nursemaid to him.

She tightened her arm around his thin shoulders—not because it was her duty, but because the boy needed such comfort.

At last, the craft bumped to the ground. The sand sifted and settled, opening a view to the ocean on one side and the steep slope of cliffs on the other.

Iscariot cracked open his door, washing in the smell of salt and burning oil.

They all climbed out.

Once Elizabeth's feet felt the sand, another note struck her keen senses.

A whiff of sulfurous brimstone.

She faced the seaside cliffs of that ancient volcano, knowing what lay far beneath it, protected by an ancient sibyl.

The entrance to Hades.

Standing beside her, Tommy stared dully out across the dark seas, likely picturing the deaths far out there, wondering about his own fate. She took his hand and gave his fingers a reassuring squeeze. She would play her role as ordered, biding her time until she could make her escape.

As Elizabeth turned her own eyes out across those empty waters, she was again struck by the hollowness of her loss. And not just Rhun. She pictured her estates, her children, her family. All gone.

I am alone in this world.

Tommy leaned against her. She gripped him in turn. He glanced at her, moonlight shining in his eyes, his gaze full of fear but also gratefulness that she was near.

He needed her.

And I need you, she suddenly realized.

Iscariot joined them, stepping forward amid a flutter of emerald wings, the moths released from a hold in the side of the craft. She refused to shy from the unspoken threat and kept her back stiff.

"It is time," he said and took Tommy's shoulders.

He turned the boy to face the cliffs—and his destiny.

6:12 A.M.

Erin held Christian's heavy head in her lap as Jordan idled their listing boat toward the dark dock of the oil platform. The three of them were alone on the boat. Rhun and Bernard had slipped into the water when they were a hundred yards off and swam to the dock on their own. From a distance away, she saw a small scuffle of shadows, a strangled cry—then Rhun had flashed a signal that it was safe for them to continue to the dock.

Jordan nudged the boat forward.

The pair of Sanguinists had made it clear that she and Jordan were to hang back until the way ahead was clear. Rhun's and Bernard's keen senses would pick out and dispatch any threats.

"Keep down," Jordan warned her as they fell under the shadow of the platform above. He kept one hand on the wheel, the other on a rifle, the weapon dropped by one of the men Bernard had killed earlier. She ducked her head low over Christian, watching Jordan.

Jordan's eyes surveyed every strut and catwalk above, clearly not fully trusting the Sanguinists to keep them safe. The weight of the massive structure seemed to press down upon them. Far above, electric lights blazed, but the lower area was mostly dark, a shadowy world of concrete pillars, steel stairs, and a crisscrossing maze of ramps and bridges.

The Zodiac limped past the bulk of a huge luxury hydrofoil docked in a neighboring berth.

Jordan looked at it closely—and perhaps a bit enviously. "Guy's got bank," he mumbled, with a weak attempt at levity.

She gave him a quick smile to let him know that she appreciated the gesture. A minute later, the Zodiac bumped to a stop at a steel dock.

Jordan held out an arm, his palm down, urging her to remain low. He watched closely for several long breaths, then waved her up.

Erin shifted higher. The salty wind felt good against her face.

Jordan hopped off, shouldering his rifle and quickly tying off the boat. He then crouched next to her in the boat. They were to await Rhun and Bernard's return.

It did not take long.

A shadow shed from above and landed silently on the steel treads of the dock. Rhun joined them, followed a moment later by Bernard. Both had knives bared and bloody. Erin wondered how many men they had killed tonight.

Bernard sheathed his blade and helped Erin to haul Christian quickly from the boat, then the cardinal carried his body from there.

"The way up should be clear," Rhun said. "But we must take care when we reach the structure on top."

He led them to a long metal staircase that corkscrewed around the neighboring concrete pillar and rose to the platform above. Once on the stairs, Rhun passed Jordan a machine pistol. He must have confiscated it from one of the guards.

Jordan shouldered his rifle and took the more agile weapon.

"Don't fire unless you must," Rhun warned. "My blade is more silent."

He nodded, as if they were talking about their golf swings.

As they climbed higher and higher, Erin concentrated on hanging tightly to the cold slippery metal rail. Winds whipped at her in sudden gusts. She came across one landing slick with blood and stepped gingerly around the stain, trying not to picture the slaughter.

Ahead of her, Jordan's boots ascended more confidently. Behind her, the cardinal seemed to have no trouble climbing while carrying Christian over his shoulder.

Rhun had disappeared above again, but his presence was plain. She heard a soft thud somewhere over her head. Moments later, they reached the top of the winding stairs. The electric lights seemed too stark and cold after the shadows below.

Rhun stood over the body of another guard.

Jordan joined him, crouched low, his pistol high.

Erin huddled with Bernard at the top of the stairs while the other two made a fast canvass of the immediate area. Up this high, the winds crashed against her, whipping her hair, snapping her leather jacket.

Finally, Rhun and Jordan returned.

"Place is a ghost town," Jordan said. "Must keep only a skeletal crew here."

Rhun pointed to the towering superstructure. "There's a doorway over there."

They sprinted as a group across the open decking. The structure ahead appeared to be a rendition of an old sailing ship's forecastle, down to the tall windows, faux rigging, even a bowsprit with a figurehead. It looked like a ship cresting upward out of a steel sea.

Rhun led them to a door. He creaked it open, revealing a long corridor. He ushered them across the threshold, shutting the door behind them, but he held them at the entrance.

He lifted up a hand and shared a significant glance with Bernard. Erin guessed that they must have heard something, possibly a heartbeat or some sign of a life. With a nod from Bernard, Rhun rushed forward like a hound loosed upon a fox. He vanished into the shadows. Distantly a door slammed, accompanied by a crash of what sounded like pots and pans.

Rhun returned a moment later, slipping out of the darkness and waving them onward.

Jordan glanced hard at Rhun.

"A galley cook." Rhun lifted his arm, revealing a green bottle of wine. "And I found this."

Bernard quickly took it.

Erin knew the wine could be consecrated and used to help Christian heal. She hoped that it would be enough.

"I hear no one else," Rhun said. "Not a scuff, breath, or heartbeat."

Bernard concurred. "I believe we are alone here."

"Let's be careful anyway, just in case," Jordan warned.

As they headed down the corridor, Erin realized the significance of the lack of any living presence. "Does that mean that Tommy isn't here?"

Or Iscariot or Elizabeth.

She pictured the helicopter that had attacked them.

Had the others been aboard it? If so, where had they been headed?

"We must search thoroughly to make certain," Rhun said. "And if they are not, we must try to find where they've gone."

"And why Judas absconded with the First Angel to begin with," Bernard added, shifting Christian's weight on his shoulder. "How is the boy a part of his plan?"

His plan for Armageddon, Erin reminded herself.

The passageway ended at a large salon, lined by bookcases on both sides with arched windows overlooking the sea below. A large ship's wheel stood before the windows. From the display cases holding nautical bric-a-brac, it looked like a museum.

Rhun crossed to a large hearth set amid the shelves and held out his hand. "Still warm."

"The boss clearly left in a hurry," Jordan said. "He must've been on that other chopper."

But why?

"I will tend to Christian here," Bernard said, carrying his body to the fireplace and lowering him to a couch. "Go learn what you can."

Erin was already moving, spotting a set of elevator doors to the right, framed in a frilly grille of brass. Other doors stood closed along the walls, likely leading to a maze of rooms and corridors. Ignoring them, she crossed instead to the ship's wheel. It marked the symbolic post of the captain of this steel-locked ship. The towering windows offered a commanding view of the sea, looking east toward the distant coast, where the stars had begun to fade with the approach of the new day.

Sensing time was running out, she glanced to the right, to the nearest door. Perhaps the captain kept his most precious spaces close to his command post.

She headed to that door and found it locked.

Jordan noted her frustration as she tugged on it.

"Allow me," Jordan said. "I have a key."

She turned to him. *How—?*

He lowered his rifle, aimed at the lock, and fired.

The blast made her jump, but the result made her smile. The handle was blown off, leaving a hole through the door.

She easily pushed it open, revealing a private study lined by walnut wainscoting in a high Victorian style, with a botanical mural intricately painted on the wall, depicting lifelike flowers, leaves, and twining vines, mixed with butterflies and bees. It looked less decorative than instructional, like something one would find in a Renaissance text on botany.

Erin made straight for the massive writing desk, a solid affair with well-turned legs and a leather top covered with papers.

Jordan followed her inside.

Rhun stepped to the doorway, drawn by the commotion.

"Be careful," he warned. "We don't know—"

Suddenly the delicate paintings along the wall burst to life. Leaves fluttered from branches, flowers spun delicately from stems, a scatter of butterflies and bees wafted off the wall.

The entire motif was a deadly collage.

It filled the air in a dazzling kaleidoscope of movement and color.

And swooped toward Rhun.

41

Jordan charged the few steps to Rhun and shoved him out the door, punching one palm to his chest. Caught by surprise, the priest tripped backward and landed flat on his ass in the next room.

Jordan slammed the door shut in his face with a certain amount of satisfaction.

"Stay out there!" he yelled through the door. He grabbed an umbrella from a neighboring stand and jammed its tip through the hole he had blasted through the door, plugging the stinging cloud in with him and Erin. "I'll see about ridding the room of these buggers! Until then, stay out, Padre!"

Jordan turned away, imagining Rhun was not happy.

Too bad.

A flower petal drifted to his cheek—and stung him, piercing the corner of his lip. He grabbed it, crushed it in his fingers, and threw it down.

As if angry at this assault, more of the creatures fell upon him, silver stingers penetrating any exposed skin: face, hands, neck. He battered at them, seeing Erin under attack, too. He headed toward her through the cloud, doing his best to protect his eyes. While the buggers might not be toxic to humans, he and Erin could still be blinded by their stingers.

Erin huddled by the large antique desk and swatted at the air around her with a binder from the tabletop. He heard a litany of curses, saw spots of blood dribbling from countless punctures on her arms and face.

She slapped at her throat, and a butterfly crumpled to the ground.

Taking a clue from her example, he swept off his long jacket and batted at the air. He joined her, using the coat like a matador against a thousand angry bulls. Whipping it in a fury, he cleared some breathing room around her.

Still, she pulled the collar of her own jacket up over her head and formed a tent around her. She leaned down, scattering papers under her palms, plainly searching for any clue to the whereabouts of the others.

He peeked over her shoulder. The papers looked to be written in a hundred languages, many of them ancient. "Just grab everything!" he suggested. "We can sort through it later!"

"Not until we neutralize the threat here. If anything escapes with us, they'll go straight for Rhun, Bernard, or Christian."

Jordan knew she was right. The buggers seemed tuned to attack *strigoi*. A moment ago, Erin had not set off this trap by entering. Even his rifle blast had failed to wake them up. It was only when Rhun crossed the threshold that they rose up.

"Let's see if I can't knock this load down a bit," he said. "You keep searching."

He reversed his tactic. Instead of using the coat to batter the threat away, he used its length and bulk like a huge net. He cast it out, scooping coatfuls of the fluttering horde out of the air. He forced them to the floor and stamped them under his boots.

Erin called to him as he worked. "Most of these papers have the letterhead of the same company. The Argentum Corporation."

Jordan recognized the name. "Big conglomerate!" he called back. "Does all kinds of stuff, including arms manufacture. Sounds like a business a man like Judas would get himself involved with."

He continued his steady assault. He bashed, battered, and crushed his way throughout the room until the air began to clear. Then his hunting became more focused, picking individuals out of the air with a snap of his coat.

Rhun called through the door. "How are you faring?"

"Just finishing some light housekeeping!"

Erin waved to him. "Jordan, come see this."

He joined her, brushing a trail of blood from his eyes. She pointed to a piece of Argentum company correspondence: a grayish-silver envelope with an embossed letterhead in the corner, depicting an old-fashioned anchor.

"I keep seeing these anchors all over this place," Erin said. "And remember Rhun's text from Rasputin, the one that warned him that the symbol of an anchor was connected to Judas?"

"Yeah, the guy clearly has a nautical fetish."

"It's not *nautical*. It's *Christian*." She traced the shape of the cross that made up the center of the anchor. "This is a crux dissimulata. Ancient Christians used it as a secret symbol, back when Christians were persecuted for their faith and a cross would have been too dangerous to display outright."

Jordan slapped a small brass-and-silver bee to ruin. "Must be why he chose it for the logo of his Argentum Corporation."

"He still loves Christ," Erin said. "And with this immortality, he can never escape his guilt. It's no wonder he is fighting so hard to bring Him back."

"But how?" Jordan asked.

She pushed the papers away. "There is nothing here but corporate financials and normal correspondence. Nothing points to his plan. But it must be here. Somewhere in this room."

"He wouldn't leave something like that out in plain sight. He would've hidden it." Jordan pointed to the desk drawers. "Search for something locked, something concealed."

With only a few stingers still in the air, Jordan searched the walls, removing the framed paintings.

"Nothing in the drawers!" Erin called to him.

Jordan reached a gilt-edged portrait that looked old. A second glance at its subject matter revealed it was a painting of Iscariot, little changed from today, but here he was wearing a Renaissance outfit, his arm around a dark-skinned woman in an expensive-looking gown. Her fingers held a small Venetian mask.

As he tried to lift this portrait, he found it was actually *hinged* to the wall.

Jordan's smile matched the one worn by Judas in the painting.

He pulled it back to reveal the face of a modern safe with a digital lock.

"Erin!"

She glanced up, her eyes widening. "That's gotta be it!"

"Let's see if I can get this open."

"I don't think blasting it with a rifle will help this time."

Jordan rubbed the tips of his fingers and blew on them. "Just needs a little safecracking."

She looked doubtfully at him.

"Ever the skeptic, Dr. Granger." Jordan took the flashlight out of his pocket and played the beam across the numbers on the white numerical keypad, tilting it back and forth to illuminate them from different angles. "I can get this one open in six tries."

"Really? How?"

"Science," he said. "Breaking into this safe will be all about science."

She raised an eyebrow.

"Look closely at the numbers." He shone the flashlight on the digital keypad again. "Do you see the colored dust on a few of the keys?"

She leaned forward. "What is it?"

He held up his free hand, which was coated with the same glittering flakes. "Guy has a hobby he dotes on. Likely tinkers and handles his creations often. Forgets to wash his hands when he is in a hurry."

"Makes sense," Erin said.

"The guy is full of himself, grown confident in his security. Punches the same numbers over and over. But he's also plainly paranoid. I doubt he lets his maid clean his hidden safe."

Jordan pointed to the number seven. "That button has got the most dust on it, so I'm betting it's the first number."

"And the other three?"

"If you look close enough, you can see dust on the numbers nine, three, and five."

She bent to look. He liked having her close, and he liked looking intelligent for a change, too.

"So." Here he needed a bit of good fortune. "If there are no repeated numbers and the code is four digits long, starting with the number seven, that leaves me only six possible variations."

"Clever," Erin said.

He tapped his head with a finger. "Logic."

And hopefully *luck*.

He tapped out the various combinations, starting with 7935. Nope. On his third attempt, the light on the front of the safe blinked from red to green.

He stepped back and let Erin do the honors.

She grabbed the handle, turned it, and swung the door open.

Jordan stared over her shoulder. "More paper."

A stack filled the space, held down by a blocky glass paperweight.

Erin picked it up, lifting the block toward his flashlight. Hanging in the center of the crystal was a brown leaf.

"There's writing on it," she said. "Herodian Aramaic."

"Can you translate it?"

She nodded, squinting a bit, turning the block this way and that. Finally, she sighed and spoke the words written there. " '*After His words, written in blood, are lifted from their prison of stone, the one who took Him from this world will serve in bringing Him back, sparking an era of fire and bloodshed, casting a pall over the earth and all its creatures.*' "

Erin turned her face to Jordan, her voice dry and breathless with fear. "This is where Judas came upon his purpose. He wasn't pulling this plan out of thin air. It's a prophecy."

"Why do you say that?"

"The leaf. It's plainly old, preserved to protect it. The ancient seers of the past were often known to write their predictions upon leaves."

"So what does that mean? It's destined to happen? We can't do anything about it?"

"No, it's why the seers wrote them on *leaves*. A reminder that destiny is not written on *stone*. But Judas—as guilt-ridden as he was—would surely have latched firmly upon this prophecy as his ultimate destiny."

"But we still don't know what he's planning," Jordan reminded her.

She nodded and slipped the first sheet of paper from the pile.

Jordan noted the old sheet was also stained with flakes of emeralds, purples, and crimsons, proving it was often handled, likely recently.

Erin stiffened, unable to speak.

"What is it?" he asked.

As answer, she held out the page toward him, revealing what was drawn there.

42

Tommy stopped at the dark tunnel in the cliff face, balking at entering. The soft stink of rotten eggs flowed out of the darkness like a foul breath. Behind him stretched the soft sugary sand of the beach. Overhead, the sky was dark, shining with stars and a few pale silver clouds, lit with the promise of morning.

A cool wind brushed through his hair but failed to hide the stink with the sea's salt and algae.

I don't want to go in there.

An emerald-winged moth landed on one of the boulders, winking its wings at him. Elizabeth stood at his shoulder, her eyes on other moths that flitted about in the gusts, their delicate flights disguising their danger.

One of Iscariot's henchman bent his bulk past Tommy, entered the tunnel, and clicked on a flashlight. Black volcanic walls, streaked with yellow, stretched beyond the reach of the beam.

The flat of a hand pushed into the center of his back, allowing no other recourse.

"Follow Henrik," Iscariot ordered.

Elizabeth took his hand firmly in hers. "We'll go together."

Tommy took a steadying breath, nodded, and took one step forward, then another. It was how you got through hard times: *you had to keep going.*

Behind him, Iscariot spoke to the *strigoi* who piloted the helicopter. "Ready your brethren. Have them haunt the tunnels behind us. We must not be disturbed."

With that final order, Iscariot followed, trailed by his second bodyguard. Tommy realized he had never learned this other's name, not that it would likely matter. He sensed he would never be seeing the sky again.

Once a fair distance into the narrow tunnel, Elizabeth shed her veil and gloves and pushed back the hood of her cloak. One of the moths fluttered into her hair, tangling its tiny legs for a moment, then flew away again.

She did not seem to care.

Tommy did, recognizing the unspoken threat from their captor.

To calm and distract himself, he counted the moths, observing subtle differences in them. A few were smaller, one had a long tail, another had flakes of gold mixed with the emerald.

. . . nine, ten, . . . eleven . . .

There were probably a dozen, but he couldn't find the last one to make it that even number.

Elizabeth ran her fingertips along the wall, her eyes studying the side passages that crisscrossed their path and the blind caves that opened up every now and again. It was a maze down here. Tommy had read the myth of Theseus in school, of his struggle against the Minotaur in the labyrinth of Crete.

What monsters are down here?

Elizabeth must have been thinking of another story. She glanced back to Iscariot. "In Virgil's *The Aeneid,* the hero Aeneas comes to Cumae, speaks to the sibyl there, and she guides him to the land of the dead. The path we take now is very much how it's described in that book."

Iscariot waved his arm around as if to encompass the entire volcanic hill. "He also states there are a hundred paths to that pit, which considering this pocked mountain and its wormed-out holes, is likely true."

She shrugged, changing her tone as if she were quoting a poem. "*'Easy is the descent to hell; all night long, all day, the doors of dark Hades stand open; but to retrace the path; to come out again to the sweet air of Heaven—there is the task, there is the burden.'*"

Iscariot clapped his hands once. "Truly you are the Woman of Learning."

Despite his praise, worry clouded her silver eyes. A bright green-gray moth landed in her black hair again, and Tommy reached up to take it off.

"No," she warned. "Leave it be."

He drew his hand back.

As they continued, going ever deeper, the branching of the tunnels slowed until they reached a long steep passageway so foul with sulfur, Tommy had to cover his mouth and breathe through his sleeve. The temperature also grew warmer, the walls damp. Tommy heard the echoing rush of water.

Finally the passage bottomed out, reaching a wide underground river. It bubbled and steamed, a geothermal hot spring. Tommy's eyes stung from the sulfur; his cheeks burned from the heat.

"Looks as if we've reached the river Acheron . . . or perhaps Styx . . . or its many countless names in the histories of man," Elizabeth commented. "But apparently no ferryman is needed here."

"Indeed," Iscariot said.

An arch of rock spanned the river leading to a dark cavern beyond.

Tommy looked to Elizabeth, suddenly terrified to cross. The hairs on his arms shivered, his heart pounded in his ears.

Henrik roughly grabbed his arm at the foot of the bridge, ready to drag him across if necessary.

Elizabeth slammed the big man back as if he were a gnat. "I will not have the boy mishandled."

Henrik's eyes flashed with fury, but he stayed back, getting a confirming nod from Iscariot to obey her.

Another moth landed on Elizabeth, this time on her shoulder, its wings brushing under her ear. She refused to acknowledge it, but Tommy understood the message here.

I cross, or he'll kill Elizabeth.

Swallowing back his terror, Tommy headed over the bridge, flanked on one side by Henrik, on the other by Elizabeth. He moved slowly across the steam-slick rock bridge, coughing against the sulfur, squinting from the heat. Black water, looking like oil, bubbled and popped, roiled and churned.

Elizabeth strode along at his side as if passing through a garden, her back straight, her chin high. He tried to emulate her confidence, her stiff swagger, but he failed. Once he saw the far side of the bridge, he rushed to it, happy to escape the burning river.

For a moment, he was alone, all the others behind him, even Henrik with his flashlight. Ahead, the pitch-dark room smelled oddly of flowers, the perfume cutting through the stink of the sulfur.

Curious, he headed deeper, wanting to find the source.

Henrik and the others finally caught up with him. The large man directed his light high, revealing an arched ceiling of volcanic rock, covered in heavy soot. The walls held many iron sconces, bearing fresh bundles of reeds. Someone had prepared this place.

"Light the torches," Iscariot ordered.

Henrik and his partner set about igniting the tar-soaked bundles, each setting off in opposite directions, slowly revealing more of the large cavern. Other tunnels led out from here.

Tommy remembered Iscariot's description of the hundred paths to Hell.

In the center of the room, a large black stone, slightly slanted but polished flat, sat like a black eye staring back at him. He had difficulty looking at it, sensing a *wrongness* about it.

His gaze skittered past it to the far side as the last torches were lit.

What he found there, bound to an iron ring in the wall, was a woman in a white dress. Her skin was brown and smooth, her cheekbones high. Long black hair spilled over her round bare shoulders. Torchlight glinted off a splinter of metal hung round her neck.

Unlike the black stone, Tommy's eyes couldn't look away from her. Even from across the chamber, her gaze glowed at him, drawing him closer, capturing him, like a whisper of his name spoken with all the love in the world.

Iscariot stopped him with a touch on his shoulder. He stepped past Tommy to face the woman across the gulf of the room, but the sadness in his voice made that gap sound infinite and impossible to cross.

"Arella."

6:58 A.M.

Judas stopped near the altar stone, unable to approach her closer. It had been centuries since he had last seen her in the flesh. For a moment, he considered forsaking everything and rushing to her side and begging her forgiveness.

She offered him that path now. "My love, there is yet time to stop this."

A moth fluttered before his eyes, breaking the well of her dark gaze with emerald wings. He fell back a full step. "No . . ."

"All the centuries we wasted. When we could have been together. All to serve this dark destiny."

"After Christ's return, we can spend *eternity* together."

She stared at him sadly. "Come what will, that will never be. What you do is wrong."

"How can that be? For the centuries that passed following your revelation of my purpose, I collected bits and pieces of other prophecies, to understand what I must do, how I must bring about Armageddon. I sought seers from every age, and each confirmed my destiny. Yet it wasn't until I learned of the boy, of this immortal so like me yet so different, that I recalled something *you* drew, my love. One of your earlier predictions before you fled my side. I had forgotten about it, considered it of little worth."

He turned to the First Angel. "Then came this wondrous boy."

"You see shadows I cast and call them real," she countered. "They are but one path, a ghost of possibility. No more. It is your dark actions that give them flesh, that imbue them with significance and weight."

"It is right that I do so, for even the slimmest chance to bring Christ back."

"Yet all of this you've built up in your mind's eye alone, basing so many deeds on these prophecies you stole from me. How could anything good come from such a shattering of trust?"

"In other words, an act of betrayal." He smiled, almost swayed by her earlier words, but now delivered. "For you see, I am the *Betrayer*. My first sin led to the forgiveness of *all* sins, by Christ dying on the cross. Now I will sin again to bring Him back."

She sagged along the wall, baring her restraints, clearly recognizing his resolution. "Then why have you trapped me here? Only to torment me by forcing me to watch?"

Iscariot found the strength at last to cross fully to her. He breathed in the scent of lotus, of the skin he once kissed and caressed.

He reached and touched her bare collarbone, daring such a violation with only one finger.

She leaned toward him, as if to sway him with her body where her words failed.

Instead, he slipped that finger into the loop of her gold necklace, tightened his fist around it, stirring the silver shard between her perfect breasts.

Her eyes darted to his, filling with understanding and horror. She pulled away, smashing her back flat against the wall.

"No."

He yanked hard and broke the chain. He stepped back with his prize, letting the gold slither between his fingers until he held only the silver shard.

"With this blade, I can slay angels to wake the very heavens."

She turned to Tommy, but her words were for Judas. "My love, you know nothing. You move in the dark and call it day."

Judas turned his back on her words and strode to the boy, prepared to fulfill his destiny.

At long last.

7:04 A.M.

Elizabeth watched Iscariot grab Tommy by the arm and pull him roughly toward the black stone in the room's center. She sensed a pall of evil around that black altar, so great that even the rock floor beneath it looked unable to bear its unholy weight, the ground breaking away from it in a scatter of thin cracks.

Tommy cried out, not wanting to get near it.

His plea ignited something inside her. She lunged forward, ready to rip him free.

Before she could take two steps, she heard a whispered order echo from the dark tunnels that branched out from here, hinting at another spider in this black web, someone staying hidden for now. The voice struck her as familiar, but before she could ponder it, four figures—two each from the tunnels to either side—burst before her, baring fangs.

Strigoi.

They were hulking beasts, bare chested and tattooed with blasphemies. They bore scars, with self-inflicted bits of steel in their flesh. They formed a wall between her and Tommy.

Beyond them, Iscariot dragged the boy to the black stone. Its slanted surface was polished smooth by the many bodies sacrificed upon it. A slight hollow had been worn near the bottom, as if a thousand heads had rested there, baring their throats to the roof.

Fueled by terror, Tommy ripped out of Iscariot's grasp. He knew what was to be asked of him. The boy was no fool.

"No. Don't make me do this."

Iscariot stood back and lifted his arms, the silver shard flashing in the torchlight. "I cannot force you. You must make this sacrifice of your own will."

"Then I choose not to."

Elizabeth smiled at his tenacity.

"Then let me persuade you," Iscariot said.

The remaining moths fell upon Elizabeth, on her cheek, the nape of her neck, several on her arms and shoulders.

"With a thought, they will kill her," Iscariot promised. "Her blood will boil. She will die in agony. Is that what you *choose*?"

Elizabeth suddenly realized Iscariot had not asked her to play nursemaid to the boy to keep him calm, but to win over his heart so that Iscariot could wield her like a weapon. To her horror, she realized how well she played into that trap.

Tommy's eyes met hers.

"Do not do this for me," she said coldly. "You are nothing to me, Thomas Bolar. Nothing but an amusement, something to play with before I feed."

She showed her fangs.

Tommy cringed from her words, from her teeth. Still, his eyes never turned from hers. He held her gaze for a full breath, then turned to Iscariot.

"What do you want?" Tommy asked.

Damn it, boy.

She narrowed her eyes on the wall of *strigoi* before her, calculating their young strength against her own. She weighed how long it would take the stings to kill her. Could she break Tommy free in time? Her sharp ears heard shuffling from beyond the boiling river behind her.

More *strigoi* lurked in the tunnels back there.

Tommy would never make it outside alone.

"Lie down on this table," Iscariot said. "That's all you must do. I will do the rest, and she will live. This I swear to you."

As the boy stepped forward, she called again to him. "Tommy, we may not leave this room alive, but that does not mean we must submit to the likes of him."

Iscariot laughed, from deep in his belly. "You Bathory women! If I've learned nothing, it's that your allegiances are as fickle as the wind."

"Then my blood ran true!"

Elizabeth spun to one side, her form a blur. She tore out Henrik's throat before he could glance her way. The other *strigoi* came at her, the closest grabbing her arm. She ripped his limb from its socket, tossing him aside. Two others leaped high and pounded her to the floor. She heaved against them, succeeding in pushing them back a pace, but more beasts poured from the neighboring tunnels and pinned her arms, her legs.

She struggled but knew it was futile.

She had failed—not just in not breaking Tommy free, but in not *dying*. With her death, Iscariot would have no further emotional hold on Tommy. The boy could yet refuse him.

Iscariot must have realized her ploy.

She watched a moth crawl across her cheek, then gently rise on soft wings and drift away.

He needed her alive.

7:10 A.M.

"No more!" Tommy yelled and faced Iscariot. Tears streamed down his face. "Do whatever you're going to do!"

"Climb on top," he was told. "On your back. Your head at the lower end of the slab."

Tommy crossed to the black stone, every cell in his body screaming for him to run, but he mounted the rock and twisted around to lie on his back, his neck coming to rest in a hollow at the base of the altar—and he knew it was an altar.

Below his head, a large black crack steamed with sulfur, more foul than even the river. His lungs crinkled up against it. Hot tears spilled from his cheeks. He turned his head enough to find Elizabeth.

He knew she did not understand. He had watched his mother and father die in his arms, their blood boiling from their eyes—while he lived, cured of his cancer. He could not let another die in agony in his place again. Not even to save the world.

She stared back at him, a single tear rolling from her angry eyes.

She also did not know the goodness inside her. He recognized she was a monster as surely as those that pinned her, but somewhere deep inside, something brighter still existed. Even if she didn't see it yet.

Iscariot knelt next to him and dragged a rope net over his body, weighted at the edges with heavy stones. He fastened the four corners to iron rings driven into the floor. Once done, Tommy could no longer move, and only his head remained free.

Tilted with his legs high, blood rushed down, flushing his face even hotter.

Iscariot placed a cool palm on his cheek. "Be at peace. It is a good thing you do. Your worthy sacrifice will herald Christ's return."

Tommy tried to shrug. "I'm Jewish. So why do I care? Just get it over with."

He wanted to sound brave, defiant, but his words came out a strained whisper. A flash caught his eyes as the silver shard, stolen from the woman, was lifted high. Torchlight glimmered along its sharp edge. Everything else in the room disappeared except for that small blade.

Iscariot leaned to his ear. "This may hurt and—"

He stabbed the shard into Tommy's neck before he could even brace for it. Though that was likely the goal, to spare him pain.

It failed.

Tommy screamed as fire lanced into him, radiating throughout his entire body. Blood welled down his throat, washing as hotly as fiery magma. He writhed and bucked under the netting, fierce enough to break one corner free. He twisted his head to see his blood flowing across the stone, over its edge, and dripping into the black crack below.

He wailed from a pain that refused to subside.

His vision closed around him, darkness filling the edges. He wanted that oblivion, to escape this pyre of agony. Under his back, he felt the stone tremble. The rock ground and cracked.

Distantly, Iscariot extolled in a booming voice, "The gate is opening! Just as foretold!"

The bound woman responded, her very voice beating back the edge of his pain. "There is yet time to show mercy. You can end this!"

"It is too late. By the time all his blood is cast below, no one can end it."

Tommy felt himself sinking into darkness—only to realize that *darkness* was rising to take him. A black mist roiled from the crack below, enveloping him in its dark embrace, swirling around him like a living thing. With every drop of his blood, more blackness surged upward and flowed into the world.

He stared toward the source, watching the crack below him split wider. He flashed to the chamber in Masada, to another crack splitting the earth, to other smoke rising from below.

No . . . not again . . .

Then the ground shook—same as before—jolting with great quakes, strong enough to break mountains. The boiling river surged up from its banks in a great font, splashing high and crashing back down again. During all this, a massive rumbling grew louder and louder, filling the world and bursting outward.

Tommy let it wash over him—until there was only silence and darkness.

And he was gone.

43

As Erin crossed the main salon, her stomach suddenly churned, as if she were getting seasick. She weaved on her feet, her hand slapping atop a display case to keep her balance. She turned back to Jordan as he closed the door to the private office, making sure no stray butterfly or bee sailed out with them.

His gaze met hers as the entire platform began to ominously tremble, like a herd of elephants were rampaging across the deck.

"Earthquake!" Jordan yelled, rushing toward her.

Erin turned to see Rhun and Bernard helping Christian to stand. The cardinal must have managed to revive the young Sanguinist with the freshly consecrated wine, at least enough to get him up on his feet.

A huge jolt bumped under her, tossing her a foot in the air. She landed on one knee as Jordan skidded beside her. Books fell from the shelves. Fiery sparks blew through the grate of the cast-iron hearth.

Jordan picked her up as the rig shook ever more violently.

Steel groaned through the walls. A tall, thin display cabinet toppled with a crash of glass. Jordan rushed her to the others.

"We have to get off this rig!" he yelled above the low roar.

Seemingly oblivious, Bernard's gaze remained fixed on the tall windows. Erin turned to see what so captured his attention. Off to the east, the horizon had brightened with the new day, rising in a steam of pinks and oranges. But the beauty was marred by a black cloud pushing through it, churning high and spreading outward, as if trying to eat away the day.

"A volcanic eruption," Jordan said.

Erin pictured the direction in which Iscariot had flown with Tommy. Her fingers crumpled the one sheet of paper in her hand, holding an old drawing. She had come out here to show it to Rhun and Bernard.

Were they too late?

As if punctuating this worry, a loud shake rose through the rig, throwing them to the floor. The lights went out. *Crack!* The deafening sound of stressed rock echoed up from below. The entire deck began a slow tilt.

She pictured one of the platform's concrete legs shattering at the knee.

"Move!" Jordan bellowed. "Now!"

He grabbed her arm. Rhun and Bernard slung Christian between them.

They fled out of the salon and down the central passageway. The shaking continued, throwing them against the wood-paneled walls. The darkness amplified her terror. They finally reached the exterior doors and fled into a world of swaying steel and crumbling concrete. An arm of a crane swung past overhead, unmoored and unmanned.

"The hydrofoil!" Jordan said, pointing to the stairs as they tumbled forward. "We need to get down to it! Get as far from this heap as possible."

Christian broke free from the others. "I'll . . . I'll see to it."

Even in his weakened state, he was fast, vanishing in a blur of black down the stairs. Bernard followed at his heels, while Rhun kept with Erin and Jordan.

The trio hit the staircase at a dead run, hurdling steps, sometimes tossed. Debris rained around them, crashing to the water below. Erin saw the surrounding seas had gone strangely flat, no waves, just a trembling surface like a pot about to boil. That more than anything drove her faster. She hit the next landing hard, slamming her belly against the far railing and bouncing away.

Around and around they fled as the platform above continued its slow tilt, crushing down upon the pillar on that side, compressing concrete with loud blasts of rock.

Another violent quake tossed her high, throwing her toward the rail. Her fingers scrambled to grab hold before her body heaved over the side—then Rhun's iron fingers grabbed her leather jacket and jerked her back to the steps, back to her feet.

"Thanks," she said, huddling for a breath.

Then they rushed onward again as the world crashed around them. Another pillar on the far side exploded with cracks, skittering upward.

But a new noise intruded through the chaos: the high-pitched rumble of an engine. A final turn around the pillar, and they reached the dock. Several sections of its length had been blasted away by falling debris. They hopped across the open gaps as the hydrofoil slipped backward out of its berth. The ship had not escaped unscathed: a length of catwalk had slammed across its stern deck and still rested there.

Suddenly an arm scooped around her waist and yanked her forward across the last of the dock. A length of twisted strut fell like a spear and pierced cleanly through the section of dock where she had been standing.

Rhun again.

Jordan hopscotched around the length of deadly steel to join them.

The hydrofoil backed next to the dock, allowing them to scramble aboard, ducking under the catwalk.

"Go!" Jordan screamed toward the cabin ahead.

The engines roared, thrusting the ship forward, knocking Erin back into Jordan's arms. They both looked upward as the craft fled from beneath the toppling platform. Giant steel pieces of shrapnel rained around them, but they finally escaped the deadly onslaught and made it to open water.

"Don't slow!" Jordan yelled. "Give it everything!"

Erin failed to understand his urgency, until a glance back showed the entire platform falling toward them, ready to crush them. Christian heeded Jordan's warning, racing ahead, lifting the ship up on its twin foils, skimming across the water.

She watched in horror and awe as the platform struck the sea, casting up a huge wave, sending that wall of water chasing after them. But by now their speed was such that they easily outran it. The tidal wave faded behind, sinking back into the sea.

Erin finally allowed herself to breathe, gasping, wiping a tear from one eye.

"C'mon," Jordan said. "Let's join Christian and Bernard."

She nodded, unable to speak.

They climbed into the pilothouse, saw Christian at the wheel, Bernard at his shoulder. They both faced forward, staring toward the coastline.

A black cloud filled the world ahead, rolling toward them. At its heart danced a small fountain of fire. Definitely a volcano. Already ash flakes began to fall, collecting on the glass like foul snow.

Erin knew this section of Italy's coast was a geothermic hot spot. She pictured the ruins of Pompeii and Herculaneum in the shadow of Vesuvius. But even that deadly mountain was but a small blip compared to the monster lurking under that entire region, a super-volcano called Campi Flegrei, with a caldera four miles wide. If that sleeping dragon ever blew, most of Europe would be destroyed.

A chunk of ash slipped down across the window, leaving a sooty streak.

Bernard leaned closer to the same. "It's crimson colored," he said.

Erin joined him, noting he was right. The streak was distinctly dark red.

Like blood.

It was probably just due to the color of the regional rock, known to be rich in iron and volcanic copper.

Still, Erin quoted a passage from Revelation 8: *"The first angel sounded, and there followed hail and fire mingled with blood, and they were cast upon the earth."*

Bernard glanced at her. "The start of the end of the world."

Erin nodded, quoting what followed. *"And the third part of trees was burnt up, and all green grass was burnt up."*

She pictured the caldera of Campi Flegrei. If that ignited, far more than a *third* of Europe would burn.

"Can we stop it?" Jordan asked, unwilling to give up without a fight.

"There may still be time," Bernard said. "If we can find the First Angel, perhaps we might yet right this wrong."

"But he might be anywhere," Rhun said.

"Not necessarily," Jordan countered. "If Iscariot did something to trigger this—and that's a big *if*, by the way—then he can't have gone far with the boy. The attack helicopter was headed east. It's only been ninety minutes since he shot us down."

"And Iscariot would have needed time to prepare once he reached the coast," Rhun agreed. "He likely timed it to match the rise of the new day."

Bernard pointed to the dance of lava at the heart of the ash cloud. "He must be near there, but where?"

Erin reached to the inner pocket of her jacket and removed the drawing she had stolen from the safe. She flattened it on the ship's chart table. "Look at this."

The drawing depicted two men—one older, one younger—in a sacrificial pose with an angel looking over the man's shoulder, her face concerned, and rightfully so. A stream of blood ran down the younger man's side and dripped into a black crack near the bottom of the page. A hand with four claws protruded from that crack.

"What's it mean?" Jordan asked.

Erin tapped the two men. The older of the two had dark hair, the other lighter. Otherwise, they looked fairly identical, like they could be related to each other.

She pointed to the younger man, maybe an older boy. "What if that's Tommy?"

Rhun leaned at her shoulder. "It looks as if his blood is being spilled onto the floor, into that black fissure." His dark eyes met hers. "You think he's being sacrificed by Iscariot?"

"And his blood is being used to open a door. Like your Sanguinist blood opens your hidden gates."

"And that thing with the claws coming out?" Jordan asked. "That can't be good."

7:26 A.M.

Bernard stared at the demon climbing from the pit and despaired. How could they hope to stop Armageddon if it had already begun? He turned toward the smoke and conflagration. Where to even begin?

He voiced that aloud. "If you're correct, Erin, this still does not tell us *where* the sacrifice is taking place."

"Yes, it does."

He stared harder at her.

She circled a finger across the five symbols that ringed this sacrificial tableaux: an oil lamp, a torch, a rose, a crown of thorns, and a bowl. "Five icons. I knew they weren't just decorative. Nothing in this drawing is here by chance."

He studied them, knowing she was right, nagged by the familiarity of those same symbols, but unable to place them. Then again, he was not as steeped in ancient history as Dr. Granger.

She explained, "These symbols represent five famous seers out of the distant past. Five women, five ancient *sibyls*."

Bernard gripped the edge of the table. *Of course!*

"From the Sistine Chapel," he said, awed. "Those five women are painted there."

"Why?" Jordan asked.

Bernard reached and took Erin's hand gratefully. "They are the five women who predicted the birth of Christ. They came from various times and places, but each prophesied his coming."

Erin touched each symbol, naming them aloud. "The Persian Sibyl, the Erythraean Sibyl, the Delphic Sibyl, the Libyan Sibyl . . ."

She stopped last at the symbol at the top. "The bowl always represents the Cumaean Sibyl. It is said to represent the nativity of Christ." She studied the coast. "She made her home outside Naples. And according to numerous ancient accounts—from Virgil through Dante—it is said her throne guarded the very gates of Hell."

Referring to the claw rising from below, Bernard said, "I believe he seeks to release Lucifer, the Fallen One."

"That's how he intends to trigger Armageddon," Erin said.

Ash lashed against the window like sleet as they drew ever nearer the coast. The sky above had closed off with smoke, keeping the day from showing its face here. Bernard quailed against the doom that must surely follow.

Jordan cleared his throat, his nose close to the drawing. "So if everything in this drawing is important, how come there's an angel looking over Judas's shoulder, doing nothing but looking sad?"

Bernard pulled his attention from the burning coastline back to the drawing.

"Her face," Jordan continued. "It looks a lot like the woman painted in Iscariot's office. Like they could be the same woman. In the oil portrait, Judas had his arm around her, like they were man and wife."

Bernard peered closer at the drawing with Erin. He examined the face, then a shudder of recognition swept through him, turning him cold.

How could this be . . . ?

Erin noticed his reaction. "Do you know her?"

"I met her once myself," he said softly, going back to that warren of tunnels beneath Jerusalem, to the woman shining with such grace at the edge of that dark pool. He remembered her lack of heartbeat, yet the fierce heat that flowed from her in that cold cave. "Back during the Crusades."

Erin frowned at him, plainly doubtful. "How . . . where did you meet her?"

"In Jerusalem." Bernard touched his pectoral cross. "She was guarding a secret, something buried far below the Foundation Stone of that ancient city."

"What secret?" Erin asked.

"A carving." He nodded to the sketch before them. "It was the history of Christ's life told through His miracles. The story was supposed to reveal a weapon that could destroy any and all evil. I sought it out at great cost."

Screams of the city's dying filled his ears even now.

"What happened?" Erin asked, sounding far away.

"She found me unworthy. She destroyed the most crucial part before I could see it."

"But who is she?" Jordan asked. "If she was around during the Crusades, then again during the Renaissance with Judas, she must be immortal. Does that mean she is a *strigoi*? Or someone like Judas or the boy?"

"Neither," Bernard realized aloud. He pointed to the wings drawn over her shoulders. "I believe she is an angel."

He stared at Erin, his eyes welling with tears.

And she found me unworthy.

44

Rhun stood at the pilothouse door as the hydrofoil raced toward the shore. Following Erin's advice they had plotted a course northwest of the city of Naples, aiming for a dark bay in the Tyrrhenian Sea, in the shadow of the volcanic cone that the Cumaean Sibyl made her home.

Black waves churned past their hull, and ash blasted Rhun's bare face. It did not smell of blood, only of iron and cinders and sulfur. When he wiped it from his brow, grit coated his fingertips.

The quakes had stopped, but the eruption continued, churning smoke and ash into the world, jetting sprays of fiery lava into the darkness beyond the rim of the cone. Erin had told them that this caldera lay in the center of a larger supervolcano called Campi Flegrei. She warned that if this smaller burning match set off that monstrous well of magma beneath it, much of Europe was doomed.

How much time did they have?

He raised his eyes to the sky for an answer—and found none. Sunrise was upon them, but under the cloak of the volcano's shroud, it remained a moonless night. The lights of the ship tunneled through the black snow.

Inside the cabin, Erin and Jordan covered their noses and mouths with scraps of ripped cloth, like thieves in this endless night, protecting themselves against the ash fall.

Jordan shouted and pointed his arm. "To the left, is that a helicopter parked on the beach?"

Rhun saw he was correct, slightly irked that the soldier had noted it first. With Rhun's sharper eyes, he picked out its unique shape, its markings, both a match to the aircraft that had attacked them.

"It's Iscariot's helicopter!" he confirmed for the others.

Christian turned the hydrofoil toward it, sweeping his lights across its bulk.

In return, gunfire spat at them, taking out one of their lights, chattering across the bow. Jordan and Erin ducked. Christian gunned the engines, looking as if he intended to ram the chopper as they beached.

"Hold tight!" Christian called out.

Instead, Rhun stepped free of the door, moving to the bow. He heard sand and rock grind under the fins—and the ship jerked to a sudden halt. Thrown forward, Rhun leaped high, using the momentum to fly over the bow rail and across the remaining strip of water. He landed smoothly on the soft sand near the helicopter. He spotted a shift of shadows and fell upon it. The gunman wore a pilot's leathers and bared the fangs of a *strigoi*.

Rhun slashed his *karambit* across the beast's throat, slicing with the blessed steel down to bone. The pilot fell to his knees, then his face. A pool spread across the sand as black blood attempted to boil the holiness out of the cursed body, taking his life with it.

Rhun did a fast canvass of the ash-covered beach—then waved everyone to shore.

As they clambered to him, Rhun looked from the dead body to the dark sky. With day turned to night, any manner of creature could walk free.

Jordan picked up something glittering out of the black ash. "One of Iscariot's moths." He played the beam of his flashlight across other bits of brightness that glittered under the light, like a scatter of emeralds in dirt. "The moth in my hand looks intact. I bet the gears and clockwork couldn't handle all this ash."

"Still, be careful where you step," Erin warned her companions. "They're likely still full of poisonous blood."

It was sound advice.

Christian especially searched the ground, looking wary.

Rhun joined him. "How do you feel?"

After a nervous lick of his lips, he said, "Better. A little wine, a little fresh air . . ." He waved sardonically to the dark snowfall. "Who wouldn't feel as strong as an ox?"

Rhun cast him an appraising look.

Christian straightened, going serious. "I am doing . . . okay."

Rhun certainly could not fault his handling of the ship. He had gotten them back to the coast in under twenty minutes.

Beyond Christian, Bernard searched the beach, likely looking less for evidence of Iscariot's whereabouts as for the reinforcements he had summoned while en route. The team could not expect much immediate help, only from those Sanguinists within easy reach of Naples. Rome was too far for them to get here in time.

Erin called out, her voice muffled by her mask. She and Jordan had moved closer to the cliffs. "Footprints! Over here in the sand!"

Rhun joined them, bringing Christian and Bernard.

She pointed as Jordan swept his flashlight. Even dusted with ash, the fresh tracks were plain, crisply impressed into the soft sand. She glanced up, her face streaming with sweat. The very air here burned. "Looks like they headed into that nest of boulders."

Rhun nodded and took the lead. He forced his way between the rocks until he reached the mouth of a narrow tunnel that broke into the cliff face. Despite the ash fouling the air and caking his nostrils, he smelled the breath of brimstone coming from this tunnel.

Jordan shone his light inside, revealing a long throat of black rock, streaked with yellow veins of sulfur.

"This must lead beneath the volcanic hill," Erin said. "Likely burrowing toward the ruins of Cumae and the sibyl's throne to the northeast."

And below it, the gates of Hell.

Bernard touched Christian's shoulder. "You remain here with Erin and Jordan. Await the arrival of those I've summoned. Once here, follow our path." He nicked a finger with a blade. "I'll leave blood for you to follow."

Erin stepped up. "I agree Christian should stay here, to lead the others, but I'm coming now. I know the sibyl and her local history better than anyone. You may need that knowledge in that maze below."

Jordan nodded. "What she said. I'm coming, too."

Bernard conceded, too easily. Rhun wanted to argue more stridently, but he also knew how futile it was to thwart Erin.

They headed inside, leaving Christian to guard their rear, to ready any reinforcements.

Rhun led the way, trailed by Bernard. He noticed how Jordan kept Erin safely ahead of him. Free of the rain of ash, the two had tugged off their masks, breathing easier, but their faces streamed with salt and sweat.

Rhun shifted farther ahead, needing no light. He sniffed at the air as he came to any crossroads. Through the stink of sulfur, Rhun's sharp nose picked out other scents: older sweat, a familiar perfume, a musky cologne. The distinct trail led him through the darkness as surely as any map.

The passageways twisted and turned. His shoulders scraped the sides, but he did not slow. Bernard kept to his heels or strode alongside when he could. Plainly Bernard had noted the trail ahead, too, while in turn marking their own path with drops of blood.

Rhun tuned out that crimson note, while trying his best not to listen to the frightened beat of Erin's heart. Yet, despite her fear, she kept going, unflagging in her determination and will. Jordan's heart also raced, but Rhun knew it was more in fear for her safety than his own.

Behind him, the beams of their flashlight bumped along, illuminating the way in short bursts. As they moved ever deeper, he noted tendrils of blackness snaking along the ceiling, looking like the smoky curl of living vines. The deeper they went, the thicker the tendrils grew, seeming to rise from the depths below.

He wafted a tendril to his face and coughed its foulness back out as he sniffed. It reeked of sulfur, but also of rotting flesh, of corruption, of the darkness of an ancient crypt.

He shared a worried glance with Bernard.

Then Bernard's gaze snapped forward.

Distracted, with his senses addled by the dark smoke, Rhun almost missed it. A scuff of bare feet, a whisper of cloth—then the others were upon them, blades flashing in the dark.

Strigoi.

A trap.

Rhun and Bernard met the sudden charge with silver and swiftness, their movements a synchronized blur. The two had fought alongside each other many times in their long lives. They felled the first two easily enough—but more surged from tunnels ahead, stirring the darkness with their damnation, filling it with the hiss of their ferocity.

Luckily, the tunnels were narrow, limiting how many could reach them at any one time. Instead, the pack seemed more determined to hold them back, to wear the Sanguinists down. Perhaps, for Iscariot to be victorious, it did not require killing the Sanguinists. He merely had to hold them in check, to buy himself enough time to complete his task here.

Which offered Rhun hope.

If Iscariot sent these beasts to thwart them, there must be something worth *thwarting*.

Maybe we are not too late.

Rhun gritted his teeth and fought on.

Gunfire erupted behind them. A glance back showed more *strigoi* appearing to their rear. Either they had lain in wait, or others had circled this maze to come behind them. Jordan's machine pistol tore through the first bodies. Erin had a pistol out, too, popping past the soldier's shoulder.

"Help them," Bernard said. "I can hold the front."

But for how long?

Rhun turned and added his blade to the battle in the rear, the trio working efficiently together. Erin slowed them with well-placed shots to knees and legs. Jordan strafed heads, blasting apart skulls. Rhun took out anything that got close.

They held their own, but time ticked away.

Surely that was Iscariot's goal.

Then past the mass of *strigoi*, figures in black robes swept into view, cutting through the rearguard, their silver crosses flashing in the darkness.

Sanguinist reinforcements.

Christian led them, blades in both hands. He cut a swath through the remaining *strigoi* to join them. Jordan clapped him happily on the shoulder.

More Sanguinists swept past to join Bernard.

Rhun followed.

Bernard pointed to the surrounding labyrinth of passages. "Spread out. Clear our flanks!"

Moving again, Rhun redoubled his efforts, slashing *strigoi* and forcing the party ever forward. Ahead the tunnel widened, revealing a subterranean river, a bridge, and a torchlit cavern beyond.

Rhun and Bernard drove the remaining *strigoi* over the edge of the river and into the boiling water below, where they were swept away. The Sanguinist reinforcements swelled behind them, bolstering their rear.

Erin joined Rhun, pointing through the sulfurous steam of the river. Vague shapes moved out there, but there was no mistaking the silhouette of a sacrifice.

"Hurry!"

Together, the team raced across the slick stone of the arched bridge.

As soon as Rhun's foot touched the floor on the other side, the very air changed, going as cold as a tomb in the dead of winter. Erin and Jordan's breath blew white as they gasped at the change. But far more chilling was the horrific sight that awaited them.

In the room's center, a pale shape lay pinned under ropes atop a black stone. A cloud of dark fog enveloped him completely, churning and swirling, reaching the arched roof and stretching to every tunnel, snaking out tendrils, questing for the open air.

The place reeked of doom and corruption.

The familiar gray figure of Iscariot stood limned against that dread force, a triumphant expression on his face.

Beyond the altar, a woman hung from the wall, her dark skin shining, her eyes seemingly aglow.

"It is she!" Bernard said, clutching his sleeve.

Rhun ignored the cardinal, spying the one final figure in this grim theater.

To the right, Elisabeta lay on the floor, in a pool of black blood, but little of it seemed to be her own. She struggled beneath a half dozen *strigoi*. Others were dead around her. A handful of moths lay twitching on the cold stone, their wings frosted brittle by the cold.

Her eyes found his, full of terror—but not for her own life.

"Save the boy!"

7:52 A.M.

Jordan drew closer to Erin, taking swift inventory.

In that moment of stunned incapacitation, a flurry of *strigoi* rushed from the closest tunnels to either side. Bernard took those on the left; Rhun charged to the right.

Jordan pushed Erin forward, out of those pincers.

He aimed for the only other direct threat in the room.

He had his machine pistol up and rushed the gray-suited figure. As Iscariot turned, Jordan skipped any witty repartee. He fired three fast bursts into the man's chest, clustered on his heart.

Iscariot collapsed backward onto the floor, bright red blood soaking through his jacket and white shirt, spreading across the stone.

"Owed you that, bastard," he mumbled, rubbing his own chest.

Still, he kept his weapon trained on the man. Iscariot was immortal, would likely heal, but how long would it take? It had taken the boy some time to recuperate. He hoped for the same here, but he kept watch. A trail of crimson blood ran across the black rock as if aiming for that black swirl.

The blood froze before reaching it.

Erin stepped in that direction, plainly wanting to help the boy.

He stopped her with a hand on her arm. "Hold on."

She glanced at him. "Do you think it's poisonous?"

"I think it's something *way* beyond that," he said. "Let me go first."

As he moved closer, he felt the ever-present burn in his shoulder go cooler. With every step, his legs turned leaden. It was as if whatever force roiled up from below could stanch that fire inside him—and take all his strength with it. His chest suddenly ached, drawing his fingers to where he had been shot. He looked down, expecting blood.

"Jordan?"

"I can't . . ."

He fell to his knees.

7:53 A.M.

Rhun heard the gunshots, watched Iscariot fall, incapacitated for now. Behind him, Bernard fought before the mouth of a tunnel, keeping *strigoi* bottled on that side. Rhun leaped over those holding

Elisabeta captive. While in the air, he reached down and ripped two of her assailants off her, tossing them forward into the pack coming at him.

He crushed moths under his heels as he landed, the creations strangely weakened by the inimical cold.

Then he barreled into the pack, his blade flashing.

Strigoi fell, blood pouring over rock.

Claws ripped and teeth gnashed at him, but he fought on and drove the pack back to the tunnels. Finally, they seemed to lose their will and fled into the darkness.

Taking advantage of the lull, he swung around. Elisabeta fought her four remaining captors, whirling like a trapped lioness, weeping from a hundred cuts, as did her assailants.

For the moment, it was a stalemate.

He leaped forward to break it.

45

Erin pulled Jordan back from the cold pyre of black smoke. He regained his strength enough to stand, but he still rubbed his chest. Was he exerting himself too much after his recent ordeal? She was relieved to feel his clammy hand grow warmer in hers.

A voice rose from beyond the cloud. "You can go no nearer."

It came from the woman chained to the wall. She wore a simple white dress and leather sandals, looking like she had stepped off an ancient Greek urn.

Erin circled the black cloud enough to see her face better. Unmistakably, it was the woman from the drawing, from Iscariot's oil painting, and likely the woman Bernard saw in Jerusalem. She was tied to an iron ring mounted in the stone, seemingly as much a prisoner as the boy.

But what was she?

Her musings were interrupted as Rhun hurled a *strigoi* high into the air, sending it flying across the fog above the altar. Hitting that cloud, a scream ripped from the beast's throat. The body immediately froze in a posture of agony. For a moment, Erin thought she saw smoky darkness explode from its lips and nostrils, swirling to join the blackness above Tommy. She remembered Elizabeth's drawings in her macabre research journal, how she had described the same smoky essence connected to the *strigoi*.

Then the body struck the far wall and shattered like a china plate. Aghast, Erin took a full step back.

How were they ever going to save the boy? Was the boy even alive?

As if reading her fears, the woman spoke. "I can reach him."

Erin stared at her.

She lifted her bound arms. "Free me."

Erin shared a look with Jordan.

Jordan shrugged, keeping his gun pointed at the fighting across the room. Rhun battled alongside both Bernard and Elizabeth to rid the cavern of the last of the *strigoi*.

"At this point," he said, "any enemy of Iscariot is a friend of mine."

Still, Erin hesitated, remembering the oil painting, with Iscariot's arm around her, looking lovingly upon her.

"Someone has to go in there and save the boy," Jordan reminded her.

She nodded, hurried over, and using a dagger from Jordan, she sawed at the thick rope that bound the woman's hands to the iron ring. Jordan continued to guard over her.

The woman's eyes met Erin's as she worked, shining with peace amid the bloodshed.

Erin swallowed, knowing whom she sought to free, but needing confirmation. "You are the Sibyl of Cumae."

Her chin dropped slightly in acknowledgment. "That is one of many names I've carried over the centuries. For the moment, I prefer Arella."

"And you will help the boy?" She glanced to his thin form on the stone.

"I must . . . as I helped another boy long ago."

Arella's hands finally broke free, and she brought her palms together as if in prayer, her index fingers inches from her face.

Jordan and Erin stepped back, sensing something building within this other.

A golden light suddenly washed from the sibyl's body, driving them farther back. A corona of that light brushed against Erin, warming the cold out of her bones, like the buttery warmth of a summer sun, smelling of grass and clover. Erin drank it in. Joy filled her, reminding her of the moment the Blood Gospel had transformed from a simple lead block into a tome that held the words of Christ.

She suddenly found the word to describe what she felt.

Holiness.

She was in the presence of true holiness.

Next to her, Jordan smiled, surely feeling the same. For one moment, in the midst of the battle, there was peace. She leaned against him, sharing warmth and strength and love with him.

"Is there anything we can do to help?" Erin asked.

Her grace turned fully upon Erin. "No. Neither you nor the priests can save the boy. Only I can."

The woman—Arella—drifted from the wall and headed toward the towering pyre of cold darkness. The few wisps of blackness at the edges burned away as her radiance drew closer. Other tendrils withered back into the cloud, as if fearful of her touch.

Then she pushed into the cloud itself, her radiance shining brighter, battering back the darkness that swirled around her. Her glow swept upward to either side, feathering out into the blackness, forming a familiar shape.

Erin pictured the old drawing from the safe.

Wings.

How could such a being exist on Earth?

She realized that it had been far easier for her to believe in *strigoi*, in the presence of unholy evil made flesh, than to accept the presence of good. But she could not deny what she witnessed now.

Arella stepped to the altar, to the boy's side.

The darkness closed down around her, tearing away at her brilliance.

A cry rose from the far side. "*No . . . Arella . . . no . . .*"

Iscariot rose to his feet, blood soaking through his shirt. He backed away, falling into a tunnel behind him and disappearing.

Jordan moved to chase after him, but Erin gripped his arm, wanting him close.

"He knows he's lost, but the boy may need us."

Jordan grimaced in frustration, but he nodded, keeping his gun pointed at that tunnel.

Arella knelt on the rough floor. Her wings bent and formed a protective shroud around the boy. Tommy lay on his back with a heavy net covering his body. His skin had a waxen, grayish hue, as if he had already died.

We are too late.

Erin's throat closed.

But the sibyl touched his pale face, and color bloomed there, spreading from her fingertips, promising at least hope for the boy.

Arella lifted his head from the stone, cradling his neck, exposing a bright silver shard that pierced his pale throat, blood seeping from the wound. Her other hand cast a corner of the net free. It looked as if it had already been ripped loose. Her arm slipped within and gently eased the boy's thin body out.

But the darkness was not about to let its prey escape so easily. As she gathered him up and stood, darkness coalesced into black claws that drove themselves deep into her light, ripping and shredding.

Arella gasped, falling to a knee.

The back of her dress tore, revealing black scratches across her shoulders.

Erin reached to help, but her arms fell, and she knew that there was nothing she could do.

Arella struggled back to her feet, lifting the boy in her arms. Her golden light was dimmer now, eaten away at the edges into a tattered lace. She hunched against the storm, as it grew ever fiercer about her. The cloud closed tighter, trying to stifle her glow, ripping at her like a shredding ice storm.

Arella took a halting step, then another.

She seemed to concentrate the last of her glow around the boy, leaving herself defenseless against the onslaught.

She took yet another step—then finally fell out of the darkness, onto her knees, cradling the boy in her lap. Her dress was rags, her skin mottled with black pocks and dark scratches, her black hair gone a ghostly white.

Erin rushed forward as the woman toppled to her side. She grabbed Tommy by the armpits and hauled his limp form farther away from the darkness.

Jordan scooped up Arella and did the same.

"We need to get them out of here," Erin said. "As far from this foul place as possible."

By now, the fighting had ended in the room.

Any remaining *strigoi* seemed to have fled along with Iscariot's retreat.

Rhun and Bernard joined her, but the countess pushed between them, coming swiftly to the boy's side.

"His heart," Elizabeth said, her eyes truly scared. "It weakens."

Rhun nodded, as if hearing the same.

"He cannot heal with this still in him," Elizabeth warned.

Before anyone could urge caution, the countess grasped the shard, pulled it from the boy's neck, and hurled it across the room. Blood continued to flow from Tommy's wound.

"Why isn't he healing?" Erin asked.

They turned toward the discarded blade.

From a tunnel near its resting place, a figure appeared, melting out of the darkness.

Iscariot glared at them with a cold fury.

He then gazed at the drape of Arella on the ground and quickly recovered the shard from the floor. Distracted by grief, Iscariot cut himself on the blade. It sliced into his finger, which spilled golden drops of light instead of blood.

With a cry of shock, he fell back.

Jordan fired at him, sparking rounds off the stone.

Rhun rushed forward, sweeping across the room with the speed only a Sanguinist could muster, his *karambit* flashing silver in the torchlight.

Then Iscariot was grabbed and thrown back into the tunnel.

And another came out to confront Rhun in his stead.

8:06 A.M.

Rhun drew to a sudden stop, frozen by shock and disbelief. He stared at the monk, at the familiar brown robe, tied with a rosary, his spectacled countenance looking forever boyish.

"Brother Leopold?"

Back from the dead.

Leopold lifted a sword, his face set and severe.

Rhun gaped at him. His mind tried to explain Leopold's actions, the fact that he still lived. A thousand explanations flitted through Rhun's head, but he knew each one to be false. He must face the harsh truth.

Here stood the Sanguinist traitor, the one who had been in league with Iscariot all along.

How many deaths lay at the feet of this one, someone he called friend?

Faces and names flashed through Rhun's silent heart. All those he had mourned. Others he barely knew. He pictured the train engineer and his coworker.

But one name, more than any, ignited the fury inside him.

"Nadia died because of you."

Leopold had the good graces to look pained, but he still found justification. "All wars have casualties. Better than you and I, she knew this and accepted it."

Rhun could not stomach such platitudes. "When did you begin to betray the order? How long have you been a traitor?"

"I have *always* served a higher purpose. Before I took my Sanguinist vows, before I drank my first cup of Christ's blood, I was already set on this path by the *Damnatus*. To help bring Christ back to the earth."

Rhun frowned. *How could that be? Why was Leopold not burned like other* strigoi *who sought to deceive the order by swearing false oaths?*

Rhun found his answer in the shine of devotion in the other's eyes.

Leopold had not sworn falsely when he took his vows. With all his heart, he had *believed* he was serving Christ.

"We mourned you," Rhun said. "We buried your rosary with full honor in the Sanctuary, as if you had fallen in service to Him."

"I *do* serve Him," Leopold said firmly. "If I did *not,* why does consecrated wine still bless me even now?"

Rhun faltered. *Was Leopold's devotion that absolute?*

"You must see the truth of my words," Leopold pleaded. "You can join us. He will welcome you."

Astonishment filled Rhun. "You wish me to leave the Church and join this betrayer of Christ? A man who joins forces with the *strigoi*?"

"Have you not done the same with the *strigoi*?" Leopold motioned to Elizabeth. "The heart must follow what it knows is right."

Rhun was stunned—which was what Leopold in all his cunning had wanted.

He lunged at Rhun, swiftly, savagely, leading with his sword.

Rhun pivoted at the last moment, his instincts reacting faster than his mind. Leopold's sword sliced his side, through his armor, cutting to his ribs. Reacting as heedlessly, Rhun slashed out with his *karambit*.

Leopold stumbled back and dropped his sword. He clutched his throat, blood pouring through his fingers. He fell to his knees, knocking his glasses askew. Still, his eyes remained on Rhun—shining not with anger, nor with sorrow, only devotion.

46

With a hand at her throat and tears in her eyes, Erin watched Leopold's body slump to the ground. She remembered a gentler man, the studious crinkle to his eyes, his wry self-deprecating humor. She pictured waking in the tunnels below Rome, sure she was dead, only to find him gripping her hand, using his medical skills to revive her.

The man had saved her life.

Yet his secrets had killed so many.

Suddenly the ground gave a violent quake, as if a fist had slammed into the floor beneath their feet. The black cloud around the altar writhed and churned, shredding and whipping. The gnash of rock and rumble of falling boulders echoed from all the tunnels.

"Time to move, people!" Jordan yelled.

Erin helped Elizabeth with Tommy as they fled for the bridge. Rhun led the way, while Bernard and Jordan followed with Arella slung between them. The ground continued to tremble. Ahead, a crack skittered across the arch of rock spanning the river, which splashed higher from its stone banks.

"Hurry!" Erin cried out.

They sprinted. Elizabeth quickly outdistanced her, even while burdened with the boy. She swept over the bridge, passing even Rhun who raced now at her heels. They joined the handful of Sanguinists guarding the tunnels back to the surface, meeting Christian there.

Erin ran, hitting the steamy wall of sulfurous heat, scorching after the chill of the cavern. She feared the slipperiness of the rock, but she did not slow—especially as a chunk of the bridge fell away, splashing into the boil below. More cracks skittered underfoot.

Suddenly a large quake sent her sprawling. At her fingertips, the span ahead of her fell away. She measured the impossible gap as a roil of steam and water blasted up from below.

Then Rhun came winging through it like a dark crow. He landed next to her, scooped her to her feet, then into his arms, and leaped headlong over the gap. He crashed with her on the far side, taking the impact on his shoulder and rolling her to safety.

Jordan . . .

Bernard came leaping over with the sibyl in his arms. Jordan sailed next to them. Both men landed on their feet—though Jordan had to skip several steps to keep his balance.

Behind them, the entire span cracked into pieces and crumbled into the river.

Heat and steam parched Erin's skin and burned her lungs.

"Keep going!" Bernard commanded.

As a group, they raced back through the maze. Nagging fears chased her ever upward. She felt the continuing trembles underfoot. She pictured the darkness churning below. Why wasn't it stopping?

Were they too late?

Were the gates of Hell still opening?

8:15 A.M.

Rhun rushed alongside Elisabeta as she carried Tommy in her arms, the prophesied First Angel. He remembered her calling out to him as he first entered the cold cavern.

Save the boy!

He knew from the anguish in her voice that it had not been prophecy that had fueled her need to protect the boy. She cradled Tommy against her chest, her mouth set in a worried line. The boy's heartbeat stumbled along, weak but determined, matching Elisabeta's expression. Rhun watched her every step, ready to catch her if she faltered. Blood seeped from a thousand cuts, but she seemed to draw from a well of strength far deeper than just that of a *strigoi*.

It was that of a mother resolved to save her child at any cost.

Erin and Jordan followed them, trailed by the cardinal, who carried the dark-skinned woman. He remembered the golden light spilling from her, remembering Bernard's belief that she was an angel. Still, she clearly knew Iscariot and had some relationship with him. But why would an angel seek out the Betrayer of Christ?

Why would anyone?

Rhun stared down at the blood staining his sleeve.

Leopold's blood.

So much remained unknown.

Finally, they reached the tunnel's end and escaped through the nest of boulders to the beach. The sky remained black, hiding the sun. He glanced to Elisabeta. For now she remained safe from this hidden day. But she fell to her knees with the boy in the sand. The risen sun still plainly taxed her, sapping even her great strength.

Rhun searched the sky. The smoke had spread to the horizon. Whatever Iscariot had set in motion, taking the First Angel from the temple had not stopped it.

Looking equally worried, Bernard joined them and lowered the woman to the sand. She did not open her eyes, but one arm moved feebly, brushing at her face as if to remove cobwebs.

She still lived.

Elisabeta gently placed the boy near her, resting his head on the sand, examining the wound on his throat. It continued to seep blood, though perhaps slightly less. But was that because he was healing or simply running out of life?

Elisabeta held his hand. Rhun had no doubt that she would kill anyone who tried to harm the boy. He remembered her fierce protectiveness of her own children, even while she murdered the children of others. Her loyalties were inexplicable to him.

Wind stirred her cloak and a shaft of filtered daylight fell upon her cheek. Rhun rushed toward her, but her skin did not burn. Evidently, there was enough foul ash shrouding the air to allow *strigoi* to walk under this dread sky.

He pictured the ash cloud circling the world, waking horrors long slumbering in crypts, graves, and other sunless places.

Elisabeta sensed this change, too, lifting her face to the gray sky. Even overcast with ash, it was the first daylight sky she had looked upon with her naked eyes in centuries. She examined it for a long moment before returning her attention to the wounded boy in the sand.

Bernard stepped to Tommy's other side. He shed his suit jacket and unbuttoned his bloodstained white shirt, revealing his hidden armor. He unzipped a waterproof compartment over his heart and pulled free a simple leather-bound book.

Rhun gaped at what he held.

It was the Blood Gospel.

8:21 A.M.

Spotting the Gospel in Bernard's hands, Erin knelt by the boy's head. She sensed the centuries of prophecy weighing down upon his pale brow. Ash settled into his hair, still boyishly soft. More flakes landed on his cheeks and lips. She reached and wiped them away, leaving an iron-rust smudge across his skin.

He did not move under her touch, his breathing shallow and too slow.

Christian joined her.

"What's wrong with him?" Erin asked. "In Stockholm, he recovered much more quickly. Why isn't Tommy healing now?"

"I don't know," Bathory whispered softly, glancing at her, grief shining in her eyes, catching Erin by surprise at its depth. "But I heard Iscariot say that blade he used could slay angels. Even now, I hear his young heart continuing to fade. It must be something about that knife."

The countess stroked hair back from the boy's forehead.

Bernard dropped to a knee. "Let me put the Gospel in Tommy's hands," he said. "Perhaps its grace will save him."

Bathory scowled at him. "You place your hope in another holy book, priest? Has the other served us so well?"

Still, the countess did not resist as Bernard drew the boy's hands to his chest. Even she knew any hope was better than none at all.

Bernard reverentially placed the book into his hands. As leather touched skin, the cover glowed golden for a brief breath, then went dark.

Tommy's eyelids fluttered open. "Mom . . . ?"

The countess leaned over him, a tear falling to the boy's cheek. "It's Elizabeth, my brave boy," she said. "We are free."

"Open the book, son," Bernard urged. "And save the world."

Prophecy echoed through Erin.

The trio of prophecy must bring the book to the First Angel for his blessing . . .

She stared from Rhun, to Jordan, to Bathory.

Tommy struggled to sit, to fulfill his role, too.

Bathory helped him up, letting his thin back lean against her side, treating him ever so gently.

Tommy settled the book in his lap and opened it to the first page. He leaned down weakly, struggling to read the ancient words in Greek found there.

"What does it say?" he asked hoarsely.

Erin recited the words for him. *"A great War of the Heavens looms. For the forces of goodness to prevail, a Weapon must be forged of this Gospel written in my own blood. The trio of prophecy must bring the book to the First Angel for his blessing. Only thus may they secure salvation for the world."*

As they watched, waiting, ash fell on the opened pages.

Nothing else transpired.

Tommy looked up at the roiling sky, then out to the choppy leaden sea. "What else am I supposed to do?" he asked, sounding so lost and forlorn.

"You are the First Angel," Rhun said softly. "You are destined to bless this book."

Tommy blinked ash away from his long lashes, looking doubtfully at him. He turned to the one person he plainly trusted most.

To Bathory.

The countess wiped blood from his throat, revealing the wound was still present. Worry filled her voice, grasping for any hope. "It may be so."

"I'm not an angel." Tommy scowled. "There's no such thing as angels."

Bathory grinned at him, showing the barest points of sharp teeth. "If there are monsters in the world, why not angels?"

Tommy sighed, his eyes rolling a bit—not from disdain but growing weakness. He was clearly fading again.

Bathory touched a palm to his cheek. "Whether you believe or not, what harm is it to abide their wishes, to bless this accursed book?"

Bernard gripped his shoulder. "Please, try."

Tommy gave a defeated shake of his head and lifted a palm over the open pages of the Gospel. His hand trembled with even this small effort. "I bless . . . this book."

Again they waited as ash fell, and the ground still trembled.

No miracle presented itself. No golden light, no new words.

Uneasiness rose in Erin.

They had missed something—but what?

Jordan frowned. "Maybe he needs to say some special prayer."

Christian surveyed the blasted landscape. "Or maybe it's this cursed place."

Bernard stiffened and grasped Christian's arm in thanks. "Of course! The Blood Gospel could only be transfigured above the holy bones of Peter in St. Peter's Basilica. We must take the boy to Rome. Only there must the book be blessed!"

Tommy suddenly slumped against the countess, his brief strength blowing out like a spent candle. A drop of blood rolled from his wound, still unhealed.

"He will never make it to Rome," Bathory said. "I can barely sense his heartbeat."

Rhun glanced at Erin, confirming this.

A small sigh drew Erin's attention past her shoulder, to where Arella lay in the sand. The woman had rolled to her side, but now fell again to her back, but not before her eyes glowed at Erin, full of the same sadness seen in the drawing, the same sorrow as she had looked upon Iscariot.

Erin understood that message, the one not heeded by Judas.

You are wrong.

As if the sibyl knew she was understood, her eyes finally closed, and her body went slack.

Worried, Erin shifted next to her and took her hand, finding it warm. She noted damp sand covering her fingertips. A glance to her side—where Arella had been leaning—revealed a symbol drawn in the sand.

It was a torch—hastily drawn, shaded with the ash, depicting a bundle of rushes, bound and set aflame.

Behind her, Bernard said, "We can bandage the boy here, put pressure on his wound en route. He will . . . he *must* survive the flight to Rome."

Christian pointed to a second helicopter parked on the beach. It must have been brought in by the cardinal's reinforcements. "I'll grab the first-aid kit. There should be enough fuel in that chopper to make it to Vatican City. It's no more than an hour's flight. Once in the air, I'll alert the doctors on staff to be ready for us."

Bathory scoffed. "The boy bears no natural wound. It cannot be cured through your modern medicines."

For once, Erin found herself agreeing with the countess. Even without Tommy's healing powers, the wound should have begun to clot.

She considered the symbol again.

You are all wrong.

As Christian ran for the first-aid kit, Bernard tried pouring consecrated wine onto the wound, murmuring Latin prayers. He wiped it clean with his sleeve.

Blood welled up, flowing thicker now.

Erin noted a faint golden glow, only evident because of the gloom. Perhaps it marked his special angelic essence, the miracle that sustained his life, the same miracle that possibly saved Jordan in Stockholm.

"You do not know what you are doing," Bathory said, pushing Bernard's hands off the boy. She pointed to Arella. "*She* carried that blade that cut him. She must know more about it. Wake her."

Erin tried, shaking the woman's shoulder, but she got no response.

"We must remove the boy from these cursed sands and take him to Rome," Bernard demanded as Christian returned. "There we will save him."

Erin flashed to Arella's earlier warning.

Neither you nor the priests can save the boy. Only I can.

Erin turned to Bernard and voiced aloud what she grew to believe. "You are all wrong."

As if hearing her own message spoken aloud, Arella stirred. Her arm weakly flopped to Tommy, to his bloody throat. With her touch, a drop of blood stopped welling up from his wound. It hovered there. Then those fingers slipped away, and the drop swelled and rolled down his pale skin.

"She can heal him," Erin insisted.

Bathory nodded. "It is an angelic weapon that pierced him. It will take an angel to heal him."

"How?" Bernard asked.

Erin stared at the symbol, knowing it was important. The woman wouldn't have drawn it without purpose. The sibyl *never* drew anything that was not important. She pictured the sketch found in Iscariot's safe.

"A *torch*!" Erin drew the others to her and pointed to the sand. "It was one of the five symbols depicted on the drawing, representing the five sibyls."

"What of it?" Bernard asked as Christian returned.

"She's trying to tell us where to go, how to heal him. The flaming torch is the symbol for the *Libyan Sibyl*, another of the seers who prophesied the coming of Christ. According to the mythology of that area, the waters are said to have miraculous healing properties. Some believe Christ stayed there with Mary and Joseph after fleeing Herod's slaughter."

"I know those stories," Bernard said. "But the Libyan Sibyl made her home in Siwa, an oasis in the deserts of present-day Egypt. Far across the Mediterranean. The boy will never make such a long journey and live."

Erin recognized this truth and remained silent.

Taking this as acquiescence, Bernard drew straighter. "We'll take them both to Rome." He waved to Christian. "Carry the boy. I'll take the woman."

Bathory stepped between Christian and Tommy. "You shall not."

Bernard looked upon her with fury. "If the boy cannot be healed *here,* if he can't reach Siwa, what then?" he pressed. "At least if we can get him to Rome, to St. Peter's Basilica, he may yet live long enough to bless the book and reveal its secrets."

"So you don't really care if the kid lives or dies?" Jordan asked, placing a hand on Erin's shoulder. "As long as he delivers the goods."

Bernard's angry expression answered that.

Erin joined Bathory. "This child's life is more important than any secrets."

Bernard confronted them, waving an arm to the spreading pall in the sky. "Ash still falls. What has been broken has not been set to right. We have seen the gates of Hell cracking open beneath the boy. It has slowed, but it is inevitable. What has been opened must be closed. We have until the sun sets this day to stop it."

"Why sunset?" Erin asked.

Bernard looked to the skies. "I have read the stories of this place. If the gates of Hell are cracked open during the day, they must be closed before the day's last light or nothing will close them again. This is more important than any *single* life, including the boy's. Unless we *act* now, innocents beyond counting will surely die."

"But it is that *act* that I find suspect," she said.

Jordan kept to her side. "I'm with Erin on this."

The countess stood firm. "As am I."

Rhun looked uncertainly at them, hovering between them and Bernard, who had the weight of a dozen Sanguinists at his back. "So what do you propose to do, Erin?"

"We forget about the Gospel, about prophecy, about saving the world. We turn all our strength to saving this one boy, a child who has suffered beyond measure. We owe him that much. He was afflicted with immortality because of a single act of trying to save an injured dove. He is that dove to me. I will not let him perish."

Bathory's cold hand found hers. Jordan's warm fingers grasped her other.

"Siwa's healing waters were said to be so strong that the sibyl herself used them to regenerate herself, to keep herself immortal." Erin stared down at the woman, wondering how an angel could look so ashen and frail. "We can still get them there before sunset. Heal them both."

"The boy will surely die before you reach there," Bernard argued. "Rome is only—"

Rhun cut him off. "How do you plan to cure the boy in Rome?"

"We have doctors. We have priests. But even if there were none, the most important thing is blessing the book at St. Peter's."

Rhun frowned his dissatisfaction. "What makes you certain that the book will reveal its secrets in Rome?"

"Because it must." The cardinal touched his pectoral cross. "Or all is truly lost."

Rhun's gaze moved from Erin to Bathory. "Bernard, you place too much weight on reaching St. Peter's."

"It is where the Blood Gospel was opened and returned to the world."

"But the book was taken *there* based upon the words of both Erin and Bathory Darabont. Yet, now, here we stand, with Erin again and another of the Bathory family, both telling you to take the boy to Siwa. While we do not know with certainty *who* the Woman of Learning is, in this instance it does not matter. They both command the boy be taken to Egypt."

"Not just us," Erin added, and she pointed to Arella. "Another woman does, too. An angel who, by your own word, found you unworthy in the past."

Bernard fell back a step from her words, but they only seemed to inflame his anger. "Rome is *only* an hour away," he insisted. "We go to St. Peter's and get the boy whatever care he needs. If I'm wrong, he can be prepped there for the long journey to Siwa."

"By then it may be too late," Erin said, waving to the cloaked sun.

Christian headed off, eyeing those same skies. "Whatever you decide to do, I'll get the bird warming up. You tell me where to go."

"Christian is right," Jordan said, as ash fell ever heavier around them. "This foul air may make the decision for us. If the ash gets any thicker, no one's going anywhere."

Recognizing this truth, they all headed after Christian. Rhun carried Arella, while Bathory kept possession of the boy. Moments later, the helicopter's engine sputtered coarsely on the beach, choking on ash, before rumbling loudly to life. Erin shielded her eyes from the sand and ash kicked up by the rotors.

It became impossible to talk.

Once at the helicopter, they all climbed in. Bathory passed Tommy to her, while Bernard helped Rhun settle Arella across a row of seats. Christian barely let them find their seats before gunning the stressed engines. He lifted them off the beach and turned them over the leaden waters, fleeing the maelstrom of fire and smoke.

"Where to?" Christian bellowed back.

"Rome!" Bernard called out, staring across the cabin, daring them to argue.

Bathory glanced to Erin with a glint of mischief in her eye. Erin leaned away, fearing the worst. But she was not the countess's target. Moving in a swift blur, Bathory twisted to her neighbor, wrapped one arm around his waist, and crashed open the door next to him. Neither were buckled in yet, and both Bathory and Bernard went tumbling headlong out the door, still clutched together.

Erin leaned over in her harness, as Christian tilted the helicopter, the door banging open and closed in the wind. She saw the pair splash into the water below, then come sputtering up, still fighting.

Jordan reached and caught the door and got it latched. "Guess that settles it," he said, grinning, plainly appreciating Bathory's bold move to break the stalemate.

The three of them looked at one another.

Christian stared back at them, a question shining in his green eyes.

Erin leaned forward and touched the young Sanguinist's shoulder. "Siwa," she said firmly.

Christian glanced to Rhun, to Jordan, getting confirmatory nods. He turned back around and shrugged. "Who am I to argue with the trio of prophecy?"

47

December 20, 8:38 A.M. CET
Cumae, Italy

Judas stood vigil in a crevice up the cliff face. He remained locked deep in shadow, hidden from the sharp senses of Sanguinists on the beach below, shielded by the stink of sulfur and the rumble of the earth as the gates of Hell threatened to open. He had barely made it out of the lower tunnels before the passageways collapsed around that smoky cavern, sealing it off. Now not even the Sanguinists could reach those gates in time.

There was nothing anyone could do to stop the inevitable.

Still, moments ago, he had watched the helicopter thump into the heavy pall of smoke and vanish, taking the boy and Arella with it.

His heart panged at seeing her brought so low, recognizing how much she had risked to rescue the boy. He pictured her ravaged body, her hair gone white. Still, even from this distance, he recognized her beauty as she lay in the sand.

My love . . .

From the rocks, he now spied as the cardinal and the countess waded from the leaden waves, their clothing clinging wetly to them. Both their eyes were on the skies, where the helicopter had vanished.

But where were the others going?

He had watched Bernard and Elizabeth plunge from the craft, clearly jettisoned like so much unwanted baggage.

"You have doomed us all!" Bernard's shout echoed up to him.

As answer, Elizabeth simply brushed sand from her wet clothing.

"We will go after them!" the cardinal insisted. "You have changed nothing!"

She took off a boot and dumped out sand. "Can you not admit the possibility that you were wrong, priest?"

"I will not let you judge me."

"Why not? You created me as much as Rhun. Your meddling with prophecies in the past forced Rhun and I together."

Bernard's shoulders grew rigid at Bathory's words. He angrily stalked away, rallying the other Sanguinists and retreating from the beach, putting the countess again in chains.

Judas waited a full quarter hour before climbing down, scaling the cliffs back to the beach. He had a specific goal in mind. He had witnessed Arella writing something in the sand, saw how it had affected Dr. Granger and the others. He crossed to that spot now, to where Arella had lain so still. He noted the depression in the sand where her head had rested.

He knelt and brushed his fingertips across that hollow.

Worry for her ached in him.

He saw what she had etched in the sand. He would recognize her handiwork anywhere, having spent a century recording her words and sketching what she had drawn. He looked upon what was inscribed here now, with as much of an eye to prophecy as at any other time.

A flaming torch.

He smiled, understanding.

She had drawn the others a map, telling them where to go.

Certainty calmed his mind. He knew all the symbols associated with her throughout the centuries, including this one.

She had lured them to Siwa.

He stood, thanking her, a conviction firming inside him. He knew this message had been left in the sand for *him* as much as them.

She was calling him, too.

But why?

PART V

. . . Behold, an angel of the Lord appeared to Joseph in a dream and said, "Rise, take the child and his mother, and flee to Egypt, and remain there until I tell you, for Herod is about to search for the child, to destroy him." And he rose and took the child and his mother by night and departed to Egypt and remained there until the death of Herod. This was to fulfill what the Lord had spoken by the prophet, "Out of Egypt I called my son."

—Matthew 2:13–15

48

Jordan leaned his forehead against the window of yet another helicopter. The constant drone of the engine and the endless expanse of featureless sand lulled him into a drowse. The persistent burn that etched his left shoulder, tracing fire along his tattoo, kept him from sleeping. It wasn't so much painful as an annoyance, an itch that couldn't be scratched away.

Still, he rubbed it even now, barely aware he was doing it.

But someone else was.

"Is something wrong with your shoulder?" Erin asked.

" . . . mm . . ." he said noncommittally, not wanting to bother her with such minor complaints when they had greater worries.

Like the boy draped across the seats next to Erin.

She cradled Tommy's head, one hand holding a folded gauze pad to his neck. During the five-plus hours of travel, her efforts had seemed to slow the bleeding, but she still had to regularly swap out gauze pads for fresh ones.

But at least they were almost to their destination.

After leaving the beach, Christian had returned to Naples and secured their same jet, freshly refueled, and lifted off immediately for the small city of Mersa Matruh along the Egyptian coast, where they transferred to their current helicopter, a former military craft turned civilian charter. From there, Christian piloted them south over the sands.

Jordan had seen a lot of desert in his tours in Afghanistan and Iraq, but nothing the size of this one. It was as if he had traded the battleship gray of the Mediterranean Sea for this tan Saharan Ocean. No matter how long the helicopter flew, the ground below never changed.

But worst of all, the ash cloud continued to pursue them, chasing them across the sea and out into the desert. According to reports on the radio, it was spreading in a wide swath, moving faster than weather patterns predicted. They had escaped European airspace just in time, before most of the area was locked down due to the foul air.

By now, he had little trouble believing the ash blew straight out of Hell.

But at least the boy still lived—though barely. His breathing was shallow, his heartbeat so faint Jordan could not discern a pulse, but Rhun assured him it was there.

Finally, something caught Jordan's attention out the window, near the horizon, a stripe of green.

He rubbed his gritty eyes and looked again.

Still there.

At least my eyes aren't playing tricks on me.

He stared at Rhun, at the woman sprawled next to him, covered with a navy-blue blanket. Like Tommy, she never stirred. It was upon her unspoken word that they were all out there.

Let it not be for nothing.

If the kid died, Erin would be crushed, knowing it had been upon her urging that they made this long detour to nowhere with a dying boy.

Jordan turned back to the window and watched the green stripe grow larger.

According to Erin, Siwa was an oasis, not far from the Libyan border. It had flowing water, palm trees, and a small village surrounding it. Ancient sites also dotted this emerald of the desert, including the ruins of the famous oracle's temple, and a cluster of tombs, called Gebel al Mawta, or the *Mountain of the Dead*.

Hopefully, they would not be burying their two passengers at that last site.

Not knowing what they might face in Siwa, Jordan turned to the one person who had those answers. He stared at the blanketed body of the sibyl across from him—only to discover her gazing back at him, her eyes open.

He stiffened in surprise and touched Erin's arm.

She glanced over and had the same startled reaction as him. "Arella . . . ?"

Erin looked down at Tommy, but he was still out.

Rhun freed the harness that held the woman secure and helped her to sit up.

She kept the blanket draped around her shoulders despite the warmth of the cabin, plainly still chilled, still recovering. She weaved a bit shakily as she sat.

"How do you feel?" Jordan asked, speaking loudly to be heard over the noise of the helicopter.

She turned to the window, staring at the stretch of trees sweeping toward them. "Siwa . . ."

"We're almost there," Erin said.

Arella closed her eyes, breathing deeply. "I smell it."

As they watched, color slowly returned to her, darkening her skin away from its ashen gray. Even her ghostly hair had begun to gather shadows. She was plainly reviving, like a dry plant after watering.

"She must be gaining strength as we near the oasis," Erin whispered next to him.

"It comes from the water," Arella said, opening her eyes again, some of the glow shining there once more. "It's in the very air."

Jordan glanced out. He saw palm trees rushing under them now, along with flowering bushes, courtyard gardens, and glints of blue water from fountains and man-made pools, all likely spring fed from the local aquifer.

Farther ahead, two milky-blue lakes framed the village. He spotted fishing boats and the zip of a jet ski, so incongruous here in the middle of such a large desert. Beyond the lakes, a series of taller, flat-topped mesas split the desert.

Christian circled the lake to the west and swung out toward one of the neighboring hills. Atop it sat a tumble of crumbling stone buildings, the ruins surrounding an old tower. It pointed at the sky like an accusatory finger.

It was all that was left of the oracle's temple.

Erin had instructed Christian to take them here.

Jordan looked back at Arella, who continued to stare out, a tear streaking down one perfect cheek.

"I have not seen it in so very long," she said.

Jordan didn't know how to reply.

"This was your home?" Erin asked.

The woman bowed her head in acknowledgment.

"That would make you both the Sibyl of Cumae *and* Sibyl of Libya." Erin's eyes widened with sudden insight. "Those *five* symbols, the five seers who predicted Christ's birth, they're *all* you."

Again a lowering of a chin answered her. "I made my homes in many places in the ancient world." She stared eagerly out the window again as Christian circled toward the ruins. "This was one of my favorites. Though it was, of course, once much grander. You should have seen it in the days of Alexander."

"As in Alexander the Great?" Rhun asked, surprise in his voice.

Erin looked at Arella. "History says he came here. That he consulted you."

She smiled. "He was a beautiful man, with curly brown hair, shining eyes, so young, so full of the need to find his destiny, to make it come true. Like so many others who came before . . . and after him."

She grew pensive.

Rhun imagined she was thinking of Judas.

Arella sighed. "The young Macedonian came to confirm that he was the son of Zeus, that his fate was one of conquest and glory. Which I told him was true."

Jordan knew Alexander had created one of the largest empires in the ancient world by the time he was thirty and died undefeated in battle.

"What about the other *son of a god*?" Erin said. "Legends say the holy family came here, after fleeing Herod's wrath."

She smiled softly. "Such a handsome boy."

Rhun shifted nervously. Jordan didn't blame the guy. Was she remembering Christ as a boy?

Erin studied Arella. "The Bible states that it was an angel that came to Mary and Joseph and warned them to flee to Egypt, to escape the slaughter to come. Was that also you?"

Arella smiled. The woman turned to the window, gazing out at the trees and lakes. "I brought Him here, so that He could grow up in peace and safety."

From his Sunday school classes, Jordan knew about Christ's *lost years*, how He had vanished into Egypt shortly after He was born, only to reappear at about the age of twelve, when Jesus visited a temple in Jerusalem and scolded some Pharisees.

Erin stared out the window now, too, likely picturing Christ as a boy, running those streets, splashing in that lake. "I want to know everything . . ."

Arella said, "Even I can't claim that. But I will share with you Christ's first miracle. To understand all, you must start there."

Erin's brows drew down in puzzlement. "His first miracle? That was when he turned water into wine, at the wedding in Cana?"

Arella turned sad eyes upon Erin. "That was *not* his first miracle."

2:07 P.M.

Not his first miracle?

Erin sat stunned, wanted to ask more, but that secret must wait. She had scolded Bernard for putting such secrets above the life of a boy. She refused to do the same.

"What about Tommy?" she asked, placing a palm over his cold forehead. "You said back in the cavern that you could save him. Is that true?"

"I can," Arella agreed. "But we must do it forthwith."

The sibyl turned and leaned to Christian, speaking rapidly and pointing farther to the west, past the ruins of her temple.

Christian nodded and tilted the aircraft in that direction.

Below their skids, they swept over a village of mud-brick houses that had stood for nine hundred years, some continuously occupied. Erin tried to imagine living in the same house, generation after generation. Her current university apartment was younger than she was. It certainly did not have the breathtaking accretion of history that surrounded her now.

Then again, more than anywhere, Egypt held a sense of timelessness and mystery, a land of grand kingdoms and fallen dynasties, home to a multitude of gods and heroes. She touched the piece of amber in her pocket, remembering Amy's fascination with this country's history. Like every archaeologist, Amy had wanted to someday oversee a dig in Egypt, to make her mark here.

But unfortunately for Amy, that someday would never come.

Erin kept a hold on Tommy's shoulder as the helicopter banked for a turn past the temple ruins.

Never again, she promised.

The temple swelled before her. The walls were tumbled, the roofs gone, and the rooms open to the ashen sky. Even in its current state, a hint of its original grandeur remained. Had the woman seated across from her really lived within those stone walls and determined the fate of the world with her prophecies? Had she convinced Alexander the Great that he could conquer the world? Had she met Cleopatra when she bathed in these waters? If so, what had she told the queen?

Erin had a thousand questions, but they would all have to wait.

Christian skimmed past the ruins and out toward a section of the outlying desert.

Where was Arella taking them?

The woman continued to navigate for Christian, her back to them.

Rhun gave Erin a puzzled look, just as confused, but she shrugged. They had come this far based upon the word of this angelic woman. It was too late to distrust her now.

The helicopter skirted past the occasional broken hill and flew over undulating dunes of sand. Overhead, the sky continued to grow a deeper gray as the ash cloud moved farther upon them.

Finally, the helicopter began to lower. Erin searched for any landmarks, but it appeared they were picking a random stretch of dunes on which to land. Their rotors tore ribbons of sand from the closest ridges.

The pitch of the engines changed, and the helicopter hovered in place.

But why here?

Jordan sounded no happier. "Looks like the hundreds of miles of desert we've already flown over."

Erin was tempted to agree with him, but then her eyes began to detect subtle differences. The closest ridge of dunes did not follow the pattern of the surrounding desert. She glanced out both windows to confirm it. The ridge curved completely around, to form a circle, framing a giant bowl a hundred feet across and about twenty deep.

"Looks like a crater," Erin said, pointing Jordan to the raised lip all around.

"Another volcano?" Jordan asked.

"I think it might be a meteor strike."

Erin looked to Arella for an answer, but the woman simply directed Christian down.

A moment later the skids touched the sand. The helicopter came to a rest, canted slightly at an angle inside the bowl, not far from the center. Christian kept the rotors turning, as if deliberately blowing sand from the crater.

That's one way to excavate.

Golden-tan sand whirled in the wash of the rotors, momentarily blinding them.

Then the engines finally stopped, the rotors slowing. After so many hours of constant droning, the silence rushed over her like a wave. The blown-up sand settled, pattering to the ground like a golden rain.

Arella finally faced them again, placing a hand on Christian's shoulder, thanking him. "We may go now."

Rhun cracked open the door and hopped out first. He held them back, ever wary, which Erin knew was well warranted.

"There is nothing to fear here," Arella assured them.

After Rhun confirmed this with an all-clear, the woman climbed out next, followed by Erin.

Once on her feet, Erin stretched, drawing in a deep breath, sucking the dryness deep into her lungs, smelling the rocky scent of pure desert. She let herself bask for a moment in the heat. Sand meant the luxury of time at excavations—hours spent in the sun digging to free secrets long buried from the patient grains that had concealed them.

She didn't have that luxury now.

She squinted at the sun. This late in winter, it would set at five o'clock, less than three hours from now. She recalled Bernard's warning about the gates of Hell opening, but she pushed such fears aside for now.

Tommy certainly did not have even those three hours.

She turned as Jordan's boots hit the sand next to her, helping Christian carry Tommy's body into the desert, into this strange crater.

"Where are we?" Christian asked, his eyes narrowing in the sunlight, even though it was dimmed by ash to a harsh glare.

"Don't know," Erin said softly, feeling like she should whisper for some reason.

She studied the sides that curved up around her, noting the ridgeline was not as smooth as she had thought from the air, but looked rather more jagged, forming a natural palisade at the bowl's rim. Heat radiated underfoot, more than she would have expected from this ash-covered day. It shimmered across the sand-filled crater, dancing with motes of dust.

Arella stepped away from them, heading toward the center of the crater. "Quickly with the boy" was all she said.

They followed her, mystified and confused—especially when she dropped to her knees in the sand and began digging with both hands.

Jordan cocked an eyebrow. "Maybe we should help her."

Erin agreed. As Christian stood with Tommy in his arms, she joined Jordan and Rhun, digging shoulder to shoulder, scooping out the hot sand. Thankfully, the deeper she dug, the cooler the sand became.

Arella knelt back, letting them work, clearly still weak.

A half foot down, Erin's fingertips hit something hard. A heady mix of anticipation and wonder rolled through her. What lay hidden here? How many times had it been buried and uncovered by passing sandstorms?

"Careful," she warned the others. "It might be fragile."

She slowed her movements, removing smaller amounts of sand, wishing that she had her digging tools, her whisks and brushes. Then a flake of black ash fell and stung her eye, reminding her that they needed to hurry.

Her pace picked up again, the others following her example.

"What is it?" Jordan asked, as it became clear that a layer of glass lay beneath them, swirling and rough, natural, as if something had melted the sand.

"I think it's impact glass, maybe secondary to a meteor strike." Erin tapped the surface with a fingernail, making it clink. "There's a large deposit of such meteoric glass out in the Libyan desert. The yellow scarab on King Tut's pendant was carved from a chunk of it."

"Cool," Jordan mumbled and returned to his labors.

Erin took a breath to wipe her brow with the back of her wrist. As Jordan and Rhun continued to clear the sand off the glass, she realized *who* worked so hard to free what lay buried here.

They were the prophesied trio . . . together again.

Taking heart in that, she redoubled her efforts, and in a few more minutes, they had cleared enough sand away to reveal edges to the glass—though more extended outward. Erin glanced all around.

Was the entire crater *glass*?

Had some meteor hit and melted this perfect bowl?

Was that possible?

It seemed unlikely. When the meteor hit Libya twenty-six million years ago, giving birth to Tut's pendant, it had scattered broken glass for miles around.

With no answers at hand, she returned her attention to what they had exposed. It was as if someone had taken a diamond-tipped knife and cut a perfect circle in the glass floor here, forming a disk four feet across.

It looked not unlike a plug in a bathtub.

Erin bent to examine its surface closer, cocking her head at various angles. The disk was translucent amber, darker on one side than the other, the two shades split by an S-shaped line of faint silver, forming a melted version of a yin-yang symbol.

She noted the same pattern extended outward from here.

The glass on the eastern half of the crater appeared to be dark amber, the western half distinctly lighter.

But what was this in the center?

"Looks like a giant manhole cover," Jordan said.

She saw he was right. She carefully fingered the edges of the large plate of glass, feeling enough of a ridge that someone might be able to lift it free if they were strong enough.

"But what's under it?" Erin glanced to Arella. "And how does this help Tommy?"

Arella turned her face from the skies to the north and nodded to Erin. "Place the boy near my feet," she instructed. "Then lift the stone you have uncovered."

Christian gently lowered Tommy to the sand. Then he and Rhun took to opposite sides of the disk-shaped plug. They grabbed hold with the very tips of their fingers and lifted it cleanly up with a grating of glass and sand. The plate looked to be a foot thick and must have weighed hundreds of pounds, reminding Erin yet again of the herculean strength of the Sanguinists.

Carrying it at waist height, they stepped it over a few paces and dropped it to the sand. Erin crawled forward and looked down at what was revealed. It appeared to be a shaft, with a mirror shining back at her from a few feet down, reflecting the sky and her face.

Not a mirror, she realized.

It was the still surface of dark water.

She glanced to Arella. "It's a well."

The woman smiled, stepping closer, growing visibly stronger, more radiant, her body responding to some essence from this well.

Arella knelt reverentially at the edge and plunged her arm down. When she drew it back, silvery water spilled from her hand.

It must be a natural spring, possibly once a part of the neighboring oasis.

Arella moved to Tommy and dripped water from her fingertips into the wound in his neck, then gently washed his throat. The blood cleared from his skin, stopped seeping from the cut, and even the wound's pink edges began to knit together.

Erin stared in amazement. The scientist in her needed to understand, but the woman inside simply rejoiced, sagging to her knees in relief.

Arella returned to the well, cupping her palms full of water. She lifted the double handful over Tommy.

Erin held her breath.

When the clear water splashed onto Tommy's pale face, his eyes startled open, as if suddenly woken from a nap.

He sputtered and wiped his face, looking around. "Where am I?" he croaked.

"You're safe," Erin said, moving closer, hoping that was true.

His eyes found hers, and he relaxed. "What happened?"

Erin turned to Arella. "I can't explain it, but maybe she can."

Arella stood and wiped her hands on her shift. "The answers are writ in the glass. The story is here for any to see."

"What story?" Erin asked.

The woman swept her arm to encompass the entire crater. "Here lies the untold story of Jesus Christ."

49

Rhun turned in a slow circle, gaping at the sand-washed crater, picturing its foundation of mysterious glass. Even as he'd helped Erin and Jordan clear the opening to the well of healing waters, he had felt a slight burn from the glass. He wanted to dismiss it as heat from the sands, from the baking sun, but he recognized that familiar sting, from his centuries of gripping his cross.

The glass burned with *holiness*.

He felt the same from the well . . . and from this strange angelic woman. When she brushed past him to heal Tommy, water dripped from her fingertips, splashing to the sand with such holiness that he had to take a step back, fearing it.

Christian clearly felt the same, eyeing her with a glance of wonder and awe.

Rhun trembled, sensing the sheer weight of the crater's sacred nature.

His very blood, tainted as it was, burned against the godliness of this place.

"We must clear the sand away!" Erin called.

She was already on her knees brushing away a test patch, revealing the edge of something etched higher on the glass. She waved them to spread out in a circle around the well.

Everyone set to work, even Tommy.

Only Arella hung back, showing no interest in digging. Then

again, she already knew the secrets buried here for ages. Instead, her eyes remained on the ash-tinged skies, staring to the north, almost expectantly.

"It's easier if you don't fight the sand," Erin said. "Work with its natural tendency to flow *down*."

She demonstrated, shoving sand between her legs like a dog, pushing it to the lower slope. Rhun and the others followed suit. The grains of sand burned under his palms with a heat that came from more than the sun overhead.

Rhun dug down to the glass bedrock of the crater. More of the design that Erin had revealed appeared, incised deeply into the exposed surface. He brushed grains away, recognizing an Egyptian style to the artwork. He pushed aside more sand to reveal a square panel holding a single scene.

The rest of the team unearthed similar tableaus, etched into the golden surface. They formed a ring of panels around the wellspring, telling a long-hidden story.

They all gained their feet, trying to understand.

Seemingly drawn by their confusion, Arella stepped to the panel closest to Erin. She bent down and gently brushed dust off a tiny figure. The small body faced them, but the face was in profile, typical of Egyptian design.

"Looks like hieroglyphics," Tommy mumbled.

But the tale here was not of Egyptian kings or gods. On the glass, a boy with curly hair wandered up a stylized dune with a pool of water waiting on the far side.

But it was not *any* boy.

"Is that Christ as a child?" Erin asked.

Arella lifted her face to them. "This tells how a young boy went alone into the desert to find a hidden spring. He was not yet eleven years old, and he played among the sands, among the pools, as boys do."

Rhun's blood stirred at the thought, of Jesus as a boy, playing in the desert like any other innocent child.

Arella stepped to the next panel, drawing them with her. Here the curly-headed boy reached the pool. A bird rested on the opposite bank, with etched lines radiating out from its body.

Erin studied the drawing, a crease pinching her brow. "What happened?"

"You are the Woman of Learning," Arella said. "You must tell me."

Erin dropped to a knee and traced the lines in the panel, picking out further details. "The boy is carrying a sling in his right hand, stones in his left. So he was hunting . . . or maybe playing. Acting out David's fight with Goliath."

Arella smiled, radiant with peace. "Just so. But there was no *Goliath* here in the desert. Just a small white *dove* with brilliant green eyes."

Tommy let out a gasp, staring over at the woman. "I saw a dove like that in Masada . . . with a broken wing."

Her smile wilted into sadness. "As did another long before you."

"You're talking about Judas . . ." Tommy dropped next to Erin, taking a closer look at the bird. "He said he saw one, too. When he was a boy. The morning he met Jesus."

Erin glanced at Tommy, then Arella. "The dove has always been the symbol of the Holy Spirit for the Church."

Rhun struggled to understand how this one bird could possibly bind the three boys together. And more important, *why?*

Arella simply turned away, her face impassive, moving to the next panel, making them follow.

On this square of glass, a stone flew from the boy's sling and struck the bird, leaving one wing clearly broken.

"He hit the bird," Erin said, sounding shocked.

"He had meant only to strike near it, to frighten it. But intentions are not enough."

"What does that mean?" asked Tommy.

Erin explained. "Just because you want something to happen a certain way doesn't necessarily mean that it does."

Rhun heard the grief in the beat of Tommy's heart. The boy had already learned that lesson well.

As did I.

The next panel told a grimmer end to this childish play. Here the curly-headed boy held the dove in his palms, its neck hanging limply.

"The stone did more than break its wing," Erin said. "It killed it."

"How he wished he could take back his action," Arella said.

Rhun understood that sentiment, too, picturing Elisabeta's face in sunshine.

Tommy turned to Arella, one eye narrowed. "How do you know what Jesus did, what he thought?"

"I could say that it is because I am old and wise, or that I am a prophetess. But I know these things because the child *told* them to me. He came rushing back from the desert, covered in sand and soot, and this was His story."

Erin turned wide eyes upon the woman. "So you did more than lead the holy family to Siwa. You stayed here, looking after them."

Arella bowed her head.

Christian crossed himself. Even Rhun's hand went unbidden to the cross around his neck. This woman had known Christ, had shared His early triumphs and sorrows. She was far holier than Rhun could ever hope to be.

Arella waved her arm around the crater. "Jesus stood then where we stand now."

Rhun pictured the well and the pool it must have once held. He imagined the bird and the boy along its banks. But what happened after that?

Arella moved along the ring of panels. The next revealed the boy casting his arms high. Rays, inscribed into the glass, shot upward from his palms. And amid those beams, the dove flew high, wings straight out.

"He healed it," Erin said.

"No," Arella said. "He restored it to life."

"His *first* miracle," Rhun breathed.

"It was." She did not sound exulted by this act. "But the light of this miracle caught the dark eyes of another, someone who had been searching for him since the moment the angel came to Mary with his joyous message."

"King Herod?" Jordan asked.

"No, a far greater enemy than Herod could ever be."

"So not a man, I'm guessing?" Erin said.

Arella drew them to the next panel, where the boy faced a figure of smoke with eyes of fire. "It was indeed no *man*, but rather an implacable enemy, one who ambushed the boy not because of his hatred of the Christ child, but because he sought always to undo His father."

"You're talking about Lucifer," Erin said, her voice hushed by dread.

Rhun stared at the glass, at the dark angel challenging the young Christ child—as Satan would do once again, when he would tempt Christ in the desert, when the Savior was a man.

"The Father of Lies came here, ready to do battle," Arella explained. "But someone came to the boy's defense."

She stepped along the ring of art to reveal the boy now enfolded in the wings of an angel, just as the sibyl had enfolded Tommy that very morning.

"Another angel came to help him." Erin turned to Arella. "Was it you?"

The other's face softened. "Would that it had been, but it was not."

Rhun understood the regret in her voice. What a privilege it would have been to have saved Christ.

"Who was it then?" Erin asked.

Arella nodded to the panel. It was still partially obscured by drifting sand. Rhun helped Erin clear it, the holiness burning his palms.

Erin pinched away a few final grains, noticing that it wasn't only wings that guarded over the boy, but a sword, clutched in the hand of the angel.

Erin looked up at Arella. "The archangel Michael. The angel who fought Lucifer during the war in Heaven. The only one to ever wound Lucifer, striking him in the side with a *sword.*"

Arella took a deep breath. "Michael was always Heaven's first and best sword, and so it was this time. He came down and shielded the boy from his former adversary."

"What happened?" Jordan asked.

Arella bowed her head, as if unwilling to say. Rhun listened to the whisper of wind against sand, to the humans' heartbeats. Sounds as eternal as the sibyl herself.

When he was certain that she would speak no more, he stepped by himself to the next sun-warmed panel. It depicted an explosion emanating from the boy, the lines shattering out from his thin form, stripping anything else off the panel.

Rhun lifted his face and swept his gaze around the crater. He tried to imagine a blast fierce enough to melt sand to glass. What could survive that? He pictured the angel's wings shielding the mortal boy from the backlash.

But what of Christ's defender?

Rhun turned to Arella. "How could Michael withstand such a miraculous blast from the child?"

"He could not." She sighed softly, turning her back on the ring of art. "Michael was rent asunder."

Rent asunder?

"All that remained of him was his sword, left abandoned here in the crater."

Rhun reached the last panel. It showed only a chipped sword embedded point down in the crater. He scanned the arc of this story, trying to comprehend it fully.

Christ's merciful act of restoring the life of a simple dove had resulted in the very destruction of an angel. How had the boy been able to forgive himself? Had it haunted him?

Rhun found himself on his knees before this last panel, covering his face. He had destroyed Elisabeta, a mere woman, and it still plagued him across the centuries. He was responsible for destroying her life and all those lives that followed in her bloody wake. Yet, in this moment, his hands did not hide his grief and shame, but his *relief,* recognizing the small measure of comfort offered by this tale.

Thank you, Lord.

Simply knowing that Christ himself could make a mistake lightened his own burden. This realization did not forgive Rhun's sins, but it made them easier to carry.

Erin spoke up. "What became of Michael's sword?"

"The boy came to me afterward, carrying a splinter of that sword in his hands."

Arella touched her chest.

"That was the shard that you wore," Erin said. "The one used to stab Tommy."

She looked apologetically upon the boy. "It was."

A piece of that angelic sword.

"Where is the rest of it?" Jordan asked, ever the warrior.

Arella's serene voice grew shaky, as if the memory troubled her. "The boy told me that he had sinned when he killed the dove . . . and sinned again when he brought it back. That he was not ready for such responsibility of miracles."

"So you're saying Christ's first miracle was a sin?" Jordan asked.

"He thought it was. But then again, in many ways, he was simply a scared, guilt-ridden boy. The truth is not for me to judge."

Erin urged her to continue. "What happened after that?"

"He told me the rest of his story." She waved an arm. "Then I calmed the boy and put him to bed, and I searched for the truth behind his words. I found this crater, the sword in its smoking center. Searching farther out, I discovered Lucifer's footsteps to the south, stained by drops of his black blood."

Rhun looked to the south. Now brought to his attention, he discovered a taint cutting through the holiness from that direction, faint but present.

Were those drops still out there?

"But of Michael," Arella continued, "I found no trace."

"And his sword?"

"It remains hidden," she said. "Until the First Angel returns to Earth."

"But isn't that me?" Tommy asked.

Arella's dark eyes lingered on Tommy for a silent moment, then she spoke. "You carry the best of him within you, but you are *not* the First Angel."

"I don't understand," Tommy said.

Erin glanced at Rhun.

None of them did.

No wonder the boy could not bless the book.

Bitter disappointment coursed through Rhun. All the deaths to bring Tommy here had been in vain. So many had suffered and bled and died in pursuit of the wrong angel. And with the gates of Hell continuing to open, the world's doom was now certain.

They had failed.

"Helicopter," Christian said, stiffening in warning next to him.

Arella turned her eyes to the north, where she had been gazing frequently, as if she had expected as much. "So they all come at last. To see if what was once broken can be mended."

"And what if it can't?" Erin asked. She noted the sun sitting not far from the horizon. Sunset was little more than an hour away.

Rhun dreaded the answer.

"If it cannot"—Arella brushed her hands across her soiled white dress—"then the reign of man on Earth is over."

50

If I only had their ears . . .

Jordan cocked his head, trying to discern any sign of a helicopter's approach, but all he heard was the swish of wind across sand. He tried his eyes, but he found only a featureless tan horizon, sand dunes spreading in all directions, and a few flat-topped hills in the distance. Above him, the sky had turned a dark gray, the sun a wan brightness through the murk, sitting low this time in winter.

Jordan sized up their team's ability to resist an attack—in case it was an assault force winging their way.

Who am I kidding? he thought. *Of course it's an attack.*

His team certainly had no cover out here in the open, and the two Sanguinists were their best defense—and offense, for that matter.

But how many were coming?

If it was Iscariot, the bastard had boundless resources: men, *strigoi*, even the monstrous *blasphemare*.

He turned to Christian. "How about flying to someplace more defensible?"

"The bird is almost out of gas, but even if it weren't, it's not fast enough to outrun the machine that approaches."

Jordan pictured the hellfire missiles shot at them.

"I see," he said with a sigh.

He swung his machine pistol up from his shoulder. He had

little ammunition left. Erin checked her pistol and shrugged. Same boat as him.

Jordan gave her what he hoped was a reassuring grin.

From the expression on her face, he failed.

Then he heard a distant *whump-whump*. His eyes picked out a dark mote in the glare off the sands. A small commercial helicopter swept toward them, coming in low and fast. It could hold at best five or six enemies. And it certainly had no missiles.

That was at least a small blessing.

The pilot seemed to be pushing the craft beyond its limits. White smoke trailed behind it. Jordan widened his stance and lifted his pistol, aiming for the cockpit. If he could take out the pilot, maybe the chopper would crash and solve all his problems.

As the helicopter sped closer, Jordan sighted on the right side of the bubble-shaped front, where the pilot should be seated. He moved his finger to the trigger.

"Wait!" Christian pushed his gun barrel down.

Jordan backed a step. "Why?"

"It's Bernard," Rhun answered. "In front, next to the pilot."

Okay, now I want their eyes, too.

Jordan wouldn't have recognized his own mother at that distance. "Is that good news or bad news?" he asked.

"He's not likely to shoot us, if that's what you're asking," Christian said. "But I don't think he's going to be happy with us either."

"So mostly good news, then."

The helicopter aimed straight for them and made a rough landing at the crater's rim, teetering at the edge, smoke boiling out of the back of the engine as it coughed to a stop.

Bernard hopped out, accompanied by a massive pilot, a true beast of a man in a flight suit. The latter ripped off his helmet, revealing a shock of dark red hair. From the cabin behind them, two women joined them. The first out had her long gray hair tied in an efficient braid, wearing Sanguinist armor. The second wore jeans and a silver shirt, covered by a long cloak. That cloak billowed into wings as the woman broke away from the others. Jordan noted the flash of chains binding her wrists.

Bathory.

She came scary quick, swooping down the slope, half skidding on her backside, showing little concern about the indignity of her approach. Her face was a mask of concern, her eyes fixed to one member of their group.

"Elizabeth!" Tommy ran up to meet her and hugged her hard.

She tolerated it for a moment—then roughly pushed his chin up, examining his neck.

"You look well," she said, but her terseness belied her true feelings.

Jordan leaned to Erin. "I don't get what the boy sees in her."

Bernard reached them, eyeing Tommy, too. "You were able to heal them both," he said gruffly, glancing at Arella. "Very good."

The two other Sanguinists flanked behind him, backing him up, both stone-faced.

Bernard pointed to the large man. He was even larger up close, a true tank of a man, with a barrel chest and thick arms covered in mats of curly red hair.

"This is Agmundr."

The newcomer thumped a meaty fist against his chest and flashed a grin at Christian. He lifted his other arm proudly toward the smoking aircraft.

Christian sighed and shook his head. "So it looks like you trashed another helicopter. I thought I taught you better, Agmundr. It's not a Viking warship. It's a finely tuned piece of machinery."

"It vexed me." Agmundr's voice rumbled out in a deep-throated Nordic accent. "Too slow."

"Everything vexes you," Christian scolded, but they grasped each other's forearm in a warm shake, earning Christian a slap on the back that almost dropped him to his knees. Jordan liked this Agmundr.

Bernard indicated the other Sanguinist. "And this is Wingu."

The woman was black and stood taller than Jordan. Up close now, he saw her gray braid was decorated with feathers and wound by a colorful bead tie. Her face was stern, pocked with tribal scarring, small dots across her cheeks.

She gave them a simple nod, but her dark eyes took in everything.

"We have little time for pleasantries," Bernard said, scanning the skies behind him. "We must bring the boy to the book. If he can be healed here, perhaps he can bless it here."

"It *is* a holy site," Erin said. "Possibly holier than St. Peter's."

Bernard frowned at the crater.

"This is where Christ performed his first miracle," Erin explained. "When he was a child."

Wingu spoke in a deep whisper, "I can sense great holiness here."

Bernard slowly nodded, clearly feeling something, too, but he straightened and motioned to Tommy. "Then let us see if the book can be blessed upon this ground."

Bathory let Tommy join them, but she looked reluctant. Not that she could do anything about it. Though she could walk under this ash-shrouded sky, she was clearly drained by the sun overhead, or maybe it was the holiness underfoot. Either way, she must know she could not resist the Sanguinists gathered here, on holy ground that gave them strength.

Bathory studied the pictures as she stepped across the ribbon of art. Her interest finally drew Bernard's attention to the same. He did a double take, then moved closer himself, turning in a circle, his gaze sweeping from panel to panel, as if he were speed-reading.

He turned to Arella. "This is the story you destroyed in Jerusalem." He strode to the last panel, bending a knee to touch the sword depicted there. His voice was full of anguish. "Why did you keep this from me?"

"The world was not ready," she explained simply.

"Who are you to judge what the world is ready for?" Bernard stood, moving toward Arella with a hand on the hilt of his own sword.

Jordan touched his rifle.

Rhun blocked Bernard. "Stand down, old friend. Leave the past to the past. We must now face the present and the future."

"If we could've possessed such a weapon . . ." Bernard shook his head, as distraught as Jordan had ever seen him. "Imagine the suffering we could have spared the world."

"And all you would've wreaked," Arella said. "I walked the mosque after you left Jerusalem. I saw what your forces did in the name of God. You were not ready. The world was not ready."

Rhun touched his pectoral cross. "We have no time for this," he reminded them. "The sun will be setting in another hour."

His words seemed to finally break through Bernard's anger and anguish. "You are right." He reached to his armor and removed the

Blood Gospel again and held it out. "Please, my child. Before it's too late. You must bless this book."

Looking worried, Tommy took it. The book looked huge in his small hands. "This didn't work last time. And remember, I'm not the First Angel."

Bernard gave them a baffled look. It seemed the cardinal was suffering one long day of surprises, most of them bad. Jordan knew how that felt. "What does he mean?"

Erin ignored him. "Try anyway," she urged the boy. "You can't do any harm."

"Okay," Tommy said doubtfully. He opened the book and lifted his palm over the pages. "I, Thomas Bolar, bless this book."

Everyone leaned forward, as if expecting a miracle.

Again nothing.

No golden light, no new words.

It seemed this blasted place had worn out its potential for miracles.

4:04 P.M.

"As Tommy said," Erin offered, sensing the defeat among the Sanguinists, "he's not the First Angel."

"Then who is?" Bernard asked.

Erin knew she was missing something, but she felt as if she were struggling with a jigsaw puzzle in the dark, shifting pieces blindly. "Arella said Tommy carries the best of the First Angel *inside* him. So I think he's still key to this puzzle."

Rhun stood a little straighter upon hearing this. She imagined he had been thinking of all the lives spent to bring Tommy here.

They can't have died in vain.

Still, she let that go. It was the Sanguinists' job to wallow in sin and redemption. She had a real problem that needed solving, and she could not let herself be distracted.

"If the First Angel is inside Tommy," Jordan said, "how do we get him out?"

"Maybe he has to be cut out," Bernard said.

Erin scowled at him. "I think we'll save that as a last resort." She stared at Tommy. "Maybe an exorcism could release the angel."

Tommy gulped, looking no happier about her suggestion than Bernard's.

Rhun's shoulders tightened. "You do not exorcise angels, Erin. You exorcise demons."

"Maybe so. But maybe not."

They were all in new territory here.

Erin looked to Arella. "And you cannot help us?"

"You have all the answers that you need."

Erin frowned, beginning to understand the ancients' frustration with their oracles. Sometimes they could be downright obtuse. But Erin knew the sibyl was telling her the truth. Somewhere inside Erin was the answer. As the Woman of Learning, it was up to her to puzzle it out from here. She also had to trust that Arella's silence served a purpose, and the sibyl wasn't playing coy just to frustrate them.

Did that mean something, too?

"Maybe we need to take Tommy to Rome after all," Jordan said, "now that he's better."

"No," Erin said. "Whatever is to come, it must happen in this place."

She turned in a slow circle, knowing the answer lay somewhere in the sandy golden crater. Her eyes went from the panels to the uneven glass edges that looked like splashes of water frozen into ice along the crater's rim.

"Are you sure it must happen here?" Jordan pressed.

Plainly he was seeking any excuse to escape this desert and get her somewhere safe. She appreciated that sentiment, but with the gates of Hell relentlessly opening, nowhere on Earth would be safe for much longer.

Support for her position came from the most unlikely spot.

Agmundr grunted. "The woman is right. We must stay here."

"Why?" Erin turned to him. "What do you know?"

Agmundr pointed to the north. "Nothing mystical. That Chinook helicopter that I thought was following us . . ." He glanced at Bernard. "I fear we failed to outrun it after all."

Erin looked at the smoking chopper. It looked like a horse that had been ridden into the ground.

Agmundr cocked his head. "From the sounds of its engines, it'll be here shortly."

Rhun and the others clearly tried to listen for it, but their blank faces told her that the Viking must have sharper hearing.

"Are you certain?" Bernard asked.

Agmundr lifted a heavy eyebrow, plainly wondering how the cardinal could doubt him.

Jordan grimaced, and Erin put her hand on his arm.

"Nothing like a little more pressure," he said.

"I work best under pressure."

Of course, maybe not this much pressure.

4:08 P.M.

Rhun envied Erin and Jordan, appreciating how they found comfort in each other, how a simple touch could slow a troubled heart.

He glanced at Elisabeta, who pulled a protective arm around Tommy after Wingu undid her chains. In the battle to come, they would need every resource. Rhun sensed Elisabeta would do everything to keep the boy from harm.

Her gaze met his. For once, he read no animosity, only concern for the boy under her arm. How different their fates might have been if he had met her as a simple man, instead of a tainted *strigoi*. Then again, perhaps it would have been best if he had never met her at all.

"How many soldiers can a Chinook carry?" Christian asked, drawing Rhun back to the moment.

"It's a troop carrier," Jordan answered. "Fifty or so. More if you pack 'em in tight."

Fifty?

Rhun scanned the dark sky. He finally spotted the olive-green bee against the gray sky. It was indeed a large craft with rotors front and back and a long cabin stretched between. Its engine pulsed with strength and menace.

Rhun considered their small group. The Sanguinists here were all seasoned warriors, but they numbered too few.

Jordan tracked the aircraft with his weapon, but he didn't fire. "Armored," the man mumbled as the craft flew closer. "Figures."

The massive helicopter circled the crater from a distance away, sizing them up, taking account of the situation. Then it slowly settled to the ground, a good hundred yards beyond the crater rim.

It kicked up a giant cloud of sand, obscuring its form. But Rhun made out a ramp lowering from the rear of the helicopter. Shadows tromped down it. He counted two score. So less than fifty. But they looked strong, fit, and fierce, some in leather armor, others in uniforms of different armies, and a few in simple jeans and T-shirts. They were clearly no disciplined fighting force, but they did not need to be.

He listened for heartbeats from them—but found none.

All *strigoi*.

Rhun stepped forward, shielding Erin and Jordan behind him. He had led the pair to this moment—back inside the mountain of Masada, when he had revealed his nature to them. He had set them on this bloody path, and he could do no less than give his life to protect them now. But he feared that it would not be enough.

Then again, he was not alone this day.

Christian drew to one side of him, Bernard on the other, and flanking them all were Agmundr and Wingu. Elisabeta hung back with Tommy, crouching from the threat, showing sharp teeth.

Upon some silent signal, the entire pack of *strigoi* began to lope across the sand at a speed that no human could ever match, racing under this dread gray sky.

Erin's heart skipped faster, but she held her ground. Jordan stood calm next to her, his bravery evident with every strong beat of his heart.

Rhun drew his blade and waited.

He picked out his first target: the biggest warrior, a tall man in the middle. Christian followed his gaze, nodded, and picked another for himself. Rhun watched the others choose their targets.

With discipline and training, the Sanguinists could break the first wave of attackers. Additionally, his group had the advantage of fighting on holy ground.

It might weaken the others enough.

It might.

Then another hatch dropped from the flank of the helicopter and dark beasts poured out of the shadows and into the grim light.

Rhun's fragile hope faded.

Blasphemare.

He spotted gray jackals with long noses and large ears, howling as they ran, their cries piercing the day. Behind them came a pride of black-coated lions flowing with a sinuous grace, like oil across the sand.

Each was twisted into a fearsome and monstrous incarnation of its natural self, born of black blood and cruelty.

He tested their heartbeats, finding them slow and deep, attesting to their age and strength. Even without the *strigoi*, Rhun doubted that his forces would stand against these creatures for long—if at all.

Rhun swallowed once and whispered a quick prayer.

They were doomed.

As had been foretold the day he was turned, he would die fighting.

But Erin deserved a better fate.

4:31 P.M.

It had to be blasphemare, *too.*

Jordan groaned. He gripped his machine pistol more firmly, knowing it was little better than a popgun against these beasts.

The countess drew Tommy back behind her. "Don't paint the devil on the wall," she told him.

What does that mean?

Tommy was equally baffled and voiced it aloud. "Huh?"

The boy looked at the menagerie hauling ass toward them. It sure looked like the devil was all around them. And this was no painting, but a slavering, howling horde in all its cinematic glory.

"It means . . . *have hope*," she explained.

It was odd to hear the countess talking of hope when Jordan himself couldn't seem to muster more than a scrap of it. Still, it was nice of her to try to comfort the kid.

The *strigoi* horde reached the crater's rim first and rather than flooding over the edge, they parted and swept outward, encircling the bowl, trapping them completely. Or perhaps they also sensed the holiness of this sand-and-glass valley.

The countess hissed low in her throat, pulling Tommy farther behind her. The Sanguinists moved to match the *strigoi* maneuver, ringing everyone in a protective circle.

Arella spoke near Jordan's ear, making him jump, coming upon him so quietly.

"The countess speaks wisdom," Arella whispered. "All can yet be won."

Before Jordan could ask her what that meant, Arella grabbed Tommy from behind Bathory and yanked him toward the open mouth of the well—and pushed him into it. He cried out as he splashed clumsily into the water.

Bathory was upon her in a flash, knocking her away. But a splash from the well washed across her boots. She cried out and fell back, as if it had been molten lava.

Arella returned to the well's edge as Tommy floundered below.

"Beware," she warned. "Only those imbued by angels can touch these waters. All others will be destroyed. Even humans."

With those dire words, she dove into the water, catching Tommy's arm and dragging him below.

The countess hung back, looking stricken.

No wonder the well had been so firmly sealed and left to the sand and ages.

"At least the boy is safe from immediate harm," Rhun consoled her.

Yeah, but what about us?

Jordan widened his shooting stance. He stared up at the horde gathered around them. *Strigoi* hissed and drew long curved swords. *Blasphemare* crowded in by their hips and shoulders. At least the bastards hadn't brought guns—then he remembered *why* they didn't carry such weapons.

They preferred to eat their prey alive.

51

Movement drew Erin's eye to the crater's edge, to where a giant in brown leather stalked forward, edging into the bowl. The *strigoi* was black skinned, shaven headed, pierced with steel, dragging a long broadsword behind him. He bent to pinch some of the sand and cast it away in disgust, likely sensing the holy ground. He spit where he tossed the grains, sneering and looking down at them.

At her.

A chill swept through her.

He continued another step, then another into the crater.

He didn't come alone.

A pair of *blasphemare* lions padded to either side of him, staying close, their eyes searching, tails swishing grains. Their manes were black rather than tawny, ruffled by the hot desert wind. Their eyes shone toward her with a dread crimson under the ash-covered day. They snarled, showing fangs that better fitted something saber-toothed. Black claws dug deep, kicking sand back in a posture of pure feline threat.

The giant swung his sword in an easy figure eight through the air, the long blade an extension of his muscular arms.

Suddenly Erin wished she had not insisted her group come to Siwa.

Still, she pushed such thoughts down and firmed her grip on her gun. No matter the outcome in the next few minutes, she knew it was *right* to come here. Her guilt lay not in bringing everyone here but in failing to solve the mystery of these sands in time, the riddle hidden behind Arella's calm eyes.

Around her, the Sanguinists had drawn their swords. Bernard carried an antique curved blade that shimmered like water, made of Damascus steel, edged with silver, likely deeply blessed. Christian brandished a curved blade, too, but his was modern, a *kukri* out of Nepal. Agmundr drew a longsword from a sheath across his back. Wingu raised two shorter blades, one in each hand, swinging them with grace and power.

Rhun simply had his *karambit* in hand, its hooked edge as lethal as any *blasphemare* claw.

The giant *strigoi* took a final step forward, drawing the lions at his hips—then stopped again.

From behind him, a familiar silver-haired figure stalked into view. Iscariot had changed out of his usual gray suit into leather armor, bleached white, tailored gracefully to his muscular body.

Jordan swung his machine pistol toward him.

Iscariot noted the motion, and a shadow of a derisive smile etched his features. The man had plainly recovered from the last time Jordan had shot him with that same weapon.

Iscariot lifted an arm and released an emerald-winged moth into the air.

The Sanguinists shifted warily, their eyes upon its flutter. How many of those poisonous creations had he brought with him? With enough of them, he could fell the entire group of Sanguinists without stirring his army.

But the moth flew only a few feet into the crater before spiraling to the ground, shattering a wing to iridescent scales as it crashed. Whether from the contamination of the ash in the air or from the blowing dust of sand, apparently its delicate cogs could not handle this harsh terrain.

Or maybe again it was the holiness found here.

No matter the cause, at least one threat had been neutralized.

Not that it would likely change the final outcome.

Iscariot's voice carried easily down into the crater. His gaze swept over them, noticing who was missing. "It seems you have lost your two angels."

Erin willed herself to keep her gaze fixed on the enemy and not let it twitch toward the well where Arella had vanished with Tommy. She hoped that the boy would get away, that the spring led out to some secret exit, some distant pool. Tommy's immortality should keep him alive, even drowned underwater.

"We may have lost our angels," Jordan called back. "But I see you found your demons."

Iscariot laughed and gestured to the Sanguinists. "You have your own *demons*, Warrior of Man."

"*Friends,*" Jordan countered. "Not demons."

Iscariot frowned at them, clearly having no more patience. "Where are you hiding him?" he asked, leaving no doubt he was talking about Tommy.

Iscariot must know, as long as Tommy was loose, that his plan to unleash Hell on Earth remained threatened.

Silence stretched for several breaths.

Judas's eyes settled on Erin and remained there. He lifted an arm and pointed to her. "No one is to harm her," he called out loudly. "She is mine. She will give me my answer."

A wave of snarling and hissing swept along the crater's rim.

"Kill the rest!"

4:34 P.M.

Far down the throat of the well, Tommy kicked as hard as he could, heading even deeper. The initial shock after the strange woman tossed him down here and dragged him under had faded. Now he just tried to keep up with her. Despite the sudden dunking, he oddly trusted her.

He didn't know if she was really an angel, but she'd saved his life, so for now, he would give her the benefit of his doubt.

To either side, the walls of the well felt like beach glass, still rough, but too smooth to be rock. He pictured that explosion etched above, of a battle between Lucifer and Michael. That same blast must have gone deep under the earth, sealing off that pool where Christ had stood and melting everything around it to glass.

He wanted to disbelieve that story, too, except for two things.

One, the water grew ever warmer the deeper he dove.

Two, beneath him, lighting his way, a golden glow beckoned, outlining the woman's sleek legs.

He chased after her until his lungs were bursting, his ears stinging from the pressure.

Down, down he went.

Finally, he reached the bottom, desperate for air.

She pointed to a side cavern that opened a few yards off. With his lungs burning, he ducked through the short passageway, pushing off the smooth walls and kicking off the bottom. The source of the light came from there, drawing him like a moth to a flame.

But it wasn't a *flame* he sought.

Air.

He had dived with his father off the Catalina coast, into sea caves that pocked that island, remembering ducking through rock to find a cave sloshing with water below and a pocket of air above.

He prayed the same would be found here, some secret cave where he could hang out with this woman until the battle ended, and it was safe.

Safe . . .

How long had it been since he had felt safe?

His lungs screamed as he scrabbled the last distance, worming through the entrance to the cave. His vision began to close down, squeezing narrower, dancing with sparks. He knew he didn't have enough air even to make it back to the surface. He was committed now. His father had once said that the most important thing in life was finding the right path and committing to it.

Somehow, Dad, I don't think this is what you meant.

Panic lent his arms and legs extra strength. He popped into the small cavern, lined by gold glass and littered with loose sand below. Knowing there must be air above—*why else drag him down here?*—he pushed hard off the bottom.

He shot up—and his head crashed against the ceiling.

He pawed the roof, searching for even a bubble, some tiny breath of air.

There was none.

4:35 P.M.

Strigoi and *blasphemare* poured down the sides of the crater like a foul wave.

Jordan gripped his gun tightly, trying to ignore the dark giant barreling toward them, in the lead, flanked by the pair of shadow-maned lions.

Erin aimed at one of the beasts.

Jordan swung to a different target, knowing his weapon would do little against what was surging over the crater's rim. He had to trust the Sanguinists to handle that first wave.

Instead, he aimed to the side, near the edge of the sandy bowl. He waited for the dark army to reach there—then fired.

The spatter of hot round pierced the fuel tank of their helicopter.

The explosion ripped the craft apart in a fiery blast, sending the rotors cutting a swath through the *strigoi* and slamming into the far crater wall. The sudden blast and resulting damage shattered the initial charge, sending *blasphemare* loping away, hissing and howling at the smoking wreckage. Several *strigoi* struggled in the sand with severed limbs. Others were clearly dead.

Rhun glanced approvingly toward him.

Jordan used the stunned moment to swing his weapon toward Iscariot, who remained at the crater's edge. He steadied and aimed for the guy's center mass, not trusting a head shot from this distance, especially as limited as Jordan was on ammunition. He dared not waste a single round.

He squeezed the trigger, intending to drop the guy again, if only for a short time. Temporarily leaderless, maybe the army could be routed.

But as he fired, the huge bulk of a jackal swerved in front of Iscariot, taking the rounds across its shoulders, saving the bastard. Black blood flowed from the beast's side, but it didn't look bothered as it stalked back and forth, keeping its master protected.

Iscariot retreated down the rim's far side, further sheltering himself.

Coward.

Closer at hand, the dark giant recovered quickly, lunging forward again to close the distance, rallying those nearest to him. He snarled, showing long fangs.

Agmundr met the challenge, bounding in front of him.

Giant against giant.

It was no contest.

Fueled by holiness, Agmundr swung his longsword so fast it sang through the air. He cleaved the *strigoi*'s head clean off its shoulders, the snarl still fixed to that skull as it flew away.

Jordan strafed the horde charging to the left.

Wingu and Christian leaped to the right.

Rhun and Bernard guarded their rear.

Elizabeth kept near the well's edge, neither threatening nor helping, simply guarding Tommy's retreat to who knew where.

Erin fired behind Jordan's shoulder, popping a lion clean through the eye, sending it rolling to Agmundr's feet, where a whirl of his huge blade caught the beast in the throat.

Jordan felt bad for the damned creature. It hadn't asked to be turned into what it was. But pity only brought you so much mercy.

He kept firing.

Agmundr faced the second lion, dancing before it, both adversaries looking for a weakness—then a massive jackal barreled into the Viking, blindsiding him, sinking powerful teeth into his thigh.

Jordan shot the beast in the shoulder, but it didn't even flinch.

Growling, Agmundr fell to the sand and rolled onto his back. The jackal released its hold of his thick leg and lunged for his throat. Jordan fired at its face—only to find his weapon empty.

Screw it . . .

He rushed forward with his gun raised, ready to use it as a club. Before he could bring it down, snapping jaws darted under Agmundr's sword. Yellow teeth ripped deep into the Viking's throat.

Agmundr bucked once from the assault—then went limp, as the jackal ripped upward, taking out the man's entire throat.

Cold blood splashed Jordan's arm.

He fell back.

The jackal turned toward him, blood and slather dripping from its gray muzzle onto the gold sand. Its massive haunches bunched— then it sprang straight at him.

His entire world became yellow fangs and a terrifying howl.

4:36 P.M.

Rhun spun to Jordan's defense. From the corner of an eye, he had watched Agmundr fall, and the soldier leap to help—only to face the same jaws that took the mighty Viking's life.

Rhun slammed into the huge jackal's side. Its jaws snapped shut less than an inch from Jordan's face. The beast skidded in the sand, sliding around to face him, nails digging through sand to scratch the glass beneath.

Rhun held his bloody *karambit* in front of him and prayed for the strength to protect the others. The very air was full of blood as Christian, Bernard, and Wingu continued their dance among the dark horde. The crimson mist sang to his own blood, begging him to drink lustily from that font.

Rhun held his breath against it.

Across from him, the jackal's angry red eyes locked onto his. Gray hair bristled down the scruff of its hunched neck. A snarl revealed yellow teeth set in a powerful jaw.

As it lunged, Rhun kept firm in the sand and thrust out his arm, ramming his *karambit* between the pointed teeth and deep into the creature's mouth. With all the force that he could muster, he drove his blade up through the roof and into its brain—then yanked his hand out.

The beast collapsed, black blood frothing from its mouth to stain the sand. Its front paws scratched at its jaws, whimpering from the pain.

Pity rose in Rhun at the sight of one of God's creatures turned into such a suffering monstrosity. Finally, that crimson glow dulled to a sightless brown, as the beast was freed of its curse.

Rhun had no time to rejoice in its release.

A heavy force bore him to the sand from behind, slamming his face into the jackal's dark blood. Claws raked his back, shredding through his armor and skin, a long claw catching on his rib.

Rhun screamed—as a lion roared in triumph atop him.

52

Panicked, Tommy floundered in the flooded cavern. He clutched both hands over his mouth. Unable to stop himself, he convulsed a lung full of water into his body, setting his chest on fire. His arms and legs kicked out blindly, striking the sides of the cavern as his body fought to expel that fire, to cough, to gag. But there was nothing to replace it but more water.

He fought until he could fight no more and hung motionless.

Drowned.

But he was the boy who could not die.

His lungs ached, but they no longer struggled to force out the water. He opened his eyes again and stared around him, wanting to cry.

Knowing now he would not die, he searched the cavern.

The woman must have drawn him down here for some reason.

He remembered her pointing him to the cave.

Why?

The source of the cavern's light rose from an upwelling of glass in the room's center, like a miniature volcano. It was so bright that he had to shield his eyes against it. Still, he spotted something silver at its heart.

He leaned deeper into that glow, able now to make out a foot or two of thin silver sticking out of the block, topped by a wider, shielded hilt. He noted the grip was indented, for fingers to clutch it firmly.

His right hand reached to do just that—then he remembered the story above, of Archangel Michael's sword. He looked closer and could even make out the long notch along one side, where a shard had been chipped from it.

His other hand rose to his neck, remembering that pain.

He reached a single finger and touched the round knob at the hilt's end. As his skin brushed the metal, power fired through him, like touching a raw electric wire—only it left him feeling *stronger*. He felt like he could shatter mountains with his fists.

He studied the blade. Most of its length looked buried in the sandy glass.

Like King Arthur's Excalibur.

Tommy knew what was expected of him. An angel had carried this sword, and it was up to the First Angel to free it, to return it to the sun, to be used against the darkness above.

But he withdrew his hand.

He didn't want to touch it.

What did he care about the world above? He had been kidnapped, tortured, and kidnapped again—only to be finally sacrificed on an altar.

He suddenly realized the sword could end that misery.

It can free me.

The blade could deal a wound far greater than the stab to his neck. He could bring both wrists to its edge, drag them swiftly down, cutting deep.

He could die.

I could see Mom and Dad again.

His mother's face rose up in his mind, as he remembered how she would tuck her short curly hair behind her ears, how her brown eyes almost glowed with concern whenever he was hurt. A look he saw often while battling his cancer. He also recalled how she would sing him lullabies in the hospital, even when he was probably too old for them, how she would make him laugh, even when he knew that she wanted to cry.

She loved me.

And his father no less. His love was more practical: trying to cram as much life into those few last years. Tommy got to drive a Mustang convertible, learned to shoot pool, and when he was too weak, his father would sit cross-legged next to him on the couch and help him slay zombies in *Resident Evil*. And sometimes they had talked, really talked. Because they both knew there would come a time when they couldn't anymore.

He knew one other certainty.

I was supposed to die first.

That was the deal. He was sick; they were well. He would die, and they would live. He accepted that deal, made rough peace with it—until the stupid dove had ruined everything.

He stared at the sword and made a decision.

They could fight this war without him.

He reached for the sword, ready to cut a bloody path back to his parents' arms. He hovered his hand over the hilt's grip, preparing himself. Once ready, he snatched hard to the silver handle.

A jolt rang through him. Below him, the blade glowed brighter and brighter, ramping up to a supernova. He squeezed his eyes shut, fearing the brilliance would blind him. The light pierced his lids and filled his skull.

Then it slowly faded again.

He opened one eye, then the other.

Between his legs, the glass had melted away. In his hands a giant sword glowed a dull orange. Its weight held him anchored to the sandy bottom.

He brought his thumb to its edge. It sliced deeply before he even knew he'd made contact. Blood spilled upward in a red cloud. He followed that trail, knowing how easy it would be to draw that edge over his wrist.

A sting at best . . . then it would be over.

He moved the blade toward his wrist.

Who would miss me here?

He turned his eyes from that impossibly sharp edge to the roof above him, picturing the hot desert. He remembered cold fingers lifting his chin, touching his throat, making sure he was safe.

Elizabeth.

She would miss him. She would be angry.

He pictured the others: Erin, Jordan, even the dark priest Rhun.

They had risked everything to bring him to this desert, to save his life. And right now, they might be dying.

Dying for me.

4:39 P.M.

Out of bullets, Erin snatched up Agmundr's longsword. She needed both hands to lift it. She swung from her hips, bringing her arms and the blade into the air, slicing the space between her and the nearest *strigoi*.

The monster laughed, took a step back, and charged toward Christian, ignoring her.

She searched for someone to attack.

None of the *strigoi* or the *blasphemare* would come near her, obeying Iscariot's order that she not be killed. His troops kept their distance until he came down to claim her.

Maybe that's my better weapon.

A howl of a lion swung her around. Yards away, Rhun struggled, pinned under one of the shadowy *blasphemare* lions. Jordan rushed to his aid, swinging his pistol like a club.

She dropped the heavy sword and ran toward them both.

Jordan got batted away like a horsefly, claws ripping clean through his leather jacket, almost tearing off a sleeve. He landed on his back. But the distraction allowed Rhun to roll free, losing a large swath of skin.

The lion lunged at its escaping prey.

And Erin did the stupidest thing in her life.

She jumped between Rhun and the lion, spreading her arms and hollering, throwing out her chest like a showboating prizefighter.

The lion dropped low, hissing, haunches high, tail swatting angrily.

"Can't attack me, can you?" she challenged it.

It curled black lips and snarled, backing away, especially as Christian slid to her side to back her up.

He glanced at her. "Didn't know lion taming was on your résumé."

She smiled, letting her guard down too soon.

The lion launched itself, expertly hitting Christian, while raking her shoulder with its claw as it passed, knocking her aside.

Erin fell to her knees and grabbed her wound. Hot blood seeped through her fingers and ran down her arm and chest. She realized the error of her ways. Iscariot said she couldn't be *killed*—but he said nothing about *maiming* her.

To the side Rhun and Christian battled the lion.

Jordan called her name.

The world had slowed down.

She collapsed sideways into the sand. Its grittiness under her cheek comforted her. She was in the desert. She loved the desert.

4:40 P.M.

Jordan ran toward Erin and skidded on his knees to her side. He knew he was too late to help her. Blood poured out of her shoulder and soaked the golden sand.

Erin raised her head.

Her caramel eyes met his—then looked past him.

Wonder filled her face, inexplicable from all the blood, howls, and screams in the air. She raised a bloody hand and pointed over his shoulder.

Jordan turned to see what she meant.

What the—?

Out of the mouth of the well, a single curl of orange flame rose from the darkness below. It twisted like a tight whirlwind, perfectly straight to the dark sky.

Jordan couldn't take his eyes off it.

Even the battle slowed, as a wary, fearful calm spread outward.

Eyes and faces turned toward it.

When the flame sprouted as long as his arm, a hand came into view below it, as if pushing the fire upward. The spit of fire continued to rise. The strange torchbearer was dragged up from below with it, lifted free of the well, and gently lowered to its edge.

Tommy.

As his feet touched ground, the fire snuffed out to reveal a silver sword held aloft, a few licks of flame still traced it, dancing brilliantly along its length.

The boy's eyes met Jordan's.

Fire danced there, too.

"I think this belongs to you!" Tommy yelled, half boy, half something dreadful.

The kid—if he was still a *kid*—twisted back his arm and flung the sword high. It spun end over end. Jordan wanted to duck, but instead his left arm rose on its own. The hilt landed perfectly in his palm, as if it was always meant to be there. The low burn in his tattoo flared to flaming life. Through a rip in his jacket and shirt, he saw the curled tracery of his old lightning scar blaze with an inner fire.

Strength flowed into his body.

Jordan danced the sword around him in a pattern of fire and steel, as if casting some arcane spell. He had never wielded a sword in his life.

A lion roared, turning to go after Erin again.

Jordan thought, and he was there, blocking it.

He slashed the sword across the lion's paw, as it swiped at him in irritation.

As soon as the blade pierced its skin, the creature roared in agony. Flame followed the line where the sword had cut it—then swept up the leg and over its body. Maddened by pain, the lion leaped back and fled through the dark army, forging a flaming path through them, igniting everything in its wake.

Jordan checked out the sword.

It was one hell of a weapon.

Or make that *heaven* of a weapon.

Jordan spun in a circle, catching a *strigoi* on the arm, another on the thigh. Both howled as flames spread from their wounds. He swept outward, moving on legs that defied bone and muscle.

As swift as any *strigoi*, any Sanguinist.

Creature after creature fell before his blade.

Then he headed deeper—after his true enemy.

Iscariot.

4:42 P.M.

Judas watched the Warrior of Man stalk across the field of battle. Beasts fled from his path, scattering out into the desert. Those few that stayed were hunted by the others. He saw the countess grab the boy; the angelic glow in the child's eyes faded after relinquishing the sword to its bearer on Earth. The boy hugged hard to the ancient creature.

Judas felt no fear.

It had come to this moment.

He had spent centuries trying to find a purpose in his long life, centuries again to bring the world to this brink of damnation, where he could die.

And now the time was upon him.

The soldier would kill him, but only if he put up a fight. He was not a man to strike down an unarmed opponent. So Judas bent and picked up a discarded blade, an ancient chipped scimitar.

His last bodyguard tried to join him, lifting an assault rifle. The man's partner, Henrik, had died in the cavern back in Cumae, but this one had lived, escaping with him.

"Go," Iscariot ordered.

"My place is always at your side."

"Forgive me." Judas swung the sword and decapitated the man. He stepped away from the body. No one would interfere with his destiny.

The Warrior of Man's eyes widened in surprise, but he didn't slow down.

Others closed behind him, including Dr. Granger, holding a sopping rag to her shoulder.

"Stay back, Erin," Jordan called. "This is my fight."

The woman looked as if she wanted to argue, but she didn't.

Judas lifted his bloody sword into a guard position. "How often must I kill you, Sergeant Stone?"

"I could ask you the same question."

His sword shone white-hot in his hands, sparking with spats of fire. Judas shivered in anticipation.

The soldier circled him, suspicion plain in his face, as if he suspected some trick.

You must play your role, Warrior. Do not disappoint me.

To ensure that, Judas lunged for him, and the man parried. He was unnaturally quick. Knowing this, Judas fought harder, no longer needing to feign incompetence. He had been trained under many different sword masters over the centuries.

He attacked again and again, enjoying the true challenge, his last. It was fitting to find a worthy opponent. But that was not his destiny. He allowed his guard to drop, as if by accident.

Jordan struck.

The blade pierced Judas's side.

The same place where a Roman soldier had stabbed Christ on the cross.

Judas offered a quick plea of gratitude before he fell to his knees. Bright red blood poured from his wound. It soaked through his shirt. He dropped his sword.

Jordan stood before him. "We're even."

"No," Judas said, reached to his leg. "I am forever in your debt."

He fell to his side, then rolled to his back. Gray sky filled his vision. He had done that. The world surrounded by ash and blood. The sun was minutes from setting. Nothing could stop what he had started.

My death heralds my success.

He took it as a sign, his reward for opening the gates of Hell and bringing about the final Day of Judgment.

The burning pain in his side was unlike anything he had ever experienced, but he drank it in. He would soon be at peace. He welcomed it. He let his eyes drift closed.

Then a shadow fell over him, bringing with it the smell of lotus blossoms.

Arella.

He opened his eyes and looked upon her beauty, another reward for fulfilling his destiny.

Her warm hands took his. "My love."

"It came to be just as you foretold," he said.

As she leaned over him, her tears fell onto his face. He savored each warm drop.

"Oh, my love," she said, "I curse the vision that brought you to this."

He sought her dark eyes. "This was Christ's will, not yours."

"This was *your* will," she insisted. "You could have walked a different path."

He touched her wet cheek. "I always walked a different path. But I am grateful for the years that we walked that path together."

She struggled to smile.

"Do not blame yourself," he said. "If you can grant me but a single favor, grant me that. You are blameless in all this."

Her chin firmed, as it always did when she held her feelings inside.

He reached up through the pain and curled a strand of her long hair around his finger. "We are but His instruments."

She placed her palm against his wound. "I could fetch water from the spring to heal you."

Fear shot through his body. He searched for clever words to persuade her against such a path, but she knew his ways. So he settled on one word, placing all his will into it, letting the truth shine in his eyes.

"Please."

She bent and kissed his lips, then fell into his arms one last time.

4:49 P.M.

Erin's throat tightened as an angel wept for Judas.

Arella cradled him and stroked his gray hair back from his forehead while murmuring words in an ancient tongue. He smiled up at Arella, as if they were young lovers instead of two ageless creatures caught at the end of time.

Rhun touched Erin's shoulder, looking to the darkening sky.

His single touch reminded her that, while the battle was won, the war was not over. She looked to the sun, sunk deep into the horizon to the west. They were nearly out of time to undo what Iscariot had set in motion.

She stared at the man who had started all of this.

Iscariot's blood flowed from his side, weeping out his life. In the growing darkness, she noted the soft glow shining within the crimson, remembering seeing the same when he had accidentally cut his finger in the cavern under the ruins of Cumae, by a sliver of the same blade that slew him now.

She remembered Arella, casting out the same golden radiance when she rescued Tommy. And even Tommy's blood had glowed faintly on the beach in Cumae.

What did that mean?

She looked from Tommy, who stood still by the well, to Judas.

Did that mean they *both* carried angelic blood?

She remembered that *both* Tommy and Judas had also encountered a dove, symbolic of the Holy Spirit, an echo of the bird Christ had killed. And both were about Christ's same age at that time.

And then Arella's words earlier.

Michael was rent asunder. You carry the best of the First Angel within you.

Erin began to understand.

Tommy didn't carry *all* of Michael inside of him, only the best, the most shining and brightest, a force capable of granting life.

Another vessel carried his worst, his darkest, with a force that killed.

She saw that the shine of Iscariot's blood was distinctly darker than Tommy's blood.

Two different shades of gold.

She turned and gazed across the crater, at the glass exposed by their digging, at the round plug that once sealed the well. Like the crater itself, one half was dark gold, the other lighter.

She remembered thinking it looked like an Eastern yin-yang symbol.

Two parts that make a whole.

"We need them both," Erin mumbled.

She peered at Arella. Earlier, the sibyl had stayed silent because she knew Iscariot needed to come here, too. Had Arella even drawn that symbol in the sand so he would know to come to this place?

Bernard drifted closer to Erin, his clothes ripped and bloodied, but he must have sensed the growing understanding inside her. "What are you saying?"

Rhun looked on, too.

She drew the two with her, along with Jordan. They needed to hear this, to tell her she was wrong.

Please, let me be wrong.

Rhun turned that dark, implacable gaze of his upon her. "What is it, Erin?"

"The First Angel isn't Tommy. It's the archangel Michael, the heavenly being rent asunder. Split in *two*." She gestured to the crater's glass. "He must be reunited. We must fix what was broken here."

That was Arella's warning to them—or the reign of man would end.

"But where's his other half?" Bernard asked.

"In Judas."

Shock spread through the group.

"Even if you're right," Jordan asked, "how are we going to get them back together?"

Erin focused on Iscariot, dying on the sands.

She knew that answer, too. "Their immortal shells must be stripped from them."

Jordan gaped at her. "They have to die?"

She lowered her voice to a whisper. "It's the only way. That's why the sword was left here, why we had to come here."

"Iscariot has already received a mortal wound," Rhun said. "So the blade must afflict one upon the boy?"

"Do we dare do that?" Jordan asked. "I thought we decided in Cumae that Tommy's life was more important than even saving the world."

Erin wanted to agree. The boy had done nothing wrong. He had tried to help an innocent dove, and in return he had seen his family ripped from him, and he had suffered countless tortures. Was it right that he must die here as well?

She could not send this child to his death.

But it was also *one* life against the lives of the just and unjust around the world.

Jordan stared at her.

She knew if she gave him the word that he would carry it out, reluctantly but he would. He was a soldier—he understood about sacrificing for the greater good. The needs of the many outweighed the needs of the one.

She covered her face.

She could not watch more innocent blood be spilled. She had watched her sister sacrificed to false belief. She had caused Amy's death because of her own ignorance of the danger she had put her in. She would not take another innocent life, no matter how much her mind told her that she must.

"No," she gasped out, decidedly. "We can't kill a boy to save the world."

Bernard suddenly moved toward Jordan, going for the sword. But Jordan was as swift now and lifted the blade to the cardinal's chest, its point over his silent heart.

"This will kill you as surely as any *strigoi*," Jordan warned.

Bernard glanced at Rhun to back him up, to join him against Jordan. The cardinal wanted that sword.

Rhun folded his arms. "I trust the wisdom of the Woman of Learning."

"The boy must die," Bernard insisted. "Or the world dies with him. In horror beyond earthly imaginings. What is one boy against that?"

"Everything," Erin said. "Murdering a boy is an evil deed. *Every* evil act matters. *Every* single one. We must stand against each and every one, or who are we?"

Bernard sighed. "What if it's neither good nor evil, only necessary?"

Erin clenched her hands into fists.

She would not let Tommy be murdered.

"Erin." Jordan's worried blue eyes met hers. He nodded over to the well.

Tommy made a placating motion with his palms toward Elizabeth, keeping her there. He then stalked over and studied each of them.

"I know," he said, looking exhausted. "When I touched the sword and decided to bring it out of the well . . . I knew."

Erin remembered the fire in his eyes as he held the sword.

"It's about choice," he said. "I have to *choose* this, only then will all be set right."

Hearing this now, Erin realized how close they had come to ruin. If she had unleashed Jordan or if Bernard had grabbed the blade, if either of them had thrust the sword into the boy without his consent, they would have lost all.

This thought gave her a small measure of comfort, but only very small.

What Tommy was saying meant that the ending would be the same.

A dead boy on the sands.

"But Iscariot didn't agree to be stabbed," Rhun warned.

Erin stiffened, realizing Rhun was right.

Have we already lost?

Jordan swallowed, lowering the sword, knowing Bernard could no longer force the matter. "I think Judas did agree," Jordan said. "During the fight, he was matching me move by move. Then suddenly he let his guard down. I didn't realize it at the time, just reacted, stabbing him."

"I suspect he always sought death," Rhun said.

"So then what do we do?" Jordan asked. "From here I mean?"

Erin saw how his eyes could not even meet the boy's.

Tommy shifted, apparently to keep his back to Elizabeth, glancing over his shoulder to be sure, to keep her from seeing. Tommy noted Erin's attention. "She will try to stop it from happening."

Tommy lifted the tip of Jordan's sword and placed it to his chest.

He looked up at Jordan, trying to smile, but his lower lip trembled with his fear, struggling to look so brave, so sure in the face of the unknown.

Jordan finally found the boy's face, too. Erin had never seen such agony and heartbreak etched in the hard, wry planes of his face.

"I can't do this," he moaned.

"I know that, too," Tommy said quietly, his voice quavering. His eyes looked toward the west, to the sun, to the last light he would ever see.

A wail rose from beside the well. "Noooo . . ."

Elizabeth rushed toward them, suddenly sensing what was about to happen.

Tommy sighed and thrust himself upon the sword—taking the last light of the day with him as he died.

53

Rhun caught Elisabeta around the waist as she ran up to them.

Tommy collapsed to the ground, sliding off the blade, spilling red blood across the dark sand. A bright golden brilliance pooled there, too. Across the crater, a similar radiance shone from that side, a darker gold that framed the figures of Judas and Arella.

"Why?" Elisabeta sobbed, clutching him.

Rhun drew her down next to the boy.

The sword had pierced his heart clean through. Rhun heard now its last feeble quiver, then it stopped.

Jordan crashed to his knees across from him, dropping his sword, clutching his left side.

Erin leaned down. "What's wrong—?"

Rhun felt it a moment before it happened—a welling of great power beyond measure—and threw his arm over his eyes, shielding Elisabeta with his body.

Then came a bright explosion.

Glory seared his eyes.

His blood boiled in his veins.

Elisabeta screamed in his arms, the sound echoed by the others in a chorus of pain and fear.

Brought low by this radiance, on his knees, Rhun begged for forgiveness as he prayed through the pain. His every sin was a blight against that holy brilliance, nothing could be hidden from it. His greatest sin was a blackness without boundaries, capable of consuming him fully. Even this light could not vanquish it.

Please, stop . . .

Finally, after what felt like an eternity, the light gave way to a merciful darkness. He opened his eyes. Lifeless bodies of *strigoi* and *blasphemare* were scattered around the crater; even those that had fled beyond it had fallen dead at the explosion. Rhun stirred as pain still raged in his body.

It burned with the holiest of fires.

He searched the crater. Erin was crouched over a fallen Tommy, with Jordan kneeling next to her, holding his shoulder. They both looked shaken up, but unharmed by the brilliance. Being untainted, they had likely been spared the brunt of its force.

Elisabeta lay crumpled in his arms, unmoving.

She was *strigoi,* without even the acceptance of Christ's love to shield her from that fire. Like the other damned creatures, she must be dead.

Please, he prayed, *not Elisabeta.*

He gathered her to his chest. He had stolen her from her time, from her castle, imprisoned her for hundreds of years, only to have her die in a lonely desert far from anything or anyone she had ever loved.

How many times had his actions cursed her?

He stroked short curly hair from her white forehead and brushed sand from her pale cheeks. Long ago, he had held her just so while she lay dying on a stone floor at Čachtice. He should have let her go then, but even now, deep down he knew he would do anything to have her back.

Even sin again.

As if in response to this blasphemous thought, she stirred. Her silver eyes fluttered open, and her lips warmed into a hesitant smile. Her gaze was momentarily lost, displaced in time and place.

Still, in that moment, he knew the truth.

In spite of everything, she loved him.

He touched a palm to her cheek. But how had she survived the burning brilliance in her cursed state? Had his body shielded her? Or was it his love for her?

Either way, joy filled him as he fell into her silver eyes, letting the desert fade around them. For the moment, she was all that mattered. Her hand rose. Soft fingertips touched his cheek.

"My love . . ." she whispered.

5:03 P.M.

Erin looked away from Rhun and the countess. Her gaze was still dazzled by that blast of light, swearing for a moment she saw a sweep of wings sailing upward from the sands. She gazed up at the stars.

Stars.

She straightened and turned in a slow circle, watching the pall clear from the night sky, spreading outward in all directions. She pictured the darkness being swept clean, all the way back to Cumae.

Had they succeeded in closing that opening gate?

Jordan stood up next to her. He flexed and stretched his left arm, shaking the limb a bit, reminding her of a more immediate concern. She remembered him crashing to his knees and clutching his side, like he was having a heart attack.

"Are you okay?" she asked.

He looked down at the boy, at the blood.

"When he fell, it felt like something was ripped out of me. I swore I was dying."

Again.

She examined Tommy's pale face. His eyes were closed as if he were merely slumbering. Back in Stockholm, the boy's touch, his blood, had resurrected and healed Jordan. She noted the pool of blood here no longer glowed. It simply seeped coldly into the sand.

She reached over and squeezed Jordan's hand, feeling the heat there, glad of it. "I think whatever angelic essence Tommy imbued in you was stripped back out during that blast of light."

"Where's the sword?" Jordan asked, glancing around at his feet.

It was gone, too.

She again pictured those wings of light. "I think it's been restored to its original master."

Bernard joined them, his eyes on the skies. "We have been spared."

She hoped he was right, but not all of them had been so lucky.

She dropped to a knee and touched Tommy's blood-soaked shirt. She brought her fingers to his young face, looking even younger in death, his features relaxed, finally at peace. His skin was still warm under her fingertips.

Warm.

She placed her full palm to his throat, remembering doing the same with Jordan. "He's still warm." She reached down and tore open his shirt, ripping buttons. "His wound is gone!"

Tommy suddenly jerked, sitting half up, pushing away from her, clearly startled, his gaze sweeping over them. The fear there faded to recognition.

"Hey . . ." he said and stared down at his bare chest.

His fingers probed there, too.

Elizabeth burst away from Rhun and landed on her knees, taking his other hand. "Are you fine, boy?"

He squeezed her fingers, shifting closer to her, still scared.

"I . . . I don't know. I think so."

Jordan smiled. "You look fine to me, kiddo."

Christian joined them with Wingu. The pair had finished a fast canvass of the crater and its rim to make sure all was safe. "I can hear his heartbeat."

Rhun and Bernard confirmed this with nods.

Relief shattered through Erin. "Thank God."

"Or in this case, maybe thank *Michael*." Jordan slipped an arm around her.

The countess scolded Tommy. "Don't ever do something like that again!"

Her seriousness drew a shadow of a smile from Tommy. "I promise." He lifted up a hand. "I'll never impale myself on another sword."

Christian moved closer to Erin. "His blood doesn't smell . . . *angelic* anymore. He is mortal again."

"I think it's because we released the spirit inside him. So it could rejoin its other half." She glanced over to Iscariot. "Does that mean Judas is healed, too?"

Christian shook his head. "I checked as I made my circuit with Wingu. He lives yet, but only barely. Even now I can feel his heart about to give out."

Rhun fixed his eyes on Judas. "His reward was not life."

5:07 P.M.

For the first time in thousands of years, Judas knew his death was near. A tingling sensation spread from the wound in his side and coursed through his veins like icy water.

"I'm cold," he whispered.

Arella drew him tighter into her warm embrace.

With great effort, he lifted his arm in front of his failing eyes. The back of his hand was covered in brown age spots. His skin hung in loose wrinkles from his bones.

It was the fragile limb of an old man.

With trembling fingers, he felt his face, discovering furrows where there had once been smooth skin, around his mouth, at the corners of his eyes. He had withered to this.

"You are still beautiful, my vain old man."

He smiled softly at her words, at her gentle teasing.

He had replaced the curse of immortality with the curse of old age. His bones ached, and his lungs rattled. His heart lurched along like a drunken man walking in the dark.

He stared at Arella, as beautiful as ever. It seemed impossible that she had ever loved him, that she loved him still. He had been wrong to let her go.

I have been wrong about everything.

He had thought that his purpose was to bring Christ back to Earth. All his thoughts had been directed toward nothing else. He had spent centuries in service of this holy mission.

But that had not been his purpose, only his conceit.

Christ had granted him this gift, not to end the world, not as penance for his own betrayal, but to undo the mistake that Christ Himself had made as a boy.

To fix what was broken.

And now I have.

That was his true penance and purpose, and it was better than he deserved. He had been called to restore life, instead of bringing death.

Peace filled him as he closed his eyes and silently confessed his sins.

There were so many.

When he opened them again, gray cataracts clouded his vision. Arella was a blur, already cruelly fading from his sight as the end neared.

She hugged him tighter, as if to hold him there.

"You always knew the truth," he whispered.

"No, but I hoped," she whispered back. "Prophecy is never clear."

He coughed as his lungs shriveled inside him. His voice was a croak. "My only regret is that I cannot spend eternity with you."

Too weak now, Judas closed his eyes—not onto darkness, but onto a golden light. Cold and pain receded before that radiance, leaving only joy.

Words whispered in his ear. "How do you know how we shall spend eternity?"

He opened his eyes one last time. She blazed through his cataracts now, in all her glory, shining with heavenly grace.

"I am forgiven, too," she intoned. "I am called at last home."

She drifted up from him, away from him. He reached for her, discovering his arm was only light. She took his hand and pulled him from his mortal shell and into her eternal embrace. Bathed in love and hope, they sailed to their final peace.

Together.

5:09 P.M.

No one spoke.

Like Erin, they had all witnessed Arella bursting to light, washing the crater with a warmth that smelled of lotus blossoms. Then there was nothing.

Judas's body remained, but even now it was crumbling to dust, stirred by the desert wind, mixing with the eternal sand, marking his final resting place.

"What happened to him?" Tommy's voice was tight with worry.

"He aged to his natural years," Rhun answered. "From young man to old in a handful of heartbeats."

"Will that happen to me?" Tommy looked aghast.

"I wouldn't worry about it, kid," Jordan answered. "You were only immortal for a couple months."

"Is that true?" He turned to the countess.

"I believe so," Elizabeth said. "The soldier's words are sound."

"And what about the angel?" Tommy studied the empty spot in the desert. "What happened to her?"

"If I had to guess," Erin said, "I would say that she and Judas were taken up together."

"He would have liked that," Tommy said.

"I think so, too."

Erin threaded her fingers through Jordan's.

He tightened his grip. "But that means we're out of angels here. Isn't at least *one* of them supposed to have blessed the book?"

Erin turned to Bernard. "Maybe they already have. The skies are clear overhead again."

Bernard reached through his shredded clothes to the armor beneath. He tugged the zipper, looking ready to rip it clean off. Finally, he got it open and pulled free the Blood Gospel.

He held it atop trembling palms, his eyes worried.

The leather-bound volume looked unchanged.

But they all knew any truth lay inside.

Bernard carried it to Tommy and placed it reverently in the boy's hands, his expression apologetic. "Open it. You have earned it."

He sure had.

Tommy dropped to his knees and put the book on his lap. With one finger, he slowly lifted the cover, as if afraid of what it might reveal.

Erin watched over his shoulder, equally unnerved, her heart racing.

Tommy lowered the cover to his knee, revealing the first page. The original hand-scrawled passage glowed with a soft radiance in the dark, each letter perfectly clear.

"Nothing new is there," Bernard said, sounding forlorn and distraught.

"Maybe that means everything is over," Jordan said. "We don't have to do anything else."

If only . . .

Erin knew better. "Turn the page."

Tommy licked his upper lip and obeyed, lifting the first page and exposing the next.

It, too, was blank—then darkly crimson words appeared, marching across it in finely scribbled lines. She pictured Christ writing those Greek letters, his quill dipped in His own blood to enact this miraculous gospel.

Line after line quickly filled the page, far more than the first time the book had revealed its message. Three short cantos formed, accompanied by a final message.

Tommy held the book up to Erin. "You can read it, right?"

Jordan placed a hand on her good shoulder. "Of course she can. She's the Woman of Learning."

For once, Erin didn't feel the urge to correct him.

I am.

As she took the book, a strange strength surged from the cover through her palms. The words shone brighter before her eyes, as if she were always destined to read what was written here. She felt suddenly possessive of the book, of its words.

She translated the ancient Greek and read aloud the first canto. *"The Woman of Learning is now bound to the book and none may part it from her."*

"What does that mean?" Bernard asked.

She shrugged lightly, as clueless as he was.

Jordan slipped the book from her hands. As soon as the Gospel was lifted from her fingers, the words vanished.

Bernard gasped.

Erin quickly took the book back, and words blew back to life.

Jordan flashed a grin at Bernard. "Still doubt who she is?"

Bernard simply stared at the book, looking anguished, as if the love of his life had been torn from him. And maybe it had been. Erin remembered how she had felt when sent back to California, deemed unworthy to be involved with this miraculous book.

"What else does it say?" Tommy asked.

She drew in another breath and moved to the second canto. *"The Warrior of Man . . ."* She glanced at Jordan, hoping it was something good. *"The Warrior of Man is likewise bound to the angels to whom he owes his mortal life."*

With the uttering of the last word, Jordan suddenly flinched, ripping away the rest of the torn sleeve from his left arm. He gasped. The tattoo traced there had turned to fire, glowing golden. Then in another breath it blew out, leaving only the blue-black lines of ink on his skin.

He rubbed his arm and shook his fingers. "I can still feel that burn down deep. Like after Tommy revived me."

"What does that mean?" Erin asked, looking to the others.

From their expressions, no one knew.

Christian offered the only counsel. "Jordan's blood still smells the same, so he's not immortal or anything."

Jordan frowned at him. "Quit smelling me."

Leaving that mystery for now, Erin turned to the third and final canto and read it aloud. *"But the Knight of Christ must make a choice. By his spoken word, he may undo his greatest sin and return what was thought forever lost."*

She faced Rhun.

His gaze met hers, his dark eyes as hard as obsidian. She read some understanding in that dark glint, but he remained silent.

Tommy pointed to the bottom of the page. "And what's that written at the bottom?"

She read that, too. It was separate from the three cantos, clearly some final message or warning.

"Together, the trio must face their final quest. The shackles of Lucifer have been loosened, and his Chalice remains lost. It will take the light of all three to forge the Chalice anew and banish him again to his eternal darkness."

Jordan sighed heavily. "So our work isn't done yet."

Erin held the warm book in her hands and reread that last passage several times. What was this *Chalice*? She knew that she would spend many long hours trying to pick meaning out of those few lines, to wring some sense out of them.

But that could wait for now.

Jordan stared over at Rhun. "What's all that about your greatest sin?"

Rhun remained silent and turned to the empty desert.

Bernard answered, "His greatest sin was when he became a *strigoi*." He took firm hold of Rhun's shoulder. "My son, I believe that the Book is offering you mortal life, to restore your soul to you."

But would he take it?

Erin read that final canto again.

The Knight of Christ must make a choice . . .

54

Rhun felt Bernard's urgent fingers on his shoulders. The cardinal's breath brushed his neck when he spoke. He heard the shift of cloth and the creak of leather armor as his mentor shifted his stance. But what he didn't hear was a *heartbeat*.

Rhun's chest was just as silent.

Neither of them was truly human, nor mortal.

His blood still burned from the blast, reminding him of another essential difference between them and all humankind.

We are cursed.

Though blessed and bound to service in the Church, they remained tainted creatures, best left to the dark.

He took in Bernard's words, wondering if they could be true. Could his heart stir again? Could he have his soul back? Could he rejoin a simpler world, one where he might father children, where he could feel the touch of a woman's hand without fear?

He seldom allowed himself to entertain such a hope. He had accepted his lot as a Sanguinist. He had served without question for long, long years. His only possible escape from this curse was death.

But then he met Erin, who questioned everything and everyone. She gave him the will not only to challenge his fate—but to hope for something more.

But dare I grasp it?

Elisabeta stepped before him, turning his eyes from the desert to her soft face. He expected rancor, vitriol that he should be offered this gift. Instead, she did something far worse.

She touched his cheek. "You must take this boon. It is what you always wanted." Her cold hand lingered there. "You have earned it."

He stared into her eyes, seeing that she truly wished this for him. He gave a small nod, knowing what he must do, what he had truly earned.

He moved her hand from his cheek and kissed her palm in thanks.

He turned to Erin, to the book shining gently in her hands, where it had always belonged.

To each, their place.

He knew all he had to do was touch that book and state his greatest sin, and it would be taken from him, allowing a soul to return to the damned.

Erin smiled at him, happy for him.

Bernard followed him, clearly thrilled to witness this miracle. "I am so proud of you, my son. I always knew that if any of our order were to be restored to grace, it would be you. You will be free."

Rhun shook his head.

I will never be free.

He lifted his hand over the book, remembering that moment when he writhed in the holy brilliance of an angel restored, where his every sin was exposed—including his *greatest,* that black blight beyond any forgiveness.

The words of the Gospel echoed through him.

. . . he may undo his greatest sin . . .

He turned his face up to the heavens. His friends were wrong. Rhun knew his greatest sin, as did the one who wrote those words upon that page.

He placed his palm there now. "I take it upon myself to give up my greatest sin," Rhun prayed. "To let it be undone and give back that which I had stolen."

Erin looked troubled at his words—as she should be.

Behind him, he heard Elisabeta gasp and then crash to her knees.

Erin whispered to him. "What have you done?"

As answer, he glanced back to Elisabeta. She clapped her hands over her mouth and nose, as if she could hold back the hands of fate. But black smoke seeped between her fingers, expelling from mouth and nose, and formed a dark cloud in front of her startled eyes. Then in a breath it spiraled downward and vanished from this world.

She moved her hands from her mouth to her throat.

And screamed.

She screamed and screamed.

The sound rang across the desert again and again.

Rhun took her in her arms, calming her, holding her.

"It is as it must be," he said. "As it should always have been."

He watched her anguished, frightened face grow pinkish. And for the first time in centuries, he heard her heart beat again.

Rhun lost himself in the rhythm of it, wanting to weep.

Elisabeta's eyes were wide upon him. "This cannot be."

"It can, my love."

"No."

"Yes," he whispered. "Destroying your soul was my greatest sin. Always."

Her face grew redder, not with returning life, but anger. Her silver eyes darkened into storm clouds. Sharp nails scratched down his arm. "You made me mortal?"

"You are," Rhun said, hesitant now.

She shoved him away, her strength the barest fraction of her former might. "I did not wish it!"

"W-what?"

"I did not *ask* you to turn me into a beast, nor did I *ask* you to return me to this." She held out her arms. "A frail and mewling human."

"But you are forgiven. As am I."

"I care nothing about forgiveness. Yours or mine!" She retreated from him. "You play with my soul as if it were a trinket that you can give and take at will. Both then and now. Where is my *choice* in any of this? Or does that not matter?"

Rhun searched for words to explain it to her. "Life is the greatest gift."

"It is the greatest curse."

She turned and stalked away, heading for the open desert.

Tommy chased after her. "Wait! Don't leave me!"

The boy's lonely and plaintive cry stopped her, but she did not turn to face Rhun again. Tommy ran up to her and hugged her from behind. She pulled him forward and drew him closer, her shoulders quaking as she cried, her chin on his head.

Bernard touched Rhun's shoulder. "How could you have squandered such a gift on her?"

"It was not *squandered*."

Anger blew through him. How could Bernard be such a fool? Did he not understand that the greatest sins are those that we commit ourselves, not those that are committed upon us?

The countess kept her back toward him.

She would come to understand and forgive him.

She must.

5:48 P.M.

Erin closed the book and stepped away from the others. Jordan moved to follow her, but she asked for a moment of privacy. She stared up at the stars, at the rising moon as she strode across the crater, to the only place where there were no bodies, away from the chaos of emotions behind her.

She needed a moment of peace.

She reached the open well.

The holiness here, likely born from the sword preserved below, had kept the fighting away from this spot. She glanced back to the carnage, to both beasts and *strigoi*.

Their group had paid a terrible price, but they had come through it. Just not all of them.

Her eyes fell upon poor Agmundr, picturing his huge grin.

Thank you for protecting us.

She remembered Nadia on the snow, even Leopold on the floor of the cave. They had met their ends far from the lands of their birth and those who had loved them.

Just like Amy.

She knelt by the edge of the spring and peered into the clear water. Stars reflected there, a wash of the Milky Way shining brightly back at her, reminding her of both the smallness and majesty of life. The stars above were eternal. She listened to the swish of sands across the surrounding dunes, whispering as it had for millennia past.

This spot had long been a peaceful, holy place.

Erin surveyed the panels that told the story of Christ's first miracle and what followed. It was a reminder that *anyone* could make an error, take a misstep. Like Christ, she had not known the deadly consequences of her actions in Masada, how the events would bring death and ripples across time.

She looked back at Bernard as an uncharitable thought crossed her mind. So much bloodshed could have been spared if the cardinal had not kept so many secrets. If she had known the importance of the deadly information that she had shared with Amy, Erin might have been more cautious. Instead, the secrets that the Sanguinists had kept from her had cost Amy her life and the lives of others.

She focused on the book in her hand. While she would accept the mantle of the Woman of Learning, she would no longer allow truths to be kept from her. The Vatican authorities must throw open their libraries and reveal all their secrets, or she would no longer work with them.

The book was now bound to her, and she would use it to break down all doors.

She owed that to Amy.

She reached to her pocket and slipped out the marble of amber. She held it up to the moonlight, revealing the delicate feather inside. The amber had trapped it as surely as her memories held Amy: forever preserved, never free to float away.

While she would never forget her student, perhaps she could let something go.

She tilted her palm forward until the amber slid down to her fingertips. Then it tumbled off them and fell into the spring. She leaned forward and watched the marble break the reflection of stars and vanish into that eternity.

Now part of Amy would always be here in Egypt, at rest in one of the holiest places on Earth, near ancient secrets that might never be discovered.

Erin stared into that well, making a promise.

Never again.

No more innocent blood would be spilled to preserve the secrets of the Sanguinists. It was time for the truth to shine.

She gripped the book and stood.

Ready to change the world.

CHRISTMAS DAY

12:04 A.M. *CET*
Vatican City

Buried far below St. Peter's Basilica, the Sanguinists gathered in the cavernous vault of their order, their holy of holiest places, simply named the Sanctuary. They came in their greatest numbers every year to celebrate a midnight Mass in honor of the birth of Christ.

Rhun stood at the edge of the congregation. Others of his order filled the space, unmoving, in silent vigil. Not a breath nor a heartbeat nor even the rustle of a robe disturbed the utter peace. He drank in the quiet, as he knew the others around him did, too. The world above had grown ever louder across the centuries, but here he found the calm peace that his battered spirit so longed for.

Above him, the roof soared, its smooth and simple lines drawing his eyes up toward Heaven. The cold stone had been hewn smooth by thousands of hands in the early years of the Church. It contained none of the adornments of regular churches. This space spoke to the simplicity of a Sanguinist's faith—hard stone and simple torches were enough to lead the damned creatures to Him. Although he was deep beneath the streets of Rome, he felt closer to Him in his glory here than anywhere else.

This Christmas Mass was also known as the Mass of the Angels. Never had it felt more appropriate to Rhun than on this holiest of nights so soon after he had walked with angels.

The smoky fragrance of incense drew his gaze from the roof to the center of the room. There, he found the holiest of priests walking with slow grace through their congregation. The head of the Order of the Sanguines wore simple black robes tied with a rough cord. He eschewed the costumes of cardinals and bishops and the pope— preferring to clothe himself as a simple and humble priest.

Yet, he was so much more.

He was the Risen One.

Lazarus.

Without him, they would be condemned to live out their existences as foul beasts, murdering innocent and guilty alike until they met their deaths at the end of a sword or a ray of sunlight. The Risen One had found another road for them to tread, a path of holiness and service and meaning.

Rhun knew now that it was no *sin* to be a Sanguinist.

He had made the right decision in the desert. His existence now served God, and that had been his truest wish since his earliest days. He had strayed from that path when he corrupted Elisabeta, but he had been given a chance to wash that sin clean. Now he could serve Christ again without a shadow on his conscience.

Lazarus passed by him.

Rhun stared at his long fingers, knowing they had touched Christ. Those shadowed eyes had stared at Him. That stern face had spoken to Him, laughed with Him.

Two other Sanguinists flanked Lazarus.

A man and a woman.

They were said to be even older than the Risen One, but their names were never spoken. In fact, the ancient pair was seldom seen, not even among the Cloistered Ones, the order's elders who spent their time in eternal prayers and meditation. Rhun had once longed to join the Cloistered, but he had been drawn back into the world of the living instead.

The man carried an ancient cross, its wood turned from brown to gray with the passing of the centuries. The woman swung a silver censer of incense. Delicate smoke wafted into the room, filling Rhun's nostrils with frankincense and myrrh. The holy scent surrounded him, settling on his robe and his hair and his skin.

A chant began, and Rhun's voice rose in harmony with the other Sanguinists. Their beautiful chorus resonated through the vast chamber, hitting subtle notes beyond normal hearing. In the Sanctuary, gathered here with his order in the long darkness, he did not need to hide his otherness and could truly sing.

Lazarus stopped in front of the ancient stone altar and raised his pale hand to form the sign of the cross. *"In nomine Patris, et Filii, et Spiritus Sancti."*

"Amen," answered the congregation.

The familiar routine carried Rhun away. He neither thought nor prayed. He simply existed in each moment, letting the chain of them draw him ever forward. He belonged here with his brothers and sisters of the cloth. This was the pious life that he had *wanted* when he was a mortal man, and the life that he had *chosen* as an immortal one.

And so they came to the Eucharist.

Lazarus spoke the words in Latin. "The Blood of our Lord Jesus Christ, which was shed for thee, preserve thy body and soul unto everlasting life. Drink this in remembrance that Christ's Blood was shed for thee, and be thankful."

He held the ancient chalice high that they might all look upon the source of their salvation.

Rhun answered with the others and lined up to receive Holy Communion.

When he stood in front of the Risen One, Lazarus met his eyes, and a faint smile chased across his face. "For you, my brother."

Rhun tilted his head back, and Lazarus poured in the wine.

Rhun savored the silkiness as it flowed down his throat, spreading through his limbs. Tonight it did not burn. On this holiest of nights, even for one such as he, there was no penance.

Only His love.

Rome

2:17 P.M.

Tommy flipped through the channels on Elizabeth's tiny television. Every single one showed a Christmas celebration in Italian. It had been like that all day—nothing to watch. He sighed and clicked it off.

Elizabeth sat stiff-backed on the sofa next to him. He had never seen her slouch, and she wouldn't let him lounge either.

Both feet on the floor at all times, he had been sternly lectured.

"Had you expected different programming?" she asked.

"Not expecting. Hoping."

Besides, he was Jewish and didn't celebrate this holiday, but he'd missed Hanukkah, too. The only acknowledgment of the season to reach him came from a most unexpected place, a Christmas card sent to him by Grigori Rasputin. Somehow the Russian had discovered that he was staying at this apartment in Vatican City.

Elizabeth had scowled upon finding the card taped to the apartment door.

Written on the front of the envelope was *Merry Christmas, my angel!*

The card showed an angel, complete with a golden halo.

He didn't know if it was a threat, a joke, or sincere.

Considering that guy: *probably all three.*

He handed Elizabeth the remote control, but she set it down on the coffee table. He had instructed her on how to use it, and she was a quick learner. She was curious about everything in the modern world, and he was glad to teach her.

After leaving the deserts of Egypt, Tommy had ended up in Rome, at an apartment supplied by the Church. He'd had his blood tested several times since he got back, but otherwise everyone left him alone. He was just some orphaned kid now. He had been offered other temporary accommodations, a place to himself until he was returned to the States, but he preferred to stay with Elizabeth.

Bored, he asked, "Want to learn how to use the microwave?"

"Is the microwave not a device for cooking meals?" She tightened her lips. "That is servant's work."

Tommy lifted an eyebrow toward her. She clearly needed to learn far more about the modern world than just its technology. "Don't you think you'll need to cook for yourself?"

Her eyes darkened. "Why should I waste time on such trivialities?"

He waved his arm around the room. "You can't live here forever. And when you leave, you'll have to get a job and earn money and cook for yourself."

"The Church has no intention of letting me go," she said.

"Why? They're letting me go." He was being sent to his aunt and uncle in Santa Barbara, a couple he barely knew.

"You are but a child. They see you as no threat. So they will send you to this California without fear."

He sighed, trying not to whine. Elizabeth hated when anyone complained. He finally just blurted it out. "I don't want to go."

She turned to him. "You will go."

"I don't know those people. At all. I think I met them once."

"They will care for you, as their familial duty requires."

But they won't love me, he thought. *Not like Mom and Dad.*

"When do you depart?" she asked.

"Tomorrow." He hung his head.

She tapped his chin. "Sit straight. You'll crook your back."

Still, he saw she did that to hide her shock. Apparently no one had told her.

"I just found out this morning myself," he said. "Merry Christmas to the both of us."

She frowned at him. "Why should I feel anything other than happiness that you are to be reunited with your family?"

"No reason," he mumbled.

He stood and walked into the kitchen. He had nothing else to do. He didn't have anything to pack, just a couple of outfits that Christian had brought him and a handful of books that Erin had given him before she and Jordan left for the States themselves.

"Tommy. " Elizabeth stood and crossed to him. "You might find it difficult to live with these people, but they are your family. It is better than being trapped here . . . with me."

He opened and closed a cupboard, not that he needed anything, just to do something. He slammed it a bit too loudly.

She turned him by the shoulders and grabbed his chin. "Why are you so angry? What? You wish me to weep at your farewell? To beg you to remain with me?"

Maybe a little.

"No."

"Such displays of hysteria did not happen when I was a girl," she said. "I have seen much such silliness on your television, but I find it crass."

"It's fine," he said.

She touched his arm. "I shall miss your presence. You have taught me much and brought me joy."

He guessed that her words were like a modern woman falling on the floor weeping.

"I'll miss you, too," he said.

She pulled a gray box out of her pocket and placed it in his hand. "For a parting gift, since you do not celebrate Christmas."

Tommy took off the wrapping carefully. It was a prepaid cell phone.

"If you are ever in need of me," she promised, "call and I will come."

"I thought you were a prisoner."

She scoffed. "Like they can ever keep me caged."

Tommy felt tears threatening and struggled to hold them back.

She bent to stare him in the face. "There are few in this world who are trustworthy. But I trust you."

"Same here."

That was why he had stayed here with her. The others were loyal to their beliefs, but she was loyal to him.

He hugged her, to hide his tears.

"Such foolishness," she said, but she squeezed him even harder.

10:12 A.M. CST
Des Moines, Iowa

Erin sat on the carpeted stairs of Jordan's parents' house. She was hiding out from action in the living room below, taking a moment to brace herself from the Christmas morning chaos. She inhaled the sugar of fresh-baked gingerbread and the burnt allure of freshly brewed coffee. Still, she stayed put.

She lingered on the stairs studying the pictures hung on the neighboring wall. They showed Jordan at different ages, along with various brothers and sisters. His entire childhood was immortalized here, from baseball games to fishing trips to prom.

Erin didn't have a single picture of herself as a child.

A glance below revealed Jordan's nieces and nephews bouncing around the living room like popcorn, full of sugar from the treats in their Christmas stockings. It was the kind of thing that Erin had only ever seen in movies. When she was a child, Christmas was a day of extra prayers, not presents or stockings or Santa Claus.

She stuck one hand in the pocket of her new fleece robe. Her other arm was in a sling. Her shoulder was almost healed from the lion attack. Jordan had just changed the bandages up in her bedroom and was already back down, dragged below by his nephew Bart. Erin had promised to follow right after, but it was peaceful on the steps.

Finally, Jordan poked his head around the corner, discovered her, and joined her on the steps. He tucked the edges of his new robe between his legs as he sat. Both of their robes had been gifts from Jordan's mother.

"You can't hide forever," he said. "My nieces and nephews will hunt you down. They can smell fear."

She smiled and bumped him with her elbow. "It looks very merry down there."

"I know they're a bit much."

"No, they're fun." She meant it, but his family seemed so normal, so very different from hers. "Just takes some acclimatizing."

Jordan stroked the back of her hand with his thumb, the simple touch reminding her why she cared so much about him. "Are you telling me that you've faced down lions and wolves and bears and all kinds of undead, but you're afraid to go in there with four little kids, their exhausted parents, and my mother?"

"That pretty much sums it up."

He pulled her into his arms, and she rested her cheek against his flannel-covered chest. His heart thumped steadily under her ear. She savored the sound, knowing how close she had come to losing him. She tightened her arms around him.

He rumbled at her. "You know . . . we can always move to a hotel, a place with *one* bed for the *two* of us?"

She smiled up at him. His mother had insisted that they sleep in separate bedrooms when they arrived yesterday. "It's damned tempting. But it's sort of fun seeing you in your native environment."

A child's voice piped up from below, demanding, "Where's Uncle Jordan?"

"It seems Miss Olivia is growing impatient." He tugged her to her feet. "C'mon. They don't bite. Except maybe the little ones."

Her hand felt warm and safe in his as he led her down the last steps and into the noisy living room. He guided her past the decorated Christmas tree to a couch.

"Best to stay out of the combat zone," Jordan warned.

His mother, Cheryl, smiled at her. She sat in a brown leather chair with a knitted afghan over her knees. She looked pale and frail.

Erin knew that she was battling cancer, and no one was sure if she would see another Christmas.

"My son's right," Cheryl said. "Avoid the tree until the madness dies down."

"Grandma!" Olivia shouted, near the top of her lungs. "Can't we open presents now?"

A similar chorus rose from the other children.

Cheryl finally lifted a hand. "All right already. Dig in!"

Like lions on a downed gazelle, the kids dove into the presents. Paper tore. Squeals of delights filled the air, and one disappointed voice called out, "Socks?"

Erin tried to imagine what kind of person she would be if she'd grown up here.

Olivia dropped a plastic unicorn into Erin's lap. "This is Twilight Sparkle."

"Hello, Twilight."

"Uncle Jordan says that you have stitches. Can I see? How many are there? Does it hurt?"

Jordan saved her from the grilling. "Olivia, the sutures are under the bandages, so you can't see them."

She looked crestfallen, as only a disappointed child could look.

Erin leaned closer. "There are twenty-four stitches."

Her eyes got huge. "That's a lot!" Then one eye narrowed suspiciously. "How did you get 'em?"

Erin honored her own commitment to the truth. "A lion."

Jordan's mother almost dropped her coffee cup. "A lion?"

"Cool!" Olivia extolled, then handed Jordan another plastic pony. "Hold Applejack."

She ran to get more of her toy horses.

"Clearly you won her over," Jordan said.

Olivia returned and stacked ponies on Erin's lap, reeling off names: Fluttershy, Rainbow Dash, and Pinkie Pie. Erin did her best to play with them, but it was as foreign to her as aboriginal tribal customs.

Cheryl spoke over Olivia's head. "Jordan tells me that he's been assigned to a special protection unit at the Vatican."

"That's right," Erin admitted. "I'll be working with him."

"Mom," Jordan said, "quit trying to worm information out of Erin. It's Christmas."

Cheryl smiled. "I just want to thank her for getting you reassigned to somewhere safe."

Erin thought back to the number of near-death experiences the two of them had survived since meeting at Masada. "I'm not sure *safe* is the right word. Besides, if it was entirely safe, Jordan wouldn't want to do it."

His mother patted Jordan's arm. "Jordan never takes the easiest path."

Olivia was done being ignored and tugged on Erin's sleeve. She pointed an accusatory finger at Erin's nose. "Do you even know how to ride a horse?"

"I do. I even have a big mare named Gunsmoke."

She remembered Blackjack and felt a twinge of sorrow at the loss.

"Can I meet Gunsmoke?" Olivia asked.

"She lives in California, where I work." Erin corrected herself. "Where I used to work."

Erin had spoken briefly with Nate Highsmith last night, wishing him a happy holiday. He had already met with one of the alternate graduate professors she had suggested and seemed mostly okay with her departure. Now, no matter what happened to her, he would be fine.

"What do you do?" Olivia asked. "Are you a soldier, like Uncle Jordan?"

"I'm an archaeologist. I dig up bones and other mysteries and try to figure out the past."

"Is that fun?"

Erin looked over at Jordan's relaxed and happy face. "Most of the time."

"That's good." Olivia poked Jordan's knee. "He needs more fun."

With those profound words, the girl headed back to her toy pile under the tree.

Jordan leaned over and whispered in Erin's ear. "He certainly *does* need more fun."

Erin smiled into his blue eyes and spoke the truth. "So do I."

AND THEN . . .

Far beneath the ruins of Cumae, Leopold floated in and out of dark consciousness. For the past handful of days, he had ridden waves of blackness and pain, rising only to fall, over and over again.

Rhun's blade had cut deep enough to kill him, but he did not die. Every time he felt certain that he would sink into that final blackness, ready to accept the eternal suffering for his failure—he woke again. He would force himself to drag his body and feed on the corpses left in the cavern with him, along with an occasional unlucky rat.

Such frantic beasts offered little sustenance, but they gave him hope.

He had thought himself sealed down here following the quakes, with no chance of escape. But where a rat crawled, he could dig. He just needed his strength back.

But how?

Beneath him, he heard stones rumble far below, gnashing together like giant teeth, as if calling him to duty. He dragged open his heavy eyelids. The torches had long since sputtered out, leaving the smell of smoke. But it was barely noticeable against the stench of sulfur and the rot of bodies.

He reached to a pocket and removed a small flashlight. Leopold's numb fingers fumbled with it for long agonizing seconds before he clicked it on.

The light dazzled. He closed his eyelids against it and waited until its brightness no longer cut at his eyes. Then he opened them again.

He searched the floor around the black altar stone. The net that had held an angel was still there. The cracks that had been opened by that same angel's blood had closed again. The writhing darkness was also gone, bottled back up.

All signs of my failure.

Weak as a kitten, he rolled to his back and reached to the inner pocket of his robe, to what lay heavily there. The *Damnatus* had charged him with this second task. The first was to grab the sibyl and imprison her here.

That duty had to be done *before* the sacrifice.

His second responsibility had to be done *after.*

He did not know if it mattered now, but he had sworn an oath, and he would not forsake it even now. From his pocket, he pulled out a cloudy green stone, a little larger than a deck of cards. It was a prized possession of the *Damnatus,* discovered in the Egyptian desert, traded by many hands, hidden and uncovered over and over until it ended up in the palms of the Betrayer of Christ.

And now into mine.

He lifted the stone to the light. He watched the darkness inside shiver and shrink from the brightness. When he moved the beam away, the blight inside grew, shimmering with dread force.

It was a thing of darkness.

Like myself.

He knew the rumors about this stone, how it was said to hold a single drop of Lucifer's blood. He did not know if that was true. He only knew what he had been commanded to do with the stone.

But do I have the strength to accomplish it?

Over the past days, he had abided the darkness and pain, fed to sustain himself, growing incrementally stronger, hoping for the might of muscle and bone to fulfill the last task asked of him by the *Damnatus.* The necessity for such an act had never been revealed to him, but he knew that if he did not attempt it now, he would grow weaker from here on, starving slowly in the darkness.

He turned the stone to study the strange etching on one side, inscribed faintly into the crystal.

It was in the shape of a cup—or perhaps a chalice. But this was no cup from which Leopold had so often consumed the blood of Christ. He knew the cup depicted here was far older than even Christ Himself, and that this stone was but a sliver of that greater mystery, the key to its truth.

He lifted the stone high and brought his arm down hard, slamming the crystal to the rock floor. He succeeded in chipping it, but that was not enough.

Please, Lord, give me the strength.

Leopold repeated the action over and over again, weeping from frustration. He must not fail again. He raised his arm and crashed it down. This time, he felt the crystal break within his hand, splitting into rough halves.

Thank you . . .

He twisted his head enough to see. He turned his hand. The crystal had been broken through its heart. Black oil flowed across the emerald glass and found his skin.

He screamed as it touched him.

Not in pain, but in utter and complete rapture.

In that glorious moment, he knew the rumors were true.

He watched the drop of Lucifer's blood sink into his flesh, claiming him, consuming him fully with its darkness, leaving behind only purpose.

And a new name.

He stood, full of dread strength now, his pale skin as black as ebony. He lifted his face and howled his new name at the world, shattering stones around him with his voice alone.

I am Legion, destroyer of worlds.